ALL THE SKILLS

— BOOK THREE —

ALL THE SKILLS

— BOOK THREE —

HONOUR RAE

Podium

Podium

ALL THE SKILLS

— BOOK THREE —

PART 1
HIVE LEADER
(IN TRAINING)

CHAPTER 1

Arthur did not like sitting astride Instructor Athena's dragon, Brooks. He was large and orange, with a thick neck and a particularly bony ridge that poked him in all the wrong places even through the padded saddle. His two large wings were meant for gliding rather than quick maneuverability. He turned as ungainly as a barge in a too-small river.

He was also one of those dragons who didn't speak to those he thought of as "outsiders." He hadn't spoken so much as a word to Arthur in all the weeks of training class.

The last reason Arthur disliked riding Brooks during practice drills: Brixaby became incredibly, obnoxiously jealous.

His purple-black dragon buzzed near Brooks's left shoulder, giving the older dragon the evil eye with bloodred eyes instead of what he should have been doing, which was watching the rest of the class in flying drills.

Four months into the six-month training course for new dragon riders, only Brixaby and the two purples were not yet considered large and strong enough to carry their riders.

Arthur suspected that Lilac, the paler of the two purples, who had scales the color of her name, would be able to carry her rider soon.

He wasn't looking forward to that day. Brixaby would be nearly frothing with jealousy.

With a steady diet of card shards—as many as Arthur could get his hands on—Brixaby had grown more than eight times the size he'd been as a hatchling.

Unfortunately, he had started at the size of a sickly sparrow, so that wasn't saying much.

As a flying animal, he was also light boned. Arthur could carry him on his shoulder.

No other way to put it: Brixaby was nowhere near the size needed to safely carry a rider.

Like any good partner to a strong-willed dragon, Arthur was already thinking of ways to soothe his ego. In Brixaby's case, that meant bribes.

"Brooks," Arthur said, reaching down to touch the orange scales. They were a particularly . . . unpleasant color that reminded him of spoiled oranges. "Turn to the west. The wing is making another pass."

The large dragon under him made no sound of acknowledgment other than to slowly, laboriously beat his wings. Arthur got the impression the dragon was rolling his eyes. Some dragons did not like listening to anyone else other than their rider.

This was ironic considering Brooks's core card centered around transforming the quality of sound.

Arthur wished that Instructor Athena were there with him to help direct the dragon. But just as the rest of the class was doing formation drills . . . he was in training, too. As a Legendary rider, he was expected to train to be in charge.

Not that anyone ever explained how to do that, Arthur thought. *They act like bonding with a Legendary gave me a special leadership card.*

Unfortunately, the few leadership skills he managed were all low rank and not much help yet in a combat setting.

Below them and to the right, the class came into view.

It was a double-diamond formation—one stack above and just forward of the other. That was a simple shape in theory, not so much in practice. Though the dragons were hatched within a few days of one another, there was a huge variety in size, wing length, and weight. Flying out in the open with unpredictable wind patterns while keeping in a tight formation was not easy at all.

His class had only been able to somewhat manage the feat over the last few days.

"Brix," Arthur said, interrupting the dark little dragon who was glaring at Brooks and not so subtly flexing his claws. Brooks ignored him. "Do you think it's time?"

"What? Yes? Yes!" Brixaby snapped out of his distraction and twisted into a hovering circle. Unlike orange Brooks, Brixaby was built in the body shape of a purple and some of the blues. That meant he had four wings, each with the ability to twist from side to side as he flapped. That gave him the ability to hover in place or shoot backward or nearly vertically in the air like a hummingbird. He might be small, but he could zip rings around the competition.

His draconic eyesight was better than Arthur's too. He gazed up into what looked to Arthur like endless blue sky. "Yes, they're ready."

Then Brixaby gave an evil chuckle.

"Give them the signal."

Brixaby concentrated for a moment, and Arthur knew his ridiculously deep voice was currently echoing in two dragons' heads far above them. That had been a gift from a mind-mage card Brixaby had absorbed a few months ago.

The card had been meant to inject subconscious thoughts into the minds of its victims to influence their actions. Brixaby had absorbed an aspect of that, which meant he could speak into the minds of other sentient beings within normal shouting distance. It made communication and passing along orders a snap. Especially since it was one way, as Brixaby had bragged several times. Humans and dragons could hear his orders, but they couldn't talk back.

Also, since Brixaby had quite the voice . . . his "shouting distance" was farther than most.

Arthur wished more than once he could find an Empathy card to feed to Brixaby . . . but so far had come up empty.

"Here they come," Brixaby said with satisfaction.

Shielding his eyes against the sun, Arthur spotted two dots plummeting down from high above.

These were the two purples in the class. The only ones aside from Brixaby who were still too small to carry their riders. Purples generally didn't fill a combat role during scourge-eruptions. Traditionally, they were couriers or independent rescue units to evacuate those who couldn't get out of the way. So they were excused from all but the most basic formation flying.

Since Instructor Athena had given Arthur charge of the group today—he was supposed to know how to train a formation in combat when he couldn't fly with them and was in training himself—he decided that the purples would play the "scourglings." Their job was to upset the formation flying below.

Lilac and the other purple, Tofu, had cow bladders filled with black paint clutched in their claws. Their job was to sweep by at full speed and splatter as many dragons as they could. The black paint would be the "scourge-rot."

The class had done these practices before, with one diamond formation trying to disrupt the other. Then, the terms of engagement had been known ahead of time.

This was going to be a surprise.

Arthur's only concern was for Cressida and Joy. As Joy was a Rare, she took up the protected middle spot in the lower diamond.

Joy was a pink meta who was often alerted by useful quests that could be anything from running an errand for an elderly neighbor to, one time, alerting the hive leaders of a rare nighttime scourge-eruption. She was almost precognizant, and her quest card might give her the heads-up something was coming.

Arthur waited with a held breath. There was no alert from the approaching double-diamond formation.

At the very last second, a rider on a brown looked up, saw the two diving purples, and yelled out a warning.

That brown dove down—an instinctive reaction to an attack from above. Unfortunately, he held the middle point in the diamond, which opened a hole for the two purples to fly through and sink their claws into their bladders of paint.

It exploded into a fine mist, dusting most of the dragons below and around in "scourge-rot."

The worst was Joy and Cressida who were splattered directly.

Arthur and Brixaby cheered as the formation disintegrated into chaos; rides cursing and dragons scattering in every direction.

They probably shouldn't have celebrated. It was, technically, a failure as the class had trained on how to break off smoothly into smaller formations to deal with scourgling attacks.

But the prank—and the lesson it brought—was worth it.

At least, until a screamed roar rang out.

One of the greens, Morrice, had gotten splattered all down his side. He retaliated by twisting his head and opening his mouth. A green beam erupted from between his jaws and struck Lilac straight on.

The little purple screamed, back arching in agony. Already, odd green splotches were starting to erupt from between her scales.

"NO! STOP!"

That shout came from their instructor, who watched the whole show from the ground. She had a vocal stunning ability. It was normally powerful enough to knock anyone for a loop—but she was on the ground, and the entire flock of dragons was several hundred feet up.

At that distance, her yell was only a loud yell.

It didn't stop green Morrice from following the staggering purple down, lining up for another shot.

"Brix—" Arthur started, but Brixaby was already gone.

His dragon had been a natural flyer right out of the shell, and he'd worked hard on leveling his flying skills since then.

He was a blur as he shot down, using the ground's natural pull and his streamlined body to every advantage.

Brixaby was a touch too far away to stop the green. Instead, he put himself in between the two dragons just as the second beam went off.

It hit Brixaby, and Brixaby's natural magic nullified it. The green was only an Uncommon—the two tiers of difference between them helped.

But nullification wasn't the only one of Brixaby's powers.

With a snarl, Brixaby sent a green beam back right at the attacking Morrice. He had been close enough to pick up the dragon's spell, and now he had it for the next twelve hours.

Unfortunately, the knack for targeting came with practice. The beam missed.

What a shame, Arthur thought. He would have liked to see Morrice get a taste of his own medicine.

"LAND! RIGHT NOW!" Instructor Athena roared.

Arthur barely had time to grip the saddle under him before Brooks folded his wings and shot to the ground with more alacrity than he'd ever shown before.

It turned out he could move quickly after all . . . but only when obeying his rider.

By the time Arthur made it to the ground and dismounted Brooks, purple Lilac had landed and was being attended to by her concerned rider. Splotches of lichen were actively growing up between her scales. The little purple rolled over and over on the ground.

"Itchy! Itchy! Itchy! Lilac is itchy! Make it stop! Silvy! Make it stop!"

"It will be okay. Lilac, calm down. You'll be all right!" Silvy turned pained eyes to Arthur. "She'll be all right, won't she, sir?"

Arthur froze.

This was his fault. Well, it was Morrice's fault. But Lilac had been following Arthur's orders. And—

His hesitation caused Silvy to fear the worst. Her eyes widened, and she screamed. "Healer! Healer!"

"No, she'll be fine—" Arthur scrambled to fix his mistake but knew it was too late. Silvy was panicked, and that was transmitted to her dragon, who started to wail.

"Is Lilic dying? Lilac doesn't want to die! Silvy! Help!"

"No, no, you'll be fine," Arthur said. "Look, the healers are nearly here." He pointed to the trio of two men and one woman who were running from the hive entrance.

Unfortunately, Silvy and Lilic were now too worked up to listen.

Arthur stayed a few more moments until the healers had arrived. He knew he'd be no more help here.

Instead, he turned to his own dragon, who was buzzing around the landed Morrice and threatening to tear his card out of his "useless, rotten green core."

It was a common threat, but Arthur thought Brixaby meant it this time . . . and he wasn't sure he would stop him.

Instructor Athena was already walking up to the pair, but Arthur beat her to it.

"What were you thinking?" he demanded of Willard, Morrice's rider.

The boy hadn't dismounted yet and made a point of looking down his nose at Arthur.

"My dragon was reacting to an attack. You set *scourglings* on us, sir," he sneered. "Out of the whole formation, we were the only ones to fight back. We ought to be commended."

Arthur saw red. He opened his mouth, but Instructor Athena got there first. "Rider Willard, dismount and address your superior properly!"

That was what she was annoyed about? Decorum?

Willard made a face but dismounted. After his feet hit the ground, he stood with his back straight, though he smirked at Arthur.

The howls of the very distressed, itchy purple sounded in the air again. Arthur wanted to punch Willard.

It took every iota of self-control not to scream in his face. Instead, he kept his voice level and cold. His father, he remembered, always sounded scarier when he was cold.

"If you can't tell the difference between a scourgling and a dragon, you have no business being up in the air. Instructor Athena." He turned to the woman. "This pair has proven themselves to be a liability in combat. I don't want them anywhere near this class."

"Yes, sir." The instructor nodded. She had been paying deference to him since the moment Arthur joined the class.

She turned to Willard. "You have displeased your Legendary superior, rider. You're done for the day."

Willard sneered and started to turn.

"I didn't excuse you," Arthur snapped. Then he turned again to Athena. "My apologies, Instructor, I didn't make myself clear. I don't want this idiot or his idiot dragon in this class ever again."

He heard several gasps around him—the rest of the riders had dismounted and circled to watch the show.

Pretending he hadn't heard them, Arthur went on. "Willard and Morrice can make themselves useful tending the dragon-soil pits—Morrice is a nature dragon. Fertilizer should be up his alley. Then, when the next class is up to this level in a month or two, hopefully, they will be mature enough to join and complete their training."

Athena was silent for a moment. Arthur wondered if he'd overstepped, but he didn't want to show weakness by looking at her for confirmation.

Willard, however, had gone white around the lips. "You can't do that!"

"You'll find that, as your better in rank, he can," Instructor Athena said, which was not exactly a vote of confidence, but whatever. She looked back to Arthur. "If this is your wish, sir."

She was giving him an out. A loophole where he could modify his order and say something like, if Willard and Morrice behave themselves, with water rations for dinner, they could return after a week.

Arthur wasn't even tempted.

"No, that is *not* his only wish," Brixaby interrupted, buzzing in between them. Willard took an instinctive step back. "In addition, I want Morrice to write a letter of apology to Lilac—hmm. You have no reading skill, do you? Fine. Morrice will *dictate* the letter, and Willard will write it. You may as well include the rest of this class in your apology too, as you've forced Arthur to kick you out, and that will leave the formation of one dragon pair short—"

He was interrupted by a sound that froze everyone in place.

Alarm gongs.

The sound of a scourgling eruption in progress somewhere within the kingdom.

And as newly minted flyers—even brand-new ones—the class was now required to respond.

CHAPTER 2

Arthur was unsurprised when a messenger dragon immediately dropped out of the sky to take him to Valentina.

Usually, the purples and some of the smaller blues acted as couriers. This time, however, it was a young red dragon, big enough to carry several people but lacking a rider.

"Valentina wishes to see the Legendary pair at once," the red said with an absent nod to Brooks. With a start, Arthur realized the newcomer red was a Rare dragon, just like Brooks.

It wasn't something he could put his finger on—no markings or badges to designate a Rare versus a lower-tiered Uncommon. It was just a feeling he had been able to identify ever since bonding with Brixaby.

Odd. Arthur thought that he recognized all the Rares in the hive by sight now, if not by name. This red was new.

"Of course," Arthur said and turned to Athena for last-minute instructions.

It shouldn't have surprised him much to find her staring at him expectantly instead.

There was a blank moment.

"What are your orders for the class, *sir*?" Athena said pointedly.

It was a tacit reminder that he was in charge of the class, even though he was as green as everyone else.

Arthur paused and swept his gaze over the rest of the waiting riders and dragons. The expressions ran the entire rainbow of emotions between anticipation, anxiety, and dread for the upcoming scourge-eruptions. Then there were the two most downcast faces of all that belonged to the purple riders.

Lilac would be out for the rest of the day even if she wasn't dealing with the aftermath of being hit by Morrice's card power. The other purple, Tofu, looked shaken. And who could blame him after what happened to Lilac?

Everyone else, though, was capable. Arthur didn't intend to sit this eruption out, so he wasn't about to tell his classmates to do the same.

And there was a saying that the best part of leadership was delegation.

"Instructor Athena." Arthur pitched his voice to carry to all surrounding him. "Please prepare the class to best help with the eruption. I'll be meeting with Leader Valentina and will return shortly."

"Very good, sir." Athena saluted him, and most of the others did too.

The marked holdouts were the few he suspected were friends with Willard and Morrice.

Paying them no mind—because he was certain Athena had noticed and would be chewing them out momentarily—Arthur quickly alighted onto the red's neck. The dragon had a saddle already fitted, though it was an impersonal one without any markings to show that someone owned and took care of it.

Did this dragon not have a rider at all?

That was unusual for a hive as small as Wolf Moon. Rare dragons were thin on the ground and somewhat precious.

Well, no harm in being friendly. Arthur waited until the dragon had taken off into the sky—usually the most labor-intensive moment of flight—before he spoke. "I'm Arthur, and this is Brixaby. Can I have your name?"

"Shadow," the dragon grunted, which was an unusual name for a red, whose natural magic usually involved high energy of different forms. Fire. Heat. Occasionally plasma. Shadow had a deep-ruby red hide with no hint of orange, which usually tended to mean energy manipulation.

Arthur was trying to find a polite way to ask about his card's power and his rider—if any—when Shadow curtly spoke again.

"Brixaby, sir. You'd better hold on."

Brixaby grumbled something under his breath, but he settled down on Arthur's shoulder, and his tail squeezed possessively around Arthur's neck.

"Brix, let me breathe—"

Then, without warning, Arthur was wrapped in velvet darkness. But it wasn't as if he were looking at a moonless night at midnight or being dropped in a torchless cave. There was a quality to this darkness, like there were shapes just out of reach—

And in the next moment, they stood on a wide balcony Arthur recognized as the entrance to Valentina's dwelling. Due to the angle of the sun against the stony tip of the hive's peak, this part of the balcony was in shadow.

New Counterfeit spell obtained: Shadow Transport
Time Remaining: 59 Minutes 59 Seconds

"Ohh, a transport power." Brixaby had recovered before Arthur and eyed the other dragon with a bit more respect and a lot more greed. "That is quite useful. Tell me, are you in any other Legendary retinue?"

Arthur wanted to scold Brixaby, but he wondered the same thing.

Shadow just shrugged. "I'm not allowed."

"Not allowed?" Brixaby asked. "Why no—"

He was interrupted by a loud call from within the room beyond. "Brixaby! Arthur! Stop wasting time and attend to my rider this moment!"

That voice came from Elissa, Valentina's dragon. Arthur's eyebrows rose, and he wondered how the giant of a dragon had fit herself in that room.

He turned back to Shadow. "Thank you for the transport." He flipped a purple token to the dragon, who caught it out of the air and, by the puff of purple-black smoke, used his card's power to transfer it to one of the saddlebags. Tokens like these worked as payment for the usual purple and blue couriers and their riders.

Basic food and shelter were guaranteed for all rider pairs, but those tokens and any card shards collected during scourge-eruptions could be traded for additional luxuries like better rooms and tastier food over and above the usual rations.

Though Shadow took the payment, he made no move to leave the balcony. Arthur exchanged a confused look with Brixaby as they walked into Valentina's rooms.

One look inside told him that Valentina was having one of her bad days. Her blue-steel-colored dragon had squeezed in, it seemed, by force of personality and the destruction of much furniture. Though she was squished and puffing out unhappy clouds of fog, she was curled around Valentina, who sat in a chair, her knuckles white around the top of her cane. Valentina's wrinkled face was unusually lined. Arthur suspected it was from pain.

There were potions and card-anchor spells to help with that sort of thing, but the one time he mentioned it, Valentina had sharply refused. She was afraid it would slow her in battle.

Because no matter what, if Legendary support was called in, she would be required to attend. Even if she was on death's doorstep itself.

Despite her obvious discomfort, the old woman stared up at Arthur with a challenge in her eyes.

"So, I understand your class is officially available to attend the eruption. Feeling your oats, young man? Think you are ready?"

"We are," Arthur said, though in reality, he had no idea. "Most of the class could have technically attended the one the day before last, but now all of the riders except Brix and the two purples can ride their dragons."

"And you think that that is enough to protect you from the scourglings? Oh, to be young and foolish again." She snorted. "You are to be there for no more than two hours. Your dragons may be enthusiastic, but none of you have stamina yet. In fact, I'd send orders to hold you back . . . but this is going to be a bad one."

"Why is that?" Arthur asked. Valentina complained a lot, but unlike Whitaker, she often dropped words of wisdom—and sometimes valuable information.

Whitaker simply piled paperwork on him—usually overdue forms that Whitaker should have taken care of himself, months ago.

"Because this eruption is right on the edge of Guardian City. Nowhere physically near our hive, thank my dragon's card." She reached with her cane to poke at Arthur's chest. "You know why an eruption in a city is bad?"

"Other than the staggering cost of life?" he asked dryly.

Her eyes narrowed. "If I were looking for obvious answers, boy, I'd ask an Uncommon yellow!"

Arthur resisted the urge to sigh. The thought that a lot of people were about to die was enough to remind him that every moment counted. He cut to the chase. "Because scourglings grow fastest when they feed on complex life, and especially *magical* life. An eruption in the middle of a field ready for harvest is much less dangerous than one in the middle of a town. The corruption brought by the scourge would destroy the harvest and sterilize the land, but there wouldn't be many people . . . or if there were people, they'd probably be farmers without cards. That won't be the case in a city. The scourglings might consume enough pure magical power in the form of cards to raise a demi-scourgling."

Elissa spoke. "If that happens, you and that little dragon of yours must be prepared to fight."

"I can fight," Brixaby declared. "I can't *wait* to face a demi-scourgling."

"Then you're a fool," Elissa said.

Brixaby hissed back, though it was under his breath. He would never say as much, but he was intimidated by the older Legendary.

Ignoring the byplay, Valentina nodded. "I'm glad you understand. Your main objective is to secure any large sources of cards and keep them away from the scourglings. This is important, over and above rescuing civilians."

Arthur's breath caught.

Valentina must have noticed because she glared at him. "You understand why this is important."

"I do," he said.

She pressed the point. "Eating a single schoolyard filled with carded noble's children is bad. Eating a card library may raise a demi-scourgling that will wipe out the entire city—"

"I understand, Valentina."

But privately, he thought he could still save a bunch of kids if it came to it. He would have a whole class of dragons behind him.

"Hmm." She didn't look like she fully believed him, but that was not his problem. Every moment of delay was one too many. "You are to take Shadow for this run. He's already been told what I've told you."

"What about his rider?" Arthur asked.

"Dead, so rest assured that this dragon knows the consequences of faffing around in a scourge-eruption." The direct look she gave him said she guessed his motivations.

Arthur just calmly looked back. "Brix and I know our duty. We'll act with integrity and honor." Which to him meant putting people first, cards be damned.

A deep rumbly voice spoke up from behind them. It was Shadow, who had, living up to his namesake, crept up in the shadows. "Pretty words from someone who hasn't flown a scourge-eruption before."

Brixaby bristled. "What do you mean?"

"It means to watch your tail. Everyone knows you two are newer than spring-time lambs out in the field. Anyone who's hoping to get a Legendary card—or if the rumor is to be believed, two cards—they're coming for you."

Brixaby clenched his claws. "Then they'll get a surprise." He sounded like he was looking forward to it. "Meet us back down at the class, Rare." Then he placed one of those claws on Arthur's shoulder.

In the next moment, Arthur was enveloped by velvet darkness with the . . . things crawling out of reach, only to emerge a moment in orange Brooks's long shadow. The class was still on the ground nearby, standing in formation and waiting for his return.

"Was that necessary?" Arthur asked his dragon.

"Only necessary until I copy the green dragon's portal spell in a few minutes," Brixaby said. His booming voice carried, and the rest of their classmates came to attention as they noticed they'd arrived. "Then we won't need him at all."

"We still will for me to fly."

Brixaby ignored that.

Joy bounded up, her hide painfully pink in the bright sunlight. "Brix! Brix! I just got a quest to help you save a noble's card library." She wrinkled her nose. "But . . . I don't understand. Are we saving cards or are we fighting scourglings?"

Arthur answered for his dragon. "Both."

CHAPTER 3

Arthur was very aware of the hive's adult dragons streaming through the newly opened midair portals that led to the eruption. And that every moment he held his class here on the ground meant that many fewer dragons helping out.

It possibly meant that many more people being killed by scourglings.

It also meant that good cards and shards were being lost.

Arthur's first instinct might be to save, but for many dragon pairs . . . this was an opportunity to gain wealth. Those dragons and riders were glaring at him as if he were holding them there to keep them poor.

Or maybe it had to do with Willard and Morrice.

Ignoring them, Arthur put on a calm facade and waited, as if with infinite patience, for the class to organize on the ground in preparation for a double-diamond formation: one diamond on top of the other.

Cressida and Joy were to take Morrice's old position at the head of the bottom diamond. It would allow Joy, who had no direct combat cards of her own, to be protected.

It would also allow her to lead the way.

As usual, Brixaby grumbled a little at that. He was the Legendary-ranked dragon here. He felt it was his duty to lead everything.

His grumbles quieted when Arthur pointed out that Cressida and Joy were part of Brixaby's retinue. That meant, in a way, he was leading.

They also had a quest card, which had already hinted at what they were about to face.

Arthur had pulled Cressida aside and asked her about it as soon as he told the class to start forming up.

Cressida's mouth pulled in an expression of distaste. "The quest said to locate Noble Woodmours's personal card library and protect it at all costs. It has a nice reward, too," she added with a sigh. "Ten Rare shards and one free attribute point."

Arthur's eyebrows rose. He hoped he and Brixaby would be able to get in on that quest. The Counterfeit Siphon card that linked them together had allowed them to join a quest or sometimes get one of their own when Joy or Cressida were actively holding a quest.

Sometimes it worked, sometimes they got nothing at all.

It was annoyingly random, but that was a meta card for you.

"Valentina told me to guard any card stashes from roving scourglings," Arthur said. "Your quest likely came from that. So why do you look like you've just been told to suck a rotten egg?"

Cressida glanced around to see if anyone was paying attention. Of course, they were. The two of them were the highest ranked in the class, having a private discussion. Everyone was watching and trying to look like they weren't.

Noticing this, Cressida took a half step closer to him and lowered her voice. "I haven't had personal dealings with the Woodmours, but from what I've heard from my family . . . they are not kind to their renters."

His mood immediately darkened. "How so?"

"They were granted rich, arable land, but rumors say renters—the people who turn and toil the fields—regularly starve to death. That shouldn't happen. Even my father, Lord Icehouse, ensures his tenants are fed, and our fields are frozen over for fully half the year."

With some shame, Arthur realized he had never thought deeply of the plight of the Common folk outside of border villages where he'd grown up. Even the poorest in the inner kingdom had a leg up on people trapped at the border. After all, they could leave, and their land wasn't actively trying to poison them.

Clearly, he had been wrong.

And he wasn't too happy to hear the quest was nudging them to protect some rich jerk's library.

But . . .

"There has to be a reason," he said. "None of the card caches in the area can be allowed to fall to the scourglings. So why this one?"

Cressida winced, and he knew she was thinking about the scholars' library. "I don't know. That's all the quest said."

"Come on, come on, come on, we're all formed up! Hurry!" Joy called to them, literally dancing from foot to foot.

She was right. It was time.

Arthur clapped Cressida on the shoulder. "If you get anything else"—*Like a better quest*, he did not add—"or if his quest updates with more details, let me know."

He glanced around and saw that Shadow was nearby. The Rare dragon had slunk in so quietly that neither Arthur nor Brixaby—who was buzzing around the still-grounded formation, making adjustments to ensure everyone was perfect—hadn't noticed.

He went to Shadow, who gave him a nod and bent to allow Arthur to climb aboard. The dragon didn't mention Brixaby's little trick. Arthur suspected he was embarrassed about it.

With Instructor Agatha taking up a mirrored position in the back to watch for stragglers, and the two lone purples watching the rest of their class jealously, Arthur made the signal to take to the sky.

By this point, most of the adult dragons had already gone through. Their class joined a line of purples and blues with wolf heads emblazoned on their chest straps. These were teams of the Lobos, the rescue and evacuation group. Many of them were already on their second or third round bringing evacuees to the hive.

Not everyone saved could be brought to the hive, and not everyone brought was allowed to stay. But newly orphaned children, craftspeople who just lost their guild or workshop, nursing mothers, and people of means or with important political connections were usually always welcomed.

In return, the Lobos were given tokens by the hive. This was their pay and recompense for the fact they could not kill scourglings and harvest them for shards and cards.

It wasn't a bad life. Arthur had a guilty thought that if Brixaby had been a Common purple instead of a Legendary one, he could have been happy in the Lobos.

Two shimmering green dragons held open the edges to a rip in the sky. Arthur signaled the double diamond forward to the rip, with him and Shadow in the lead and Brixaby holding on to his shoulder.

He felt Brixaby's claws tighten as their linked Counterfeit Siphon card picked up the portal spell.

New Counterfeit spell obtained: Spatial Portal
Remaining Time: 11 hours 59 Seconds

Then after a moment of dimensional turbulence, which felt like being buffeted on the inside as well as the outside, they were above Guardian City.

And it was a horrific sight.

No one had yet discovered a rhyme or reason to where the scourge chose to erupt, or even if it was a choice at all. Only that they occurred at least fifty miles inward from the kingdom's border. It was as if the things were as repulsed by the deadened lands as normal people.

They could erupt in the middle of an empty forest or tundra or lake as easily as they could in the middle of a city.

But when they did erupt within a city . . . it was bad.

The sharply peaked cone had already grown equal in height to some of the grand five- or six-story buildings around it. Coming in from above, Arthur saw down into the mouth of the thing: dark, like an open throat. A throat that was expelling cartfuls of dirt and freshly hatched scourglings every second. The cone had already fully engulfed one building, and by the wreckage, the weight at its base had knocked over another building, which had a cascade effect on the rest around it.

Some of the debris was actually clods of dirt rolling down the sides of the peak, making the cone larger and larger by the moment. Some opened like blooming flowers, shook the dust off, and were revealed as animal-shaped scourglings that ran down the rest of the slope to the city streets.

As high up as they were, the people running from the destruction looked like ants. Some were on horses or pulled livestock behind them. Others had carts that were quickly overwhelmed by other fleeing people or got stuck in the debris.

All around, dragons in various large formations, in pairs and trios, and even working alone dove to use card powers on emerging scourglings.

Arthur saw one spit green acid on a small pack of wolflike scourglings pursuing a family. The wolf-scourglings went down with unnatural whistles instead of howls. The dragon landed to rip the remaining wolves to ribbons . . . and to harvest any cards and shards within the creatures. Both dragon and rider pointedly ignored the family who, after failing to get their attention, continued running for their lives.

Arthur gritted his teeth, hating to see it.

But he couldn't escape the fact that this was the main draw of a scourge-eruption and a large part of the reason why people and dragons put their lives on the line each and every eruption. Not only duty, but wealth.

Scourglings had card shards within their cores. Some of the stronger scourglings—or the ones who had found an unlucky human and eaten their heart deck—had full cards tucked within.

It was why every hive attended every scourge-eruption no matter where it appeared within the kingdom. For a healthy rider and dragon to sit one out would not only be shameful, but they would also be leaving income out for another dragon to harvest. Most dragon riders supported families back home for this reason.

For Arthur and Brixaby, it was especially important. Brixaby only grew after ingesting magical cards or the shards.

Brixaby could—and had—absorbed a full card and had more than tripled in size from about equal to a sparrow to a respectable parrot.

For him, absorbing a card allowed him to add portions of its power permanently as his own instead of temporarily, as with their Counterfeit Siphon.

Unfortunately, that process destroyed the card completely and forever took it out of circulation from the world.

Arthur had mixed feelings about that.

On one hand, the card Brixaby had recently consumed and destroyed was one the Mind Singer desperately wanted. Also, the king was very much opposed to his subjects creating sets of cards. Arthur had nearly been executed learning that lesson.

On the other hand, forever destroying a card—and therefore any possibility a set could be completed—felt like a desecration on a base level. He could not pinpoint why, exactly. But it felt like by allowing the destruction of viable cards, he was somehow betraying the cards in his own heart.

So, after the Mind Singer's card, he fed Brixaby only card shards.

Brixaby grumbled a little and demanded Rare shards if he wasn't allowed to consume whole cards. He still grew with them, though at a slower pace.

It meant that Arthur's dragon literally consumed more money to grow than even his generous stipend allowed.

Brixaby needed card shards, and they were conveniently running rampant in the streets below him, hunting people.

He knew he should turn his formation toward Noble Woodmours's holdings, but . . .

One of his riders, Senda, who sat on her yellow dragon Starshine, suddenly pointed and screamed. A large building was tipping over—whether by the shaking ground from the rapidly growing cone or someone's errant card power.

Bad enough that the debris was falling on people, but it also blocked several city streets and choked off a way to escape for hundreds as they fled.

A dark mass of scourglings, perhaps sensing an opportunity, quickly headed in that direction.

"We're not going to leave those people!" Senda yelled. "They're trapped!"

She started to turn Starshine's head to fall out of formation and fly to their aid.

Brixaby had anticipated this. With a burst of speed thanks to his Flying Sprint skill, he was suddenly at Starshine's nose.

"What do you think you're doing?" Brixaby snapped.

"Our duty!" Senda said, even as her dragon recoiled from Brixaby's anger. Starshine was only a Common with a basic light-condensing spell. She was no match for an annoyed Legendary. "I'm not going to sit here and let people die because you say we need to save some fancy noble's card collection—"

"I agree." Arthur pitched his voice loud enough to carry to all. "But we are a formation, which means we go together."

He heard some of the dragons murmuring his words to the riders up and down the diamonds.

He caught a glimpse of Cressida's pinched face. She was clearly torn.

"If we help contain the scourglings here, then there's less of a chance they'll get to Woodmours's library, right?" Arthur called.

It was a thin excuse. He knew it, and he knew she knew it.

But better than letting people die.

Cressida nodded, and Joy looked excited.

"Top diamond, fall to the rear!" Arthur called. "Cressida, you and Joy lead the way."

He wanted to give Joy every chance he could for her card to pick up a new quest or modify the existing one.

Besides, Joy might not have a combat card, but Cressida did.

Though the process of switching out the upper and lower layers of the diamond had been shaky at best during formation drills, right now the entire class moved well, smooth and practiced. It was a basic formation, and Shadow knew what to do, easily sliding into the middle rear spot—the most protected.

"Ready cards!" Joy called back, her voice high and excited.

Around and in front, the dragons and riders of the double diamond mentally reached for their cards. Arthur didn't have anything specific to help, but he caught Brixaby flexing his claws as if preparing to rip the shards out of some scourglings.

"Dive!" Joy shouted.

As one, the young dragons turned their wings to spill air.

And at the almost exact same time, the erupting cone admitted a great gout. Scourglings and debris flew into the sky to rain down upon the entire city.

CHAPTER 4

Arthur watched as erupted debris rained down in slow motion. It was a mass of dirt and dust, punctuated by sharp rocks and boulders almost as big as a horse cart.

To his shame, he froze in horror.

Judging by Brixaby's sudden stillness on his shoulder, he had too. But Arthur was riding a veteran dragon who was used to sudden dangers on the battlefield.

"Ware above!" Shadow boomed out. "Earth cards, shield your formation!"

They only had one dragon with earthen powers, Char, who was born with a disintegration power, which he colloquially called a quicksand power. This was because his rider had a wellspring-type card. Together, they created an effect that liquefied most substances to create quicksand under people's feet.

At Shadow's call, brown Char surged up with a burst of speed. Other adult brown, tan, and orange dragons, who traditionally had the powers of material change, did the same. The falling storm of rubble and boulders began to burst into harmless dust.

But even all those dragons working together couldn't manage all the debris. Boulders were falling. They looked like they were coming down slowly, but that was only an illusion due to size. And several of them were falling toward their class's formation.

"Brix!" Arthur called and pointed up.

The little dragon understood. He buzzed closer to Char—close enough to fall within his aura.

Suddenly, rocks threatening to land on their heads burst like fireworks Arthur had seen at the end of festivals.

Brixaby was only temporarily copying Char's power, but he had the strength of a Legendary behind it. That gave a not-insignificant boost.

Harmless dust rained down. Arthur covered his eyes to keep from getting blinded. It clouded the air and made it almost impossible to see.

But rocks and dirt were not the only things expelled from the eruption. The moment Arthur found himself cloaked in dust, he heard the terrible whistling coming from above and around.

Scourglings. Some would surely fall to their death from being blasted that high and then hurtling back down to the ground. Others, however, would have wings.

"Dive!" Arthur called, knowing that at any moment, their formation would break apart as the rest of his class came to the same conclusion and then moved to protect themselves. They were still in training, and they had not practiced using card powers cohesively during battles. They were more likely to hit each other or other nearby dragons than scourglings.

His call was taken up a few moments later by Cressida and Joy from their place in the diamond.

"Dive! Dive! Follow me!" Joy sang out.

Brixaby's speed meant he had no problem returning to Arthur. His claws sank into the protective pad Arthur had sewn into his shoulder to use as his perch.

Together, their class of dragons swooped below the worst of the dust cloud. They even kept their formation, though it was ragged.

Arthur looked up. The whole sky above was dark with dust. Dragon pairs all over the city who had used earth powers to break up the worst of the boulders were still working on dispersing the cloud.

But they hadn't gotten everything.

Several boulders had devastated buildings and streets, in addition to the scourgling survivors that now chased fleeing people.

Arthur wished he and Brixaby could be one of the independent fighters he saw diving after those scourglings now, or one of the noncombat Lobo rescue teams who ignored the scourglings and simply flew down to scoop up people running for their lives.

If Brixaby were larger . . .

Wincing, he turned from the sights below to focus on his class. They were his responsibility.

Joy and Cressida continued to lead the way forward. The other dragons tightened up the formation again into a passable double diamond. Soon, they were flying between the buildings, toward the collapsed barrier that cut so many people off from escape.

A small crowd had formed at the base of the debris—some digging for survivors but most trying to escape. He saw people scaling the mountain of debris, desperate to get farther away from the ever-expanding eruption.

Arthur called to Char and his rider, "Fly ahead! See what you can do to open a way for them!"

The rider signaled he understood with a raised hand, and the two peeled off. Char's ability to reduce stone into dust would help clear a path. Maybe they could even find survivors in the rubble . . . though Arthur didn't hold out much hope.

One of his blue riders, a girl named Tamya, screamed and pointed to the road just to the south.

A giant scourgling mass had taken the form of a dark, twisting mass of . . . roots? Worms? It was something that tumbled along end over end with hundreds of legs, most ending in sharp teeth that mindlessly snapped in all directions.

The mass was one block away and tumbled ever closer, as if it could smell the people trapped just ahead.

Cressida yelled, and a bear made of flame galloped through the air ahead of her. It continued down as if on a steep downward slope and struck at the mass with giant flame claws.

At the same time, Starshine, the yellow dragon, opened her mouth. Light so condensed that it was a heated beam pulsed in a line, striking the mass in the middle.

Several other dragons who had area-of-attack powers did the same, though with more limited effect. A spear of ice missed the scourgling mass completely and instead hit a nearby wall.

We'll have to work on accuracy, Arthur thought absentmindedly. But his heart had swelled with pride for his class.

Though not all of the card powers hit or were effective, they had started to attack at once. No hesitation.

One dragon flew over and spat out a tiny flurry of snowflakes that burned when they hit the mass. That seemed especially effective. It still rolled forward but with small freezer-burned chunks left behind.

"Turn and hit them again!" Arthur called. "Strafing run!"

Then the diamond formation passed over the scourgling mass and turned in a tight circle, guided by Joy and anchored in the middle by Shadow's excellent flying. Then they headed straight on for another pass, flying low, just above the tops of the buildings.

Though the scourgling mass was looking ragged thanks to the attacks, it continued to doggedly roll forward as if it wasn't completely aware of them at all.

Until, just as the first few dragons flew over it again, the entire thing blew apart.

At first, Arthur thought someone had lobbed some kind of explosive power at it, though he didn't remember anyone having that type of card. Then, as he caught a flash of dark misshapen parts of the scourgling jabbing into dragon flesh, he realized he'd just led the formation into an attack.

On instinct, he reached for his Phase In, Phase Out card, worrying that Brixaby might not have the presence of mind to do the same. They had access to each other's cards, as the borders that defined his heart deck and Brixaby's core were thin, but they hadn't had much practice at it.

He didn't have the chance to activate the card. In the next second, velvety darkness and odd crawling figures—were they closer than before?—surrounded them.

He, Brixaby, and Shadow erupted out of the dark side of the downed building several hundred feet from the impact. The veteran dragon had whisked them away.

"What?" Brixaby buzzed straight up in surprise, looking around to get his bearings. "Why are we here?"

Arthur, though, had twisted to look back toward the formation. It was in complete disarray.

Some dragons were down on the ground, and some were still aloft and screaming with pieces of dark shards sticking out of scales and flesh. The few who seemed to be untouched were flying, scattered and confused.

Joy's distinctive pink hide was still visible in the air, though from this far away, Arthur couldn't see if she was bleeding.

Meanwhile, the scourgling that had been a mass was now scattered everywhere. It was reduced to hundreds of mobile sticks with teeth on each end, snapping this way and that as it flailed in random directions. Some of the snapping sticks recombined with others and started, once again, rolling toward the crowd of trapped people.

"Take us back, Shadow," Arthur said.

"I cannot. My orders are to keep you safe," Shadow said and added, as if sensing Arthur's growing outrage, "You are a Legendary rider. There is only one of you and many Commons and Uncommons."

Arthur didn't give a damn, and he was about to reach for the Shadow Teleport power himself.

At that moment, Brixaby let out a roar and launched off his shoulder, not at Shadow, but at several scourglings which had recombined and were tumbling their way.

"No, Brix!" Arthur yelled.

But his dragon acted like he was possessed. Although he didn't have a strict combat card to fight the scourglings, he had strength and agility thanks to Arthur's Master of Body Enhancement card.

Brixaby fell on the scourglings with teeth and claws alone. When one stubborn mini-mass detonated again, Brixaby simply let it phase through him, using Arthur's card power. Then he fell on the split pieces and ripped them to shreds.

Meanwhile, the initial shock had worn off the rest of the class, and those who could were fighting back.

Cressida, who, by the looks of things, had saved herself and Joy completely by using her shield power, sent another flame bear to great effect among the scattered scourglings. Her summon batted them with ghostly claws the size of dinner plates, or else bowled straight through larger masses. Nothing stood in its way.

Starshine was once again beaming her condensed light on small recombining masses and burning them to cinders. Even Keelfree, who had the burning snowfall charms, was peppering some of the remaining scourge. A few had landed and, like Brixaby, were using teeth and claws against the things before they could reform.

"Dragons should not fight on the ground," Shadow commented pointedly. "That's where we are most vulnerable."

Cupping his hands around his mouth, Arthur called out, "Form up! Take to the sky!"

Brixaby finished with the last of his scourgling and quickly returned with his claws full of Common card shards—his harvested haul. Each piece of the scourgling was good for one shard.

Arthur took them with a grimace. Common. A good portion of his class had been injured by a *Common*-ranked scourgling.

Well, a card shard was a card shard. He dropped them into his Personal Space.

Only one dragon couldn't fly. He was the blue who had badly thrown a spear of ice. Luckily, he was small enough to crawl upon the back of an orange dragon who, much like Arthur and Brixaby, didn't have many combat skills.

The orange dragon did have long claws, which were now inky wet with dark scourgling blood, and a smug look on his face.

Fully half of the class was injured, but most were also pocketing new card shards.

The remains of the scourgling mass were trying to recombine again. Under Brixaby's direction, the dragons swooped down to collect litter from the streets—chunks of broken masonry, fallen rocks, and furniture spilled from smashed-open homes. They then dropped these on the recombining scourglings to squish them from afar.

It was a lot safer than using untested power so close to trapped people and their own classmates. It saved on mana too.

Shadow flew in wide circles above, allowing Arthur to sit and watch and feel useless.

Even if he had a card with long-range abilities, he had been lectured time and time again that his place as a Legendary rider was to stay out of the fight except in the direst circumstances. It was a minor faux pas that Arthur allowed Brixaby to join in on dropping stones on the scourglings. They were meant to save up their strength.

Arthur didn't like it, and he didn't agree with it. But Instructor Athena had not followed them through the rip in the sky because *he* was the ranking rider. That meant he was in charge.

This was how the hive trained their riders. Sink or swim. Fight or die.

He wondered if this was Valentina's and Whitaker's decision or if this was simply how things had always been done.

If it is, he thought, *that's another thing I mean to change.*

In the back of his mind, he again saw a horrific scene when he was twelve years old: a pink dragon being torn apart by two others. Finding the rider's corpse was how Arthur had gotten his Return to Start card.

It wasn't unusual for dragons not to return from scourge-eruptions. The missing were always logged as simple casualties. More and more often, Arthur wondered if it was really that simple. And if the people in charge knew better than to ask too many questions, and if Uncommon and Common pairs were considered that disposable . . .

A triumphant shout came from behind him. Arthur turned to see brown Char, who he had set to clearing the debris, had finally succeeded.

A thin column of broken stone and brick melted away before his eyes. Some additional stones fell into the new gap, but the waiting crowd didn't care. They surged forward, some sobbing with relief to get that much farther away from the scourglings and battling dragons. Some folks had the presence of mind to call out thank-yous to the brown and rider.

Char and his rider bowed their heads, not out of acknowledgment but out of simple exhaustion. Arthur didn't need an extra mana sense to know they were depleted. They had saved perhaps a hundred people but at the cost of becoming useless for the fight to come. It was worth it.

Meanwhile, the class was finishing up with the final pieces of the scourgling mass. No more dark twig pieces so much as twitched.

Arthur waited for the last of it to be harvested and then called the dragons back into formation, though several were visibly bleeding from the surprise explosive attack.

Arthur pointed to his riders. "You, you, you, and you . . . oh, and you. Fly back through the Wolf Moon Hive rip and return for healing. You're done for the day."

To his surprise, he didn't receive any backtalk. Most of the riders looked exhausted, and no one wanted to see their dragons bleeding and hurt.

Arthur turned to Cressida. "How's your mana?"

"A little more than half gone," she admitted. "Summoning Wicker for so long, and throwing that shield around me and Joy really took it out of me."

Arthur hesitated. Although Joy wasn't bleeding, if Cressida's mana had fallen that dramatically, she might not be able to protect herself and her dragon if there was another attack.

But he wanted her around. If he weren't in this class, she would be the leader, as a Rare rider. As such, she was his second-in-command.

She was also someone he trusted.

As if on cue, Joy spoke up. "Arthur, my quest just updated!"

"Tell me," he ordered.

"Now it has a twenty-minute timer. The rewards haven't changed, though." She sagged. "That's a bummer."

Her quest update must have sparked something through her aura. Arthur and Brixaby both picked up a version of the quest themselves.

New Quest: An Ally Calls for Aid
An old ally from the past once helped you out and now needs assistance in turn. Will you help them in their hour of need?
Rewards: Vital information/Access to Noble Woodmours's card library

An ally?

Marion? Arthur thought. He didn't know where his friend had gone after Brixaby had hatched, but with his connections as an ex-prince, it wasn't hard to imagine him winding up on a powerful noble's land.

Beside him, Brixaby whooped in happiness and buzzed loop-the-loops in the air. The dragon didn't care about Marion, but he loved quest rewards.

"What are we waiting for?" Brixaby boomed as he came out of his loop. "Let us go get—I mean *save* some cards!"

CHAPTER 5

After many of the dragons were sent back to the hive for healing, they only had enough to form a single diamond formation instead of the previous double diamond. Arthur placed Cressida at the top point, with himself anchoring the position in the middle.

Two dragon pairs flew on his direct right and left: a red with the power of fire that, for some reason, bloomed into flower shapes, and Tamya, who'd first seen the scourgling mass coming. She and her blue Len had fine control over salt water. Holding the back line was an orange dragon who, like Arthur and Brixaby, did not have combat power. Instead, their specialty was to create lifelike, and sometimes tangible, illusions. It was impressive for a Common, though the orange could not pull the trick often without exhausting herself.

"Cressida, lead the way to Woodmours," Arthur said.

With the pink pair leading the way, they flew over the city.

Dragons from all twelve hives were thick in the air, diving and throwing card powers to take out scourglings in groups and solo. But the city environment worked against them, with countless places for scourglings to hide. The winding, sometimes confusing, streets stopped people from escaping.

Dragons with the Lobos patch and rescue groups from other hives were still hard-pressed to lead people out of the way. Other dragons worked in teams to block streets before scourglings could break past and spill into more populated parts of the city. Unfortunately, this often trapped those who were too slow to evacuate. They were sacrificed to save the others.

Cries for help drifted up from below.

Arthur gritted his teeth, wishing he could stay and help. A small but selfishly vocal part of him also wished they dared to fly higher so he didn't have to hear these screams or see people being chased down.

But for all of the dragons who were battling scourglings at the ground level, there was an equal amount fighting scourglings on the wing in the air. Flying higher would make the entire formation a target.

Swallowing hard, Arthur looked firmly ahead and tried not to listen.

Meanwhile, the eruption continued without stopping. The cone had grown by a full third from when they had gotten there a scant few minutes ago, and its base had now swallowed up entire buildings.

"Do you think a demi-scourgling will erupt?" Brixaby asked. Unlike Arthur, he leaned his neck down and watched the streets avidly.

Arthur shook his head. "I don't know. It's our job to secure at least one of the card stashes and keep that from happening. And if a demi-scourgling does erupt . . . it'll be our job to help stop it, too."

Brixaby hummed under his breath, and Arthur was not entirely sure if the dragon was looking forward to that possibility or not.

It got better as they flew toward the edge of the city directly to the east. The worst of the scourge-eruption had not reached this area yet. People were able to evacuate at a more orderly pace, but that didn't mean they were completely out of danger.

The formation flew over a pack of swiftly running scourglings that looked like racing hounds with thin bodies and sharp heads. The beasts ran as fast as a horse could gallop.

As they glided over, the red dragon craned her neck and spat. Bouquets of wildfire drifted down. When the fire touched the scourglings, it twisted them up into living vines, thorn flames piercing flesh and burning.

"Permission to go down and harvest?" the red's rider yelled.

"No time," Arthur called back. "Good job, though," he added. "You saved lives there."

The rider shrugged, disappointment on her face that she couldn't reap the reward for her good deed.

Soon, the cobblestone roads ended and were replaced by gravel and then dirt, bordered on both sides by livestock farms. Finally, they came to rolling fields, some thick with harvest.

"Woodmours Estate is dead ahead," Cressida called out.

Arthur gestured sarcastically forward. "Oh, you mean that giant castle?"

"That's the one," she confirmed.

He figured that was it. It was easily the tallest building outside of the city. The tiny cottages and humble homes surrounding it were small, but their thatch roofs and simple gardens were well outstripped by their lord's obvious wealth. Not all of the small buildings were in good repair, either. It looked like they'd been attacked by weather and neglect rather than scourglings.

It reminded Arthur of his childhood village . . . although these people were at least allowed to keep private gardens for their own food.

The castle ahead had four main towers, bracketed by equally large buildings on all sides. It looked like a place to easily get lost inside, and that was coming from someone who lived in a dragon hive.

"How much time is left on the quest?" Arthur called out.

Joy craned her head to answer back, "Five minutes, thirty seconds."

They had traveled miles in those fifteen minutes, faster than he could have ever traveled with a galloping horse, but it still wasn't fast enough. They had only minutes left.

Arthur looked around anxiously, then scolded himself. It wasn't as if there was going to be a sign stating: Card Library is here!

The cards were likely well-defended deep within the castle. Possibly underground.

Yet . . . why were there only a few minutes left on the timer? There was no sign of life. Only a few scattered sheep on the hills. No horses or goats or the shepherds to attend to them. Not even any herding dogs left to manage the lone sheep. Had they all evacuated already?

"That courtyard is big enough to land in," the blue rider called out.

Arthur nodded but didn't give the signal to descend. "Does anybody see signs of scourglings? Do you see any people or animals?"

"I think the Woodmourses are in their touring season," Cressida called back.

"What?"

She turned almost entirely around in Joy's saddle to give him a scathing look. "*Touring season*," she repeated with emphasis. "It means the main family is likely in a summer home in a more pleasant climate right now. That's what nobles *do*, Arthur."

Arthur internally winced.

Cressida still had not forgiven him over the "By the way, I'm related to Duke Rowantree" thing. She had not gone as far as to ask to be taken off his retinue when they finally graduated, but she made it clear that she was annoyed with him on several levels for the secrecy.

While their friendship had taken a hit, she usually remained smoothly professional during class and training time. However, sometimes her lingering irritation leaked out.

He wasn't sure how to make it up to her. So far, he'd just tried to give her space.

"Are we landing or what?" the red rider asked. Then she added almost with reluctance, "Sir."

Arthur glanced down at the deserted courtyard, which was clean with no signs of anyone having left in a hurry. No sign of Marion, either.

Something felt off.

Instead of ordering the landing, he gestured with his arm for them to circle the area.

"Brixaby, I don't like the look of that courtyard. Can you check it out?" he asked.

Brixaby looked at him quizzically. "Check what out? There's no one here, which means the card library will be unguarded," he said eagerly.

"I seriously doubt they left it unguarded," Arthur replied. "Just look around the courtyard before we land. Something's not right about this."

Even if the noble was off . . . touring—whatever that meant—there should be a great deal of support staff. Arthur saw no one.

Brixaby shrugged his wings and flew off Arthur's shoulder, diving down toward the courtyard.

He pulled up just before his claws touched the brickwork and buzzed straight up again.

"Do not land in that courtyard!" he roared.

The young dragons, who had been flying in a decent diamond formation, wavered and called out,

"What's wrong?"

"What's going on?"

"What happened?"

Arthur ignored them and waited until Brixaby landed back on his shoulder.

For once, his dragon sounded shaken. "My danger sense went off just as I almost landed."

Shortly after hatching, Brixaby had partially absorbed a Legendary time card, which gave him a useful forewarning sense. However, it rarely went off. Arthur suspected that the triggering event had to be truly dangerous, which confirmed that something was wrong.

"Do you know what set it off?"

"I don't," Brixaby growled. "Only that whatever it is, it's bad."

Joy called out, "What do we do? We only have three minutes left."

Unexpectedly, Shadow spoke up. "Never forget to keep your eyes on the sky."

Arthur glanced up and saw three dragons approaching in an arrow formation: a silver in the lead, flanked by two fierce-looking reds, one of which was bristling with spikes that had flames coming out.

"I think we just found out why that quest is counting down," Arthur muttered.

He signaled for the rest of the diamond formation to keep circling the castle. Meanwhile, he ordered Shadow to fly upward on an intercept angle with the trio. As the ranking rider, it was his duty to learn what the other dragons wanted.

As they got closer, Arthur got a vague sense of the strength of their cards. "A Rare and two Uncommons?" he asked Brixaby.

"I think so," Brixaby replied. "But those two Uncommons have their cores stuffed with cards."

This was a combat trio, then.

Arthur reached down to touch Shadow's neck. "If we get in trouble, could you Shadow Teleport us out?"

"Only to another shadow, and the biggest one is by that castle. I'm told that it's dangerous," Shadow added, almost sarcastically.

"Well, let's not push them," Arthur said.

Thankfully, the silver started to slow his descent when it became obvious that Arthur was there to greet them. As all the adult dragons were of the typical body style—two wings and four limbs—they couldn't stop and hover like Brixaby did.

As a result, all of the dragons slowly circled each other as the riders spoke. It felt exactly as ominous as it likely looked.

"This castle and all its contents are now the property of Blood Moon Hive," the silver's rider called out. He was a beefy man atop an equally beefy dragon with glinting claws. Silvers were usually pure magic dragons, but Arthur had the feeling this one was unusually combat focused.

Arthur saw no reason to play stupid. "The card library, you mean?"

"Call it what you want, kid," the silver rider called back. "We are here on our hive leader's orders."

"So am I," Arthur said. "I'm Arthur, with Brixaby." That name should get some recognition, at least.

"I'm a Legendary," Brixaby said, just in case they didn't get it. "And that means I outrank all three of you. Now go away."

The silver dragon snorted, sending Brixaby tumbling end over end with a minor wind power. "You haven't even graduated training yet, hatchling."

The flame-tipped red's rider called out, "What's the matter? The kids haven't learned how to land your dragons yet?"

"You shouldn't go down there," Arthur said. "One of our group members has a forewarning card. We have reason to believe that something in that castle is dangerous."

"Of course it's dangerous. We're in the middle of a scourge-eruption. Stand aside, we have the rank," replied the silver's rider.

Brixaby bristled. "No, you don't."

"They do," Shadow said with a sigh. "You haven't graduated yet, and Blood Moon is one of the top hives. Wolf Moon is, well, on the bottom."

"Thanks for that," Arthur muttered, wishing Shadow had kept quiet.

The other red snarled. "Do you hatchlings intend to stop us?"

Brixaby growled and flexed his claws.

Arthur shook his head. "I'm warning you, don't go down there."

The silver's rider seemed to have had enough. He made a quick chopping gesture. With practiced synchronization, all three dragons folded their wings and dove as if they expected to be stopped by card powers.

Arthur didn't bother, though inwardly he was frustrated.

Yes, the castle had set off Brixaby's danger sense, but he suspected that whatever those three combat-focused dragons faced, they could handle it.

Probably some scourglings hiding in the shadows, he thought.

They were on the verge of failing the quest, but at least the card library would be protected from the scourglings. That was the important thing.

Maybe they could go back to the city and help people directly.

Surprised by the diving dragons, the rest of his class, still in diamond formation, scattered and flew to the sides to give the much-larger adults room.

Either that wasn't good enough for the silver or they wanted to send a message because a gust of wind blew several of the slower flyers sharply to the side.

Arthur signaled the rest of his class to reform and gain height. "Let's get back to the city."

"But the quest!" Joy whined. "It has . . . wow, forty-five seconds left."

"You have your orders," Arthur said, irritated with himself and the waste of time.

With mulish expressions, the class did as they were told. Arthur looked back.

The three adult dragons had taken the time to circle the courtyard once and likely not seen anything obvious. As the quest counted down to the final seconds, they swooped to land in the middle of the courtyard.

And the entire castle exploded.

CHAPTER 6

The powerful concussive blast threw Arthur, Shadow, and Brixaby end over end.

Only the fact that a dragon saddle was not built like a horse's saddle, but had straps to keep the rider firmly seated, kept Arthur from flying off into the air. The straps tightened painfully around his thighs and waist—thankfully not damaging because of his Toughened Skin enhancement.

He had just enough presence of mind to grab Brixaby off his shoulder and throw him into his Personal Space. As long as Arthur stayed alive and his card unharvested, Brixaby would be safe there.

Sudden darkness surrounded him, and for a moment Arthur feared he had somehow thrown himself into his Personal Space as well. But the darkness had a velvety quality that was familiar: This wasn't extra-spatial storage. Shadow had teleported again.

Those shadow monsters were closer than ever. Arthur saw limbs, and though he couldn't move, one reached for him . . .

In the next moment, they burst into light and chaos again, an explosion so close that Arthur felt it more than heard it.

Then a return to darkness as Shadow once again teleported with Arthur aboard.

Another monster, more bulbous than the last, reached for him again. Arthur couldn't do so much as lean back . . .

They popped back into the light, this time in the dappled shadows of the tree line across the field.

Shadow staggered in place, and Arthur had to clutch at the sharp ridges of the dragon's neck to keep from flopping to the side. The world was spinning around him in a nauseating, swooping way that didn't make sense because his eyes told him that everything was stable.

Instinctively, Arthur reached up to touch his right ear, and his hand came back slick and wet with blood. Weren't inner-ear problems supposed to cause dizziness? Had that shadow monster in the velvet dark space been real?

"What just happened?" he croaked, and though he knew his voice was working, he couldn't hear anything.

Shadow regained his feet, and Arthur felt his reply through the rumble in his body, but the words were lost.

One of the lectures that Arthur had attended in basic dragon class came back to him: always look to the health of the beast first. Though his mind was screaming with questions—*What happened? Where is the rest of the class? Where is Cressida? Is the combat trio dead? Was this a scourge attack or a heinous booby trap? What was that monster?*—he pushed them all aside and focused on performing a quick visual assessment of Shadow.

The dragon had stopped staggering and had his head up high in an alert posture. Arthur couldn't see any blood. While Arthur's inner ears had somehow been injured by the blast, he suspected that Shadow's weren't. From an offhand comment during one of the other lectures he'd learned, dragons' inner ears were more durable than a human's, as they were flying creatures and naturally had to compensate for quick altitude changes.

Speaking of his ears, Arthur heard a sudden pop in his head that followed a brief flash of pain. He worked his jaw open and closed, and noise filtered back into his brain, distorted and dim at first but rapidly growing in clarity as if something inside was focusing it.

Or, more accurately, his internal healing card was going to work. He would have to swallow his pride and thank Valentina once again for that fortuitous card.

"Where is he?" Shadow asked with the exasperated tone of someone who had already repeated himself.

"Who?" Arthur croaked.

Shadow's voice was sharp. "Your dragon, fool!"

"He's in my spatial storage space. He's safe. What happened?" He kept his sentences short because his ears were still adjusting with painful crackles and pops, though his hearing was getting clearer. For example, he could now pick out continuing explosions from the direction of the castle.

"Those idiots set off a powerful trap card," Shadow said. "They died like they lived, like looters."

Arthur glanced back to the castle, just in time to see one of the towers fall into what was left of the courtyard. This caused a cascade of other mini explosions, which sent more debris flying in all directions. The formerly grand castle was now a pile of rubble with occasional walls and two towers sticking out.

"I meant what happened back there with your teleportation," Arthur said. "You teleported us twice in a row? Those . . . those shadow things—"

"*You* try to teleport out of an explosion with shadows dancing everywhere," Shadow snipped, avoiding Arthur's last question. He added almost bitterly, "I only hope that the castle was trapped against anyone in general from stepping in the courtyard and not against dragons specifically."

That hadn't occurred to Arthur, and it should have. He needed to get over his shock, stop reacting, and try to take control of the situation.

His first step was to remove Brixaby from his Personal Space.

The moment he was free, the little dragon flew immediately upward, looking annoyed. "If you're going to throw me somewhere safe, at least follow me so I know you are safe too!"

"That's not how it works," Arthur reminded him, though he was mildly surprised that Brixaby even knew he was in the Personal Space . . . until he remembered that Brixaby's nullify magic interacted oddly with the timeless nature of the card. "My mind can visit, but my body stays out here."

"We need to fix that! And . . . you're bleeding . . ."

Arthur touched his forehead where Brixaby was looking, and it came away with blood.

"It's nothing, already healing." He dropped his hand. "We need to gather up the others. Shadow, can you fly?"

In answer, Shadow took immediately to the air.

Brixaby flew ahead of the other dragon, booming out, "Form up. Diamond formation! Gather up!"

It didn't take long to get everyone airborne again. By the looks of things, the entire class had been scattered, with most either knocked to the ground or fled there to escape the unsafe skies. Somehow, aside from minor injuries and a little deafening, all were well.

Cressida had Joy fly up next to Shadow. She looked pale with more than simple shock. "I had to use my shield to save us, and I'm almost completely out of mana."

Arthur swore under his breath, then nodded. As much as it pained him, he couldn't keep her around. The health of his riders came first.

"Then go back to the hive," he said, "and send word to Valentina what happened here. Whitaker, too, if you can find him—"

Brixaby broke in. "Do you hear that?"

Arthur hesitated—his hearing wasn't fully back to normal, but he sat still and listened. Except for the sounds of flapping dragon wings and rumbles from still-collapsing debris, he caught it: whistling. The calls from excited, hunting scourglings.

They were coming. Likely, they had been alerted to their location by the explosion.

Arthur glanced around to take in the state of his class. Though they had formed up in a very loose diamond formation, most of the pairs were already ranging out with dragons and riders searching the littered ground. No doubt searching for body parts of the combat trio—the telltale glow that they could harvest cards from.

No one else but him and Cressida, from the dawning horror on her face, noticed the scourglings yet.

"Also," Brixaby said, "we still have our quest."

Joy perked up. "You do? Ugh, that's not fair. Cressida and I failed ours."

Arthur swiftly checked the status of his quest, and sure enough, the quest to aid an ally was still active, though the timer had been removed and so had the reward for access to the card library. But the reward for vital information still remained. That was odd.

He looked again at the remains of the castle. Only dense rubble existed where the building had once stood. There was no way anybody had survived.

"The library would be well-shielded. Shadow, fly us over the top of the castle."

Occasional stones were still falling from the remains of high towers and parapets, causing miniature secondary explosions. The dragon gave him a baleful look, but Brixaby immediately buzzed ahead, and Joy followed.

Without immediate orders, the others took the opportunity to range a little farther out and keep searching for harvestable materials.

Let them, Arthur thought wearily. If they could glean combat cards from the arrogant trio, then all the better. Arthur planned on doing the same if circumstances allowed it.

"Gain altitude," Shadow barked at Brixaby and angled upward to be high over its apex of any lingering explosions.

As they flew over, Arthur realized what he thought was a great mound of debris was actually a wall surrounding a crater. And at the bottom of that crater glinted a dome of energy, so thick he couldn't see through it. He had seen something like this in Buck Moon Hive. That had been a semitransparent shield meant to keep the powers of dueling combatants away from the watching audience.

Arthur had no doubt what this particular shield was protecting. "The card library has to be down there," he said, then looked back at the direction of the whistles. They had grown loud enough that even the scavenging dragons had taken notice. Squinting, Arthur thought he caught dark movement along the tree line that stood right before the far east field.

The scourglings were massing—perhaps they sensed the card library.

"We can't let them have it," he muttered. Though he silently wondered if it was worth putting his riders' lives on the line. If the shield had protected against that explosion, it had a good chance of standing against scourglings.

But if he was wrong . . .

Brixaby, of course, had another idea. "We must get to the cards before they do. Then shovel them into your Personal Space. I just checked. There's plenty of room."

"And if a couple goes missing, that's carrying tax," Cressida said lightly.

Arthur gave her a look, and she shrugged.

"Joy is almost old enough to gain a secondary deck, and she needs some combat cards."

"I'll be the best combatant ever!" Joy confirmed.

"It's not the physical weight of the cards I'm worried about—it's the magical weight." But Arthur's argument was half-hearted. "Okay, but only if we can figure out how to get past that shield. Hey, Shadow, do you think you could teleport in there? It should be nice and dark . . ."

Shadow stared down for a moment, considering. "No, you've seen what dwells in that realm. They've caught our scent. It won't be safe to teleport there for a few minutes. Besides," he added as Arthur started to wrap his mind around that, "I can feel shadows under the dome, but . . . they're moving."

"Moving?" Arthur repeated.

The scales around Shadow's snout crinkled in the dragon version of a frown. "It's more like solid objects are moving to create shadows. I believe someone is down there. Multiple beings."

"Scourglings?" Arthur asked.

Below them, the energy dome flickered. Then, abruptly, it died altogether.

At least a dozen full-grown dragons burst up and out from where the dome had been. They were in all colors, and roaring so fiercely that Shadow, Joy, and Brixaby all flinched back in surprise.

"Hive dragons!" came the call from below.

"Kill!

"Flee! Open the portal!"

"Wait!" Arthur called, looking around wildly. None of the dragons had riders aboard. They didn't even have saddles. These were wild dragons. "We aren't here to hurt you!"

Had they been trapped down there? Captured? Were they fleeing for their lives?

One of the dragons, a menacing red with yellow eyes, was carrying something in its claws. A net with glowing rune marks and sigils woven through it.

With practiced ease, it threw the net at Cressida and Joy, who squealed in surprise.

Joy began to fold her wings into a dive, but the net expanded in the air, twice as large as the smallish pink. It closed around them both. The red dragon pulled the net taut, and the two simply . . . disappeared.

"Joy!" Brixaby roared and would have shot after them, but Shadow turned, his claws reaching out to snatch the little dragon from the air. In the next second, velvet darkness engulfed them.

It was a fraction of a second, and Arthur didn't see the monsters in the other realm before they erupted below an unbroken wall, right underneath the dragons.

"What are you doing?" Arthur yelled.

"Keeping you safe."

"Arthur!" Brixaby yelled from within Shadow's claws. "They're escaping!"

To Arthur's horror, he saw a riderless green dragon trying to rip open a portal in the sky. Unlike the hive dragons, the process was laborious. The green was already panting with the stress.

Meanwhile, the other young dragon pairs in the class were scattering, and the riderless wild dragons were paying them no heed. They flew around the green, urging him on.

A dark rip split the sky. They were going to escape, and if Cressida and Joy were somehow with them . . .

But there was more, because Arthur had *recognized* the red that had taken them.

He'd seen it once when he was twelve years old.

Arthur didn't think. He didn't have time to even fight with the buckles and straps that held him in his saddle. The moment Shadow realized what was going on, he'd just teleport again.

So Arthur grabbed his sharpest knife from his Personal Space and slashed it across the straps holding him to his saddle. He had a very high Knifework Skill, and the leather parted instantly.

Leaping from Shadow's neck, he ran, with Brixaby bellowing rage from within Shadow's claws.

Shadow called out to him, but Arthur ignored him. A moment later, Brixaby buzzed right over his head, his own claws now streaked with Shadow's blood.

Arthur yelled toward the red dragon, using every voice-projection trick that his skills would give him. "Hey, Red! Remember this?" Then he projected his Master of Skills card into the sky.

The red stopped halfway to the opening portal. Its yellow eyes focused on him.

"Take them," he said.

That was probably a bad idea. Arthur held up his hands. "Wait, we can talk—"

Other rune nets were cast from above.

Shadow reached Arthur in time to close wings around him and Brixaby, as if to shield them both.

Through the gap in the wings, Arthur saw the net fall and surround them all.

Then for a long moment that somehow felt like the time between one breath and another, there was nothing.

PART 2
A GUEST
(WHO CANNOT LEAVE)

CHAPTER 7

The next thing Arthur knew, he, Brixaby, and Shadow stood somewhere else entirely.

Gone were the rolling, fertile fields that had been scattered with debris from the castle. Now, the ground was arid and scraped raw from the wind and blazing sun overhead. But not quite dead like the scourge-ravaged lands.

They were surrounded by dragons and hostile-looking people who pointed spears, bows, and swords at them.

"Welcome to Mesa Free Hive," drawled a sardonic voice. "I am Chablis."

A dark-skinned woman stood in front of the general crowd with crossed arms. Though she was dressed in common brown-gray homespun threads that were certainly not new, they were clean. There was an air about her that proclaimed her as the leader.

Shadow snarled in reply, and so did Brixaby, who'd dropped to Arthur's shoulder.

Arthur looked around, his heart still beating fast with adrenaline from seeing Cressida and Joy disappear within the confines of a net. Though it felt like only a few moments ago, a deeper sense told him that much more time had passed.

The bright sun was high in the sky, though the portal might have transferred them across several time zones. They could be anywhere in the kingdom.

"Where is the other rider your people captured?" he said to Chablis, then looked at the other dragons for signs of nets in their claws.

"Rider?" she repeated.

"Yes," he said with an edge in his voice. "Our training class was attacked by your dragons." That last part was an assumption, but he hoped it was a reasonable one.

Someone called out from the audience, "How'd that kid link with two dragons?"

Shadow turned and snapped at the would-be heckler, showing teeth. "He is *not* my rider. He's an idiot I'm trying to keep safe!"

Arthur pressed on. "Shadow is helping me and my dragon, Brixaby. We are from Wolf Moon Hive, still in *training*."

Arthur intentionally kept his rank as a Legendary quiet. It wasn't that he didn't expect anybody else to sense it—especially if any of these people were dragon riders—but he knew that throwing around his rank would not go well with people already unimpressed with him.

It only bred resentment, and as they were severely outnumbered, that would be a bad idea.

He looked around. "One of your dragons captured a pair: a pink and her rider. They are part of my retinue. Where are they?"

The woman's eyebrows shot up. "They're safe."

"Then show them to me."

She chuckled and shook her head. "You are not in charge here, young master." This last part was said with the deepest sarcasm. "Now, what did you say your name was?"

He got the impression that she knew exactly who he was and this was an attempt to rile him up. Nobles hated it when commoners didn't automatically know them on sight.

Inwardly, Arthur activated his Charming Gentle-Person card and checked his class stats to make sure the usual ones were equipped—Gambler and Cooking. He wanted every point of Luck and Charisma he could scrape up.

This would only become a battle of strength if he failed to talk himself out of this.

"My name is Arthur, and this is Brixaby," he said, "from Wolf Moon Hive."

"Hmm . . . Arthur and Brixaby." She made a show of pretending to think. "You wouldn't happen to be the new Legendary pair, would you?"

Out of the corner of his eye, he saw some people shift around uncomfortably. "We are."

Chablis sighed. "Well, I'd hoped not. That will certainly stir up the hives more than they already have been." Then she looked over her shoulder. It must have been a signal because the red dragon he recognized earlier pushed through the crowd to stare down at Arthur.

The red inhaled, nostrils flaring. "Well, it does seem that some cubs grow up and develop teeth. Now you're a dragon rider. A stooge of the hives."

In a flash, Brixaby flew to a point right before the red dragon's nose. "Arthur is good and brave! If you don't watch your forked tongue, I'll pluck out your core card and give it to a Rare who will serve me."

The two dragons snarled at each other. It should have been ridiculous because Brixaby was about the length of one of the red's front teeth, but an indefinable sense of power rolled out from him. It was the strength of his Legendary core card, enhanced by the pair of Legendary cards he'd linked with Arthur.

Arthur suspected that sense of power was the reason why they had not been outright killed from the first moment.

No doubt, these people could manage it if they piled on them all at once, but caution had so far held them back. They probably didn't know the extent of Arthur's and Brixaby's powers—that every card that was thrown at them would be used against them. But more than enough rumors about Brixaby had gone out to make most worry. Nobody wanted to lose their cards.

Arthur was more than happy to let Brixaby play the evil card-stealing dragon while he took on a more reasonable tone.

Stepping forward, Arthur held out open hands. "I think there's been a . . . misunderstanding. Our training class was on a mission to protect a card library from the scourglings. Nothing more."

There were some scattered laughs throughout the crowd. Someone called out, "Yeah, the library was *protected* all right."

That meant it had probably been looted.

Arthur kept his expression neutral. "If the cards were kept away from the scourglings, then I'm satisfied. Meanwhile, my dragon and the rider pair you captured need to return to the eruption. We're needed in case there's a demi-scourgling."

Chablis held up her hand. "The eruption was three days ago."

Three *days*?

A pit opened in his stomach. What if he and Brixaby had been needed? What if a demi-scourgling had erupted?

Immediately, Arthur checked the status of the countdown timer for the Shadow Teleport.

As Shadow was a Rare, the Counterfeit Siphon copy effect lasted for an hour. However, that timer had long since expired. From Brixaby's slightly unfocused expression, he was checking the same.

In fact, the only thing that had not expired yet was their quest to aid an ally. Likely because it no longer had a timer on it.

Noting that Arthur was caught completely flat-footed, Chablis's lips twisted into a sarcastic smile.

"Our spies have reported back that teams were sent to your location. Not rescue teams, mind you, but *recovery* teams with express orders to harvest cards." She paused for a moment to let that sink in, then continued blithely, "Apparently, they've gone over the area with a fine-toothed comb. Several of the hives are already accusing one another of secretly holding your cards. What do you say to that, new Legendary rider?"

Arthur thought for a moment. "I suppose most people suspect the Blood Moon Hive of looting our bodies?"

There was a distinct pause, then a couple of barked laughs from the crowd.

It took Arthur a moment to realize that they had expected him to be arrogant and incensed over the thought that the hives were already fighting over his heart cards. They expected him to be a high-handed noble.

It was all too easy to imagine somebody like his cousin, Penn, yelling at the woman, accusing her of lying. Other nobles would have no problem throwing their powers around.

They were, he realized, in an awkward stalemate.

This woman and her crowd could kill Arthur and Brixaby eventually and harvest their cards, but it would come at a ruinous cost. In addition, he felt there was some other power play going on.

He had learned a lot of dragon body language over the last few weeks since he had linked with Brixaby. When the red dragon had stepped forward, he had put himself between Arthur and the crowd.

The quest had said that Arthur was to aid an old ally. Could that mean the red?

So Arthur pressed forward in the moment the surprise had given him, shrugging one shoulder. "I heard how Noble Woodmours treats his people. I wasn't there to protect his interests, just the cards from getting swallowed up by our enemy."

Chablis's gaze sharpened. "And I suppose you wouldn't mind helping yourself to some of the cards as payment?"

This was a trap. She was testing him to see if he was too virtuous. As an experienced liar, Arthur easily sidestepped. Again, he shrugged.

"There would be a certain . . ." What had Cressida called it? "Carrying tax."

She relaxed very, very slightly. Admitting that he wasn't unbelievably honorable seemed to be the right move.

Shadow suddenly broke in, his tone full of wonder. "Is this . . . Did you say this is a free hive? You actually exist?"

"Who are *you*?" the red asked, as if noticing him for the first time.

The dragon straightened. "Shadow, once linked to Rider Torres, one of Denny's retinue. Who are you?"

"You may call me Laird. And I suppose once you lost your rider, you were thrown out of your hive?" the red pressed.

"No," Shadow said with a low growl. "Once I refused to link to a rider of their choosing, I was *exiled* to Wolf Moon Hive."

Arthur flinched. He hadn't known that. Of course, he hadn't exactly asked. It was wrong to demand that a dragon share their core with somebody not of their choosing. He hadn't even thought it was possible until he met the king.

Nevertheless, he couldn't get too distracted. He looked back toward Chablis. "I need to see my people and ensure that they are safe."

"You think that we are going to allow you your combat riders?"

Riders?

"How many did you take?" he asked. Then, with worry making him desperate, added, "We haven't done anything to you. We were following orders and were no threat."

"We couldn't be sure about that," the red said. "And we took two pairs: the pink and the blue."

"Laird!" the woman snapped. Apparently she felt he had given too much information.

The dragon tilted his head in a shrug.

Arthur's heart beat fast. "The pink is a meta, and the blue has powers over sea salt. They aren't combat riders."

That caused a little bit of a stir through the watching crowd, and he wasn't sure why.

Arthur continued. "I'm not asking for them to protect me. I'm here to protect them. I was put in charge of the class, and I need to ensure they are safe."

"How like a hive rider to make demands of us." But then the woman glanced back over her shoulder to exchange glances with a few others. They were actually considering it. She turned back. "The only way we would agree to your request is if you agree to wear enchanted card locks."

As if on cue, someone stepped forward with a pair of glowing bracelets etched with rune markings.

Including the nets, this was the second enchanted item he had seen from these people. This was no simple bandit camp. They had very high-level craftsmen here. Higher than he had seen in Wolf Moon Hive.

Arthur hesitated. Not because he was planning to pull a trick on them, but because he remembered very well what it felt like to be without his skills. That had been the Mythic Lung Bai's specialty, and it had left Arthur entirely helpless.

"Brixaby will not be locked," he said.

"We did not ask for the *child* to be locked," she replied easily. "Only you, as a show of good faith."

The child? That was odd phrasing.

Before he could open his mouth to respond, Brixaby moved. Quick as a blink, he dropped down from where he had been hovering at nose level with red Laird, and landed on Chablis's shoulder.

"Then you won't mind being my mount," Brixaby said darkly, his clawed forepaw falling to the base of her throat. "Nothing happens to Arthur while he is locked, and I don't start ripping cards out of hearts . . . starting with yours."

There was a very, very ominous stillness.

With remarkable poise, Chablis said, "As long as the rider is locked, we have no quarrel."

"Of course we do," Brixaby said. "You kidnapped us."

Time to take the more reasonable position. He and Brixaby were a good team. "If I agree, you bring back my riders and we talk," Arthur said.

"Agreed" was Chablis's quick answer.

Arthur very much did *not* want to lose access to his cards, but if this was what it took to ensure Cressida and the other pair were okay, he held out his hands.

"Then bring out my people."

The two bracelets clicked on, the designs on them glowing but unfathomable at first glance. Arthur steeled himself against the sense of weakness as even his bodily attributes were locked away from him.

However, it did not seem to interfere with the basic link between himself and Brixaby. Small mercy.

Meanwhile, two more nets with rune markings covering the weavings were brought out. Arthur didn't know much about what went into an enchanted item because Wolf Moon Hive was too small to attract ultra-high-quality crafters. From the little he understood, enchanted items were different from card anchors, which were directly tied back to the caster's card. A properly enchanted item took on power of its own.

He also saw that there was a difference between the nets coming out now and the net he, Brixaby, and Shadow had been held in. That net lay off to the side, limp, with the rune markings dead or flickering. Much of the weaving looked burned. He suspected that these were not Legendary-level enchantments and had been strained almost to the breaking point by holding him and Brixaby.

That was likely the true reason why they were here now. Chablis had to let them out before the enchantment failed and they were forced out.

Laird himself took one of the new nets. And even though it looked empty inside, he plunged his clawed hand in. Things started rattling around, and Arthur heard bleating sheep, annoyed chickens, and horses inside.

Had those dragons completely ransacked the Woodmours's estate?

That would explain why there hadn't seemed to be much livestock around.

Or people, he thought, with the start of a sick feeling. Somehow, he'd have to find the leverage to get those people back . . . assuming they wanted to return, having been abused by their noble.

Finally, Laird found what he needed and yanked his claws out. Through a twist of space that didn't track correctly to any of Arthur's senses, Joy and Cressida were suddenly standing in front of them, blinking and looking confused.

Joy's wings were half spread, as if she was about to flap. She paused and looked around. "It's so bright out here."

Cressida's reaction was much sharper. "What's going on? Who are you people?"

Laird's answer was to pull out the blue Len and his rider, Tamya. Honestly, Arthur didn't know that pair very well. He didn't think they had spoken more than a couple of sentences in his presence over the last couple of months.

Both Len and Tamya recoiled at finding themselves in front of so many people, identical frightened looks on their faces.

"It's going to be okay," Arthur said, for the benefit of all of them. "This is Laird, and this is Chablis. We've been taken from the Woodmours Estate."

"Yes, you are our *guests*," Laird said with a dragon smile full of sharp teeth. "You're in our Mesa Free Hive now."

Cressida swelled in indignation, and Arthur could practically see a "How dare you" forming on her lips, which was not going to be helpful. They did not need any noble attitude at this moment.

"They've agreed to let you out of the nets, and now we're going to talk," he said.

Upon hearing this, Cressida snapped, "Fine. What is a free hive?"

Arthur couldn't help it. He grinned.

She caught his look and leveled a stern one in return. "What?"

"It's just . . . I'm glad not to be the only one in the dark for once."

"Our free hive is located on the underside of this mesa," Chablis said. "Congratulations, you are no longer in the kingdom."

Cressida whirled around to stare at her. "What do you mean?" She looked down at her feet. "Are we in the scourge-killed lands?"

"Not anymore." Chablis gave probably the truest smile he had seen so far. "You see, what you have been told about the deadened lands beyond your kingdom is a lie."

There was a blank moment as everyone processed what had just been said. Then Cressida turned to Chablis with a scowl.

"You have my attention. What does that mean?"

Chablis smiled back with an edge of condescension. "Come, I will show you."

She gestured ahead toward the lip of the mesa, and as if this was a signal everybody had been waiting for, the crowd began to melt away. Most of the dragons outright flew off. The only ones who stayed were Chablis, Laird, Cressida and Joy, Arthur and Brixaby, Shadow, and the blue pair.

Arthur glanced around, then exchanged glances with Brixaby, who had taken the opportunity to lean over to sniff at the card-lock bracelets. He tested the runes with his forked tongue.

Meanwhile, Arthur was doing his best not to let his inner discomfort show. Lung Bai's block had been so subtle that he had not truly noticed it until he tried and failed to use his skills. This was much cruder.

There was a slight but noticeable weight pressing on his heart, as if the block were a physical thing. It wasn't something that he could ignore or that could sneak up on him. And though he couldn't put his finger on it, he felt like this block was the result of a Rare power. One that was still strong enough to interfere with the Legendary cards in his heart. But if he pushed it, he felt he *might* be able to break through. That gave him a little comfort.

Brixaby tilted his head this way as he studied the bracelets. "What do these runes mean?"

"I'm not sure."

"Do not scratch or try to break them," Laird rumbled from above. "I understand that the backlash of ruining enchanted objects can be severe."

Brixaby recoiled for a moment, but just as quickly bent back to examining them. He was bent over, his tail wrapped around the back of Arthur's neck for balance. "I do like how they glow, Arthur. These would look good against my scales."

"You *want* a card lock?" Arthur asked.

"Of course not. But surely there are benign runes."

"Only if you can get them to glow red," Joy piped up, "then they would match your eyes."

Brixaby turned to her. "You think that would look good?"

"Oh yeah, super scary," Joy said, curving her neck to look at her own pink scales. "But red wouldn't work for me. Red would look good on you, too," she said to the blue dragon Len.

Len looked mildly startled to be addressed at all. He and his rider, Tamya, were trailing a few steps behind the group as if they were hoping not to get noticed.

After an awkward moment, Len bobbed his head to Joy. "As you say, ma'am."

Joy gave an exaggerated sigh and returned to Brixaby.

They continued across the length of the mesa, and that was no short walk. Arthur found it interesting that Chablis did not ask for the dragons to simply take them there, nor did any of the dragons offer. In fact, none of the Free Hive dragons had saddles on them, and though he could occasionally see some dragons swooping in the sunset, he saw very few ferrying goods.

Cressida slid up next to Arthur and looked down at the restrictive card-lock bracelets herself. She didn't look happy. "Why did you agree to put those things on you?" she asked in a low undertone. "Now you have no way to defend yourself."

"It was the only way that they would agree to let you and the blue pair out of the nets." Selfishly, he hoped that this would score a couple of points with her, but her scowl only deepened.

"How did they manage to capture you and Brixaby, anyway? Weren't you able"—she lowered her voice to a whisper and her eyes flicked to Shadow—"to use *another* power?"

He grimaced.

Shadow, walking along with them, had no concern whatsoever for Arthur's pride. "He ran out from my care and challenged the red, practically dared him to throw those nets over us."

Arthur shifted and glanced at Cressida, wondering if she would at least be slightly impressed with this.

The look she gave him said no. "You got yourself captured for me?" she said flatly.

"And Tamya and Len," he lied.

"It was for mostly you," Brixaby said, turning from his side conversation with Joy. "Even if you are still annoyed with Arthur for his terrible family—which I completely understand as they are awful and I wish Arthur was not related to them—you are still riders in our retinue. It's our job to protect you."

Arthur wished there were rocks on this flat, barren mesa. Or something conveniently deep that he could crawl under.

He risked a glance at Cressida. Her fair skin was flushed red, and she was not looking back.

Joy stopped, shivered, and then piped up. "Hey! I just got a new qu—"

"Joy!" Cressida turned to her. "Do you remember what I said the other day about oversharing?"

Joy looked briefly stymied for a moment but then brightened. "Right, right. But what if I told you that it was *really important* for me to make five friends because then something really cool would happen?"

Cressida sighed.

Arthur glanced from the bickering trio to the red dragon who was striding slowly on the other side of Chablis and not looking their way but was most definitely listening to the back and forth. They both were.

He had so many things he wanted to ask the dragon. He had wondered for so many years if it was a whim that had caused him to give a child an insanely powerful card, or did he have a deeper plan in mind?

But as curious as Arthur was, he knew that there was a time and place for those questions. This was not it.

Finally, they reached the end of the mesa. The rocky land dropped off abruptly into the air, leaving them several hundred feet above a stark desert below. Red-brown rock stretched on as far as Arthur could see to the horizon. There wasn't a tree or scrap of grass to be seen.

However, there was a strip of something else beyond it. Darker land? The deadened lands that had been sterilized by ancient scourge-eruptions? No. It didn't look quite right, either. Those had been gray. This was darker.

"So, what do you see?" Laird asked.

"We're in a desert," he said. Everybody turned to look at him with an expression that said, *No kidding.*

Arthur ignored them. "What's out there? That dark patch?"

"Deadened lands," Cressida said.

"That is the sea," Chablis told him, "though I won't tell you which one for security reasons."

Both Cressida and Arthur whipped around to peer back out. Arthur supposed, like him, Cressida had never seen the ocean either. He wished that he could be closer and get a good look.

"And," Chablis said, "you'll note that none of it is scourge-touched."

She had a point.

"You have dragons. So, I assume you worked dragon soil into the ground?" Arthur asked.

"Yes and no. We mostly use dragon soil for our crops . . . in its dried form, of course. Dragon soil is so potent that it will cause life to grow to its own detriment. People who handle it in its raw state without gloves grow tumors on their skin. That's why it is dried out for a year and a day before it's safe."

"And Legendary soil is even more potent than others," Brixaby added proudly.

Chablis continued. "*Something* would grow out in the desert if someone worked dragon soil into the sand—mostly lichen and moss—but there's only so much water to go around. The point is"—she gestured widely—"scourge-touched land does not cover the entire world except for one little kingdom. Or else the balance between living and dead would be entirely lopsided. No, the scourge covers the most arable land, which happens to be the most valuable to all humanity's kingdoms."

Cressida and Arthur spoke at the same time.

"What other kingdoms?" Cressida blurted.

"You know how many kingdoms there are?" Arthur asked over her.

Cressida turned to stare at Arthur, her eyes wide, and he could practically see the realization that he knew of other kingdoms dancing in the back of her eyes.

Chablis ignored Cressida altogether. "There are six Mythics in the world, and it is thought that each holds their own territory."

Arthur felt a sinking sensation. "There are five Mythics left, not six."

Laird stepped forward to lower his head in front of Arthur. "Are you certain?"

"I learned it in the king's palace." This was a gross simplification of what had happened that day, but Arthur wasn't about to show all his metaphorical cards.

Chablis and Laird exchanged a troubled look.

"What does that mean?" Cressida asked.

"It means that the balance between the Scourge Gods and Mythics is shifting faster than we thought," Laird rumbled, then shrugged a massive shoulder. "If the worst should happen, if kingdoms are overrun . . . Well, it may still not trouble us here. This desert is a vast, harsh place. Over there is the great sea, but it's too briny for everything but tiny shrimp and flies to live. Even the scourglings suffer and die out there." He smiled full of teeth. "I've seen it."

"Well, how do you live here, then?" That came from Tamya. She had been so quiet that Arthur had forgotten she was there.

"We have a freshwater aquifer we draw from, but if we remove too much, we risk contamination from the ocean," he explained.

"I still don't understand how you think you're safe from the scourglings," Cressida said.

Arthur thought he knew. "Because the scourglings are most attracted to life. Complex, magical life. This desert and the sea out there are basically deadened lands. They're using it as a barrier."

Chablis looked at him, then nodded, and he thought she caught a bit of respect in the back of her eyes. "He's right. Tundra, recently volcanic land, deserts like this . . . little areas we can eke out, surrounded by desolation. There are many such islands of life where the scourglings cannot penetrate, and where people live outside the traditional kingdoms. The world is vast—more vast than anybody has led us to believe. But the kingdoms teach that they are the only ones in the world—that they are the only safe harbor for humanity. That is a lie. One of many."

Arthur's thoughts raced. If this free hive wasn't the only one of its kind . . . could there be somewhere safe he could take the people of his border village? Could they find a place of their own? Or perhaps here?

Could he and Brixaby hide from the king in a place like this, should they ever need to?

Cressida crossed her arms. "Why are you telling us this?"

"Because we aren't your enemies," Chablis answered simply. "And though I'm sure you don't believe us yet, we don't actually want your kingdom to fall."

"After all, the kingdoms fight the scourglings for us," Laird added with a toothy grin.

Chablis continued. "But the whole system from the kings and queens on down is sickened with its own brand of rot. We knew that the balance had already started to shift toward the scourglings, and now I hear that it is worse than ever. Tell me, is it true that the scourge erupts more often than they have before?"

"We're in a busy cycle," Cressida said defensively.

Laird snorted. "Back when I was a hatchling, there could be weeks without an eruption. How often are they occurring now?"

Cressida pinched her lips in irritation, so Arthur spoke. "A few times a week. Occasionally twice in one day."

Chablis and Laird exchanged another look.

"That's not good," Chablis said, then clapped her hands in a change of subject. "But not something we can tackle right now. Come, let us show you our hive."

Cressida made a show of looking around. "How can you even have a hive without a former eruption zone?"

"We have not always lived in scourgling homes," Laird said dismissively. "Our hive is under your feet."

This time, they were allowed to ride their dragons, or at least Arthur was allowed to ride Shadow, Cressida on Joy, and Laird bent to give Chablis a lift.

The dragons leaped off the top of the mesa into the hot air. As they sank, Arthur was able to see the Mesa Free Hive for the first time. As the name suggested, it was carved out of the mesa itself.

The top of the rocky mesa provided shade from the sun and a measure of camouflage from the air. The inside, however, had been hollowed out into a latticework of different caves and open areas.

At first sight, it was a jumbled mix without any sense—no levels like a proper hive that he could see. Some areas were clearly meant for farming: he saw half-open caves bright with artificial light from card anchors, which was less harsh than the relentless sun. The insides were full of rows of crops.

Children sat for lessons inside other half-open caves, or out in the open, thanks to the shade from the mesa against the setting sun.

There were areas for livestock, too. He saw dragons with some of the rune-enchanted nets he'd seen before, carefully plucking out sheep and placing them into pens.

The dragons spiraled down. Unlike in a regular hive, there was no guard station or men and women on duty to check people in and out. It was completely open, likely to take advantage of the desert wind, when there was any to be had.

They landed in the shadow of the great mesa.

Arthur frowned at the livestock pens, wondering about logistics. As one of the hive leaders in training, he was aware of how much it took to keep people fed and happy. He'd spent nights updating Whitaker's books with the mind-boggling numbers. He wasn't sure how they did it.

Chablis followed his gaze and guessed at his thoughts. "We can grow enough crops here, but feeding dragons has always been the main challenge. There is just not enough water or arable acreage for livestock. It's why we're always in search of new cards."

"You raid the kingdom's farms during eruptions?" Arthur said, barely resisting the urge to add, *Like the vultures who wait for dead dragons to fall from the sky to collect their cards?*

"Not all eruptions." Laird snorted. "Our portal system is . . . subpar. We cannot get to most eruptions. And we do not take from places that have already suffered." He slanted a glance at Arthur, "only from nobles who can afford the loss."

"You mean like Woodmours?"

Laird flashed a dangerous dragon smile. "I have been waiting for years for an eruption to happen near that place."

"And I suppose you cleaned out Woodmours's card library while you were at it?" Cressida asked.

He looked at her. "Of course."

Chablis sighed. "It is a balance. Here, utility cards are much more useful than combat cards. We are so far away from the battles and protected by desolation. Why would we need someone who can shoot fireballs out of their eyes? We would much rather have someone to reinforce the walls, to help us carve out a new layer in the mesa, or to water the crops." She glanced at the blue pair, who didn't seem to be actively listening, looking into the Mesa Hive and whispering to each other.

She continued. "All children receive a card from a random draw at sixteen years of age. From there, they can earn more cards depending on our economy, which we model much like the hives."

Brixaby, who had been remarkably quiet until now, whispered in Arthur's ear. Unfortunately, his whisper was loud enough for everyone to hear. "They have a cave filled with crafters over there. I would like to see them."

Arthur glanced at his dragon. Brixaby hadn't taken much interest in human-made crafts, though he did enjoy human food. The more complex and meatier, the better.

"Ohhh, me too! Me too!" Joy said. "Brixaby, let's go together."

"Yes," Brixaby agreed, both equally cheerful and obviously false. "I want to see if they do anything differently than in Wolf Moon Hive."

The two dragons might as well have painted the words "We are up to something" on themselves. Arthur thought he saw Chablis roll her eyes, but she didn't say anything.

That was interesting, too. They had started to play nice the moment the card locks went over his wrists.

He suspected that show of intimidation before had been a bluff, and this was somehow the real sell. Though what they were selling, he wasn't sure.

Cressida hesitated, then looked at Chablis. "Are we prisoners here? Are we allowed to explore?"

The woman glanced meaningfully at Arthur's card-lock bracelets. "You may explore, but we ask that you do not leave, at least for now." She smiled. "And if you cause trouble, then be aware we do have jail cells: one for humans and one for dragons. Even dragon children."

It was the second time that she called them children. Not hatchlings. Was that . . . meant to humanize them somehow?

Arthur opened his mouth to ask, but Laird stepped in. "It's Arthur, isn't it?"

He looked up at the dragon. "Yes?"

The dragon inclined his head and then glanced at Brixaby. "Run along and look at our crafters, boy. I mean no harm to your rider, but it's past time he and I had a conversation."

CHAPTER 8

Brixaby was not worried for Arthur's safety. Well, not overly worried.

Yes, his skills were locked, but Brixaby had a sense for nullification magic and knew that if Arthur truly pushed, such as in a time of crisis, he could break through the lock with his Legendary-level cards.

Besides, if anybody in this so-called "free hive" dared to touch Arthur after they had guaranteed his safety, Brixaby would simply make an example of them. Unlike his rider, he had no moral qualms about destroying cards for his own gain.

Irritatingly enough, while he and Arthur trusted each other to take care of themselves, Cressida was waffling back and forth about her own dragon's safety. The girl was insisting on accompanying Arthur during his conversation with Laird. And yet she clearly did not like the idea of Joy going off without her.

Then again, Joy did not have any combat cards, so it would be hard for her to defend herself.

The hypocrisy of this statement didn't bother Brixaby in the least. After all, Arthur had proved himself more capable without a combat card to his name.

"Are you sure you'll be all right?" Cressida asked in a low undertone to Joy. "Wouldn't you rather come with us?"

It was vexing that Cressida thought Brixaby would allow Joy to get hurt.

"She will be with me, and I am more than enough protection for anybody," Brixaby told her imperiously. "She is part of my retinue. Therefore, you may also go and protect my Arthur."

Though he was *certain* that his rider could take care of himself, he supposed there was a certain advantage in bringing somebody along who could summon elemental flame bears.

Cressida did not look entirely happy at the duty Brixaby had magnanimously granted her.

"Brix." Arthur looked at him intently. "If you run into a problem you can't handle, you're to *Return* at once. Do you understand?"

Brixaby started to scoff—as if there was a threat he, a Legendary dragon, could not face!—but then he caught the emphasis in Arthur's phrasing.

Return? What did that?

Oh. That dratted Return to Start card. That was an instant transport back to Wolf Moon Hive, where he'd last keyed in the location—though he would be leaving Joy and Joy's rider behind. That tasted like ash on his tongue.

But Arthur was looking at him intently, so Brixaby bobbed his head. "Very well."

"Come on, Brixaby," Joy called happily, forcing the issue by rising into the air without her rider. The air currents became briefly turbulent thanks to her larger wings. Brixaby had to work to compensate for his smaller—though still vastly superior—form.

The two dragons started to fly off, but then Joy suddenly wheeled back around. "Oh, Len, of course, you're invited to come, too."

Who? Brixaby almost asked, and then remembered at the last moment that Len was the blue dragon who was as interesting as a bowl of bland porridge. Brixaby glared at Joy for extending the invitation.

Thankfully, Len shook his head and backed away, hunching his neck as if to make himself smaller. Ridiculous. He was almost twice the size of Joy. "No . . . no, ma'am. I would like to stay here with my rider, Tamya, if you please. If that's okay with you, I mean."

"Aw." Joy sagged a little, then shrugged. "Okay, but come find us if you change your mind."

"Or don't," Brixaby muttered under his breath.

Finally, *finally*, the two of them lifted into the air toward the crafting cave.

Once they were high enough not to be easily overheard—discounting card powers, of course—Brixaby spoke to Joy.

"I know why I'm going to the cave"—for all the sweet, sweet skills that would surely be on display—"but why are you going there?"

"For my quest, silly," Joy said. "I'm here to make friends."

Brixaby heaved a sigh. He suspected that Joy's quests were not as random as she pretended they were. Whenever he picked up a quest from her, it was goal based: Do this, do that, and usually required gaining a skill or accomplishing a task. Joy's, on the other hand . . .

"I have to make five new friends," she said happily.

Brixaby scoffed.

Joy glanced over at him, and her expression changed slightly to one that better suited a predator. "And if I do, I will acquire a temporary point of luck to use *whenever* I want."

"You . . ." Brixaby eyed the other dragon. That was a really good reward. "Do you suppose I could also gain that quest?"

"Don't know. It's random. Now let's go. There are lots of people in there, and I'm great at making friends." She nudged him with the tip of a wing, which *almost* sent Brixaby tumbling in the air. Because he was a naturally excellent flyer, it didn't happen, but it was a close thing.

Back in Wolf Moon Hive, the crafters were kept behind guilds with high protective walls, with many card-based restrictions carved on them. Naturally, this was to avoid any theft or craft secrets leaking out. Brixaby was not vain enough to assume he was the only one who could copy skills or techniques.

Here, however, where they had foolishly let a dragon of his caliber roam free, crafters worked out in the open. That meant if Brixaby could get close enough—within their aura—he could pick up those skills. And unlike magic or combat-oriented skills, crafting skills would become his, thanks to Arthur's Master of Skills card.

As they flew closer, Brixaby caught another interesting difference between this free hive and Wolf Moon Hive: dragons worked as crafters too.

Some of the dragon crafters had stalls set up for themselves, and the large open-air cave gave plenty of room for dragons to fly in and out while humans were forced to walk.

The stalls themselves were not made of fabric, which could be easily blown away by dragon wings, but rough stone, likely shaped by some form of earth or rock manipulation. Interesting. He noted all these details carefully, for when they returned to Wolf Moon Hive. Perhaps there would be some interest in dragon crafters there.

The other Legendary dragons would not like the change, but Brixaby hardly cared what they thought.

"Ooh, down there! Look at the pretty glass they're making!" Joy descended to land near one of the first stalls located next to the entrance.

A silver dragon with odd blue patterning under his belly, like a spiderweb, was working alongside a human by a glowing forge. The human was blowing into a thin nozzle attached to a pipe. The other end of that pipe was in a glowing-hot expanding blob of molten glass.

The silver dragon carefully held the glass in blunted claws and turned it so that when the human blew air in, the molten glass expanded evenly. Tiny wisps of smoke came up from the dragon's claws as they smoldered, but neither the dragon nor the human seemed to care.

What caught Brixaby's attention was that he did not immediately pick up any of the skills they were using. This meant that either there was something wrong with his own cards—highly unlikely even if his rider was currently card-locked—or these two were just going by normal, hard-earned experience instead of card-based skills.

How irritating.

"Doesn't that heat hurt your claws?" Joy asked, staring with wide eyes.

"No, my scales have become well-callused over the years," the silver dragon replied. "Back up behind that line." He pointed with the tip of his tail to a red line painted on the floor. "You don't want to get splattered with molten glass. That will hurt."

The human raised his lips from blowing the glass long enough to add, "We'll be with you to show the wares in a few moments. This is delicate work." Then he went back to huffing air into the pipe.

"And mind your tails and wings. If you knock any finished glass over, you will be working in here to pay for it," the silver snapped, seeing Joy turn toward their table of wares.

Joy obediently tucked her tail under her body and held her wings close.

Brixaby, who had a perfect form and did not need to worry about such mundane matters, buzzed to inspect the glassware more closely. To his delight, he realized that they were not all simple vases, but drinking bowls.

Dragon-sized drinking bowls, some large enough to hold a good deal of soup.

This had been a concern in the back of his mind as he grew larger. Yes, his form was small and still perfect, but as he consumed more card shards and grew, he would find it more difficult to eat from proper vessels.

He had grown to rather enjoy human food and did not want to eat from a trough like a lower animal.

Now that he thought of it, he'd never seen larger, dragon-sized eating utensils at Wolf Moon.

As he looked over the glassware, he found he rather liked one simple white bowl with walls as thin as a chicken egg, but it was strong when Brixaby lifted it.

Meanwhile, the crafting pair finished their work. The silver replaced the larger molten vessel in the forge to heat again.

Finally, Brixaby got a reward for his diligence:

New Counterfeit Spell obtained: Feeding the Forge
Remaining Time: 71 hours 59 minutes 59 seconds

A magical skill, and this was a Common dragon.

He was a little annoyed that he was admiring the wares of a mere Common . . . but, well, the glassware was quite good.

Wiping off his hands, the human came up to them. His face was soaked with sweat, and he was red around the cheeks, but he didn't seem out of breath.

"Can I help you two kids?"

"Kids?" Brixaby swelled. He was nearly five months old! He would be soon graduating from Wolf Moon Hive class, if this absence didn't set them back. In any case, he was no *child*.

Of course, the ever-talkative Joy jumped in before he could reply.

"These are so pretty. How long did it take you to learn how to do this? Oh no, wait! I have a better question: Is this what dragons do when they don't fight scourglings? Do you make pretty things? How did you and your rider learn to do this?"

The dragon turned from the forge to answer her, and the human took his place to manage the heat.

"He is not my rider. He's my business partner," the silver said.

Joy visibly stopped herself before she asked, *Where is your rider?* That was something that they had both learned early on not to do. There were too many dragons in the hive who had lost their linked riders in some way or another.

Brixaby shuddered at the thought.

"My rider works as a sheep herdsman," the silver added.

"That is so interesting," Joy said, and the weird thing was, it sounded like she meant it. Usually when Brixaby said that something was *interesting*, he meant the opposite.

"So," Joy continued, "does your and your rider's linked cards help more with glass blowing or with the sheep?"

That was an incredibly rude question, so Brixaby was shocked when the silver answered.

"Neither. We have a card spell to duplicate scrolls, but I found there weren't many academic pursuits here at this hive. Glassblowing marries both the logical and the creative sides of my personality. As for my rider, he was a herdsman before he came to the hive . . ." The silver continued, happy to explain his life story.

Brixaby had found that happened a lot around Joy.

He didn't know if she had a secret conversational skill or if people picked up on her friendliness and opened up in kind. The pink dragon was sitting up in interest, tail wrapped around her feet, every line of her body showing intense interest in something that was frankly boring.

He continued to browse the wares, but he found himself repeatedly drawn to the white bowl labeled "porcelain." He briefly considered stealing it and hiding it in his Personal Space, which he had access to thanks to his linked card with Arthur.

However, it was improper to hide his valuables and much more important to display them out in the open . . . which he couldn't do if it was stolen. That was a problem.

Then he saw the price tag and realized that the bowl cost one Rare shard.

He didn't have any Rare shards as he always ate them as soon as he could lay his claws on them.

After some consideration, Brixaby decided not to steal the bowl. Instead, he would ask Arthur to buy it for him. His rider was intelligent, and Brixaby was confident he'd be able to talk down the price.

Joy finally wrapped up her tedious conversation, and she and Brixaby moved on. As they left, Brixaby caught a sly look on Joy's face.

"Only four more friends to go," Joy said.

"It suddenly makes sense," Brixaby said. "That's why you were so interested in that boring dragon's story."

"Hey, Tomlin isn't boring. He's interesting. Don't talk about my new friend like that." Joy bumped him in a teasing way, and they continued on.

"Yes, yes," Brixaby grumbled. "As long as I continue to be your top-ranked friend, I do not mind if you befriend all the Commons in every hive . . . if this place can even be considered a hive—" He stopped in midair so fast that Joy crashed into him. She had been going at a walking pace, so this was no problem.

Besides, Brixaby hardly noticed. All his attention was on the gleaming, beautiful craftsmanship . . . no, work of art, in the next stall over.

"Joy," he whispered, awed. "Forget the tacky red glowing runes. Look at *that*."

Joy followed his gaze, wrinkled her snout, and then looked back at Brixaby as if to make sure they were looking at the same thing. Seeing that she was, she tilted her head.

"The . . . chainmail?"

"Yes!" Brixaby buzzed up to it, and after a moment's appreciation for the fine work, ran his claws down the hanging chainmail shirt. It was as buttery smooth as he hoped, every polished rivet gleaming in the sun. He turned and looked at the craftsman, who was nearby, working on another. "I must have this. It is exquisite! What would you charge for this, but made for a dragon? No, wait!" he realized. "I will require many sizes, as I will grow." He peered at the man. "I demand you show me how to craft this!"

CHAPTER 9

Arthur and Cressida watched their dragons fly off toward the crafting cave.

Arthur sighed. "I have a feeling that those two are going to get in trouble. But . . ." He trailed off.

Cressida sighed in agreement. "Yes, they are going to get in trouble, but we can't watch over them every second. They're growing up and would be flying freely in Wolf Moon."

"This isn't Wolf Moon, and we aren't here voluntarily," Arthur muttered, though he wasn't arguing.

He . . . wasn't even certain he was all that upset about being forcefully taken away from his home hive. He knew he should be, but he'd felt nothing but varying degrees of overwhelm and irritation back at Wolf Moon for months now.

And the idea of a hive he had not known even existed was fascinating.

Cressida visibly shook herself, then turned to look at Arthur. She tilted her head toward red Laird, who was waiting patiently for them to continue their discussion as if he had all the time in the world. Maybe he did. Arthur didn't know how long he had stalked Baron Kane's security cart before he finally struck outside his village.

Meanwhile, Chablis had made her way over to the blue pair and was talking to them in a low undertone. Arthur didn't like that—certainly didn't trust his . . . what? Kidnapper? Suddenly nice jailer? But after a moment's consideration, he gestured for Cressida to walk with him to the red dragon.

He didn't trust Chablis, but he'd waited for literal years to ask the red questions.

"So, you know Laird?" Cressida asked.

"Well . . ." Arthur blew out a breath. "He gave me my Master of Skills card."

Hearing them, Laird turned his head their way. "Yes, that was quite the day. I had no idea that the seed I planted in the border village would someday bear fruit, though I was told it would be profitable."

Cressida spoke before Arthur could ask what that was meant to mean. "So . . . you truly lived in a border village?"

"I told you that," Arthur said.

She gave him a look. "You've told me many things since I've known you. I don't know what to believe anymore."

Arthur flushed, and Laird chuckled. "Well, I, for one, can verify that I discovered this man, then a young child—"

"I wasn't that young," Arthur muttered.

"—in quite a dire border village under the Baron Kane estate. Despicable place. Ruled by a despicable man," he added.

Cressida looked at Arthur with a hard-to-read expression. "How bad was it?"

"Not the worst that I've seen," Laird answered before he could. "There are some border barons who work their people to death in mines or pluck out the pretty girls for their own uses. But Kane just lets them die of neglect and starvation, mostly."

Arthur shrugged. Those memories were like scar tissue in his mind—terrible, but hard to feel anything underneath. "He had his vindictive moments."

"I'm sure," Laird rumbled. "However, I am pleased by the reports that came out of his barony after the loss of that card. You successfully kept it away from him, for which you have my thanks."

"You told me that you would kill my family if the card ever fell into his hands." It seemed a little ludicrous now as an adult, but as a twelve-year-old child, having a dragon threaten him had been very effective.

"That was an incentive. And look what you did with yourself," Laird said brightly.

Cressida looked between them before settling on Laird. "I don't understand. Why would you give a card—a Legendary card—to a child you didn't know?"

Laird shrugged a massive shoulder. "What should I have done with it? Putting a Legendary card in my core would only poison me. Introducing a card of immense wealth into this community would poison it as well. Humans would tear themselves apart for it. Or the kingdom hives would get wind and come after us. No doubt they have their spies here, as we have in theirs," he added, with the cock of his head. "Plus," he continued, "I thought it would be funny to stymie Baron Kane. His own land would be the last place that he looked."

"He *did* look for the card in our village," Arthur said. "If he had thought to search the kids, he would've found me."

"But he didn't." Laird sounded very self-satisfied. "And now he is leveraged under painful loans to pay the value of that card back. Unless he gets very lucky in his harvests, which I doubt—you've seen how hard he works—his family's wealth will be destroyed within a generation."

Cressida asked, "Kane was using that card as payment, I take it?"

"Yes, to cover gambling debts," Laird said with a draconic smile. "That's not his only problem: I still go by every once in a while to steal the best rams and ewes from his flock. Ask any shepherd. That is devastating."

"It sounds like you know Baron Kane," Arthur said leadingly.

"I do. He is my late rider's grandson, kicked out of Blood Moon Hive for deviant behavior—and that says a lot, considering the state of Blood Moon Hive." Laird sighed. "But he had good blood on his father's side and managed to weasel his way into a barony. He is a dangerous, corrupt man. After he was shamed in the hive, my rider was never quite the same, and we dragons, unless we're killed in a scourge-eruption, we live for a very long time." Laird's smile was all threat. "We remember grudges."

So, this had all started as simple revenge.

Arthur felt like there was much more to the story—especially that line about profit—but there were immediate, pressing questions as well. "What are your plans for us here? For me and my people?"

Some of the maliciousness in Laird's demeanor drained away. He looked toward Chablis, who was talking to Tamya and Len, gesturing toward the hive.

"The Free Hive Council has been thrown into a tizzy," Laird said, drawing Arthur's attention back. "They're unsure whether to use you, kill you, or befriend you. Their hands have been tied by inaction."

"Or you could just let us go," Cressida said.

"That was also discussed." Laird made a gesture with spread wings as if to indicate the vast desert beyond. "After all, neither of you would be able to find your way back."

Arthur and Brixaby could find their way back after they'd copied one of the shimmer green's portal abilities. Of course, he didn't say so.

Laird looked at Arthur as if to judge his reaction, snorted at whatever he saw, and then gestured back toward the mesa. "What do you think of our little hive?"

"I haven't seen very much of it," Arthur admitted, but then, as the red dragon looked on, he blurted the first thing that came to mind. "Mostly, I want to know if the people I left behind in the border village—the people suffering under Baron Kane—would have a place here."

"Criminals?" Cressida asked, scandalized.

He turned to her. "Most are the families of criminals. They didn't do the original crime. They were just unlucky enough to be related to the person who did."

Laird hummed under his breath. Though through a dragon voice, it sounded like a very threatening growl. "Our resources are stretched thin, but not *that* thin. We do have some extra resources, and it has occurred to me to snatch up the peasants under Baron Kane's rule. The problem is, many have taken an oath to the king to remain there."

An oath that Brixaby could easily rip out of their heart decks, as he had done with his father. Arthur kept the lid on that, too. He sensed Laird was happy to find some leverage over Arthur—and that was what he'd been fishing for.

"I have taken my own oath to the king," Arthur admitted, "though I'm certain it's lighter than what condemned men and women were forced to give. More important to me, as a Legendary rider, I have to fight the scourglings, but . . ." He looked back over his shoulder toward where Brixaby and Joy had gone. "I also want to learn about this place."

"To be frank, Arthur, you and your dragon represent both a great risk and a hope. We don't have a Legendary card in our ranks. We could use somebody with extraordinary skills. But, as I said, having a free Legendary card in circulation is . . . a problem. Other free hives have ripped themselves apart fighting over one."

"Only if you can take it," Arthur said, resisting the urge to raise his hand to cover his heart.

"That is why the faction calling for your death hasn't won the whole council over. Most see the value of a young Legendary pair allied to us."

Arthur understood then. At least partly. There had been power plays among the kingdom hives when Brixaby had still been in the egg.

The little byplay a few minutes ago atop the mesa had been a test. When Arthur had proven to be reasonable, able to control Brixaby, and willing to wear the card locks, they'd decided to use a carrot instead of a stick. After all, killing a Legendary for his card was no simple matter.

I don't want to join a random hive outside the kingdom, he thought. Though a smaller voice added, *I don't know anything about them. Yet.*

Laird looked to Cressida. "What about you? Your Rare pink is a meta—not with a knowledge card, I take it?"

She nodded blandly. "She has random insights."

Which was a very guarded explanation of quests.

Laird shrugged. "I'll have to report that to the council, but I'm sure they'll be glad to have you. We are a free hive—a community of outcasts. Many of the dragons are like me, who lost their first rider and did not want a second. There are just as many dragon pairs who just became disenchanted with their home hive for one reason or another."

Speaking of riderless dragons . . . Arthur looked around for Shadow and realized that the dragon was gone. He felt bad for not realizing it earlier.

Laird continued. "We only wish to live freely and scrape out a little piece of safety in an unsafe world. We don't want anything to do with the kingdom's drama."

He said that, but earlier he had admitted to raiding kingdom lands. Arthur didn't point this out, but he exchanged a look with Cressida that told him she noted the same thing.

"I will allow you to settle in," Laird said. "Meanwhile, do not remove those card locks or cause undue trouble. Look around the hive, explore, and ask questions. And get comfortable with the idea that this may very well be your new home."

The dragon bunched up as if ready to leap into the sky.

"Wait," Arthur said. "You said someone told you giving me my card would be profitable? What did you mean?"

If the dragon were human, he would have had a roguish smile on his face. "We don't have a Legendary card *here*, but it doesn't mean we do not have access to them."

"What does that—"

Arthur was cut off as Laird took to the sky, the first down sweep of his wings throwing dust and grit in all directions. Raising their hands to cover their eyes, he and Cressida backed away. When Arthur looked again, he and Cressida were alone.

"He did that on purpose," Cressida said. "So you'd seek him out again. He's trying to dangle information in front of you like a worm on a hook, hoping you'll bite."

"It's working," Arthur said. "Who gives a Legendary card to a random twelve-year-old kid from the borderlands?"

Cressida shrugged, looking like she was about to say something, then paused and bit her lip. Suddenly, she turned to him. "I'm still upset with you, you know," she said. "You told me so many versions of your life, half the time I don't even know which name to call you. But . . ." Her lips pressed into a line. "But I do realize you haven't had it easy."

"My father was Duke Rowantree," Arthur said. They'd had a version of this conversation once, a few weeks ago, just after he came back from that near-disaster with the king. He suspected she had been too shocked and angry to properly listen. "That's my true last name. But my father was caught with Legendary cards from the same set. Now my uncle holds his title as duke."

"Legendary cards from the same set," she repeated. "That's treason."

"I have a pair of Legendaries," Arthur countered.

"And rumor had it that the king almost killed you," she snapped.

He almost smiled. Was that worry he heard in her voice? "But I got special dispensation."

Exasperated, she threw her hands in the air. "From what I heard, the king's moods are . . . changeable."

They hadn't spoken much about the king. Arthur had been a little shell-shocked when he came back. And every time he wanted to tell her the full story about what he went through that day, he felt the tug at his heart. It strained the loyalty he promised in the oath. Not a lot, but he didn't want to test it in case the king could feel it on his end.

Did the king think he was dead now? Or did the oath tell him that he was alive? Thankfully, it wasn't strong enough to punish Arthur for leaving the kingdom entirely.

"He is . . . uh, changeable. I'm certainly not out of danger. I have to get stronger for many reasons, but the king is certainly one of them," Arthur agreed.

Cressida looked briefly away. "Well, the bloodline of a duke is certainly more powerful than the bloodline of a baron."

Arthur's eyebrows rose.

"What?" She looked back at him. "That *matters* with the other nobles. And the Rowantree name is more powerful than the baron who lords over prisoners. It's important to high-ranked people. Were you truly twelve when you received your card?"

Arthur almost asked why it mattered, but it didn't hurt to answer. "Yeah. I left my village soon afterward and took the name of Ernest. He was my best friend at the time. He died." He swallowed hard. "So many people die out there, Cressida. Laird spoke of neglect, but those are pretty words. You wouldn't believe what it's like unless you see it. The scourge-dust blows in from the deadened lands and sickens people. Any little cut risks your whole limb rotting out from under you. Ernie died because his mother was stupid enough to plant vegetables on lands that had not fully been healed by dragon soil yet. You have to sneak that sort of thing because growing your food isn't allowed. Anyway, they didn't know until it was too late. The scourge-rot ate them from the inside out."

"Oh, Arthur," she sighed.

He hadn't spoken like this before. It was as if a crack in a dam he hadn't been aware of had formed, and everything came spilling out. "No one from a hive can understand. The people there don't have cards. *No one* has cards, so they're completely susceptible to every sickness. Families starve and die for the sins of one family member. And yeah, technically the kids can leave, but only after they turn eighteen. They know nothing of the world, have no cards, and most can't even read. Most stay just because there is nowhere else to go—" He stopped, hearing his own words turning into a rant.

She was quiet, simply put her hand on his shoulder.

. . . And he just couldn't stop speaking.

"I'm sorry I lied to you," he said. "My name really is Arthur Rowantree, but until recently, that name wasn't safe. And it still might not be safe now. The king can change his mind about me anytime." More things, long-held fears and anxieties bubbled up from deep inside him, and he couldn't stop them. "Valentina and Whitaker didn't prepare me to face the king. They didn't think I would survive, and they were right. I only got out thanks to luck. Now, the trust is gone between all of us. Whitaker is supposed to train me, but he barely does anything.

He cancels more classes than he attends, and when he does bother to show up, I'm doing paperwork I barely understand—*his* paperwork he should have done months ago."

"Valentina allows this?" Cressida asked. "She doesn't strike me as the type of woman who would."

"I think if she were even ten years younger, she wouldn't. But she's getting old," he said bitterly, "and when she dies, Whitaker is going to be in charge, and . . ." He couldn't finish because inside he desperately worried that without Valentina's influence, the entire hive would be up a creek without a paddle. Or worse, everything would fall on Arthur's shoulders.

Emotionally flailing, he sidestepped topics. "Meanwhile, have you seen how Athena treats our class? She won't teach me *anything* because she's terrified of my rank. I know I made mistakes back at the eruption—I shouldn't have let our class fly over that mass of scourge—but I don't know what to do. I don't want to make the wrong move with people's lives in the balance."

"Arthur, we saved a lot of lives back there . . . all those people who were trapped and couldn't flee—"

"I *know*, but I got our dragons hurt by a Common scourgling. If I had been thinking, I could have told another veteran group to go and save them. Then we could have searched for Woodmours's card library. If we had gotten there earlier, maybe we could have done . . . done *something*." Though he didn't know what. Then he stopped because he realized he was just kind of verbally vomiting all of his worries on Cressida.

In fact, she looked a little overwhelmed by everything.

"I didn't know this was going through your mind," she said. "You always look so confident."

"That's my Acting skill," he admitted.

She half smiled, her hand still moving up and down his forearm, almost like she was gentling a horse.

"Well, I think you did a good job. And if it wasn't you in charge, it would have been me, and . . . I don't know if we could have done any better."

"Cressida, you and Joy anchor the class. I'm so glad I have somebody to trust. If I didn't, I would've gone crazy a long time ago."

"Well, there's not much of a class now," she said. "Just me, you, and Tamya."

They both went quiet at that.

After a moment, Arthur said, "If I understand things right, Wolf Moon thinks that we're dead."

Cressida winced. "If we don't make it back, then eventually it'll just be Whitaker in charge."

"I wouldn't wish that on anyone." He'd tried to make it a joke, but it came out as more bitter than he expected.

She heaved a sigh, and her hand dropped from his arm. "You're not the only one with . . . reservations, Arthur. I was expected to either marry well or link with the Rare egg. And now that I have Joy, I'm expected to send extra card shards back to my father."

"What?" He was shocked. "I didn't know that."

"I'm to send back any children I birth, too." She shrugged as if it didn't bother her, but Arthur could tell that it did. "My stipend as one of your retinue would have more than covered what my father expected, even before harvesting from scourge-eruptions."

His fists clenched, and he forced himself to relax. Even the thought of walking up to Noble Icehouse and ripping the cards from his heart deck was tempting. He did share Brixaby's power, after all. He just had never used it.

"You could just . . . *not* send him shards," he suggested in what he hoped was an even voice.

"No, I can't." She crossed her arms, looking away. "I don't want to talk about it. The point is, I have my responsibilities back at Wolf Moon, too." She glanced at the Mesa Hive, and there was unexpected longing in her gaze. "I know they're playing nice, that this freedom to ask questions is either an illusion or a trap but . . ."

She trailed off, and silence descended between them.

"We don't have to decide now," Arthur said. "We can take our time and learn about this place. That's assuming they'll let us leave without a fight."

"Oh, please." Cressida rolled her eyes, but her next words were said fondly. "Sooner or later, Joy will get a quest to leave. Then nothing will stop her."

He smiled and tilted his head toward the mesa. "Think it's time we check on them?"

"We may as well."

CHAPTER 10

Arthur had caught glimpses of the crafting cave before his talk with Laird—enough to get a rough idea of where Brixaby and Joy were heading. But as he and Cressida walked up to the mouth of the cave, he realized that he had thoroughly underestimated its size and scope.

The cave seemed to have been dug out of half of the mesa. Yet light-based card-anchor spells kept it from being gloomy.

What shocked him more was to see dragons working as crafters. Alone. He had got the impression that perhaps they were working alongside the riders—maybe the pair had shared a card. Certainly, dragons were working alongside humans.

But many of the dragons seemed to have booths of their own, talking to other dragons and showing off wares. Some were even doing blacksmithing or working on giant, dragon-sized looms. One was doing pottery on a spinning wheel—the clay vase was quite impressive.

In fact, there seemed to be more dragons than there were humans—or maybe the size of the booths for dragons was just so much larger that they dwarfed their human competitors. Because it was clear at a glance that these dragons weren't playing second fiddle to crafting humans. They had their own businesses. A whole economy.

Arthur exchanged a glance with Cressida, who looked overwhelmed. He could see the same realizations churning behind her eyes.

"What do you think?" he asked.

She shook her head. "I . . . I don't know . . ."

But Arthur did. A slow smile spread over his face. "I think this is wonderful."

"You do?" Her tone surprised him.

"Don't you?" he asked.

She looked into the cave ahead of them. One orange dragon was working at a forge, pulling out a long sword the length of a horse and laying it across an appropriately sized anvil. When he brought down the hammer, Arthur suspected anybody nearby was in danger of being deafened.

"I don't know," Cressida replied with a frown. "There's nothing wrong with it, it's just . . ." She trailed off for a moment, shrugged, and then looked back at Arthur. "When I see a dragon do that"—she gestured to the one who was tempering a sword—"it makes me wonder what they could be doing against the scourglings with that kind of strength."

"The Mesa Free Hive doesn't regularly fight the scourge."

"I know, Arthur." Her voice took on a little impatience. "And I'm not sure how I feel about that, either. Dragons are meant to fight the scourge, aren't they?"

He was a little disappointed at her reaction. But at the same time, Cressida was a noblewoman and had grown up in a society where one's order of birth could mean the difference between a life of luxury and scraping to survive. It made sense her first instinct was to be wary of anyone testing the boundaries.

Still . . . that didn't mean she couldn't change her mind.

"What about Common dragons without combat skills?" he pressed. "Like Tamya and Len. Their combined card power deals with sea salt, right?"

She shrugged. "Yes, but their deficiencies can be corrected with the new card once Len is old enough to solidify his core. Or Tamya might be able to take a card now. I heard Athena mention they might be able to manipulate blood with the correct additional card."

Per hive policy, hatchling dragons were not allowed to take new cards. A magical beast's body was built around its magical core, which contained a single card. Dragons could have secondary and even tertiary decks, but those took time to properly develop.

Brixaby was somewhat of an exception with his natural power. But even he'd had a hard time when he tried to absorb Legendary cards fresh from the egg.

"Sure," Arthur said, starting to get annoyed now, "they can always buy a combat card, but you know how expensive those are. They'll go into debt just to be able to defend themselves in a scourge-eruption. Then who knows how long it'll take to pay it off, risking their lives the whole time—with a brand-new combat card that only one of them can absorb, by the way."

Cressida turned away for a moment, her arms crossed over her chest.

Arthur opened his mouth again, not wanting to let her stew, but then he noticed that she was looking at the cave and the dragons. After a moment, her shoulders slumped.

"I know you're right," she admitted. "But Arthur . . . it's obvious you like what you see here, and that you want to bring it back to Wolf Moon Hive—if we're allowed to go home at all," she added. "But I can tell you right now that most people, especially the nobles, won't accept it. They don't like the idea of dragons being more than beasts used to fight the scourglings. Even I didn't know how much dragons were like people until I met Joy . . . No," she caught herself with a shake of her head. "I didn't realize that dragons *are* people, and . . . I suppose I'm still getting used to that."

He remembered his father's lecture about dragons when Arthur was small. He said they were like beasts. He'd been wrong. Cressida had been wrong too, but she was trying to be better.

Forcing himself to set his annoyance aside, he shrugged. "Well, you know that I've never cared what nobles think."

She opened her mouth and closed it again. "I was about to say that you *should*, but you're a Legendary rider. Frankly, you have the luxury of not caring what they think."

If only that was true, he thought, remembering his uncle's and cousin's appeal to the king, and how close Arthur had come to execution. Because, yes, he was a Legendary rider, but the king was a Mythic.

He shook his head.

"Let's find our dragons." He made a show of looking around. "I don't see that anything is on fire or anyone running or screaming, so I don't know which direction they went."

Cressida rolled her eyes, but the tension between them was gone, and her expression was affectionate.

She held out her arm, as any well-bred noblewoman was taught to do. Arthur slipped his arm within hers, escorting her through the raucous, chaotic crafting cave.

They found Joy a few aisles in. Her bright pink scales stood out easily, even among other occasional pinks.

She was sitting in front of one of the smaller human booths and chatting up the merchant. At first, Arthur thought the jars arranged on the merchant's booth were some kind of vegetable-pickling method until he got closer and saw the dead bodies of insects and a few skeletal remains of mice and other rodents floating within.

Arthur stepped within hearing range just in time to hear Joy say in a slightly strained voice, "Oh, that is very . . . um, wow. And how long have you been doing . . . uh, this?"

"Since I was a child," the man replied intensely. "I always felt that preserving tissues was my way of reaching immortality."

Cressida stepped in. "Joy, what's going on? And where's Brixaby?"

"Oh, Cressida!" Joy turned to her rider in obvious relief. "I was just getting to know my new friend Donnie here—"

"We're not friends," Donnie said.

And just as abruptly, he turned his back on them all to start rearranging already impeccably arranged jars.

Joy frowned and in a lower voice said, "I still need two more friends for my quest, and Donnie's was the only booth without anybody in front of it. But I don't think that he's looking for friends. He asked if he could preserve one of my scales—"

"I hope you told him no," she said, alarmed.

"Yeah, I'm not shedding anyway." Joy looked at Arthur. And though dragons didn't exactly smile as humans did, the mischievousness was plain on her face. "Brixaby found his own friend. Over here, you have to see!"

She led her way down the aisle. Soon, Arthur stood in front of a booth that specialized in chainmail armor.

And behind that booth, perched on the side of a bucket filled with rusty, misshapen chain-link rivets, was his dragon.

"Uh, Brix?" Arthur asked.

The little dragon looked up, and his bloodred eyes were bright. "Arthur! Observe my masterpiece!" He held up a daisy chain of rivets that started out lumpy on the far end but quickly grew more smooth and uniform. "My skills are quickly advancing. Soon, I will overtake Dimitri's so-called mastery of this art."

"So, you're his linked partner, then?" asked a man before Arthur could figure out a reply.

He looked up to see a rotund bearded man who looked every inch the stereotypical armorer, complete with large arms and a leather vest.

"Yes, I'm Arthur," he said. "What's going on?"

The man snorted deep in his nose and swallowed, making Cressida and Joy visibly grimace. "The kid here wants to know the trade. Said I'd agree to let him work and learn so he doesn't make a fool of himself by linking chain."

Arthur's attention sharpened. "Brix, you want to apprentice to this man?"

"No," Brixaby said, using a strange pinching tool to crimp two links together. It was overly large for his small form, and he had to use both claws and a foot to press it down. "I wish to stay until I can learn the method, and then make my own glorious armor."

Dimitri rolled his eyes. "Keep dreaming. It takes a dedicated apprentice years to learn the basics of the craft. But . . . I could use the help."

"Oh!" Joy said brightly. "It won't take Brixaby years. He's—"

Cressida put her hand in front of her dragon's muzzle, stopping her from spilling secrets.

Arthur was torn. Brixaby was a mini gourmand with a taste for fine human food. Arthur had hoped his dragon would take more of an interest in cooking— skills which would allow Arthur to show off. But Brixaby had always been more interested in eating than the process of making food.

However, he wasn't going to let that get in the way of an actual crafting interest. He'd never seen the little dragon concentrate on a single task for so long before.

"I think you'll find Brixaby is a quick learner," Arthur said, wondering how long it would be until the man learned he had a Legendary dragon behind his counter. "I assume you'll pay him standard apprentice rates?"

Again, Dimitri did that deep, wet snort. This time, he ended by spitting to the side.

Cressida turned away and gagged.

"Teaching him, ain't I? That's his pay."

"Oh, really?" Arthur's voice was bland. "Is that what the crafting guild has to say about people you're . . . apprenticing?"

Dimitri scowled. "One Common shard a week. That's standard low-apprentice pay."

That was less than Arthur had made as a cook in a back-end kitchen, but this wasn't Wolf Moon Hive. "One Common shard," he agreed. "But if Brix tests up to guild-craft standard of mid-apprentice or higher, you pay him accordingly."

"Fine," Dimitri said, clearly not thinking it would be a problem.

Brixaby looked up from his work. "Do I get to eat those shards?"

"Of course," Arthur said. "You earned them."

Letting out a satisfied hiss, the dragon crimped another rivet on the chain.

Abruptly, the cave rang with a deep bong-bong-bong of large gongs.

Arthur, Cressida, Joy, and Brixaby all froze in place. Those sounded like scourgling alarms that announced an eruption.

However, no one else seemed to be alarmed. Around them, conversation cut off, and crafters started calmly putting away their wares.

"What's going on?" Cressida asked.

"New around here, ain't you? It's a card-gifting ceremony," Dimitri said. "We've all been expecting it since word of a successful raid came from up high. Kid," he said to Brixaby. "Put that chain away. You're going to want to see this." He glanced at Arthur and Cressida. "All you snooty hive folk should see the way *decent* folk deal with cards."

CHAPTER 11

It wasn't hard to figure out where the ceremony would be held. As the gongs continued to ring, echoing around the interior sandstone walls and out across the desert plain, locals turned and started filtering out of the cavern. The atmosphere was that of a relaxed festival, with people and dragons calling out to each other cheerfully.

Once outside, the dragons either took to the sky to fly up to the top of the mesa or, more commonly, bent to allow humans to ride on their backs and necks. Some people had already come prepared and strung temporary ropes around the dragons to act as handholds, though Arthur didn't see an official saddle among them.

Others who didn't want a ride to the top either used their own card power or started up a long stairway carved into the side of the mesa. It looked like quite the hike.

Cressida turned to Arthur with a frown. "Joy can't take us both at the same time," she said almost apologetically, though Arthur had not expected such a thing. "Why don't you go with her first, and then she can come back for me?"

For the hundredth time, Arthur felt a pang of regret that Brixaby was much too small to carry him. He turned to the little dragon to gauge his mood—Brixaby could be jealous whenever Arthur rode on another dragon—but paused when he saw Shadow melt out of the crowd as if he were using a kind of card power.

"There you are." Brixaby buzzed right up to the tip of Shadow's nose. "I was beginning to think that you abandoned your duty to my rider."

"Not yet," Shadow said, then turned to stiffly nod at Arthur. "Sir, I figured you would need a safe way up to the top."

Arthur couldn't say that he had grown close to Shadow in the few hours they'd worked together, but there seemed to be a new formal distance to the dragon now. "If you wouldn't mind."

"It's my duty," Shadow said stiffly.

Then, in the next second, velvet darkness surrounded them. The monsters, thankfully, were far away enough to be mere impressions.

In the following moment, Arthur, Brixaby, Cressida, Joy, along with Shadow, stood in the sheltered lee of . . . was it an impossibly tall rock wall? Arthur felt slightly dizzy from the rapid transport as he stepped back from the wall to look around.

"Shadow, what exactly are those things?" Arthur demanded. "Those shapes—are those scourglings?"

"Don't know, but you don't want them touching you." Shadow cocked his elbow. Several scales, dark as Brixaby's, stood out among the ruby.

"Where are we?" Cressida asked.

"The top of the mesa," Shadow replied.

Tearing his attention from Shadow, Arthur looked around and blinked. The top of the mesa? No, that was impossible. He had just been here a few hours ago, and it had been completely flat. Now it had completely changed.

Brixaby buzzed to gain height and a better perspective. Figuring that was a good idea, Arthur backed up a few steps, then a few steps more. He looked up, and up, and up.

It took a few seconds for his mind to wrap around it, but he realized that he was looking at the back of a large auditorium—an awe-inspiring structure that was built entirely out of red sandstone. Due to Shadow's teleporting ability, they had appeared where the sun was mostly blocked.

Joy flew after Brixaby and called down, "There is an opening over there." She pointed a claw to indicate the curved wall. Then she brightened at a passing green. "You look nice. Do you want to be friends?"

"I will sit with the rest of the dragons," Shadow said, and without another word, leaped into the sky. Arthur saw several of the larger dragons swoop to land at the very top rim of the auditorium. That functioned as their seating.

As he and Cressida came around the structure, they saw people filtering in through arched entrances—some separating from dragons who, like Shadow, decided to sit at the top. Others followed their riders and friends inside. Everyone was all smiles, and there weren't any guards at the door to check their identity. It seemed everyone was welcome.

Once they passed through, Arthur saw that the inside was even larger than he suspected, as a massive space had been carved out to create sub-levels. At the very bottom sat a stage.

"None of this was here a few hours ago," Cressida said, echoing his thoughts.

"If they have powerful enough cards, say, a few earth Rares, they might be able to raise or sink this whole structure. That way if there were any patrols from the kingdom flying above, this wouldn't give them away." Arthur was just thinking out loud, but Cressida nodded.

She looked up and waved at Joy, who was cavorting with other young dragons up in the air. Brixaby buzzed nearby, too, though he held himself slightly apart and did not actively interact with the others.

Cressida dropped her hand. "Let's get near the stage," she said. "I want to see what all this fuss is about." Then lower, "And if these people are as fair as they claim."

Arthur stopped himself right before he defended the free hive folk. He settled with a nod.

But the instinct to think the best of these people bothered him. After all, they had essentially kidnapped him and Cressida. And though they weren't being held in a cell or currently threatened, they weren't allowed to leave. The Free Hive Council had kept Arthur away from his primary duty of being available in case a demi-scourgling erupted.

And yet . . . Brixaby was already showing interest in a craft. And Arthur wasn't exactly chomping at the bit to get back to Wolf Moon Hive with all its deep-seated problems.

Just in case, he concentrated on his mental-blocking skills . . . then remembered the card-lock cuffs. How far did those go? Would they block only his skills, or the skills of mind-mages working on him too?

Deep down, he didn't think he was being manipulated. His discontent had been brewing for a while. The truth was, he wanted to find a hive that was worth leading.

And he hadn't realized how disenchanted he had slowly become with Wolf Moon until now. The schism had started when he was left out to dry before he met with the king. And it hadn't gotten better. When—*if*—he did return, he needed to find a way to fix that.

Still, as he and Cressida made their way down toward the stage, he found himself thinking, *Please be a place worth defending . . .*

The seats were filling up fast, but Cressida navigated the way with the confidence born of a noblewoman. They found a spot three rows up, which was still fairly close. The seating itself was made up of wide shallow steps. The humans typically sat on the edge and dragons lounged on the wide portions. Joy swooped to join them, cuddling up next to Cressida, even though she was as big as a horse.

"Cressida, I found my five friends. They are so nice here!"

Brixaby came down as well, sat next to Arthur, and fluffed out his four wings. "It seems they'll let anyone in for this show," he sniffed.

"You don't think that Commons and uncarded should be allowed in?" Arthur asked, frowning at his dragon's prejudices.

Brixaby gave him a look like he was being intentionally obtuse. "I think everyone's time would be better spent improving skills and crafts."

Oh. Brixaby was just put out that he couldn't work on his newest obsession. Arthur knew the feeling. There was nothing quite like leveling up a new skill.

"You know, if you stored some chain rivets in your storage space, you could be working on it right now . . ."

Brixaby gave him a startled look and then flicked two of his wings back in irritation. "I will consider it later," he said haughtily, which was as good as admitting that he had completely forgotten to use his Personal Space.

When he and Arthur had linked, they had pretty much given each other carte blanche to access Arthur's heart deck cards and Brixaby's core card, Call of the Void.

Brixaby, however, didn't often use Arthur's cards he wasn't directly linked with, and vice versa. Arthur's cards weren't stamped on Brixaby's heart, so accessing his cards was a matter of practice rather than automatic thought.

Also, Arthur felt ambivalent about using Brixaby's power, as it required the permanent destruction of cards. He hadn't found even a Common card that he was willing to take out of circulation from the world forever.

His thoughts were interrupted by Joy pointing one claw just to the side of the stage. "Oh! There's Tamya and Len. They're over there. Should they come sit by us? What do you think, Cressida? Tamya! Len! Over here!" She stood up on her hind legs to wave broadly in their direction.

Joy was being very loud, even among a crowd of chatting people—but it seemed Tamya and Len were purposely not looking in their direction.

"Are they sitting with uncarded people?" Arthur squinted to try to get a better look.

Sure enough, the pair sat with people who had the hallmarks of the uncarded. Some were frightfully skinny, and others had the unhealthy pallor of someone who had been sick multiple times in their life. He was certain that one woman had pockmark scars on her cheeks.

"Joy, settle down. There's no room for Tamya and Len to sit with us," Cressida said. "Leave them be."

Joy dropped back down to four feet again with a sigh. "I don't think they want to join us anyway," she said sadly. Joy could act like a ditz, but she was observant when she wanted to be.

"I don't want to sit with them either," Brixaby said. "They never have anything to say, and their power isn't all that interesting either."

"Their powers aren't very useful to fight *scourglings*," Arthur had a hunch about why they were sitting with the uncarded, and he wasn't sure how he felt about it. "But in a desert community by the ocean, they'll be invaluable . . ."

Cressida glanced at him, frowned, and then sent a harder look back toward Tamya and Len. Before she could say anything, Councilor Chablis walked out to the middle of the stage. She was followed by several older men and women that Arthur didn't recognize, and Laird, which he most certainly did.

"Don't tell me . . ." Arthur said.

"That's the council," Cressida murmured, having picked up on it too. "And look at that, Laird is one of them."

Arthur felt a spike of annoyance, but Laird had not told him he *wasn't* part of the council.

Smiling widely, Chablis stepped before everybody else and made a gesture at her own throat. When she spoke, her voice echoed throughout the auditorium. She had a sonorous card power.

"My people, we are all gathered today to witness the induction of these fine folk, new citizens to our free hive. By taking a card into themselves, they strengthen our hive, as we strengthen them with the gift of power and healthy life."

The crowd clapped, including the dragons, who did so with forward or backward flicks of their wings, depending on how they were built. The purples and the few blues who had four wings were especially loud. All eyes were on the group clustered to the side of the stage—the one where Tamya and Len sat.

As Arthur had suspected, Tanya and Len had agreed to join the free hive.

"They convinced them to leave Wolf Moon in just a few hours?" Cressida gave Arthur a concerned look. "Do you think it was by force?"

That redoubled Arthur's worry about influence.

"Of course not," Brixaby said, overhearing them anyway. "They're just cowards who don't want to fight and earn cards like everyone else. They want them given to them on a platter." Then he let out a long sigh, likely wishing he could be given a card to eat right about then.

"Should we stop this?" Cressida asked worriedly.

It was moments like this that reminded Arthur that Cressida had been expected from birth to be a leader, while he was still getting used to the idea. It hadn't even occurred to him that, as the ranking rider of Wolf Moon, he should have an official say in whether Tamya and Len joined the Mesa Free Hive or not. That his permission should have been asked.

And what if he didn't want to have a say?

He hesitated, weighing the options to intervene or not, but then he shook his head. "I'll talk to them later."

By then, Tanya and Len would have already accepted the card, but he could at least find out why they had decided to abandon their hive. Arthur knew why *he* was disenchanted. But what would a Common rider have to worry about?

Cressida frowned, but she nodded. "Isn't Len still too young to take another card?"

"That depends on if his secondary core has developed yet," Brixaby answered. "If he's foolish enough not to know, then he deserves to be card poisoned."

Shortly after, the clapping died down. Chablis looked over the crowd, and Arthur saw her eyes briefly land on him before moving away again.

"I will call our new residents up one by one, and they will draw a card from the barrel."

Laird leaned forward with a large apple barrel between his claws, the insides glittering with cards. Arthur winced at the sight of incredibly valuable cards stuffed together like that, but they weren't exactly paper. As hard as plate steel, they couldn't be bent. Still, it seemed like an undignified way to store so much power.

"Fate will decide your card and how you may help your new home," Chablis said to the waiting group. "Once you choose, please join the craft experts and masters who best fit your card." She gestured to another group lined up at the other end of the hall. "These men and women will help you get started in your new life."

"That barrel reeks of Common cards," Brixaby muttered, making a show of sniffing. "A few Uncommon, too."

Cressida leaned close to Arthur. "I bet none of them are combat oriented."

His Gambler class twinged. "I wouldn't take that bet."

"Still," Joy said, "it's nice to get a card at all. I would hate to be without one. Some of those people are so thin . . ."

Arthur silently agreed. Seeing those hopeful, anxious folk about to receive a card of their own, he couldn't help but think of the people left behind in his border village.

Brixaby snorted, unimpressed. "What if they pick a card they aren't suited for?"

"It'll go in their heart. They'll grow with it," Arthur answered.

"Besides," Joy said, perky and optimistic as always, "there's no rule that says they can't trade the card. So, if someone has a fear of mice but gets a speaking-with-mice card, they can trade it!"

"Who would want a speaking-with-mice card?" Brixaby demanded.

"I would! Mice are so cute with their little hands and whiskers. But Cressida said I couldn't keep any of the ones I found for a quest that one time because—" Joy was cut off as Cressida shushed her.

The first person took the stage: an older woman with wispy silver hair and a determined expression on her face. She moved like every step pained her but asked for no help crossing the stage.

Laird lowered the barrel to make it easy to reach, though he kept the top above her eye level, presumably so she wouldn't look before she picked. The woman didn't seem to care. She reached over the top and plucked out one, then brought it down and gazed at the card for a moment before she spoke to Chablis. Because her words weren't enhanced, they didn't carry to the rest of the crowd, so Chablis repeated them.

"A Common fabric-weaving charm!"

Though the card wasn't traditionally exciting, the crowd clapped and cheered as if it were first-rate. With a small smile on her stern face, the woman pulled down the neck of her shirt and pushed the card into her chest. She gasped audibly. A man with a textile badge on his shoulder crossed the stage to meet her. She met him halfway, her steps visibly more fluid.

"What happens when a card is given to an older adult who can't grow with it?" Arthur asked Cressida. "Are they healed? She looks better."

Cressida hesitated before answering. "I don't know. I've never met an uncarded adult."

Nobles, Arthur thought with fond exasperation.

The ceremony continued. Every card drawn could be put toward a utilitarian or crafting purpose, and as Arthur suspected, every one was a Common or Uncommon. No Rares and no combat cards. Which made him wonder what they did with the fighting cards. And if he and Brixaby could browse them. Though he still had a little bit of a wait until Brixaby could safely develop a secondary dragon core . . .

He was musing on this as the last person was called up and received an Uncommon Herb Gardening class card—quite the find, and one Arthur wouldn't mind copying one day.

Finally, the only ones left were Tamya and Len.

With a smile, Chablis indicated Laird could put away the barrel. A male council member stepped forward with a pretty gilded box. Chablis turned to the audience.

"Our last inductees are a young dragon-rider pair. While they are too newly linked to safely accept a new card, the council has offered this Common water-temperature alteration card as a gift—"

Arthur sensed rather than saw a flash of movement out of the corner of his eye. He wouldn't have thought much about it except for Brixaby's sudden squawk.

"Arthur! Phase out!"

His Phase In, Phase Out card was part of his heart deck and was all but stamped on his soul.

Arthur didn't think about the fact that what he was about to do was impossible with the card-lock cuffs on. He just did it.

In the next blink, a wiry man dressed in black passed through Arthur's body, a knife out in front. He had come at Arthur at an angle, a knife-edged with green slashing at his neck.

His attacker—no, his would-be-assassin—staggered forward through Arthur and past him to land on Cressida.

Or he would have.

Joy, for all her bubbles and excitement, was still a dragon. With an outraged roar, she slammed one pink-clawed limb between her rider and the staggering man. Her wing swept forward to knock him away.

It happened in a flash, and before people all around had time to do more than scream, the would-be assassin was knocked out of arm's reach.

Quick as a diving hummingbird, Brixaby darted forward and ripped a card right out of the man's heart.

He came away just as Joy started bellowing. The green-tinged knife that had been aimed at Arthur and almost hit Cressida had instead been driven between the scales of her forelimb. And those scales were starting to darken and wither.

CHAPTER 12

Joy recoiled, as if trying to distance herself from her own limb, and collided with several people who didn't move out of the way in time. In just a few seconds, the wound was visibly darkening. No, Arthur realized. It was rotting.

Chaos ensued, with people screaming and scrambling to get away from the assassin and Brixaby, who was buzzing around with the man's card in his claws.

"Who are you? What did you do to my friend?!" Brixaby roared out in a thunderous voice that didn't suit his tiny form.

The man choked out something, and his form shifted as if he were trying to cast an illusion.

Brixaby darted down and returned with a second card torn from the man's chest. The would-be assassin collapsed.

"It's poison! Joy's been poisoned! Healer!" Cressida yelled, and a bear made of flame erupted into being beside her, rising on its hind legs, round ears pinned back.

Brixaby landed on the man's chest to scream in his face. "Give me the antidote!"

The man was far beyond answering, his limbs shaking in a seizure and froth bubbling up from his lips. Meanwhile, in those few seconds, the darkening cut on Joy's forelimb had increased to a hand-width size.

The pink dragon had stopped shrieking in fear and just stared at it in shocked horror.

Arthur stepped toward her. "We need to stop the poison from spreading until we can get you to a healer. Joy, let me store you."

Joy looked at him, wide-eyed. "Poison?" she asked, clearly too shocked to understand what he said. "But it doesn't hurt."

Which wasn't a great sign, as it meant that the nerves had died.

"Let me store you in my Personal Space," Arthur repeated. "Remember, I did the same thing when you were a hatchling?"

Cressida turned to Arthur. "Yes, please. Joy, it will just take a moment, love. We'll unstore you once we have a healer."

"O-okay," Joy warbled.

Arthur reached for her and thought about his Personal Space.

Suddenly, the dragon felt as if she weighed a thousand pounds—but the weight was more than physical; it was magical, and so unexpectedly dense that Arthur lurched forward as if he'd just tried to pull a mountain into his Personal Space. And the mountain had pulled back.

"What the—" Arthur began, before remembering the card-lock bracelets. He looked down at his wrists and saw that they were bare. Then he remembered the clinking sound he'd heard right when he'd phased out.

Wait.

It hadn't occurred to him in the last frantic minute, but he shouldn't have been able to do that.

Glancing around, Arthur saw the two bracelets on the ground, as if they had fallen through his body when he'd phased out. None of this made sense.

He touched Joy again and once more felt that lurch. He couldn't store her.

"Something's wrong," he muttered.

Cressida stared at him. "What do you mean?"

A third try also failed. "I don't know. It won't work—I don't think it's me. The bracelets are off."

Meanwhile, Joy's wound was growing larger and darker. A blackened scale sloughed off to reveal shriveled skin underneath.

"My scale . . ." Joy sounded heartbroken by the loss. "I really liked that one."

Panic started to set in. Arthur looked around and saw that most of the crowd had fled. "Healer! Is there anyone with a healer card around here?"

As if in answer, he saw Laird make a flapping leap from the stage and land in the newly cleared area right by them. His presence scattered the few people who had been loitering. "What is going on here?" he asked.

"Somebody cut Joy, and they had some kind of poison card," Arthur said, not wanting to muddy the waters with the assassination claim.

But Brixaby, who still crouched on the fallen man's chest with claws digging into his skin, had no such problem. "This madman tried to kill Arthur, and Joy got in the way!"

Chablis slid down from Laird's neck. She took a hard look at Joy, which spoke of some kind of scanning power. "This dragon is under some kind of magical nullification block."

"I'm trying to store her in my Personal Space, but it's not working. Can anyone around here disperse it? Brixaby, can you do it?" Arthur asked, turning in desperation to his dragon.

Brixaby did have some natural nullification magic within his scales, but one pained look from his dragon told him that he couldn't extend that to others. It wasn't a card power. It was a function of his natural talents as a magical creature.

Joy, of course, had her own natural talents as a meta/knowledge dragon. None of which were helpful right now.

"What's going to happen to me?" Joy asked. "I don't know what to do. There aren't any quests. Cressida, help!"

Cressida, who had been standing next to her dragon to support her, twisted her hands in anxiety. "We could try to cauterize the wound until the healers get here."

"What is taking them so long?" Brixaby growled. "You there, Laird. Send for the healers, quickly."

Laird, however, looked sad. "We don't have any high-level healers in the hive. I can tell you right now that none of them could stop a poison as potent and fast-acting as this. They may be able to heal the damage afterward, if she lives."

His last words were like a bell toll.

"Fine, then she should take these." Brixaby buzzed up to Joy to push two cards right in her face. "Put these in your core."

"I can't." The pink dragon reeled back, staggering as her rapidly blackening forelimb lost strength. "My secondary core isn't ready yet."

"It doesn't matter. You still have to try. Look at the card." He shoved it in Joy's face. "It's a Rare card that works with poison, and he had this, too." Brixaby shook the second. "They were combined in the same set. One puts necrotic poison on a blade, the second is nullification magic. If you have that power, you can make them your own."

"She's a meta/knowledge dragon," Cressida said. "We can't. It's too dangerous. That's a pair of cards. It will be too strong for her, even if she did have a secondary core. We have to . . . there has to be something else . . ." Cressida looked around, frantic for another solution.

Her gaze landed on Arthur, and at that moment, Arthur realized that his duty was to be strong for them all.

And though he was unsure of what to do, he was certain that if Joy did not take those cards, then at the very least, she would lose her arm. The poison was visibly crawling up to her shoulder, and it was all too easy to imagine that it would soon head to her heart.

"You've got to try," he said, looking at Joy. "Whatever changes come . . . you can't fight it. You have to accept it."

"Arthur, she'll be adding a pair of cards to her main *core*," Cressida repeated, unsure if he understood.

But he did, all too well.

Humans could add cards and remove cards from their heart deck. Yes, there was pain and possibly some mental damage if they were taken forever, but it was possible. Dragons, however, were magical creatures built around the cards in their core. Joy was almost old enough to have consolidated a secondary core, but not quite. That meant that these cards would change her fundamentally.

"It's the only chance she has," Arthur said.

"She is part of my retinue, and I say add the cards," Brixaby snapped. "Hurry!"

Brixaby once again pushed the cards toward Joy, but Cressida snatched them away.

For a moment, Arthur thought she was going to toss them aside. Instead, her expression firmed, and she turned to the pink.

"Put these in your core, Joy. And whatever happens . . . you'll always be my dragon."

"I think," Joy said weakly, "I'd better use that point of luck I just got . . ."

The black was visibly crawling up Joy's shoulder. At some points, the necrosis rot had gotten so bad that her bone was showing. Joy leaned to press her forehead against Cressida's.

As she did, Cressida pushed the cards into Joy's chest.

The dragon had not reacted in pain with her flesh literally rotting off the bone, but the cards were another story. She bellowed, rearing back.

Cressida cringed as if hit by a backlash. Toxic green flashed over both of them—their auras briefly visible.

Joy's blue eyes rolled up in the back of her head, and she passed out. Arthur stepped forward to help push her to her side as she crumpled, so she didn't land on her damaged limb.

"It's not working," Cressida breathed. "The poison's still advancing." She was clearly on the verge of panic. "Oh no . . . oh no . . . we have to cauterize it! Stop the spreading somehow!"

"No." Arthur grabbed her and pulled her closer before she used one of her flame-bear summons to do something drastic. Arthur pointed. "Look, it's worked but . . ."

The black rot had stopped, but a new, sickly off-green was spreading down her limb, coloring the skin beneath her scales, making it an odd unpleasant juxtaposition with her vivid pink scales. As they watched, the new green swept down the still-healthy parts of her forelimb until it reached the tip of her claws. The quick of her once rosy-pink claws turned toxic green down to the tips.

"What does it mean?" Arthur asked.

"I think," Laird replied heavily, making Arthur jump since he had forgotten that the red dragon was still there, "that much depends on what you just put into your dragon's core."

Cressida paused and bit her lip. "I see them," she said, gesturing and projecting an image of the cards from Joy's deck. Arthur was surprised, since he hadn't realized that a rider could do that with their dragon's cards. Then again, these had been added to Joy's main core, not a secondary deck, and were now a fundamental part of her.

She kept the projection small and between them, so only she and Arthur, looking over her shoulder, could read them.

"Those are . . . quite the cards," Arthur said.

Necrotic Blade
Rare
Poison

Whenever the wielder of the card controls an edged weapon, that weapon will be imbued with quick-acting necrotic poison. The lightest scratch means death. The wielder of this card has automatic resistance to this poison.

Nullification Blade
Rare
Nullify

Whenever the wielder of the card controls an edged weapon, that weapon will be imbued with a nullification potion which will terminate all magical effects and buffs. The wielder of this card has automatic resistance to all nullification effects.

Eyebrows high, Arthur looked back at Joy. The black that had crawled up her forearm hadn't receded—she still needed a healer for the damage done before she became resistant. However, only the limb that had been stabbed had the extra green tinge. The rest, including her wings, were her normal eye-blinding pink.

His focus went to her new green claws. "I don't think it would be a good idea to get scratched by those."

"The little pink will live," Laird said. "It's a good thing that she seems to lean more toward meta than knowledge. A little more flexible."

"Now that that's done," Chablis said in a sardonic voice, lifting Arthur's card-lock cuffs. "Care to explain this?"

Brixaby turned to the woman, menace radiating from him like heat. "Care to explain why somebody tried to kill my rider while he was at his most vulnerable?"

With that, Brixaby darted forward.

Instinct made Arthur catch his dragon in midair as he darted toward Chablis. He didn't think Brixaby was going for her heart cards—at least he was pretty sure—but the effect was striking.

Chablis and the three human councilors who'd gathered next to her backed up hurriedly. Even Laird moved a step to the side, giving Brixaby a hard look.

"You blocked my rider's powers and then set him up to be assassinated!" Brixaby bellowed. He was so angry that he vibrated in Arthur's grip. "Arthur, let me go. I'll show them what happens when they betray us."

"No one betrayed you. That is absurd," Chablis said. "Young dragon, we would never allow your partner to be put in danger."

"Not even for free Legendary cards?" Laird asked dryly. "Utility Legendary," he said, with emphasis.

The other councilors pretended they did not hear him.

"This is ridiculous," one of the councilors, a male, said, "we gave this *kingdom* rider permission to be among us only if he kept the card locks on. He's broken our one request: The locks must stay on!"

Brixaby inhaled as if to bellow, but Arthur got there first.

He kept his voice measured but stern. "I had the right to defend myself. That assassin came out of nowhere. You are lucky that I was able to break the card locks." He looked down at Brixaby meaningfully. The dragon looked like he would happily tear out the cards from all their hearts.

"Is that a threat?" the councilor asked.

"Don't be a fool," Laird said. "A dragon who loses his rider and survives— one who is so young that he hasn't even developed a secondary core—would go insane with rage. A Legendary would be near unstoppable. I think this is less of an assassination attempt on Arthur and more of an attack on our hive."

That visibly deflated most of the councilors. Chablis, especially, seemed thoughtful. She looked at Arthur.

"For whatever it's worth, you have my personal guarantee that this attack was not ordered by our hive. We're not sure of your value to us, but we certainly were not plotting your death."

Arthur nodded, though he wasn't sure that he believed her.

"And you have my guarantee," Laird rumbled, "that we will interrogate this man and get to the bottom of it."

"That, I can agree with," another one of the councilors said.

The third remained silent and troubled as he looked at the assassin, but he did not object.

"That's not good enough," Brixaby said, "I need guarantees that my rider will stay safe. I can't look out for him forever. I have crafting to do."

"Brixaby," Arthur sighed. Deciding the dragon had calmed down enough, he adjusted his grip and allowed him to stand on his shoulder. Thankfully, Brixaby didn't take this as an opportunity to dive for the councilors.

"Yes, interrogate the man," Arthur said. "But Joy needs a healer, now—the best healing you can get for her. And I expect it to be at no cost."

Chablis leaned back as if she had been slapped. "Of course, we wouldn't charge you for that. Healing is free here at our hive."

That wasn't always the case in Wolf Moon. Another difference between the two. But her attitude annoyed him. "So far I have been brought here against my will. Then a pair of the ones I'm responsible for has been convinced to leave my hive. Now this man attacked me, resulting in the injury to a retinue rider and a friend. So forgive me if I don't expect the best out of you."

"You're lucky that I'm so forgiving," Brixaby added with a sniff.

There was an awkward silence. Arthur got the impression he hadn't made any friends with that last speech, but he had made a point.

"We will let you know what our investigation uncovers," Laird said. "But, as we have no mind-mages here, it may take some time."

Arthur filed that gem away for later, though he had no way of knowing if his statement was true or not.

Laird looked to Chablis. "Have someone gather up this assassin . . . Though I don't know what use he will be to us. You only took his cards?" he asked, looking at the downed, twitching man and then at Brixaby. "This isn't the result of poison?"

"No, he is simply weak," Brixaby said without pity. "He'll come around when he finds a way to live without his cards."

"Very well, then. Chablis, take this man into custody and send for a healer. I'll escort our guests to the visitors' quarters."

Interesting. Laird wasn't just one of the councilors. He was comfortable ordering the others around.

It looked like one of the human councilors was going to object. The old man got as far as saying, "Wait just a moment—"

Laird turned his back to him. Since he was a large dragon, it was effectively like putting a wall between himself and Arthur.

The old man fell silent. This conversation was apparently over.

Carefully, Laird moved Cressida aside from the unconscious Joy and gently scooped her up within his claws.

"Come," he said simply, crouching down in a signal for everyone else to climb on his back.

Arthur exchanged a look with Brixaby but did as Laird asked.

Despite the grim circumstances and his worry for Joy, he allowed a part of himself to feel amazed. His twelve-year-old self would never have imagined riding the red dragon who had changed the course of his life forever.

He just wished it was under better circumstances.

The guest quarters in Mesa Free Hive was a small cave filled with basic furniture. It carried a musty scent, as if no one had lived there for some time and it had been long neglected. Arthur was glad that Brixaby didn't say anything snarky about it. He only buzzed in and around as if scouting for danger.

Laird gently laid down the limp Joy on the balcony and flew off, presumably to check on the status of a healer. Instantly, Cressida rushed to her dragon's side.

"How is she, really?" Arthur asked, after looking around to ensure they were alone. He hoped that there was nobody with an eavesdropping card monitoring them.

"I don't know," Cressida said. "The link is still strong between us, but . . ."

He finished for her, "You're only connected through her quest and linked cards."

"Yes."

"She's breathing, and . . ." Cressida placed a hand on the base of her neck. "Her heartbeat is strong. But I can't tell anything else. Arthur." She looked at him, a well of emotion in her eyes. "The last thing I did before leaving Wolf Moon Hive for the class was to lecture her about collecting disgusting rodents for a quest . . ."

She trailed off, eyes brimming with tears. Unsure what to do, Arthur rested his hand on her shoulder.

"I love Joy," Cressida continued. "Even when she's so enthusiastic about everything she drives me up the wall. What if taking those cards has changed her?"

"We'll deal with that as it comes. And if she is . . . different, I'm sure you'll still love the new Joy."

Because he knew that Joy would most certainly be altered by this; small or great, he wasn't sure, but there would be some change.

Rising grief threatened to swamp him—he was fond of the little bubbly pink, too. But it was better for her to change, be altered, rather than to die.

He hoped.

There came a knock at the door. Arthur rose to answer it, letting Cressida and Brixaby sit next to Joy.

It was a middle-aged woman with a healer badge. She nodded to him and then all but pushed Arthur aside to go inspect her newest patient.

Amused, Arthur closed the door after her. He'd gotten so used to being constantly scraped and bowed to at Wolf Moon that being treated as a nobody again felt odd.

The healer took one look at Joy's ravaged forelimb and tsked under her breath. Instant green light started to spread over Joy. It wasn't too different from her newly green skin under the scales on her poisoned limb.

Finally, the healer spoke. "I was told to expect poison, though . . . It seems to be neutralized now. This is all necrotic damage, not too different from gangrene."

"Can you save her limb?" Cressida asked.

"Yes," she said, still brusque. Everybody let out a breath of relief. "But I'll be managing it for the rest of the day, rebuilding all this muscle and tissue. She will wake up ravenous, so be aware of that."

"Yes," Cressida wiped at her eyes, clearly relieved.

"No, girl. I mean, she will wake up *literally* starving. So while I work, I want you to go fetch her a meal. There are sheep in the lower paddock . . ."

While the healer spoke, Brixaby buzzed up to Arthur's ear. "Arthur, we need to speak. In private."

That was by far the quietest he had ever heard Brixaby before, and proof that he could whisper when he wanted to.

With a glance toward the balcony, Arthur left Cressida and the healer speaking and walked to the back of the room. "What is it?"

Brixaby had a devilish look in his eye.

From nothing, or specifically, from Brixaby's own Personal Space, the dragon pulled out a card.

"The assassin had a third card. And I think it's one you'll like."

Arthur read the card.

A Stealthy Class

Rare

Utility

This card grants its wielder instant Stealth Class as well as a 50% boost to natural and skill-based stealth.

Stealth Class Skills:

Silent Movement – Level 10

Heightened Awareness – Level 10

Camouflage – Level 10

Evasion – Level 10

Deception – Level 10

Concealment – Level 10

When Equipped:

+3 to Luck

+5 to Perception

CHAPTER 13

Arthur reread the card three times, hardly believing it.

Brixaby couldn't have plucked a better card for him if he had planned it. Then again, the man had been an assassin. It made sense that he would have a stealth card in his deck.

Still . . . a stealth *class* card was on a whole other level.

"Don't get me wrong, it's amazing. But how did you get it?" Arthur asked.

Brixaby's head lifted with pride. "Everyone was paying attention to Joy. I just plucked it out while the man was seizing and put it straight in my Personal Space."

Before Arthur could worry about his dragon's lack of empathy, Brixaby shot a hasty glance toward Cressida and the healer who were talking. Then he looked back to Arthur.

"What are you waiting for? Use it, and don't let that healer see."

Arthur glanced toward the two, then shifted around so his back was to them. It made it harder for any eavesdropping. "I can't put it in my heart deck," he reminded Brixaby. "Yes, the chances are low that it might affect our bond, but it's a risk I don't want to take."

"Of course," Brixaby said, looking mildly offended. "It should work just fine in your card-anchor deck. Go on. I want to see what your Master cards do with it."

So did Arthur.

Nodding, he slipped it into his card anchor. Or . . . at least he tried. He encountered a strange resistance. He was still able to do it with a little more effort, but the entire temporary deck felt as if it were weighed down. Then again, he did have a lot of power contained there.

While it was perfectly possible to upgrade a card-anchor deck, Arthur would not risk such a thing when he was newly linked to Brixaby.

Those thoughts were cut short as he received a wave of notifications.

New skill gained: Silent Movement (Stealth Class)
Due to the A Stealthy Class card and Master of Body Enhancement's
bonuses, you automatically start this skill at level 13.

New skill gained: Heightened Awareness (Stealth Class)
Due to the A Stealthy Class card and Master of Body Enhancement's
bonuses, you automatically start this skill at level 13.

New skill gained: Camouflage (Stealth Class)
Due to the A Stealthy Class card and Master of Skill's bonuses, you
automatically start this skill at level 13.

New skill gained: Evasion (Stealth Class)
Due to the A Stealthy Class card and Master of Body Enhancement's
bonuses, you automatically start this skill at level 13.

New skill gained: Deception (Stealth Class)
Due to the A Stealthy Class card and Master of Skill's bonuses, you
automatically start this skill at level 13.

New skill gained: Concealment (Stealth Class)
Due to the A Stealthy Class card, you automatically start this skill at
level 10.

New Class!
Stealth – Tier 1 Utility
You have begun to master the art of remaining unnoticed. Some say
that to be stealthy is to disappear like magic. In your case, that is
exceptionally true.
This class combines the following:
Silent Movement – Level 13
Heightened Awareness – Level 13
Camouflage – Level 13
Evasion – Level 13
Deception – Level 13
Concealment – Level 10
Stealth – Level 19
This one basic class will be the average of all skill levels. Newly learned
compatible skills may be added to the Stealth Class. However, an added

lower-level skill contributes to the overall average, possibly lowering the
entire class level.
Stealth Class – Level 13
When equipped, card wielder will learn all the Stealth Class levels at
1.25 times the normal rate in addition to existing skill bonuses.
+3 to Luck
+7 to Perception
Do you wish to combine these skills now?

Sure enough, it looked like the skills had been copied over and been slightly
enhanced, thanks to his Master of Skills and Master of Body Enhancement cards.
It seemed his Legendary Master card classes overrode the actual class card to
some degree, though it did include a two-point advantage in Perception.

The reference to magic was surely about the concealment skill. It was a magical skill, which his Master cards could not copy over. That explained the strange
warping sensation around the assassin as if light had bent around him.

Arthur would have access to that skill too if he kept this class card in his
anchor deck. But . . . there were better uses for it.

With a slight grimace, he removed the card again. Sure enough, the majority
of his skills stayed the same. However, he received an interesting notification:

Skill Downgrade:
Concealment (Stealth Class) has lost its mana-enhancement ability.
Concealment is now a utility-only skill.
Due to your Master of Skills bonuses, Concealment has been upgraded
to level 13.
Stealth Class is now level 14 (13.85 rounded up.)

He couldn't help it. He was grinning from ear to ear. He was glad that he was
turned away from Cressida so she didn't see because this wasn't the right time for
happiness.

But on a personal level, this was huge. "I kept the class and some of the skills.
If we can find more cards like this . . ."

"Well, we would if you ever allowed me to pluck more cards out of people's
hearts," Brixaby said blithely.

Arthur rolled his eyes but held the card back out to him. "Your turn."

Arthur naturally assumed Brixaby was going to consume the card. Brixaby
had the same problem that Joy did—even worse, considering he was a little
younger than her. His secondary card core was not fully developed. However,
Brixaby's particular main allowed him to consume others and add them to his
own strength.

The pity was that it would destroy the card. Arthur felt ambivalent about that, but he wasn't going to stand in Brixaby's way. He had found the card. It was his.

So he was surprised when Brixaby took the card, and, with a pained expression, stuck it into his Personal Space.

"You're not going to eat it?" Arthur asked, shocked.

"I'll hold on to it. For now," he said, not sounding entirely happy. Then he straightened. "I'm a Legendary dragon, and I'm not meant for sneaking around. I ought to be seen. Plus," he added, "it's a valuable Rare card. I might sell it at a later time for something else."

That didn't strike Arthur as quite right. It seemed that Brixaby had other ideas, ones he wasn't entirely willing to share right now.

Could it be that he was growing up?

If necessary, Brixaby could try to briefly consume the card to absorb a little power and remove it again. He had done such a thing with the Legendaries when he first hatched. But those had been extenuating circumstances. Legendary cards were on another order of power than Rare cards. Also, Brixaby himself had been newly hatched with a core card that had mostly, but not entirely, formed.

Also, consuming it and then removing it again might just damage the card. And a damaged card could rot and sprout a scourge infestation. Arthur decided not to mention the possibility.

"If that is what you want," Arthur said.

Brixaby still looked torn. This decision was hard for him. "I can eat it at any time," he said, as if trying to convince himself.

Holding back another smile, Arthur nodded and then turned away. As he did, he saw Cressida stride to the edge of the balcony and run up one of the flags. It was red, indicating an emergency.

Moments later, a blue dragon no bigger than a draft oxen flew up and asked for her request.

Arthur walked up just in time to hear Cressida order a sheep sent up immediately. The blue nodded, took one look at the still unconscious Joy, and dove down.

"I don't know how I'm going to pay for it," Cressida muttered, turning back to Arthur. "All of my coins and shards are back at Wolf Moon."

"I can cover it," Arthur said.

The healer, who was still working on restoring Joy's limb, spoke up. "This is an emergency situation. The hive will take care of basic necessities—within limits. But if you abuse our kindness, there will be consequences."

"Arthur would never," Brix said. "He pinches every single coin like a mother dragon with her first eggs."

The healer didn't respond, busy with her task.

Arthur stepped over and saw more of Joy's pitted flesh healing itself. New scales were growing at an advanced rate, replacing the blackened, dead scales. Old skin was sloughing off to be replaced by new. But there was a difference: Those black scales were replaced by green, not pink. As the necrotic damage had not spread evenly up her arm, it made for a patchy design.

"I don't think Joy will like being a part-green dragon," Arthur muttered, thinking of Joy's dislike for the green in their class, one of the few creatures she had ever spoken badly about.

He regretted his words a moment later, as Cressida's face crumpled.

"Uh, I don't mean to say—" he stammered. "I'm sure she'll get used to it." He stopped before he could dig his hole any deeper.

"I'm just glad that she's alive," Cressida said in a low voice.

There was the rapid flapping of wings, and the blue appeared, carrying a struggling sheep in its claws.

Joy gave a faint twitch when the ewe hit the stone floor. Her nostrils flared, and her eyes shot open, still blue, which stood out around her bright pink muzzle. Within a moment, Cressida was by her side.

The healer, however, hurriedly backed away.

This was just in time, as Joy twisted and got up on her feet. Her face was a mask of fierceness, entirely animalistic in a way that was not like the usual sweethearted dragon.

She shoved Cressida aside and launched herself to fall awkwardly on the sheep, thanks to her still-healing forelimb. There was a crack as the sheep's spine broke—dead instantly, which was a blessing because Joy immediately started tearing the animal open. She swallowed everything that she could get into her mouth: hunks of flesh, bone, wool. It didn't matter. Gobbets of gore flew everywhere.

"Joy?" Cressida asked, stepping toward her. The dragon didn't act like she heard her.

"Do you think that she'll share any with me?" Brixaby asked in an aside to Arthur.

"You don't want to eat that," Arthur said lowly. From where he stood, he saw the places where Joy's newly green claws sank into the animal's flesh. It was starting to go black and rot away.

Joy took a few more mouthfuls, but one of them seemed to be half blackened with necrosis. She stopped. Her eyes practically crossed, and she spat the meat to the side. "Oh . . . gross!"

"Joy?" Cressida stepped forward. "How are you feeling?"

"Hungry . . ." the dragon growled, going in for another few bites, well away from the blackening rot. The problem was, the rot was quickly spreading up the body. With a growl, Joy ripped the sheep's still-fresh head off its body and crunched it like someone would a hard candy. She swallowed it down. By then, the rest of the corpse was a black, stinking mass.

There was a barrel set to the side for rain catchment. It was old with green algae floating on the top. Joy didn't seem to care. She dunked her head in and sucked it down greedily. Coming up for air at last, she looked around, noting the shocked silence.

"Why is everybody looking at me?"

"We're not looking at you," Brixaby said. "We're staring at your forelimb."

"My what?" Joy looked down and saw her mismatched limbs. One bright fluorescent pink and the other mottled pink and tinged with toxic green. She brightened. "Oh wow! I like this! And oh, double wow! I have poison cards in my core, too. Cressida!" She turned to her rider, excited, though there was a dangerous glint in her eyes that certainly had not been there before. "These are great. Can you feel how powerful these are? Three cards! Wow!"

"I didn't link with those, dearest." Cressida looked a little worried. "How are you feeling?"

"It kind of hurts down to my claws, but this is much better than being poisoned. Now I'm the poisoner!" she said enthusiastically, sounding much like her old self, though with a new steely edge. "Wait . . . am I poisonous or venomous?"

It was too much for Cressida, who had been clearly holding herself back. She ran forward and threw her arms around her dragon in a hug.

With a feat of shocking speed and maneuverability, Brixaby darted forward and grabbed Joy's green limb before she could use it to hold her rider. "Don't prick her with these claws!"

Cressida stepped back, and Joy looked stricken. "I can't hug anyone ever again? I mean, killing enemies is really fun," she added, "but . . . what if I really, really wanna hug a friend? Or Cressida? Cressida, can we still sleep in the same bed?"

Now she sounded almost teary. But at that moment, Arthur knew she was going to be okay. She was still Joy. Just . . . with an edge.

"Of course you may still sleep in the same bed," Brixaby said disdainfully. As he should. He insisted on having his own pillow to curl up on. "I'll make you a chainmail glove to wear over your claws. Then you simply take it off when you want to kill something."

Joy visibly brightened.

"Furthermore," Brixaby said, settling back to the ground but puffing proudly. "I'm pleased with this upgrade to your capabilities."

"Really?" She looked down at Cressida, who nodded, still teary-eyed.

Joy held up her claws on her green limb in front of her face. "Yay! Oh, I wonder how many scourglings I can poison with these? Quests are going to be so much more interesting now." Then she glanced over at the disgusting blob of flesh that had been a sheep a few moments before and growled, "But . . . I could use another sheep. Or three."

Dangerous or not, Cressida threw her arms around her dragon's neck. "I'll get you more. As many as you want!"

"First, she needs to be healed to make sure that limb is as strong as the other one," the healer said. "We have to replace muscle mass, not to mention reknit several nerves." If she was affected by the emotion around her, she didn't show it. "Hold still. This may itch, but do not scratch." A new wave of healing energy engulfed Joy.

"I want to begin designing that glove," Brixaby said.

This was Arthur's chance. "And I need to speak to the council. Let them know Joy's going to make it and see if they learned anything from the assassin yet."

Cressida started to nod but then looked concerned. "What if there is more than one assassin?"

"If there is," Arthur said, "it would be pretty revealing if they struck while I'm going to speak to the council."

"If one attacks again, I will simply take their cards," Brixaby added. "I almost hope they do." With that, Brixaby buzzed off toward the direction of the crafting cave.

Cressida still looked worried.

"I'll be careful," Arthur promised her. "I have my own tricks. Stay with Joy."

Arthur headed out, too, using the door at the back of the small quarters. He wondered if he was going to be stopped from leaving, but there were no guards out there.

Nor had the council insisted he put the card-lock bracelets back on. Just as well. They hadn't worked for long.

He activated his **Stealth** skills by concentrating on them one by one. Though he could not see himself, he could tell that he had just blended in with the shadows. Perfect.

If there were more assassins—which he doubted, this felt like a one-man job—they would have a hard time finding him.

He wasn't going to speak to the council. At least not yet. He intended to find Tamya and Len and see what had driven them from Wolf Moon Hive. And what exactly had been promised to make them stay here.

CHAPTER 14

Arthur activated every skill within his Stealth Class as he explored the interior of the free hive. That, however, soon proved to be overkill. He let go of all but classic Stealth, Silent Movement, Heightened Awareness, and Concealment.

The combination of skills didn't exactly make him invisible, just unnoticed—or another bland, unremarkable face in the crowd. People glanced at him and then casually looked away with no change of expression on their faces.

It was liberating. The last few months had been quite the change for Arthur, socially. He had gone from a nobody—a common worker with a few good friends and useful skills to those who knew him—to arguably one of the most important people in the kingdom. So to be another general face in the crowd again . . . Arthur savored it.

Stealthing around was also useful because he had no idea where he was going. For years, he had grown to know the level-based layout of Wolf Moon Hive. The more common folk, the low-ranked, the general crafters, and those who were high-ranked but wanted a taste of a different life often congregated in Wolf Moon's lowest levels.

The more luxurious amenities were located on the higher levels with the upper-ranked riders and general people of importance.

However, the Mesa Free Hive's layout just didn't make any sense to him. For one thing, the mesa seemed to be made of a series of cooled lava bubbles, creating hundreds of caves with no levels stacked on top of one another. For another, they were a complete mishmash of services with no obvious organization.

Arthur passed by caves that glowed with artificial light, where crops were planted in rich deep-black soil with farmers tending to them. Other open-air caves seemed to be filled with pop-up stores where vendors hawked their wares, from fabrics and tools to all manner of odds and ends.

The most tempting caves were the open-air kitchens and food vendors. Arthur wasn't particularly hungry, but his nose picked up a wealth of spices— some in combinations he hadn't tried before, and others which seemed entirely new. It was a reminder that he hadn't truly tried to level anything within his Cooking Class since well before Brix's hatching. He missed it.

But now was not the time. Also, he wasn't sure how his new suite of **Stealth** skills would hold up under strain if he tried to grab a bite to eat. Maybe he would level these skills up a little first.

No signs pointed the way to the riders' quarters. Indeed, some of the caves he passed seemed to be entrances to barracks. He passed several that were filled with stacks of bed cots, which served as barracks. Some were filled with sleeping people. He guessed those were on a night-work shift.

There were also a few caves that were converted into communal dragon dens. He saw one with several young hatchlings playing some kind of dice game.

That was another thing about the free hive that was different from Wolf Moon: dragons and people lived together more closely. The halls were wide enough for all but the largest dragons to pass by easily. Vendors spoke to men and women as easily as they did dragons—and the dragons spoke freely back, which was not something always seen in the hive. As dragons got older, they tended to forgo speaking to strangers. Arthur wasn't sure why.

There was also a sense of . . . comfort and safety in the air. He didn't think the feeling was being imposed on him, like some kind of mental manipulation. It was simply a lack of tension. There weren't any high-ranked riders or nobles strutting about, snapping orders. Not to say that there weren't ranks altogether. Arthur passed by people with apprentice badges up to high masters.

But again, that was different from Wolf Moon. Usually, important crafters would be cloistered within their separate guilds and not interacting out in public.

Arthur was so lost in his thoughts that he didn't realize he was being watched until he felt a prickly sensation itching at the back of his neck. Still mentally holding on to the skills, he turned in place and studied the passersby.

When he spotted his watcher, he was taken aback.

A small silver dragon stared directly at him—and it looked so much like Marteen that he almost called out to them. But at second glance, he noted the slightly heavier set of the dragon's jaw and the more protruded bony eyebrows that indicated the dragon was male.

This wasn't Marteen. Just another silver mystic whose natural magic specialty likely let him see through Arthur's skills.

Sure enough, the dragon looked at Arthur intently, then raised two of his claws to point at his own eyes, and then back at Arthur in the universal signal for *I'm watching you.*

Awkwardly, Arthur waved back.

The dragon made no move, and Arthur felt its gaze as he walked away. The dragon did not stop him. Just watched.

Arthur got the feeling the dragon had been sent by the council. It made sense. Since he wasn't bound by the card-lock shackles, they'd want him under observation. If that was all they did, he'd consider himself lucky.

No one else seemed to notice him, and as he walked on, he leveled up several of his Stealth Class skills.

Skill level gained: Heightened Awareness (Stealth Class)
Level 14
Skill level gained: Concealment (Stealth Class)
Level 14
Skill level gained: Silent Movement (Stealth Class)
Level 14

He hadn't advanced his general **Stealth** skill, but as it was level 19, this took more work. However, leveling those other skills helped level his overall class skill in turn.

His exploratory adventure was fruitful . . . except he saw no sign of Len and Tamya.

After about an hour of wandering up and down caves that made no sense to him, surrounded by people he didn't recognize and who barely acknowledged him, he found himself tiring. He was thinking seriously of giving up and taking a side trip to the giant crafting cave to see how Brixaby was getting along designing his chainmail glove for Joy—when he finally spotted the particular shade of light blue that belonged to Len.

He and his rider stood in front of a seller's stall that made basic dragon tack: saddles and straps for the riders.

Wary of them running off, Arthur walked up behind Tamya. Only when he was directly behind her did he drop out of stealth.

Len made a squeak of surprise, which was a ridiculous sound for a dragon his size.

Hearing him, Tamya whipped around. Her tanned face went instantly pale as she saw him.

"Tamya," Arthur said, "you and I should talk."

Tamya half lifted her hand automatically as if to salute, caught herself, and lowered it again. Her lips pressed together. "I don't see what we have to talk about."

"We won't go back to Wolf Moon Hive," Len added, though his voice quavered. This dragon, several times Joy's size, was terrified of him. He practically shook where he stood.

Did they think he was going to rip the cards from their hearts?

"Why?" Arthur asked. "Were you treated badly there?"

Tamya stared at him. "Is that supposed to be a joke?"

"No?" Arthur looked from the rider to the dragon and back again. Both had defensive body language, and Len, especially, looked like he was on the verge of taking off and flying away. The fact he'd have to leave Tamya behind likely kept him on the ground.

"Look," Tamya said, "we have the support of the Mesa Hive now. And Len and I aren't going back. You can't make us."

Arthur held up his hands in a peaceable gesture. That was a mistake, as the two of them flinched.

"I'm not here to make you do anything," Arthur said. "I just want to understand what is going on—why a new rider who's about to graduate and start their career would abandon their home hive."

Tamya barked out a disbelieving laugh. "The first day of dragon class, Len was still small enough for me to hold in my arms. Instructor Athena gathered all of us low-rankers together and said if we were lucky, a Rare would hatch and join us soon. And that our primary duty as low-ranked riders was to ensure that Rare survived a scourge-eruption at all costs. It got even worse when *you* joined. Every day of training, it was drilled into us that Len and I were expected to die for the high-tier cards and be happy about it."

Arthur frowned. He'd seen a little of what she was talking about, though he wouldn't have categorized Athena's speech quite like that. "You're talking about formation training?"

"Yeah, where we act like scourge fodder to protect you and your pink girlfriend. We've been there for months, and not once have we been taught how to protect ourselves. Just to take orders." Her voice became high-pitched and sarcastic. "'Yes, sir. No, sir. Sure, we'll die for you, sir.'"

"I'm not saying that I agree or disagree," Arthur said, "but we hadn't finished the class yet. We'd just started practicing to fight in and out of formation. We had a lot more to learn. All of us."

Len spoke up, sounding shy. "Instructor Athena thought we'd learned enough to fight the scourglings."

"Yeah, and our *wise leader*," Tamya said, "almost got half our class killed while battling one big scourgling."

Arthur winced. "That could have gone better."

"Better?! You're not a low-ranker. You don't know what it's like for us— we're disposable trash." Tamya's voice rose as she spoke. Apparently, this had been building for a while now, and now that she had an outlet, all her resentment came spilling out. "Here, there's no difference between a high-ranker and a low-ranker. And I've seen Len happy. He's respected; we both are, for cards that no one took seriously back at Wolf Moon. Why would I go back?"

Arthur didn't necessarily disagree with her, but he had to at least try to defend himself and the hive. "Look, after training ends, you didn't have to fight if you didn't want to. You could have graduated to one of the rescue squads, done some good helping people—"

"The Lobos?!" She looked like she wanted to spit.

"There's nothing wrong with joining the Lobos—"

"There is when we don't have cards to defend ourselves!" she all but shrieked.

"Then you earn *more* cards. Everybody graduates with only the cards that they have. By that time, most dragons have formed their secondary cores. If we had been able to stay through that eruption, we would have all split the harvested shards—"

"Great, and after collecting dozens of those, we might have something good," she snapped. "Besides, the Lobos don't get shards. They're paid in jade chips that they trade for food and basic necessities. Those are given here for free."

That gave Arthur pause. He vaguely remembered some kind of transaction happening when Tess had originally brought him to the hive. But he had been too shocked by the rescue to pay much attention.

Tamya went on. "Plus, Len isn't a quick flyer like some of the blues or purples. He'll grow up large. We're just going to be scourgling fodder out there. Better stay here where we could actually do something useful with our lives, other than die for you. This hive has already promised us cards that will match the ones we already have. Len and I won't have to fight another day of our lives."

He looked into her hazel eyes and saw only resentment. And though Arthur knew it wouldn't change a thing, he had to at least try to bridge the gap between them. "You should have been treated with respect from the start. And for what it's worth, you have my word that when I go back, I want to change things. I want to make things fair for the lower-ranked dragons—"

"Well, you can do it without us." She looked at her dragon. "Come on, Len."

And without saying goodbye, she and the blue walked off.

Arthur watched them go, quietly disturbed. Tamya and Len had given no indication that they were so unhappy before. In fact, they'd been so quiet in class that he hadn't thought of them much at all.

It made him wonder who else felt the same way.

No, that was the wrong way to think about it. Who else had been *pushed* into feeling that way?

Arthur had his own issues with the training regimen. If he was told from the very start that he and Brixaby were to sacrifice themselves for somebody else, he'd be just as resentful as her.

Well, no, he corrected himself again. No, he wouldn't be quiet and meekly stew. He'd be doing everything he could to get his hands on combat or strong defensive cards to feed to Brixaby the second he could put them in his new cores.

But he couldn't necessarily fault Tamya for leaving, either.

And at that moment, Arthur knew that he couldn't stay here forever. Some way, somehow, he was going to have to find his way back to Wolf Moon. And when he did, things would change.

But first, he intended to see what this free hive was truly about.

Because he wasn't like Tamya. He didn't want to sit silent and resentful until he got the opportunity to run away. He wanted to seize this opportunity for all it was worth. Brixaby was already interested in crafting. Arthur could do with advancing his skills, too. All of them.

And there was more: Laird and the others had raided a noble's card library. Yet the Free Hive Council had only given out crafting and utility cards.

Where had the combat cards gone?

CHAPTER 15

Arthur went back the way he had come through the meandering, nonsensical hive. Tamya's words echoed in his ears, lowering his mood. Though he had not been aware that there was a problem, he knew he had failed her and Len. He was supposed to be the leader of the class—even though he was in training himself. Yet all he had done was focus on how Wolf Moon's training had failed *him*. He'd given little to no thought about the shortcomings in the lower ranks.

Rubbing his face, he sighed aloud. That must have been a bit too much for his new Stealth Class because he got a couple of curious looks before people's eyes slid away as Arthur refocused.

Then on cue, he received a new skill level in **Concealment**.

Well, he might be a screwup as a leader, but he always had his skills.

He couldn't change what had happened with Tamya and Len. She made it clear that the bridge was burned. The only thing he could do from here on out was to learn from the experience, move forward, and try to keep it from happening again.

Straightening, Arthur exhaled as if to rid himself of his guilt. As he took in a clean breath, he caught a spicy scent in the air. His stomach rumbled in approval.

He had been hesitant about going into one of the kitchens to grab a bite before, as there were things in there that could be weapons, like knives. But that silver mystic who had seen through his Stealth Class hadn't stopped him from walking where he wanted.

Perhaps he was being overdramatic. Did it matter if word got back to the council that he'd been out and about? They already knew they couldn't control him.

Following his nose, he found the delicious spicy aroma coming from a vendor who had set up a cart in an alcove, too shallow to be considered an official lava cave. The booth had a smoking grill with several battered peppers roasting upon it. Despite the alluring smell, no one waited in line for a meal.

"What is this?" Arthur asked, walking up.

"Stuffed peppers," the man replied. "We have meat, cheese, or rice. Or you could get all three for a copper."

The peppers were quite large and stuffed. That was a lot of food, but Arthur had his storage space. He figured he could take some back to Cressida as well. She wouldn't be leaving Joy's side anytime soon.

"I'll take two of the combinations," he said and stood back to watch as the vendor dipped a couple of the already-stuffed peppers into the batter and threw them onto the grill. Then the man skewered the nearly cooked-through peppers with small wooden stakes.

New Counterfeit skill obtained: Perfectly Roasted
Remaining Time: 71 Hours 59 Minutes 59 Seconds

New skill gained: Perfectly Roasted (Cooking Class)
Due to your card's bonus traits and your existing Cooking Class, you automatically start this skill at level 5.

Arthur's eyebrows rose. That was a valuable skill to have for anyone interested in cooking. Judging by the time limit left, it had come from a Common card.

Thanks to his Master of Skills card, it was now his. He hadn't had a lot of time to level his skills since Brixaby's hatching, but this would go nicely with his Cooking Class.

The vendor, completely oblivious that his valuable skill card had just been copied, took the cooked peppers by the ends of the skewers and wrapped them in wax paper before handing them to Arthur.

Arthur quickly stuffed those into his Personal Space. Because time did not move for items in there, they would come out just as perfectly cooked as they had been when they went in.

The second set of three peppers, he reserved for himself. Eagerly, he bit into one he thought might be stuffed with cheese. The taste exploded in his mouth—greasy and delicious, and satisfyingly spicy. And there was another surprise. He received a boost.

Thanks to an infusion of fire peppercorn flakes, your Fire Resistance has been increased to level 4. This is a temporary effect and will result in a temporary negative-point backlash once the effect wears off. You will then be more susceptible to burns.
Time left: 4 Hours 59 Minutes 59 Seconds.

"Is there a problem?"

The vendor was watching him closely, and Arthur hesitated before saying anything. "I have a body-enhancement card," he said, "and I just received a minor boost. Would you happen to know why?" He phrased his words carefully because asking for details on someone else's craft was, well, an easy way to get himself chased away from the vendor's booth.

At least, in Wolf Moon Hive.

So he was surprised again when the vendor beamed widely. "Oh, so you saw that little fire-resistance boost? Normally that goes right over people's heads—they still get it, though."

"You know about that?" Arthur asked, then added, still in complete shock, "You cooked it in on purpose? How?"

Mentally, he was reeling: *And you're okay with me knowing about this?*

"Oh, of course," the vendor said, "though it's more of a happy side effect than anything else. Comes from these—hold on." He started rummaging around underneath the table where he kept his supplies. Then he pulled out a glass jar filled with ground peppercorns.

"Fire peppercorns," the vendor said proudly. "They grow them at the fifth bubble, along with the rest of the minor herbs. See?"

Then, to Arthur's shock, he pinched a little bit of the ground pepper and extended it out to him. Arthur held out his palm, and the man dropped several dozen of the flakes in it.

"Give it a taste," the man said.

Shocked that the vendor was being so open about this, and a little suspicious because of it, Arthur reluctantly sniffed. Yep. Pepper. Cautiously, he took another taste.

His Fire Resistance timer refreshed.

"I add it into the batter as an ingredient. It's good stuff. Not my secret sauce, though." The man winked, and Arthur suspected that his "secret sauce" was actually his card, which showed him exactly when his peppers were roasted perfectly.

It was a sly diversion that he could appreciate. It let this man's competitors drive themselves crazy trying to find the perfect combination of herbs . . . when it was a skill all along.

"I appreciate the information," Arthur said. "I do a little cooking on the side, too, when I can. Fifth bubble, you said?"

"Yep, follow this hallway to the end, and turn right. You're in the third bubble now."

Arthur had no idea what he was talking about, but his new **Deception** skill alerted him that it would be a stupid idea to let the vendor know he was completely new to the hive. That would cause uncomfortable questions.

Thanking the man again—and tipping him another full copper, which the man looked pleased by but not utterly surprised about—Arthur continued the way he pointed while munching on the peppers. Sure enough, each one was perfectly roasted.

As Arthur walked, he tried to figure out what the vendor had meant by bubbles. He only understood once he finally looked up. He had been paying so much attention to the interior caves, which were all smaller, ancient lava bubbles, that he had failed to take in the complex as a whole.

Guess I need a few more levels in my Heightened Awareness skill, he thought, amused.

Instead of layers like in the kingdom hives, the mesa itself was carved out from old lava bubbles so large that they hadn't registered to Arthur. Not until he reached the end of one and saw the gradual downslope of the ceiling to the connecting hallway before he reached the next. And on top of the ceiling, written out in faintly glowing stones, was the number three.

The following "hallway" was still so tall that fully adult dragons could fly through, and when he exited out the other side, he saw a glowing number four on the top of the ceiling. Not hard to guess that he had just entered the next bubble in line. And that the next one after that would be bubble five.

Upon walking into bubble five, he noted that the air felt more humid and slightly cooler. Most of the smaller caves he saw were lit with artificial card light, and he heard the gentle babble of water echoing off the cave walls. There were still a few residences here and there, but it seemed this place was focused on growing things.

It made sense. Since the Mesa Free Hive had such a high population, and no exterior trade to speak of, they would need a lot of homegrown crops.

Speaking of, he wanted to know how the hive managed to keep its dragon population fed. Arthur had been doing some of Whitaker's paperwork as part of his "training." The man's recordkeeping was a mess, but Arthur had come across the amount that Wolf Moon Hive spent on animals to feed the dragons for a typical week. It had nearly bowled him over. Local nobles had entire estates dedicated just to the feeding and raising of cows, sheep, and goats, all shipped to the hive.

And Wolf Moon was a small hive.

The Mesa Free Hive must have another bubble dedicated to animal husbandry. Something well away from anybody else . . . and with a lot of air purification cards.

He let his nose guide the way to the herbs. It was difficult to pick out something individual with all the smells of growing things around him, but Arthur had been working in kitchens for years. The smell of rosemary was distinct.

That scent led him to a deep but narrow cave. The ceiling was brightly lit at the top, with dark, rich soil on the bottom. In fact . . . he knew the coloration of that soil.

"Is that dragon soil?" he blurted, kneeling to get a closer look, half horrified. He hadn't been this close to the stuff, outside its pure form thanks to Brixaby, since he was a child.

"Don't touch it, boy! Not unless you want to burn your hands or grow extra fingers on them."

The voice came from an elderly woman who was tending to a row of sage plants not far away. She gestured with her head to the side wall where several tools and supplies were hung on hooks.

"If you're here to help, grab a pair of gloves."

Her gloves went up past her elbows and were stained dark with the dragon soil.

Arthur hesitated for a moment. Then, with a mental shrug, he did as he was told.

As he stepped across the length of the cave, some trick of the air lessened the overpowering scent of the herbs. Instead, he caught a whiff of the dragon soil, which was much more acidic than it should have been.

For a brief moment, he was a little boy again, helping carry water buckets and dippers to the workers out in the field. In his old borderland village, the older teens and adults took on the dangerous task of working dragon soil into the deadened lands ravaged by the scourglings.

The work was deadly dangerous. As punishment for crimes against the kingdom, everyone was uncarded. That meant they had no defense against scourgedust, should it get too deep into their lungs or open wounds. Also, the dragon soil itself represented a threat . . . though Arthur hadn't learned that until he had been in the hive.

And what he scented now was even more pungent than he remembered as a child.

Arthur paused in the act of pulling on the gloves to stare down at the rich ground, mildly horrified. "How long has this soil been curing in the sun?"

The woman grinned at him. And though she was certainly not a young thing, she still had all her teeth. "You picked up on that fast. This soil's been curing for six months."

"But—"

"No more questions. If you're here to help and not waste my time, come over here. I'll show you how to trim the sage. Bring that pair of clippers on the wall—the ones just over there."

Arthur hesitated again. He didn't have a problem with helping, though he had come mostly to ask questions. He figured if this woman was brave enough— or crazy enough—to work with nearly raw dragon soil, he could be as well.

A few moments later, he was kneeling by her side and being shown what was dead and could be pruned away, and what was promising and alive. It wasn't as easy as breaking off the dead bits. The woman insisted Arthur cut at an angle until he reached green wood and then pat the end with a bit of the raw dragon soil. Apparently, it was to promote growth.

Soon, he received a skill.

New skill gained: Basic Herbal Gardening (Herblore Class/Alchemy Class)
Due to learning the basics of this skill from a master in this class, your starting level has been increased.
You automatically start this skill at level 8.

That was useful.

Arthur was used to doing things on his own, so he appreciated a boost when he received one.

"I came here looking for fire peppercorns," Arthur said conversationally as he clipped. "Do you know who grows them?"

"I do. I'll be along in that cave soon if you want to follow me over there. I figured you weren't here to help," she said with a mischievous smile that told Arthur she thought she had tricked him into this. Honestly, the work was worth it just for the skill alone.

And doubly worth it for the next bit of interesting information.

Arthur's next sage bush looked . . . weird. "What's wrong with this one? Is it sick?"

"Eh?"

She shuffled over immediately with a hunched back. Seeing the bush and its yellow-spotted leaves, her face broke into another grin. "Now this is more like it! It's not sick, boy! Look at the leaves!"

"They're not dying?"

"No, still alive. Not curled in at the least, and none have dropped at all!" She looked like she was ready to do a jig. "This is a new variety."

"A new . . ." He stopped, understanding dawning on him at last. Arthur glanced again at the dragon soil underfoot.

It was said that dragon soil could cause scarring burns but also odd growths—cancers that only the healers could take care of. And on plants . . .

"You're using the dragon soil to create new varieties?" he asked, a little stunned nobody in Wolf Moon Hive had thought of such a thing. They were practically knee-deep in dragon soil—curing it was a logistical nightmare all on its own.

She cackled. "Most of the new stuff is useless, but occasionally we come up with something good. Like those fire peppercorns you're interested in. That was a discovery a couple of years ago—and useful as long as you don't breed them too close. Then they'll literally light the roof of your mouth on fire."

With another cackle, she carefully took a snip of the new yellow leaf, wrapped it in a bit of paper, and noted it down with a stick of coal.

"What are you going to do with that?" Arthur asked.

"Testing, of course. Sometimes a new leaf yields a different taste. Sometimes a boost or boon, but those can be hard to spot."

Arthur grinned. "I might be able to help out with that."

The woman, who briefly introduced herself as Flossie, practically dragged Arthur out of the cave. Then she switched tactics and pushed him toward the entrance of another one about twenty feet away.

This cave seemed to serve as her personal office, or perhaps her home, as Arthur noticed a cot tucked away at the very back. It was, however, surrounded by jars filled with herbs, their lids tightly sealed—so tightly that he couldn't smell anything from them.

Most of the space—shelving, counters, and a good portion of the floor—was occupied by similarly sized jars containing herbs. The rest was cluttered with tools such as tiny clippers, scissors, tweezers, scalpels, and other pieces of vaguely alarming medical equipment.

"Sit, sit." Flossie all but shoved Arthur onto a cluttered chair. He quickly scooped up a stack of paperwork before dropping down on it, and tapped it straight, his Tidying instincts itching at the back of his mind as he took in the messy surroundings.

"Now," Flossie said, "I can offer you above-standard rates—that's what we have for all test subjects."

"Test subjects?" Arthur repeated, mildly alarmed.

She waved an errant hand. "That's what the council insists I call them, but, well, there is *some* human testing, but it's as safe as we can make it. We'll go into that later. Actually, you're coming in at a good time; it's been a while since our last subject quit, and things were starting to get backed up."

"Hold on," Arthur said. "Don't you want to know exactly what my card does first? And how I can help you?"

Flossie blinked. "Oh, of course. Forgive me, I got excited and forgot to put the harness on the dragon before jumping on." She laughed a little too shrilly for politeness's sake.

Arthur got the impression she spent far too much time with her herbs and far too little interacting with other people.

He decided to be as vague as possible about his card. "I have a card that gives me updates about the status of my body. Part of its powers includes providing me with updates on my physical condition."

"Oh!" Her eyes went wide. "I was hoping you would just be willing to record your experiences, but that is certainly helpful."

There was a pause.

"How much is the pay?" Arthur asked.

"One Rare shard per newly identified herb."

Arthur choked. It was extraordinary pay—well, it would have been if he hadn't been living off Wolf Moon Hive's Legendary-dragon stipend. Brixaby would certainly appreciate the shards. That kind of pay wasn't why Arthur had volunteered, but it didn't hurt.

He decided to be a little more candid. "The other part of my card is that I gain resistances to herbs. That means if there's something—"

"Oh, you'll be *perfect* for the poisons," Flossie said happily. She might not be great with people, but she seemed to take note when Arthur grew still. "Oh, don't worry, it won't be anything extraordinarily poisonous. We test those on rats ahead of time. Anything above LD50 is ruled out."

"LD—?"

"Also, we have one of these in case something goes wrong." She rummaged around behind some of the jars, apparently where she kept her supplies, and pulled out a tiny vivid-red vial. "This is a Rare-rank healing potion. For emergencies only."

"A healing potion?" He had seen one before, but only in the possession of royalty. And he severely doubted that this woman was royalty. "How did you get your hands on that?"

"Oh, I'm very rich and connected." She waved casually. "You have no idea how lucrative growing extraordinary herbs can be."

Arthur thought about the lengths his old cooking boss, Barlow, went to bribe growers to get the first pick of the harvest. And that had been for regular fruits, vegetables, and meats. "I can believe it."

"Excellent," Flossie said, standing. Then she proved herself no fool as she added, "But of course, before you are officially hired, I require a test of your abilities."

Flossie's test was simple. She ground up several herbs in the back of the cave, tapped the powder onto a piece of paper, and presented it to Arthur. The tiny piles were varying shades of green and brown.

"Please tell me which of these herbs has what we call 'extraordinary properties.' You may think of them as what others call"—she almost rolled her eyes—"*magical* properties."

"There's a problem with magical properties?" he asked.

"Magical properties can *only* be found in cards," she answered with the air of someone who had a very strong opinion on a very niche subject.

"Well, what about potions? Those are magical."

"Potions are made through alchemy, which is granted by a card power. What makes potions so incredibly expensive is that not only does someone have to have an alchemist card, and the practice and the will, they also have to have a compatible card with the potion they just made." She pointed back at the healing potion that she had left on the counter within Arthur's easy reach, having turned her back on him several times to prepare the herbs.

Not that Arthur had noticed or thought about stealing it . . . several times.

"The person who made that healing potion not only has a pair of Rare alchemy cards, but also a pair of Uncommon healing cards. And he can *only* make healing potions. If he wishes to make non-healing potions, he would have to have the appropriate card to infuse its magic in there."

"An alchemist can't make a blank potion and have someone else infuse the appropriate magic?" Arthur asked.

"Of course they can, but why split the cost? Plus there are other considerations, but I'm not an alchemist." She waved her hand again, her gesture flighty. "Now, what were we talking about? Oh, yes, the test. Please identify these herbs and tell me which one of these has extraordinary qualities. Don't worry, none are poisonous, and of course, you will be compensated if you indeed identify the correct one."

With a nod, Arthur looked down at the powders. He suspected he knew what the base ingredients already were.

Carefully, he tapped his finger on the first one, greenish-brown, gave it a sniff, and then tasted it.

"Sage," he said. "Not extraordinary."

She nodded. He went to the second one, which was a bright yellow.

"Turmeric," he said. "Not extraordinary."

Lastly, he examined the third.

"Cinnamon," he said, and then frowned, realizing that he had not received a notification at all. "Not . . . extraordinary."

Flossie beamed. "Excellent!" Then she yanked the papers away, stood up, and went to prepare some more. Apparently, that had been a trick test. "I'm impressed that you were able to identify those by name. Oh, the cinnamon was obvious, but not everybody can verbalize what taste they are experiencing."

"I . . . used to work as a cook," Arthur said.

Flossie returned shortly with three identical herbs, all the same reddish-brown color.

More cinnamon. He could tell that much on sight alone. Arthur glanced at her, but she just looked at him expectantly.

Arthur tested the first one—nothing.

"Still just cinnamon," he said, privately thinking it was from the same bottle as before. It had the same sharply spicy taste, the same strength to it.

He dipped his finger in the second pile of cinnamon and brought it to his tongue. Immediately, pain exploded through his body. No, it was more than pain; it was *shock*. His body seized up briefly, his back arching and the paper with the cinnamon flying away. It only lasted for a second, and Arthur relaxed, breathing hard.

Thanks to an infusion of Lightning Storm Cinnamon, you have gained a lightning resistance. This will result in a temporary 2-point backlash once the effect wears off. You will be more susceptible to lightning during that time.
Time left: 4 Hours 59 Minutes, 59 Seconds.

New body enhancement gained: Lightning Resistance
Due to your card's bonus traits, you automatically start this skill at level
3.

"Lightning?" he gasped.

"Correct. How are you?" Flossie said. He looked at her and realized that she held the bottle of healing potion in her hand, ready to give it to him. Before he could answer, she pressed her two fingers to his throat. "Ah. Normal pulse."

"I'm fine." The pain had been intense but brief, with no lingering aftereffects. "But that was, well, shocking."

"We call it Lightning Storm Cinnamon," she said. "Back in my day, teenagers around here used to dare each other to take tastes. It's harmless, though unpleasant, with very occasional heart stoppages. Very occasional," she repeated. "I wouldn't worry about it. However, I am impressed that you immediately identified it."

He shrugged, though inside he wanted to grin. Not only had he identified it, he'd gained a level 3 resistance from it.

This meant, after the backlash wore off, if he were ever to be hit by someone's lightning power or perhaps even be struck midair during a thunderstorm, he had that much more chance of survival.

I wonder if Brixaby would be interested in this.

He looked at Flossie, who watched him warily. This was, he guessed, the part where most people quit.

"What else do you have?" Arthur asked.

As far as he was concerned, this was paid resistance training.

The next thing Flossie had him test was her new batch of fire peppercorns, which was ironically what he had come for in the first place. However, this breeding was a bit too strong because it did indeed burn the top of his mouth. He didn't ask for the healing potion, knowing how expensive those were. Instead, Arthur's minor healing card almost immediately went to work.

Better yet, his Fire Resistance moved up to a permanent level 5.

After his mouth was healed, he had some tea—with no extraordinary herbs in it; he asked twice—and his mouth felt better. He then went for the next test, which was a weirdly purple apple.

Flossie cut a sliver from the apple. "It's a shame that we don't have a way of keeping this fresh. Using a bit uses the whole apple," she lamented. "But I recommend that you only take a small portion. I must tell you upfront that this one is tricky. There is no toxicity, per se, but there have been odd effects. I won't tell you about them to keep the test fair. Some people report effects, most report nothing. So, hopefully, you can finally identify what is going on."

The sliver was so thin that it was practically transparent. Arthur took a cautious bite.

Thanks to an infusion of Psychic Apple, you have gained a temporary psychic resistance and mental block which affects outside sources. This will result in a temporary 2-point backlash once the effect wears off. You will be more susceptible to mind magic during that time.
Time left: 4 Hours 59 Minutes 59 Seconds.

New body enhancement gained: Psychic Resistance
Due to your card's bonus traits, you automatically start this skill at
level 3.

He looked at her, eyes raised. "I'm getting psychic resistance." As well as a mental block, which wasn't permanent but sounded promising.

She inhaled sharply. "You're sure?"

"Yeah, that's what my card says."

"This is amazing. That explains why we received inconsistent results." She turned and started scribbling on a piece of paper.

He waited for a beat, then realized that she wasn't going to volunteer the information, so he asked, "Why?"

"Oh, it's theorized that some people are naturally more inclined to psychic resistance than others. And before you ask, it's not a card power, but more about how a healthy mind is structured. Though there is much debate among the scholars and those who study the, ugh, *humanities*." She gave a large eye roll and went back to scribbling.

A shadow fell across the cave, and the silver dragon who had noticed Arthur before poked his head in.

"Excuse me, Flossie, I need to take this boy to see the council. They have requested him regarding a matter—"

He said more, but Arthur wasn't listening. He suddenly got a flash of Brixaby's voice reaching out to him. Not in his mind, exactly, which was good because of his recent Psychic Resistance gain. But it came from the connection through his heart deck.

Arthur . . . Help . . . Along with a vague flash of the crafters cave.

He stood up, startling Flossie and the silver. "Brixaby?" Half frantic, he looked to the silver. "My dragon needs me. Which way to the crafters cave?"

"The council has requested your presence," the dragon began.

Arthur straightened and stared at the dragon, unimpressed. "My dragon comes first. Once I ensure he's safe, we will meet the council together. If you want to make it fast, then you will take me to the crafters cave."

The silver's eyes narrowed. Then he snorted. "Fine."

"Wait," Flossie said. "Your shard payment—"

"It's fine," he said. "I'll come back shortly." He paused, desperate to reach his dragon but knowing he'd kick himself later if he left behind a valuable ingredient. "Can I take the rest of the apple for testing purposes?"

"Oh, yes. It will only go bad within twelve hours. It's useless past that—"

He took it, shoved it into his Personal Space where it would stay fresh forever, and hurried out.

Grumbling, the silver dragon crouched to offer Arthur a place to sit astride him.

I'm coming, Brixaby, Arthur thought fiercely back at his dragon, hoping he could hear him.

CHAPTER 16

Arthur had flown on the backs of dragons numerous times, and he had learned that each was a new experience.

The purples—of which Brixaby was one, despite his dark scales—had four wings, all turned back so that they could rapidly beat the air. Some of the smaller blue dragons also shared this feature. Tamya's dragon, Len, was one with two regular-type wings.

However, the rest of the colors tended to have different body builds, wing shapes, and wing-beat tempos, which made formation flying particularly difficult. Some were thinner and cut through the air, while some were wide and meant for slow gliding—reds were typically famous for their long gliding powers. Browns tended to power through the air like they were trying to beat it into submission and didn't bother with currents and updrafts. The yellows, who dealt with energy—usually from the sun, though there were variations with every color such as with Shadow, who was red—tended to fly better during the day even if their card didn't use the sun's power. No one could say exactly why.

All of this was to say that the silver Arthur rode upon was unexpectedly nimble in flight. He had slim, almost knifelike wings that cut through the air. Great for the dragon, but unfortunate for the rider. His seat was a jerky, unpleasant one where he bobbed up and down constantly and moved from right to left, making Arthur feel as if he were sitting on a donkey cart with no suspension whatsoever.

Worse was that Arthur didn't have a saddle to hold on to, so he bent down and held on to the silver's neck as best he could, trying not to get in the way, and, most importantly, trying not to fall.

He couldn't wait until Brixaby grew big enough to ride. Though he suspected that Brixaby's acrobatics would take some getting used to.

Unsurprisingly, the interior of the Mesa Free Hive was designed to accommodate dragons just as well as humans. People had hallways that connected the large interior chambers, and dragons often used these. But dragons also could travel from chamber to chamber through connecting aerial tunnels. The silver used these now, and they were somewhat convoluted.

Arthur went from chamber five to three, and then crossed over, finally, to number two: the crafters cave.

Now that Arthur had seen the other large bubbles, he realized that this one was more unusual. There weren't many smaller chambers for privacy or dug-out places for residential private living units or vendor shops. Everything was a large, open-air marketplace, just underground. And it stretched on and on, with a wide mouth open to the desert at the far end.

The silver didn't have the wings to hover in place like Brixaby could. So instead, he turned about in sharp circles, scanning the floor. "Where is he?"

Arthur gazed down too. His eyes flicked back and forth. "There!" He pointed to a red banner he had noted on top of the crafter's booth the last time he'd been there.

The silver followed his finger and swooped down, aggressively moving people aside as he came in for a landing. Most of the buyers and crafters shot Arthur and the silver dirty looks, but they were more or less used to dragon antics and got on with their day.

Arthur vaulted off the silver's back almost before he touched down completely and ran the short distance to the booth. He spotted Brixaby slumped over on a back table, wings spread out and his two forelimbs pressed over his head, eyes shut.

"What happened?" Arthur demanded. "Brix! Are you okay?"

The crafter who was involved with the chainmail turned to Arthur with a frown. "I don't know. He fell sick in an eyeblink."

"Brixaby?" Arthur went to his dragon's side, hands hovering, unsure. He wasn't bleeding, and Arthur felt no wavering from the link between them. But . . . had he somehow been poisoned? Could there have been a second assassin? Why had he left his dragon alone?

Brixaby's lid slid open slightly to reveal a ruby eye. "Stop talking so loud," he grumbled.

"I was about to summon a healer," the burly crafter said, "but he insists he doesn't need one."

Carefully, Arthur scooped Brixaby into his arms. His dragon wasn't feverish but was alarmingly limp. "What's wrong, Brixaby?"

"Headache," Brixaby gritted out.

That gave Arthur a clue. Instantly, he went from worried to rueful.

"How long did you spend in your Personal Space?" he asked.

Despite his pain, Brixaby smiled a mischievous dragon smile. "Long enough to make this." With his eyes still closed, he held out a hand and pulled something seemingly out of midair. It was a chainmail construction about the length of Arthur's arm.

Arthur took it, eyebrows lifted.

He could see that Brixaby likely started from the open end of the sleeve, as the chainmail links were not quite as uniform as those farther down. It ended in a sort of mitten shape. Dragons typically had three to four fingers per limb, though again, like the wings, this varied. Pinks were likely to have five, like a human hand.

The chainmail mitten. There was one chunky portion for a thumb and a wider portion for the rest of the fingers.

"It's a prototype," Brixaby gritted out. "And not completed yet. I need to reinforce the inside. It needs more metal." He winced. Apparently, talking this much hurt.

"Wait, you did this?" The chainmail master approached and stared in frank disbelief. "When did you have the time to make this?"

"I *made* the time," Brixaby said.

"And he's suffering the backlash because of it," Arthur explained. "He over-used a card power."

"That is some card power, kid," the crafter murmured. He looked to Arthur. "You got him?"

Arthur nodded, and the crafter grunted, turning to continue his own work.

Eyes still shut and grimacing, Brixaby continued, "The areas to shield the claws need to be reinforced. If those claws at the tips wear out . . . it won't mat-ter . . . Ow . . ." He winced and covered his head again as if to press against his throbbing brain. "This is annoying. How long will I feel like this?" Brixaby asked, covering his head.

"For a while," Arthur admitted. "It will get better after a couple of hours."

"*Hours?*" Brixaby whined.

Arthur patted his back. "It's nice that you worked so hard for Joy."

"Of course I did. She's part of my retinue," he grumbled. "How can she serve me if she accidentally kills the next person by forgetting about her venom and hugging them?"

Brixaby had a disturbing point. Joy was apt to hug people on a whim.

Arthur looked again at the chainmail glove. "Do you think it will fit her?"

" . . . Perhaps."

Which Arthur translated as Brixaby having gotten so excited about the idea that he had rushed it without measuring. Not that Arthur had ever done the same thing or anything.

He looked at his dragon. "How far did you level your skill?"

Brixaby brightened at that. His red eyes slit open in a sly smile. "Level twenty-three."

That was a huge leap. No wonder he was suffering now. "Did you get any skill bonuses?"

"No, but I believe if I get a couple of secondary skills, I can get an advanced class."

Arthur nodded. That was one difference between his Master of Skills and Master of Body Enhancement cards.

Skills got bonuses by combining similar skills together into classes, which granted attribute points and additional bonuses. The Master of Body Enhancement, however, rewarded leveling up individual enhancements past level twenty . . . And probably more, but Arthur hadn't yet gotten an enhancement past that level.

That was something to think about later. Right now, he had to figure out what to do with Brixaby. He was in no shape to see the council.

A crazy idea struck him. Brixaby was experiencing a sort of mental exhaustion. But . . . could it also be a psychic backlash?

Arthur shifted his dragon around and pulled both a sharp knife and the purple apple out of his storage. He cut a thin wedge out and returned the items.

"Brix, eat this."

"I'm not hungry. Just take me somewhere cool and dark and let me be." Brixaby moaned dramatically, flopping his head over the side of Arthur's arm like a dead thing.

"Just try it. It might help." At least, he was certain it couldn't hurt. Flossie had said other test subjects hadn't come to bad ends.

Brixaby grumbled, but his nose had caught the scent of apple. He opened his mouth and allowed Arthur to place it in.

He chewed, swallowed, and went tense.

Then his head shot up, eyes wide. "What was that?!"

"Are you okay?" Arthur asked.

"I'm fine. The headache is gone. Where's my prototype? Ah." It was hanging off Arthur's arm, and Brixaby reached for it.

"No, don't!" Arthur knocked his talons away, knowing that Brixaby was about to grab it and retreat into his Personal Space again. "It's a psychic block, not a psychic heal. It's like a painkiller," he explained, seeing Brixaby didn't understand. "But your mind is still damaged."

"Perhaps *your* mind is damaged," Brixaby shot back. That was enough to convince Arthur he was feeling much better.

"Brix." Arthur shot him a glare, then glanced around to make sure they weren't being overheard. The silver was giving them baleful looks from the other end of the booth, and the crafter was entertaining a few prospective customers. Neither were close enough to easily overhear. Arthur still lowered his voice. "You have to be careful in your Personal Space. When you spend a lot of subjective time in there, you're going to get a bad backlash. It's worse when you work on crafting. I've done it myself."

"Yes, but now you have more skills . . . wait, was that an apple?" Brixaby eyed his rider. "How did an apple fix me?"

"I'll explain later, but you're not fixed. It only masks the symptoms, and I don't know how long it lasts. For now, finish Joy's chainmail in real time."

"Real time is boring," Brixaby said, but Arthur sensed he would obey him. The little dragon twisted around to look directly at the silver. "And why are you staring at my rider? He is mine. Find your own."

The silver lifted his lip in what was either a sneer or a growl. Possibly both. "The council wishes to speak to your rider. You got in the way."

Brixaby perked up. "An update on the assassin?" He hesitated, stared hard at the other dragon, then he nodded. "Yes, you may take us there . . . Er . . . What is your name?"

"Ghost," the dragon said shortly.

"Ghost, then." Brixaby smiled, all dragon teeth.

Despite the fact the silver was many, many times Brixaby's size . . . he wilted a bit.

Brixaby added in Arthur's mind, using the power he'd stolen from the mind card, *I sense Ghost is unusually strong for an Uncommon. I may want him serving me in my retinue.*

CHAPTER 17

Brixaby must have truly been feeling better because, as Arthur seated himself on Ghost, Brixaby landed on Arthur's shoulders, twined a tail around the back of his neck, and complained that he was hungry.

"How long has it been since you've eaten?" Arthur asked.

Brixaby thought for a moment. "What counts? The last time my body ate . . . or the time my mind spent in Personal Space?"

That was a good question. Arthur had no idea. So, instead of answering, Arthur took out one of the grilled peppers stuffed with meat and handed the skewer over. Thanks to the timeless nature of his Personal Space, the pepper was still hot off the grill and steaming.

Brixaby took the skewer with a happy rumble and took a big bite. However, as Ghost took off into the air, little bits of meat and pepper fell down Arthur's shirt. He kept having to brush bits off his tunic, and it left spots of grease behind. This probably wasn't the best way to meet the council, but he was past trying to impress these people.

Meanwhile, silver Ghost took a series of upper tunnels that twisted too fast for Arthur to keep track of. The dragon made jerky turns that made him feel like his head was about to snap off his body. Ghost knew where he was going, though, and abruptly, they emerged outside into the late afternoon air.

Brixaby hissed in discomfort at the bright sun, and Arthur shielded his eyes. He quickly replaced his hold a moment later when Ghost immediately shot up, almost vertically. They flew so close to the sheer wall that Ghost's stomach nearly scraped the rock. Arthur had to hang on as if his life depended on it. Somehow, though, Brixaby managed to keep hold of his stuffed pepper skewer.

Finally, just as their momentum slowed, they crested the top of the mesa.

The vast arena was gone again. It had probably sunk into the complex and been reburied to leave a flat, rocky plain.

But it wasn't unoccupied.

Red Laird stood at the top, wings extended to give Chablis some shade. The rest of the council was nowhere in sight.

Ghost flew in to land, dropping them out of the air with a bone-rattling jolt.

"Thank you, Ghost," Arthur muttered, gratefully sliding down. He rolled his shoulders, feeling like his joints had been loosened by the ride. From the slight drain on his mana, his internal healing card was doing some work to mitigate bruises.

"Yes, *thank you*, Ghost," Brixaby said loudly. "You are a most useful fellow. With many interesting cards, I'm sure." He eyed the other dragon as if trying to assess what was in his cores.

Ghost just grunted.

Laird rumbled to the silver dragon, "Took you long enough to bring them here."

"There were complications," Ghost muttered, looking away. "The little dragon overextended himself."

Laird peered down at Brixaby. "That can happen with a Legendary card? I'm surprised."

Brixaby popped the last of the pepper into his mouth, chewed, and swallowed before he answered, "I became the equivalent of a low journeyman in chainmail arts within a couple of hours," he said smugly. "What did *you* accomplish today?"

"I interrogated an assassin," Laird replied evenly.

Chablis scowled. "Not that there's much left to interrogate. The man is practically insane, thanks to you ripping the cards right out of his heart."

"Yes," Brixaby said, "the idea was that he would suffer."

"It's hard to interrogate a man who is babbling, weeping, and insane," Chablis said.

Inwardly, Arthur winced. But outwardly, he shrugged. He had to be hard at this moment. He had to let these people know he would give no quarter to anyone who threatened his life, Brixaby's life, or anybody under them. "But you were able to get something useful from him? Is that why you brought us here?"

"We were at least able to discover where he hails from," Chablis said with a glance at Laird. "We believe the man works for another free hive, to the south."

That was interesting. Arthur had been thinking on and off about who would be willing to kill him . . . and came up with a distressingly long list. Everybody from the king, to other Legendary riders, possibly Valentina and Whitaker— though they were long shots, as they needed him more than he needed them. At the top of the list, of course, were Lional and Penn Rowantree.

Unfortunately, all of these people had a motive but almost zero opportunity. How would they know he was here in the Mesa Hive?

No, it was more than possible this was some sort of convoluted plot from the council itself. But . . . another free hive?

"Why would another free hive want to assassinate me?" he asked, then, a moment later, answered his own question. "For my Legendary cards?"

"I honestly don't know," Chablis said. "They shouldn't even have *known* you were here, but . . ." She exchanged glances with Laird. "We keep a loose communication between all of the free hives, mostly as a safety precaution in case any of the kingdoms choose to exterminate us. It's possible something leaked out."

"Wait, has that happened before? A kingdom exterminating a free hive?" Arthur asked, feeling a chill. "Why would a kingdom do that?"

"Power and greed, of course," Laird said. Then he added, considering, "Or they just get annoyed with us raiding the noble libraries—"

"Laird," Chablis said, but Laird ignored her and powered on.

"Most of us have been making some concessions to the kingdoms to keep that from happening, but this hive we speak of has been acting so oddly recently, that there have been fears that they may be trying to break off to form their own kingdom—that's been tried before, too. It doesn't bode well without a Mythic."

Arthur felt like they were finally getting to the meat of the conversation. "What concessions?"

Chablis and Laird exchanged grim looks. Then Chablis sighed and nodded to the dragon. For some reason, to Arthur, it looked like a performance. He suspected the two of them planned on telling him this all along.

"The concession is that we don't allow anyone in the free hives to use combat-focused cards. As I said, we raid noble libraries—and mostly those raids are unofficially requested. Either a noble grows out of control or so powerful that they threaten their sovereign or they're so incompetent that they threaten the kingdom's security. But the king or queen can't be seen to move against them directly, so they use us as an outside influence."

Something clicked into place, and Arthur suddenly knew what that concession was. "But you don't get to keep all the cards you steal, do you?"

Brixaby perked up, listening carefully.

"No," Laird said. "We can't be seen as a threat to the kingdom hives. Our payment for staying alive is to return combat cards to the kingdom." There was a note of disgust in his voice, though it was so quiet that Chablis didn't react to it.

"But you let Joy and Cressida in," Brixaby said. "Cressida has a flame-bear summon. You saw it after the assassin attacked."

"They aren't official members of the hive *yet*," Chablis said, with emphasis. "Besides, even if it was the pink who had the summon card, dragons are different. You are built around your core cards. We mitigate this by offering any dragon who joins us crafter, utility, and other support-oriented cards as soon as they become official residents of the hive." She added, perhaps seeing the look on their faces, "This is no bad thing. You've seen it: we get along very well with our support and utility-focused cards. We have built a stable, productive life out here in the desert. We don't need combat."

They don't need combat, right up until the point that they do, Arthur thought, well aware that he was being a giant hypocrite. His deck so far did not have a single combat-oriented card. Though, he meant to fix that.

"And of course," Laird added with a grim smile, "those of us with combat cards in our core can get around the edict fairly easily."

Of course. Laird was part of the group who went on raids. That also explained why there had been no people riding the dragons during that noble raid. And if anybody witnessed the raid, they could only report that wild dragons had done the deed. There would be no one to blame except for the kingdom hives, and no one with sense blamed the hives overtly. They were the only thing that kept the kingdom from disaster during a scourge-eruption.

The checks and balances felt thin to Arthur. Easily breakable. But at least he finally understood them.

"That raid where I met you," he said, looking at Laird, "was that *officially* sanctioned?"

"No," Laird said with an evil draconic smile, "that was for my own pleasure."

Brixaby broke in. "Yes, yes. Very interesting. So, you believe another free hive has tried to kill Arthur? Point me in their direction. I'll teach them a lesson."

"We don't know if the assassin's actions were sanctioned by the hive or not," Chablis said.

"Easy." Brixaby flicked his tail. "Point me the way to their council, I'll start ripping out cards and find out."

Laird and Chablis both shuddered. Arthur watched them, thinking. He wasn't sure if he believed that the assassin came from another free hive, but it was better than the assassin coming from this council. He, Brixaby, Joy, and Cressida were essentially still captives here.

"So, you brought me and Brixaby here to tell us that you know nothing for certain," he said.

"We wanted to give you an update, in good faith," Chablis said.

Arthur's **Acting** and **Deception** skills pinged at him. "No, you brought us here because you hit a wall with the assassin, and you want something from us."

Laird let out a chuckling hissing sound, and Chablis closed her eyes briefly for a moment in exasperation. Then she opened them again. "The man might return to his senses if you give his cards back to him."

"Those cards belong to Joy." Arthur felt no need to hide that. Anybody who had been watching would have seen what happened.

"Yes, but there were others, weren't there?" Chablis asked. "Your dragon took more than the two."

So, not only had they been watching, they had been watching *closely*. But Arthur wasn't interested in giving back the Stealth Class card. He wanted to save it for Brixaby when he could safely add it to his core.

This was why he was taken completely by surprise when Brixaby said, "Then let me speak to the assassin. I'll determine if he's worthy of getting a card back."

It took every ounce of self-control not to turn and stare at Brixaby. Instead, Arthur kept his face blank and crossed his arms, silently signaling that he would be behind whatever his dragon wanted. Even if, secretly, he wondered what, by all the cards, Brixaby was up to.

"All right," Chablis agreed, so fast that Arthur had no doubt that had been the hope all along. She turned and said, "Follow me."

They walked perhaps only a hundred feet before the woman stopped and studied the ground, making a parting motion with her hands. A single crack split the baked red earth and then moved away. A moment later, Arthur was looking at a perfectly cut entrance to a shadowed stairwell leading down.

The opening was much too small to fit a dragon the size of Laird. Arthur hesitated for a moment, wondering if this was a trick. By bringing them up here, he had been separated from Joy and Cressida. And Chablis had some kind of earth card power. Was it wise to descend that tunnel with her?

He exchanged glances with Brixaby. The dragon gave him a nod toward the staircase. He seemed eager. Arthur highly doubted that he was going to give the Stealth card back—and that mental trick Brixaby used only worked one way, so he couldn't ask what he thought he was doing. His only option was to trust his dragon.

So that's exactly what he did.

Arthur followed Chablis downstairs. A few steps in and the air became noticeably cooler. Then, as the darkness closed around them, with only an occasional sputtering card-anchor light to guide the way, it was almost frighteningly cold.

At the bottom sat a row of barred metal cells. There were no guards around, and three of the four cells were also empty. The one at the very end wasn't.

Sitting there, slumped against the back wall, was the assassin.

In his mind, Arthur had unconsciously built the man up to the point he wouldn't be surprised if the assassin had a mustache to twirl. But upon seeing him again . . . he looked just like a man. A few years older than himself, with short scruffy blond hair and a somewhat unremarkable face.

Arthur would have had trouble picking him out of a crowd, except for the fact that he was currently rocking back and forth, knees drawn up to his chest, and hugging himself.

"Do you know who I am?" Arthur asked.

Slowly, the man stopped his rocking and smiled. "Yes." His eyes were too bright. "You . . . You are the traitor. The liar. The one who betrays. The one who does not keep his word."

The man should have had no cards to aid him, but in a flash of a second, he was on his feet and running straight at Arthur, hitting the bars and reaching through with a clawed hand. It wasn't a card power. It was a strength borne of insanity.

Arthur backed a step, and the fingernails missed him by a hair.

Brixaby let out a fearsome roar. The man, however, didn't seem to hear it. His face was twisted in a snarl, and though it looked like he wanted to scream, instead he began to chant in a singsong voice, "Liar, liar, liar . . ." His sweet voice was as if he was reciting a nursery rhyme. "Arthur Rowantree is a liar . . ."

"The man is insane." Chablis sighed. "Now you see what happens to some who lose their heart decks."

Arthur didn't answer. The man was *singing*.

"How long did you say the other hive had been acting oddly?" he asked, voice strangled.

"A couple of months. Why?"

The timeline fit.

There was someone else who likely wanted to hurt Arthur and everybody around him.

His instinct was a guess, a gamble, but Arthur had always been a good gambler. His bet was that the Mind Singer had sent this assassin.

CHAPTER 18

Arthur didn't pay strict attention during the rest of the visit, stunned and horrified by his revelations.

The former assassin had retreated to his corner, huddling with his knees drawn up to his chest, rocking back and forth. Brixaby, meanwhile, stared at Arthur as though trying to bore a hole through his head. It was clear he had reached the same conclusions.

In the meantime, Chablis hinted again that the assassin would be more reasonable—read: sane—if he were given one of his cards back.

Brixaby's head snapped around at her. "I've considered things, and my answer is no. He attacked my rider; he gets no mercy."

Arthur highly doubted that Brixaby had ever genuinely considered returning the card. He just wanted an excuse to come and see what the fuss was about.

Forcefully shoving his shock to the back of his mind, Arthur added, "Besides, won't he be that much harder to imprison if he has his card back?"

"That depends on the nature of the card," Chablis responded pointedly. "I don't suppose the two of you will tell me what you took from him?"

Arthur glanced at the man who was now muttering to himself in a singsong voice, then looked away again, shaking his head. "It wasn't combat, so it won't violate your hive's terms with the kingdom."

"Could we stop you even if it was a combat card?" she sniped and then looked away, pressing a hand against her temple as if she were getting a headache. "Be aware we're still determining if having the power and prestige of a Legendary card in our hive is worth the problems."

Arthur gave her a bland look. "You could send us home."

He'd called her bluff. She turned away.

* * *

He and Brixaby only spoke once Chablis had led them outside and Ghost had taken them back down to their room.

The moment he dismounted from Ghost to the balcony, Arthur turned to Brixaby. "Personal Space?"

Speaking at the same time, Brixaby said, "Arthur, join me."

They both stopped, surprised that they'd come to the same conclusion.

With a dragon's grin, Brixaby landed on Arthur's outstretched arm. Arthur added him to his Personal Space, and a moment later, allowed his mind to follow.

The first thing he spotted was a crate full of baby chicks and turkey poults tucked away in a corner. His plan had been to either resell them once hatching season ended and the price increased or gift them to his father or his old village the next time he visited. Livestock in the borderlands was invaluable.

He looked around and found Brixaby. The dragon possessed a natural nullification magic that resisted the time restrictions, so the little dragon flapped around in a peculiar stop-start motion, freezing one moment and moving the next.

Once again, Arthur extended his arm—though it was truly only his mind present here—and when Brixaby landed, he was free of the time restrictions. He moved normally.

Brixaby took a moment to look around the room, then snorted. "Next time, either you visit my Personal Space or learn to tidy yours."

"That won't work, Brix. I don't have your time nullification—wait." Arthur blinked. "Are you telling me yours is organized?"

"I stole shelving from empty riders' quarters back at the Wolf Moon Hive," said Brixaby casually.

A grin spread across Arthur's face, only to vanish moments later.

"The Mind Singer," he said grimly.

"The Mind Singer," Brixaby echoed. All his amusement was gone as well.

Arthur heaved a sigh. "I guess she told the truth about leaving the kingdom."

"Yes, and now she may be building a base of power," Brixaby growled under his breath, his tail flicking back and forth like an irritated cat. "That's what *we* should be doing. Here, using this free hive if we have to."

"What do you mean?" Arthur asked, though he had a sinking feeling he already knew. "Take over this hive?"

"Why not?" Brixaby proposed. "As Legendries, we were destined to rule the Wolf Moon Hive anyway. But they don't have anyone of our rank here, so I won't have to wait for Elissa to die."

"There's always Whitaker and his dragon," Arthur pointed out.

Brixaby gave him a look that told him what he thought about Whitaker.

Sighing, Arthur shook his head. "The Mesa Hive won't just step aside and let us take over."

"What could they do to stop us?" Brixaby challenged. "You heard it yourself. They don't have combat cards here."

"Some of them *do* have combat cards," Arthur countered. "Even if they don't practice with them." He sighed again. "What are we going to do, Brix?"

The dragon shrugged. "The Mind Singer's our responsibility. Well, yours, but . . . I suppose mine now too, since I consumed one of her sister's cards."

Arthur looked at his dragon, taken aback. "Why do you sound happy about it?"

"Because I am," Brixaby's draconic smile reached his bloodred eyes. "I like having an enemy that I know about. Better than some faceless shadow council or more politics from your terrible family. I'm a dragon. I kill scourglings."

Putting in that light, the problem did seem straightforward.

"There's nothing that says she won't stop at just one hive," Arthur reasoned.

"Scourge-eruptions don't stop at one city unless they are snuffed out," Brixaby said with a shrug. "I'm a Legendary-ranked dragon, and the Mind Singer is only a Rare scourgling. We'll kill it when the time is right."

Arthur nodded, though he felt sick inside.

Brixaby was right about one thing: the Mind Singer was his responsibility. But despite the fact she was only a Rare rank, Arthur knew he and his dragon weren't strong enough to face her.

They emerged from Arthur's Personal Space. Only a blink of an eye had passed in real time.

Ghost, in the middle of turning his head to address them, ordered, "You are to stay in this room tonight. Council's orders. Don't make me catch you out of it."

With that gruff command, he took off from the balcony.

"Pushy Uncommon," Brixaby said. "He'll make a fine addition to my retinue."

Arthur didn't bother arguing. He didn't intend to leave again for the night, anyway.

He walked into their assigned room to find Joy sprawled across the bed. Arthur stopped short, amused by the sight.

Joy was so large that her pink tail trailed off the end, and her head rested in Cressida's lap. Her damaged arm was cradled on a pillow. The muscle and scales had been regrown, though now the limb was a mix of vivid pink and toxic green.

His amusement quickly drained away as he realized there was only *one* bed, and he and Cressida had been assigned to the room.

He swore he didn't make any noise, but Joy snorted awake. Brixaby immediately flew to her, pulling out his chainmail sleeve from his own Personal Space. Joy exclaimed in surprise and happiness, sitting up to carefully hug Brixaby with her wings.

"Arthur?" Cressida asked, voice sounding raspy. He suspected that she had been dozing. "What's wrong? You look like you swallowed a fish."

There was a lot wrong, starting chiefly with the Mind Singer. But Arthur's brain had locked on to a more immediate issue. "I, uh, need to order some blankets. I can sleep on the floor tonight. Brixaby and I."

"What?" she asked, looking around. Then she froze, seemingly coming to the same realization. "Oh."

"I'll order blankets," he declared like it was an epic quest, backing out onto the balcony. That's where the signal flags were kept to call for a courier. He wondered if this qualified as an urgent request.

To his surprise, Cressida followed him out. She looked hesitant, her arms crossed around her middle. "Shadow stopped by and said that you were wanted for a council meeting," she said quietly, glancing over her shoulder to check if the dragons were listening. "I guess you made your way there?"

Arthur nodded and cast a glance back to the dragons.

Joy was currently pulling her sleeve over her verminous arm, and neither dragon was paying attention to them.

"What did they say?" Cressida asked.

Arthur hesitated for a moment, but Cressida was one of his retinue riders. She had been with him in the scholars guild and had played a part in setting the Mind Singer free. Technically, she was as responsible as he was, though he didn't blame her for what had happened.

So, he explained briefly, using as few words as possible in case someone was trying to overhear.

He hated himself a little when he saw the blood drain from her face.

Then, surprising him, she stepped forward, speaking equally softly. "Joy and I haven't received any type of quest about this. Arthur, whatever you do, do not tell this hive we're responsible for . . ." She trailed off and cocked her head to the side, indicating the Mind Singer without saying her name. "Our position is tenuous. They may decide that it's easier to kill us or turn us over to her in a bid to sue for peace."

He hadn't thought that far, but it wasn't a surprise that Cressida had. She was, after all, a nobleman's daughter.

He nodded. "I wasn't going to tell the council."

She gave him a look.

"What?" Arthur asked.

"I don't believe you." Her lips curled up very slightly in a smile. "You have a misplaced sense of justice. But I'm telling you, *don't* do it. Besides"—she glanced around again as if checking for eavesdroppers—"as I said, neither Joy nor I have received a quest about this. You'd think that we would get something to . . . I don't know, raid the other hive or stop *her*. It makes me think that it's not possible yet."

If the other hive was under the Mind Singer's control, they wouldn't be going up against just her, but all her minions as well.

"We have to get stronger," he agreed. "Joy has to recover, and Brixaby . . . he has to grow. I have so much to do."

The time just before Brixaby's hatching had been frantic. He had added cards to his heart and secondary anchor deck that he had not truly begun to explore. And now, finally, trapped in a free hive where combat wasn't allowed but crafts certainly were . . . this was the time to develop his skills and powers.

Now was the time to allow Brixaby to grow.

With that realization, he truly accepted that he could not return to Wolf Moon Hive. At least, not yet.

"We all have to get stronger," he repeated.

Cressida stared at him, and in the dim flickering light of the inner balcony, her eyes still seemed to shine. "We will. And when we're ready . . . we'll be with you." She leaned forward, and to his shock, brushed a kiss against his cheek before she whispered in his ear, "We'll make up for setting that thing free, Arthur. We'll kill her and make it right."

PART 3

(UNEXPECTED)

DUNGEON

CHAPTER 19

Two months later . . .

Arthur awoke, groggy and disoriented. Something felt wrong. Why was he sitting slumped in this chair? And what was that awful smell?

"Are you awake now?" Flossie asked.

Arthur blinked, the world snapping back into focus. A smell as sharp as dragon urine made him recoil. As he did, he realized that the older woman was standing right in front of him, holding something under his nose. A small vial. Smelling salts?

"What happened?" he muttered.

"You had a seizure," she replied matter-of-factly.

What? Arthur felt for his internal healing card. Sure enough, he found it at work, steadily drawing on his mana.

Then, as if a switch had been flipped, his memory of the last few minutes returned. He remembered eating an off-colored peach that, surprisingly, didn't taste too horrible. At least, until he lost control of his limbs.

"I had a bad reaction," he said, his voice gaining strength. He straightened up and looked around, rolling his shoulders. His muscles felt as if he had just finished an intense workout. "What went wrong? I thought you said you tested the peach for poison."

Flossie was always meticulous about such things, and it was one of the reasons Arthur trusted her. Well, to a point.

Flossie shrugged and turned back to scribble frantically in a notebook. "We did, but sometimes unexpected reactions happen." She cast him a dry look. "That is why we have testers."

Arthur preferred when his job yielded resistances rather than seizures. The past couple of months had been quite fruitful in that regard. Especially last week, when a strange mix of salts and almond flakes had granted him a resistance to drowning in salt water. He hadn't tested it out yet, but it could come in handy.

"You owe me double pay," he said dryly.

"Do I?" Flossie blinked eyes made extraordinarily large by glasses.

"Yes, I want hazard pay. You hired me to quantify the results, not to act as a poison tester."

Arthur found it easier to be blunt with her. Otherwise, she tended to completely miss nuances in conversation.

Flossie thought hard, then nodded. "Then yes, double pay today."

This meant Arthur was leaving with two Rare card shards for today. Brixaby would be happy about that.

He leaned back in the chair and let the healing card finish its work.

Flossie's crazy experiments never took up his whole day and left Arthur plenty of time to train. He left her laboratory cave a few minutes later, healed of any lingering effects from the seizure and wealthier by two Rare shards, and made his way down the twisting hallways.

Bit by bit, he was figuring out the layout of the confusing Mesa Free Hive. The trick, it seemed, was to stop trying to make it make sense.

When he got to main bubble one—a place one would think would be at the front or the end of the inner Mesa complex, but no, it was smack in the middle—Arthur didn't take the stairs up to the higher caves. Instead, he bent to get his hands dusty to help him grip better, then jumped at the cave wall.

The sheer rock wall was porous, which made sense because there were so many caves. There were lots of holes, big and small, to grab on to. Arthur started to climb.

It was risky. He'd fallen once or twice when the hand- or footholds crumbled from under him. But both times he hadn't fallen far and hadn't broken any bones. Just gained a bunch of bruises.

Now that his Rock Climbing skill was up to level 22, he had a sort of sixth sense about where it was safe to put his hands and feet.

That warning from his card only came when he was actively using the skill. If he didn't focus, he could easily overlook the little whisper of wisdom in the back of his mind that his hand- or foothold wasn't safe.

Also, he learned that to keep getting better, he couldn't just climb the same paths over and over. He had to keep pushing himself and trying new things to continue to level. Maybe there was a life lesson in there, but Arthur was too busy climbing to think about it.

His new knowledge—or was it experience?—warned him twice about weak handholds. He changed his grip, even stretching way above his head one time.

He was rewarded with Rock Climbing level 23.

Arthur grinned. His success helped lift him the rest of the way.

He got to the cave he was looking for and found a not-so-happy man with soil-stained pant knees looking down at him.

"Normal people use the ladders or call a dragon."

"Where's the fun in that?" Arthur asked, standing.

"You do have a dragon, right?" the man, Taza, asked.

"Yes, but he's still too young to fly me up. Plus, climbing gets my heart racing." Arthur would rather Taza think he liked the rush than know he was working on his skills.

Some rumors about his and Brixaby's abilities had leaked out to the general public. But they hadn't made the splash he'd feared. Most people in the hive didn't care much about fighting. So much so that Arthur had gained the impression having a combat card was like a dirty secret nobody wanted to talk about.

Cressida thought it might be because they were scarred from the places they'd left. Arthur increasingly worried it was an enforced cultural ignorance.

Despite that, Arthur liked Taza, who he'd met through Flossie. Taza didn't talk much about his life before coming to the hive, but from the hints Arthur had picked up, Taza's family had worked for a cruel noble before they managed to escape. Arthur could sympathize.

Somehow, Taza had gotten a Rare card in his youth. It had been both a blessing and a curse. The noble had forced him to use it night and day, well past the point of exhaustion. His family had been held hostage to ensure he complied. It got to the point where Taza had been on the verge of actually damaging his heart deck, which Arthur hadn't known was possible. But after Taza escaped, the card made him invaluable to Mesa Free Hive.

His card had the magical spell to make plants grow at an accelerated rate. Lots of Common and Uncommon cards could do that, too. What made Taza's Rare was that his accelerated growth spell didn't cause the soil to lose its nutrients.

Arthur had learned a lot recently. Like how growing crops could rob the soil of its nutrients. Dragon soil could be added to fix it. But dragon soil was expensive and dangerous to use. Plus, in the kingdom, it was needed to reclaim the borderland.

So someone who could use magic to keep the soil and plants healthy while wildly overproducing was worth his weight in gold.

Despite the fact his card had brought him pain for years, Taza loved being a farmer. He was happy to teach Arthur what he knew.

Arthur had shot up to level 15 in Farming in less than a week and had leveled several side skills such as Herb Identification to 11, as well as made headway into Trimming, Pruning, and Harvesting.

He thought he might be on the verge of a farming class soon.

This was all useful, though not vital in the upcoming fight against the Mind Singer. That was the reason Arthur was here today.

"Well," Taza said with a roll of his eyes at Arthur's antics, "let's get to work."

Right now, they were working on a new variety of corn that would hopefully provide a larger yield at about eighty percent of the time it took other types. It wasn't the most exciting thing, but Arthur couldn't complain if it kept people from starving.

They worked down the rows, Arthur identifying and pulling weeds, which grew rapidly in dragon soil. They both worked quickly. Taza because of his experience and Arthur because of his skills.

After about an hour, Taza thanked Arthur and paid him a simple Common shard. It was very low pay for the week. But again, that wasn't why he was here.

"I'll finish up here," Arthur said, pointing to the hoe and other tools. That was part of his job, too.

Taza thanked him and left for one of his other projects. But before he did, he used a bit of his magic to make the plants grow overnight.

New Counterfeit spell obtained: Rapid Plant Growth
Remaining Time: 59 Minutes 59 Seconds

Arthur hid his smile.

Once Taza was out of sight, he walked across the length of the space to an orchard set in the back. Among peaches, cherry trees, and almonds stood a single apple tree. It was bigger than the rest, and if someone looked closely, they would see a purple sheen to the bark.

Arthur looked over his shoulder to make sure Taza hadn't come back. Then he concentrated on his newly copied Rapid Plant Growth spell and used it on the tree.

The apple tree seemed to sigh, like it was relieved. The leaves turned toward Arthur. Then, right before his eyes, purple flowers bloomed all over—literally, up and down the trunk as well as the branches. This wasn't how normal apple flowers bloomed, but this wasn't a normal tree.

As Arthur kept feeding it power, the flowers withered, seemed to collapse in on themselves, and were replaced by the green buds of growing apples. Those grew and deepened to a dark purple as they ripened. In less than a minute, right when Arthur was almost out of mana, he had a whole harvest of purple apples that blocked psychic powers.

Arthur started picking these apples, putting them one by one in his Personal Space. He had barrels of them now. Each one was an arrow in the quiver of tricks he planned to use against the Mind Singer.

After he finished that job, he cleaned up the last of the rows of corn like he promised Taza.

Then, he made the long climb down. His next stop was to find Brixaby.

With some luck, his little dragon would be done with his crafting job, too. It was payday for both of them, which meant more Rare shards. If they were really lucky, they'd have enough for a brand-new Rare card.

CHAPTER 20

From the day of his hatching, Brixaby knew he had chosen his rider wisely. After all, the Legendary card users, the best and the brightest, had all competed for his attention. But they had to earn it—weathering a scourge-eruption and surviving a series of brutal duels, all for the privilege of approaching his egg first. Naturally, Brixaby had chosen the very best among them.

Due to his lack of combat cards, Arthur wasn't the traditional choice. However, his potential was exponential. And now, so was Brixaby's.

Despite this—and the minor detail that Brixaby had grown to respect Arthur as a person—there were times Brixaby knew his linked rider was completely mistaken.

The first instance was when Arthur had come perilously close to aiding a scourgling. Brixaby had managed to rectify that problem quite effectively by consuming its cards. The second time, Arthur had managed to upset the king, nearly leading to his execution. Arthur had resolved that issue himself . . . with a little help from the king's Mythic dragon.

But this third great mistake . . . well, it seemed it would once again fall to Brixaby to correct him. The point of contention was Arthur's stubborn *insistence* that the most efficient way to progress and grow was through the various classes offered by their cards.

This was absurd. Granted, the classes held bonuses, but to acquire new classes, Arthur was obliged to dabble in numerous skill sets. Consider his latest fascination with farming. The skills were nonsensical. Herb identification? Soil amendment? Pruning? What a waste of time.

No, despite his respect for Arthur, in this case, he was entirely mistaken.

Brixaby believed that the best strategy was to concentrate on one skill, one discipline, and master it completely. This was how he had elevated his **Chainmail Weaving** skill to level 49.

Of course, Brixaby had inadvertently picked up other skills along the way, largely due to his proximity to the craft master he'd worked beside.

He had gained **Metal Forging** and **Metal Artistry** and even acquired a few physical abilities from his Master of Body Enhancement card, like **Heat Resistance** from being around hot forges for extended periods. Not to mention the useful skill of **Focus**, necessary in proper chainmail projects.

Most importantly, Brixaby found joy in his work, even if the Mesa Free Hive didn't appreciate it.

Because they refused to fight.

Brixaby found himself growling in annoyance as he flew, just thinking about it. He had been taken aback when he discovered that all chainmail creations were sold off, not used. And he didn't know where they were sold to yet.

The chainmail craftmaster, Dimitri, had one contact who bought almost exclusively from him, leaving only a few other pieces out for display in the main booth. This mysterious contact ordered chainmail shirts tailored for human men and women, and none for dragons, even though everyone knew dragons did most of the fighting. Some chainmail constructions were peculiarly proportioned, in ways Brixaby couldn't quite comprehend. No one had limbs that long without a very odd body distortion card.

Whenever Brixaby asked about it, Dimitri simply brushed him off, saying it was none of his concern.

Brixaby had mentally sneered. *Like that's going to stop me.* Over the past few weeks, he had been observing the inflow and outflow of raw materials and finished products, not only from the man he worked with but also from the surrounding craftfolk.

The craftspeople and dragons received a large quantity of raw products from mysterious sources and put them to use, creating items that their free hive would never use: weapons of war and instruments of battle. And yet, despite the lack of visible customers, they managed to stay in business.

More crucially, they continued to purchase more food, goods, and raw materials.

Using **Arithmetic** skills, Brixaby and Arthur had worked it out. Just based on Brixaby's observations, the disparity between the goods produced and what was visibly sold was startling. And the chainmail wasn't an isolated product; it was pervasive throughout the free hive.

In fact, weapons and defense craft sales seemed to be the hive's main source of income for food and supplies.

Sure, the free hive grew its own fruit and vegetables, which was sufficient for humans. Although Brixaby enjoyed bread, fruits, and grains, his body craved meat the most. This barren mesa couldn't support large herds of livestock, even with Len and Tamya converting salt water into fresh water.

And yet, sheep, goats, and the occasional lame horse were always available for a hungry dragon to consume.

This hive was clearly a production center for crafted goods, and the sales allowed them to survive out in the desert. The question was . . . who were they selling to?

Nobody was willing to provide answers. So Brixaby had to patiently wait until he could discover the truth himself.

Finally, weeks in, that day had come. He had spent his time refining his chainmail skill. More importantly, he had *matured*.

He didn't know, nor did he particularly care, how humans knew when their heart deck was ready for its first card. But Brixaby had felt the formation of his secondary core. It wasn't as vibrant as his primary core, which, naturally, was his inner self.

This new core was slightly peripheral, a bit detached. He suspected it was somewhat similar to a human's artificial card-anchor space, where they could add or remove cards at will. Brixaby wasn't certain how this would function for him, given that his magic was based on consuming cards, but it was worth exploring. And he had the perfect card for it.

Brixaby privately congratulated himself for his cunning. He had told Arthur he intended to spend the day constructing chainmail as usual. Little did Arthur know that Dimitri had told Brixaby not to come in that day. This was the usual thing whenever the craftmaster was about to sell his stock and didn't want Brixaby to be around.

While Brixaby did feel a twinge for deceiving Arthur . . . that minuscule, barely perceptible, and *certainly* insignificant guilt was pushed to the side. It was for a good cause. Besides, surely Arthur would be happy when Brixaby proved himself right once again.

So, as soon as he had the day to himself, Brixaby flew to the lee side of the mesa, where the wind blowing off the arid desert was less harsh. There were numerous hidey holes and cutouts on the side of the steep cliff. These were the beginnings of caves, though the soil was too ravaged by the relentless sun and weather to form a sturdy permanent structure. It still provided him with some privacy.

Perched on the ledge of one of the shallow caves, Brixaby withdrew the Stealth Class card from his Personal Space. He examined it for a moment with pride. After all, he had yanked this card from an assassin's heart fair and square.

Now, it would serve as his first test of maturity.

Brixaby would never confess to feeling nervous. He was a Legendary-level dragon. What reason did he have to be nervous over a single Rare card? Absurd! Yet . . . he did triple-check his newly formed secondary core, just in case.

"What are you doing?" asked a bright bubbly voice, practically right beside him.

"Ah!"

Brixaby nearly toppled out of his shallow cave in surprise, hastily flapping his wings to regain balance as he clambered back up. He then whirled around and glowered at Joy, who was flying in tight circles just outside the cave. "What are you doing here? Why are you following me?"

"I got bored," Joy replied. "Cressida's at work. She hates it, and I feel bad for her, and I kind of want to kill something . . ." She flexed her green forelimb, now safely encased in a chainmail sleeve. Joy sighed, her head drooping. "But there's nothing around to kill."

Brixaby was particularly proud of her chainmail sleeve. It had undergone several iterations over the past weeks until Brixaby had finally created a weave so fine that the chainmail slid smoothly over Joy's green-tinged scales. He had replaced the clumsy mitten structure with something that fitted around her five talons like a glove, though he would need to continually modify and replace it as she grew.

Pink straps, chosen by Joy, wrapped around her torso to secure the sleeve and keep it from slipping down. The tips of her sharp claws were reinforced with a double weave—large then small—to ensure the sharp points did not poke out.

Joy's other limbs weren't venomous. However, over the past few weeks, her canine teeth had begun to elongate just past her lips, their tips taking on a subtle green hue. Brixaby suspected whatever she bit would have a bad day.

"Plus," Joy added before Brixaby could respond, "I got a new quest."

"Did you? To stop me?" He puffed himself up, indignant. "Well, your quest is about to fail!"

"No, not to stop you, silly. To *help* you. To be there for you. Because you're my friend."

"That's a foolish quest," Brixaby snapped, then hesitated. "What was the reward?"

"A Rare card."

"Rare?!" He growled. "That's outrageous! Why do your quests always turn out so well?" While it was satisfying that a potentially powerful meta-type dragon was devoted to him, it was equally frustrating that Joy kept receiving these high-reward quests without much effort.

It was doubly frustrating that, while Brixaby could copy her quest card, they came to him randomly. And his rewards were never so good.

Joy shrugged. "I think maybe it's because I thank the quest card? How often do you thank your cards for doing a good job?"

"I—I don't—" He sputtered. "Why would I? My cards are a part of *me*. I don't thank my tail for swishing around in the air."

"Well, maybe you should."

Brixaby felt his intelligence attribute points dwindling with each passing moment. He was about to voice his complaint when Joy decided to stop circling and landed right next to him. The shallow cave—more of a depression in the rock—was a tight fit. Brixaby scrambled, but there was just enough room for both of them. Thankfully, he wasn't pressed up against her green arm.

"So," Joy said cheerfully, "what are you doing that you need my support for?"

Brixaby thought about not telling her, given that he had made an effort to keep this from Arthur. But she was his retinue dragon, and if things went awry, he could simply make her swear to secrecy.

"I believe my secondary core is mature enough to accept a card," he said, then paused. Joy was several days older than him. "What about your core?" Not that he was nervous. He was just checking. It was prudent.

She sighed. "My primary core is still a little wacky, so I don't want to try the secondary until later. Cressida worries about it all the time. But . . . I think it's fine? I'm even more dangerous now." She flexed her venom-tipped claws. "Yeah. It feels *good*."

Joy was still Joy, just with an added edge.

"Humans." Brixaby snorted. "They're not dragons, but they always think they know more about us than we do."

Joy tilted her head. "I think it's because they're much older, so they know a lot more things. Cressida is nineteen years old."

"Really?" Brixaby was surprised. He was barely half a year old. Even one year seemed like an eternity.

"How old is Arthur?" Joy asked.

Brixaby thought for a moment. Arthur surely had told him, but it hadn't been important enough at the time to remember. "He can't be more than seven."

"That sounds about right," Joy agreed. "Tell me about your card."

With a touch of pride, Brixaby showed her his Stealth card. "I took it from the heart of the man who poisoned you."

"Oh, so we'll both have cards from him," she responded, a sweet smile gracing her features, the tips of her slightly green fangs peeking out. "I like that."

Again, Brixaby hesitated. Not from fear, of course, but from caution. "Did your quest mention that something was going to go wrong?"

"No, it just said to offer my support. As a friend." She extended a wing over him.

"I don't need your support, but . . . I suppose it would be fine to have someone witness my triumph."

And with that, Brixaby knew he could no longer delay. Holding his breath, he focused intently on his secondary core and inserted the card. There was a bit of resistance. It wasn't painful, but it felt like perhaps his new core could only fit one card in it for now. The capacity would surely grow as he did.

Within moments, it had disappeared, and he was immediately greeted with similar notifications that Arthur had described.

He had indeed gained the Stealth Class with the same suite of skills as Arthur. However, his average was a little less, as he didn't have the original **Stealth** skill until today. No matter, Brixaby planned to one day master that just as he had with his **Chainmail Weaving** skill.

Best of all, his Master of Skills card immediately took over the skills from the Rare-leveled card.

Yes, Brixaby had chosen quite well on the day of his hatching. Arthur wasn't the only one with the capability for rapid growth.

"It worked," he announced. "It actually worked! I mean, of course I'm not surprised. Hmm. And it seems I have additional attributes now."

He'd gained 7 to Perception, 2 to Luck, and 1 to Intelligence. Slightly different from Arthur's gains, though he wasn't about to complain. He'd long suspected attributes were aided by personality.

"Oh?" Joy asked.

Brixaby started to reply, but then stopped. He shifted uncomfortably, feeling . . . heavy. He assumed he would get used to having the card stretch out his secondary core after a while, but there was no need. His Master of Skills had already copied the class. The card would only drag him down now.

He took the card out of his secondary core again and spent a few moments gazing at it. He was *hungry*.

He had fully intended to consume the card after copying it. Not for any extra powers because he had already gotten what he could from it, but because consuming cards made him grow.

Then he let out a long, drawn-out sigh. He dearly wanted to eat the card, but Joy was part of his retinue, which made her his responsibility.

"Here. Take it," he said gruffly, offering the card to her.

"Really?" Joy gasped, accepting the card. "This must be my quest reward!" Then she hesitated. "Actually . . . I think this should go to Cressida."

"Why's that? You're the one with the venom." He liked the idea of a dragon in his retinue being able to sneak up on enemies before poisoning them.

"Yes, but she's been feeling so down recently, I think a card would cheer her up."

"She has?" Brixaby asked, taken aback. "What's wrong? Is she ill?"

Joy gave him a mildly annoyed look. Which for her, meant a lot. "I told you. She hates her job."

Brixaby searched his memory. Arthur must have mentioned what Cressida did for a living, but she wasn't his rider, so it wasn't important enough to remember.

"She works in the boiler room," Joy said, likely reading his expression. "She uses her flame-bear summon to heat water into steam. It's really important because it helps power a lot of things, but she's not happy. She was bred to be a noblewoman, and she says that's harder to do than any boring boiler job."

And now Brixaby eyed the card in Joy's claws for a moment, wondering if he should snatch it back and just consume it after all. He didn't particularly care about Joy's rider's problems.

But . . . if Cressida was unhappy, that would make Arthur unhappy.

"Then I'll store the card for you until you are ready to gift it to her."

Taking the card back, he reluctantly re-added it to his Personal Space.

"Thanks, Brixaby." Joy bumped the front of her muzzle against the side of his for some strange reason. "Do you want to hunt jackrabbits with me?"

"No, I must work." He straightened up in pride. "This is only the first of my planned accomplishments today."

Joy wrinkled her muzzle. "Oh. More chainmail." Then she brightened. "Do you want me to bring you a jackrabbit?"

"Yes, that would be acceptable. But don't poison it first."

Joy giggled. "I can't do that, silly. It would rot before I got it to you."

After bumping him with her tail, she took off.

Brixaby watched her fly. She was rather graceful in the air, despite only having two wings. Some of the two-wingers lumbered through the air currents, but Joy's wings were on the long side for her body size. She always seemed to float.

Also, the look of Brixaby's chainmail creation on her arm was most pleasing.

Realizing he was staring, Brixaby shook his head and took off from the ledge to buzz straight down toward the long shadow of the mesa—a gathering place for humans and dragons to trade, and just where he knew the chainmail master would be.

As he flew, he activated his brand-new stealth abilities.

He did plan on working on his **Chainmail Weaving** skill and getting it up to level 50 today. But first, it was time to find out who craftmaster Dimitri's contacts were, and more importantly, why he did not want him or Arthur to know.

Brixaby flew with his new Stealth Class fully activated. He was all but invisible to other dragons and people. But that meant he was all but invisible to other dragons and people.

"Watch where you're going," he growled, having to rely on his flying ability to quickly take him out of the path of a brown dragon.

The big, lumbering brown dragon who had almost plowed right into him mid-air flinched in surprise and looked around. After a labored moment, the brown dragon finally settled his gaze on Brixaby and squinted. "Oh, there you are. Have you ever considered painting your wings a brighter color? You're a little hard to see."

Brixaby clamped his muzzle shut before he could roar out that that was the point.

Instead, he flew on and veered to the side, closer to the walls that bordered the aerial highway between the hive's lava bubbles. He supposed he should be happy that his **Stealth** skills were so effective.

Some dragons naturally flew close to the walls, either due to preference or to give way to larger dragons. There were a few more close calls.

Brixaby could have started using his Stealth Class more sparingly, but that would have been the same as admitting he had made a mistake. He wasn't ready to do that yet.

Instead, still flapping his wings, he found he could creep directly along the walls, sort of bounding from one vertical spot to another.

New skill gained: Extreme Rock Climbing (Adrenaline Activities Class)
Due to your card's bonus traits, you automatically start this skill at
level 3.

Hadn't Arthur been working toward a rock climbing skill of some sort? Brixaby felt a brief flash of pity for him that he didn't have wings to help him along the way.

Finally, the tunnel widened out, and Brixaby arrived at the crafters bubble, which was a wider area that allowed him to stay away from other dragons. He stuck to the shadows, now clinging to the top of the domed ceiling and looking down. His naturally magnificent dark scales allowed him to blend in with the shadows.

And right below him was the stall that sold chainmail.

Twisting his head so that he wasn't staring upside down, Brixaby observed craftmaster Dimitri putting chainmail works into an enchanted net. The same type that had carried himself, Arthur, Joy, and Joy's rider here. Interesting. He wasn't aware that his craftmaster had one of those.

And it was obvious that the man had more products than he had let on. He removed more and more chainmail shirts and even several pairs of pants and greaves from boxes that had been stored under the booth tables. Brixaby supposed he should have been more curious and checked those boxes before. But they hadn't seemed important until now.

The enchanted net must have accounted for weight because after he was finally done and pulled the drawstring to shut the top of the net tight, Dimitri picked it up with merely a grunt, slung it over his shoulder, and started to walk out.

Naturally, Brixaby followed.

It was slow going because in his inefficient, human way, the craftmaster also stopped to talk to people. More than once, Brixaby considered gouging out a pebble from the wall he was clinging to and throwing it at the man to get him to hurry up. But since that might give away his position, he resisted.

It was a good thing that he was certain that this would be worth it.

Finally, Dimitri made it out of the mesa complex, and Brixaby could take to the air again. He modulated his wing movements so that the two wings on each side beat in unison instead of each cupping the air separately.

This was a much more inefficient way to fly—just like a normal two-winged dragon—but it cut down on the buzzing drone. It was, unfortunately, a distinctive sound.

So, flying in this boring, inefficient, tiring way, he was able to follow the craftmaster.

All sorts of humans conducted their business outside the main mesa complex. The location varied based on where the sun was in the sky. No one wanted to stay in the blazing heat for long, so temporary booths and picnics were often set out in the shadow of the mesa, moving as the shadow did.

Dimitri met with another human almost at the point of the tall shadow. The other human was a little odd. It wasn't the way his many golden rings decorated his ears, nose, and eyebrows. It wasn't even his shiny bald head.

To Brixaby's eye, his proportions seemed . . . off. His ears were a bit too sharp. His limbs seemed too long. He held himself not like a human but more forward, as if he was walking on the tips of his toes. Brixaby landed and crept closer, hiding behind the occasional boulder strewn across the landscape.

He wasn't able to catch the conversation between the craftmaster and the new man, but he did see the handshake and the two of them exchanging enchanted nets. Dimitri immediately loosened the drawstring, looked inside, and grunted with satisfaction. Brixaby suspected he had just seen a transfer of goods, and possibly money.

They nodded to each other again, and Dimitri walked away. Meanwhile, the tall, thin man stared after him, and then up at the mesa. His expression—as best as Brixaby could read human expressions—seemed to be contemplative.

Sometimes, when he was paying attention, Brixaby could get a feeling of when somebody was about to use a card from their heart deck. He had this feeling now.

On reflex, Brixaby popped up from behind his boulder and dropped the Stealth card. Dimitri was still walking away. Hopefully, he wouldn't look back.

"Hold it right there," Brixaby told the odd man. "I have business with you!"

The man looked at him and smiled brilliant white—his eye-teeth a little too long. "What is this? Law enforcement? That was a legitimate transaction." He had a slightly odd cadence to his voice. It was musical in a way that Brixaby had never heard before.

"Of course not," Brixaby said, trotting up to him. "I just want to know if you're interested in buying something else."

The man squinted at him. This close, Brixaby saw that his eyes were strange, too. The pupils were vertical and not round. Did that naturally happen with humans? He didn't think so.

"I suppose that depends," the man said. "Aren't you a little young to be . . . so enterprising?"

"No, just talented." Brixaby jumped to buzz up to the man's eye level, and then plucked one of his own chainmail shirts out of his Personal Space to hold it up between them.

The man's odd eyes widened. Then he reached out to take the shirt and look it over carefully. He had the air of somebody who understood what he was examining.

Brixaby preened. After passing level 30 in **Chainmail Weaving**, these shirts had become easy. He had managed to make quite a few of them in his effort to level himself up.

"How many more of these do you have?" the man asked.

"Seventeen more, in various human sizes. And ten pairs of sleeves going up from a standard human woman to a small dragon."

"I have no need for dragon sizes, only the men and women." He hesitated, then nodded at Brixaby. "My name is Jon, and I am an associate from the city-state of Evanstown."

"What is a city-state?"

"Think of it as a tiny kingdom. Speaking of tiny, I have never seen a dragon quite like you . . . I hope you don't mind me saying."

Brixaby puffed out his chest. "My name is Brixaby. You should have heard of me as I am quite impressive."

Jon chuckled. "Then show me the rest of your wares, impressive dragon."

Brixaby did, and the man checked them all for signs of quality. Not that Brixaby was worried on that account. All were up to his impeccable standard. And indeed, the man didn't set any aside except for the larger sleeves. "I have no interest in these, though if you repurpose them into additional armor, I would buy them."

"Why not?" he asked. "Don't you want to keep your dragons safe?"

"The city-state of Evanstown has no dragons."

Then the city-state of Evanstown is a pathetic place, Brixaby thought to himself.

Then they both settled to haggle on prices, which gave Brixaby a **Haggling** skill in the Merchant Class. That was most useful. Perhaps once he had completely leveled **Chainmail Weaving**, he would focus on Haggling next.

They settled on a payment of four Rare shards for the entire bunch. This was pure profit, as Brixaby had repurposed the chainmail itself from what craftmaster Dimitri had given him. Also, with these additional shards, he might have enough to finally complete that Rare card he and Arthur had been planning. Hopefully, it would be a combat variety.

With satisfaction, he tucked the shards away into his Personal Space. The man carefully folded the chainmail works and placed them within the enchanted net. "I don't suppose that an adventurous dragon like yourself would be interested in fighting scourglings for our cause?"

"No," Brixaby said. "I have many enemies to defeat first, and a hive to conquer—I mean, manage."

Jon looked up, surprised. "This hive?"

"No." Brixaby snorted. "A *real* hive, back home in the kingdom."

The man looked at him for a moment as if he was trying to decide if Brixaby was joking or not. Then he shook his head with a deep chuckle. "Well, until then, I come every second week for trade. Come visit me if you have more goods, young Brixaby." Then with that farewell said, he activated his heart card. Instantly, he was whisked away with a teleporting spell.

New Counterfeit spell obtained: Return Home
Remaining Time: 59 Minutes 59 Seconds

Ohhh. A Rare-level teleport spell. This was useful. Based on the name, that card's limitations meant he would only be able to teleport where he considered home. That was annoying, though he supposed the cave he shared with Joy and her rider could be considered a temporary home.

Brixaby gave it a try. After all, he would only have this spell for an hour.

Sure enough, he emerged back into the cave he shared with Joy and her rider. It was currently empty, which was good because Brixaby still had one more great accomplishment ahead of him today.

He retreated into his Personal Space where he had stored liberated rare metals from some crafter's stall. Gold, one of the crafters had called it. Too bad he hadn't kept a close enough eye on his product. Throwing a bar of the stuff into his Personal Space last week had been too easy.

Smelting it on the sly had been harder, but he only had to heat it to a melting point before, again, stuffing the entire crucible and tongs into his Personal Space.

Knowing that he would need to stretch himself to gain that final all-important level, he worked the odd, soft metal into a special chainmail shirt he'd set aside. It was, he suspected, not helpful for protection. But decorative, which tended to draw the eye.

He would have added it to his own chainmail, except gold clashed with the purple highlights in his dark scales.

After several hours within the mind space, he was feeling the strain that told him he needed to take a break soon.

But Brixaby did not take that break. He worked until the ache behind his eyes expanded to encompass his entire head, and the last bit of gold was woven rather pleasingly into the rivets.

Only then did he reach level 50.

Congratulations! For reaching this milestone you have been awarded the following:
+3 Dexterity
+2 Wisdom
+1 Intelligence
+25% quicker learning in all chainmail class skills.
+25% quicker adaptation to all chainmail body enhancement skills.

Ha. He had been right! There was a sizable reward for sticking to a single skill.

Brixaby felt an immediate wave of tingles wash up and down his body. The result of his new attributes, he assumed. He spread his wings and examined himself for any physical changes. Nothing was immediately apparent.

Dexterity, wisdom, and intelligence weren't among the physical attributes, but he would have liked to grow in size.

He was just pondering what a chainmail body enhancement skill was, and if that would affect his physical form, when he received another startling prompt.

Warning: No further advancement in Chainmail Weaving is possible until this skill is added to a class.

He reread it again and again, hoping he had misunderstood. But the truth was literally staring him in the face.

Classes were indeed the way to grow stronger. At least, past level 50.

Heaving a sigh, Brixaby exited his Personal Space. He was not looking forward to telling Arthur that he had been correct after all.

CHAPTER 21

From hints dropped during dragon care lectures at Wolf Moon Hive, dragons of different ranks tended to mature at different speeds. Commons and Uncommons were the fastest, with Rares reaching full adulthood slower. The average for young adulthood was six months, which was why that was used as the benchmark for graduation.

It stood to reason that Legendary-ranked dragons matured even slower.

Brixaby was likely the equivalent of a teenager and was testing his boundaries. At least, that was what Arthur told himself after an hour of fruitless searching for the dragon before he finally gave up and went back to their shared cave. One way or another, Brixaby would show up there.

And indeed he was, fluttering around the room in loops—likely working on his stamina flying.

Arthur opened his mouth to ask where he had been all day, but then stopped when he realized that Brixaby was not the only one in the cave.

Cressida sat on the edge of her small one-person cot—they had two in this room, as a replacement for the single bed. Her normally neat red hair had flyaways erupting from her bun. One side of her face was markedly redder than the other, as if she'd been out in the sun too long. But he'd known Cressida long enough to know she took care against that with creams, blaming her complexion.

"What happened? You look like you were chewed up and spit out." It was only after Arthur had spoken that he realized that hadn't been the most tactful thing to say.

She barely turned his way. "I'm fine," she said in a way that meant she wasn't.

"You smell like burned hair," Brixaby commented, still flying his loops.

Arthur debated for a moment, but anybody with eyes could see that Cressida wasn't "fine," and he wasn't going to take the coward's way out. So, watching her reaction to make sure he wasn't overstepping his boundaries, he went over and sat next to her. "Hard day at work?"

She snarled something under her breath that he didn't quite catch. Then she sighed, shoulders slumping, and straightened. "There was an accident with one of the boilers."

"Oh?"

"Some of the hot water that we heat to steam corroded through the tank walls. They're supposed to be reinforced by somebody with a metal card. But I guess they were asleep on the job," she added, frustrated.

Cold fear slipped down his spine, and he forgot that he didn't want to push. His voice grew sharp. "Cressida, what happened?"

She shrugged again as if it didn't matter, but this close, Arthur saw a fine tremor of fear shake her body.

"One second I was directing Wicker"—the name of her flame-bear summon—"to heat the bottom of the tank as usual. Then, there was a bang. Wicker reacted quicker than I did. He jumped in front of me and boiled away a jet of scalding water to steam. I hadn't even seen it coming, but he gave me an extra second to put my mana shield up. That saved me from the worst of the heat. But . . . I guess I wasn't fast enough to escape all the steam."

She touched the side of her face, which was red and likely tender. Arthur just stared, horrified. He wasn't sure what to say.

Her smile at him was sardonic. "It was close."

"But . . . I hadn't heard about any accident in the hive. Wasn't there anybody around? Did anybody else . . ." He tried to fish around for words, torn between indignation and outright fear that he had almost lost her without even knowing about it.

And he wasn't the only one. Joy wasn't anywhere to be found. She had undergone a bit of a change recently, but surely she wouldn't have left Cressida alone so soon after being in danger.

His mind was filled with images of the bubbly dragon ripping off her chainmail sleeve and happily poisoning whoever was responsible for the accident.

No. She couldn't be doing that . . . right?

"No, no one else was hurt," Cressida said briskly. She reached to smooth down some of the many flyaway hairs on top of her head, as if she'd just realized they were there. "I was alone in the boiler room. I yelled for help, but the whole cave was full of superheated steam, and it took a few minutes for someone with the appropriate card to respond."

"And the tank just . . . failed?" Arthur asked, anger growing prominent. "Just like that?"

"They said it was an accident. And at the time, I thought so too. But now that I'm here and thinking about it . . ." She shook her head. Then she looked at Arthur, and he saw the fear in her eyes. "I just don't know."

Arthur had been the subject of an assassination attempt already, and the Mind Singer had previously threatened his friends, but . . .

"It seems a little convoluted to be something that was planned," Arthur said, hoping that he wasn't just saying this to convince himself. "If this . . . wasn't an accident"—he cut his eyes to Brixaby, who was still circling around, likely not paying attention—"then what would be the point? That's the sort of thing you do to send a message."

"I can think of a message: That no matter what, no matter where we are, we aren't safe from *her*." Cressida visibly shook herself, then blinked and tried a smile for Arthur. "But . . . you're likely right. I'm just shaken."

"I don't like you working there," Arthur said.

"I don't like me working there either," she replied briskly, with a noble's quick diction. "But there aren't very many ways for me to keep useful. I don't have any crafts, and this hive doesn't fight scourglings."

"You could not work," Brixaby said as he passed over them. Arthur hadn't been sure whether he was listening or not. He seemed completely unconcerned. "Arthur and I make more than enough to feed you. And I'm certain that Joy would be sad if you were boiled alive."

"We would all be sad if she was boiled alive," Arthur said.

Despite the grim conversation, Cressida smiled. "Well, I assure you that there won't be any boiling anytime soon. That particular tank needs to be repaired and triple-checked. And the others have fire-card wielders working at them." She sighed. "Now I don't have anything to do with my days."

"You'll find something," Arthur said.

She was trying to pass off her close call, but Arthur wasn't sure he could drop it that easily. She almost died today. And he hadn't even known how close he had come to being without her. Or telling her how he felt about her.

Perhaps he was a coward because, even now, he couldn't make the words come to his lips. It was as if his throat had closed off. He swallowed thickly, trying to loosen it up again, dig down deep, and find that kernel of courage he knew must be there. But when he reached for it, it was gone.

So, instead, he just placed his hand over hers and said, roughly, "I don't want you working with the boilers again, even if they fix it."

"It's good pay."

"I don't care about the pay," Arthur said fiercely. "I want you to be safe."

They looked at each other.

There was an obnoxious buzz of wings overhead. Brixaby landed between them, causing them to separate their hands.

"If we were back at the Wolf Moon Hive, she could simply fight scourglings like everybody else," Brixaby said.

"Yes, well." Cressida cleared her throat and looked away. "Tell me how we can go back there, and I will certainly consider it."

Maybe he should just tell her. Maybe—

A thud came from the balcony of the cave. Everybody turned to see Joy land awkwardly, out of breath and grinning wide enough to show every one of her pointed teeth. And she was absolutely covered in dead animals.

"I brought tonight's dinner!" she called. "And . . . probably enough for dinner the next few weeks' worth of meals, too."

"Are any of these poisoned?" Brixaby asked before Arthur or Cressida could find anything to say.

"Nope, I killed them all the hard way. Bunnies have easily snappable necks," she said cheerily, and started unloading her burdens. She had, Arthur realized, twisted long strands into twine from the tough grass that grew in spiky bunches across the desert. She then looped this rough twine around the limbs of some of her catches and tied those to bunches around herself.

It was rather ingenious, especially since Joy didn't have a crafting skill to her name.

"Joy, that is quite a lot of animals," Cressida said weakly. Arthur noticed her staring hard at a particularly cute bunny with dark patches against white fur.

At Wolf Moon Hive, it was perfectly possible to order lesser servants to deliver a dragon's food. A rider could be delivered already prepared, butchered meat, along with a side bowl of blood pudding, which was all-important for younger growing hatchlings.

Things were a little more rustic at a free hive.

To Cressida's credit, she never complained about it, though Arthur had seen her swallow a bit hard when Joy discovered a new love for hunting.

"Yep," Joy agreed. "I killed my first three rabbits, and then I got a quest to kill twenty-five more. I didn't think I would be able to do it, except I found an entire warren and cleaned them out. The reward was this deer and her baby." She happily turned to show off a mother deer and, as she said, a young spotted fawn. Both had glassy eyes and seemed to stare accusingly at Cressida.

"That is . . . excuse me . . ." Cressida quickly retreated to the washroom.

Joy blinked in surprise, but Arthur stepped in.

"Brixaby and I can store what you don't want to eat immediately in our Personal Spaces. That way, the meat will keep fresh."

"You did have a productive afternoon," Brixaby agreed, and Arthur caught him eyeing one of the larger flop-eared rabbits. Then the little dragon swelled up, wings extended. "My day, however, was even more accomplished."

Joy turned to him. "Oh? Are we talking about that thing you didn't want to talk about?"

"Does this have to do with the fact that your craftmaster's booth was closed today?" Arthur asked dryly.

He half expected Brixaby to be chagrined after getting caught out in a lie. Instead, the dragon's scaly lips peeled back from his teeth in a very smug grin. "I found myself a buyer for my wares. And he pays very well."

With that, he flourished four Rare card shards.

Arthur's eyebrows went up. "Why don't you start from the beginning?"

As Brixaby relayed his story, Arthur felt his eyebrows climb up and up.

Cressida joined them toward the end, her cheeks a little red spotted against pale skin. He suspected she had been sick but didn't want to admit it. She must have heard some of their conversation in the washroom because she added, "And you said that this man's ears were . . . pointed?"

"Yes, he was very odd, but he was from a different kingdom without dragons, so that is to be expected," Brixaby said.

"I don't think those things are related," Arthur said. "It could be some kind of body modification card."

"Oh, one that gives pointed ears? I think that would look lovely on you, Cressida," Joy said. "I think you have a face made for longer ears."

Coming from anybody else, this would be an insult, but Joy looked like she was completely earnest.

"Body modification card or not," Brixaby said, louder, as if annoyed people weren't paying attention to him, "I now have another source of Rare shards. Arthur, if my count is correct, we may have enough to complete a card."

Arthur froze in thought, but Brixaby was right. He quickly pulled out the Rares he had been saving over the last couple of months.

It was amazing. It had taken him and his friend Horatio literally years to collect enough shards between them at Wolf Moon Hive to complete a Rare. He and Brixaby had done so in a fraction of that.

Pooling the shards, they started arranging them on the table into a complete card. Shards were . . . odd. They were slightly different sizes from one another so that even if one had the prerequisite number of shards—and that varied on Uncommons and Rares—it didn't always mean they would fit together.

And of course, the outcome of what kind of card appeared was random. Supposedly.

In this case, the shards fit together, but it became obvious they weren't going to get a card today.

"Missing a corner piece," Arthur said, shoulders slumping. Those, naturally, were the hardest to find.

Cressida cleared her throat. Then she walked to a small wooden box where she stored her small valuables—what jewelry she'd come to the hive with, and a few coins—and returned with a Rare corner piece.

"The boiler room is dangerous," she said, "but it does pay well."

"Excellent," Brixaby said. "I knew I chose well in adding you and Joy to my retinue."

"Are you sure?" Arthur asked. He almost didn't want to take it out of pride, but Cressida shoved it at him.

"Take it. And make sure it's a combat card," Cressida said.

Arthur wasn't sure how he was supposed to do that. But he wasn't strong enough to push the piece back at her. Instead, taking a deep breath, he slid the final piece into place.

The shards glowed and then flashed a uniform white before dimming again.

A new Rare card had just been born into the world.

All leaned forward to read.

Brixaby was the first to speak. "Finally," he said in the greatest tone of satisfaction. "A combat card."

CHAPTER 22

Sometimes, the abilities of cards created from shards were a complete mystery. At other times, they fit so perfectly that it was almost eerie. This combat card was of the latter variety.

Hey Man, Nice (Metal) Shot
Rare
Combat

This card grants its wielder a ballistic-telekinetic affinity to metal objects less than one centimeter in all dimensions. The wielder will have fine control of this object within one inch of their body. When charged with mana, these objects may be released and shot out at high speeds. Aim well. The wielder's control of the metal ends once it passes beyond one inch of their body.
This card grants the use of mana.

Brixaby whooped and executed a flip in midair. "This is perfect!"

Suddenly, his right forearm seemed to blink out of existence. Within a moment, he was holding a silver chainmail shirt. "Here." He thrust it at Arthur. "I made this for you."

Then, unexpectedly, he pulled it back before Arthur had a chance to reach out for it. "No, wait! I need to modify this."

There was a slight displacement of air, as if Brixaby had stepped into his Personal Space and returned, still holding the new shirt. Now the chainmail appeared more worn around the wrists. Brixaby had attached some links with openings on them so they could be easily removed from the shirt. They clinked as he buzzed up and down in excitement.

"Now it's ready. Wait, why haven't you added the card?"

Arthur was reeling inside. He looked from Brixaby to Cressida and back again. "But, you're the one with the chainmail skills. You should have this."

He had several cards that had kept him safe so far. His Return to Start and Phase In/Phase Out cards, not to mention the skills and resistances that he had been advancing over the last couple of months.

He was excited to finally add a combat card to his deck, but he wanted to keep Brixaby safe.

The little dark dragon snorted at him. "I don't need that."

"But—"

Brixaby waved a clawed hand at him. "Put it in your heart deck—we will simply share the card." Technically, this was true. He and Brixaby shared the capabilities of their heart decks.

Not all dragon-rider pairs were like this—case in point, Joy and Cressida. Still, it wasn't a perfect solution.

"But . . . it won't be your card, though," Arthur insisted. He knew that this was likely a losing battle, but he had to make sure Brixaby knew what he was giving up. "Yes, you'll have access to my card, but it won't be *your* card. It won't be imprinted on your soul. You'll have to think about accessing it, and this is a combat card, Brixaby. That means you might need it at a moment's notice."

Brixaby did not seem concerned. "Then I will simply take the next combat card we come across. Or consume it," he added after a moment.

"Arthur." Cressida laid a hand on his shoulder. "Take it from your retinue rider. It's past time. You *need* a combat card."

"I want to see you put holes in stuff with your new metal powers," Joy said, then lifted her deadly forearm and pretended to sight down it. "Pew-pew."

"All right," Arthur said, "if you insist . . ." He snatched the card from the table and shoved it into his heart before anybody could think of a true reason why he shouldn't.

He had politely refused . . . but he *really* wanted the card. It slid into his heart deck as if it was meant to be there.

Along with it came a curious sense of . . . weight? He couldn't quite define it, but this card felt different from the other—mostly utility-focused—cards. It was as if he was now accessing a different part of himself. One that had been severely underused.

He didn't have time to think about it before Brixaby was, once again, shoving the chainmail shirt at him. "I demand that you try this on and practice with it often. I will *not* have my rider miss his mark and embarrass me."

"I care about you too, Brixaby," Arthur muttered, rolling his eyes. But he grabbed the chainmail anyway. It was shockingly well made, and so much had happened within the last few moments that he hadn't had time to realize until now: Brixaby had made this specifically to keep him safe.

And somehow, he had managed to get Arthur's exact measurements because the chainmail slid over his existing shirt without feeling either tight or baggy.

Raising an eyebrow, he glanced at Brixaby but found the little dragon buzzing around him, examining his work.

"Almost there . . ." Brixaby said, and there was once again that distortion in the air before he pulled out a smooth leather patch that clipped perfectly over Arthur's right shoulder and down his arm. It was a landing pad for Brixaby.

"You know, you're almost too big for me to carry you nowadays," Arthur said. He knew that Brixaby had a habit of sneaking card shards whenever he could. He hadn't been growing quickly, but he had been growing.

"Nonsense," Brixaby said. "You will simply have to work on the strengthening aspects of your Master of Body Enhancement card. Think of carrying me as a training opportunity." Though he backwinged to settle back on the cot, watching Arthur expectantly.

They all were.

They all wanted a show. Arthur grinned to himself and accessed his brand-new card.

Instantly, he was aware of the chainmail in a way he'd never imagined. He felt every link, each woven with the others in perfect or near-perfect alignment. Brixaby had indeed done excellent work.

It took a mere thought and a trickle of mana to separate one of the already unlinked rivets from the others at the edge of the sleeve.

"Next time, you don't have to leave that gap in the rivets," Arthur said, his voice slightly distant, as most of his attention was on his task. "I can just break them myself if I need to."

It was strange. As if he were moving the rivet with an extra, invisible hand. Only there was a definite barrier when he lifted it upward. He instinctively knew that if the rivet traveled more than an inch from his skin, he'd drop it.

"Send it at something!" Joy said enthusiastically. "I wanna see how fast it goes."

Arthur nodded absently and raised his hand, choosing an object at random: his pillow.

Again, he knew what to do on an instinctive level. This card was in his heart deck. It would be a part of him forever.

It took only a moment to charge the rivet with mana.

Though there was no outward change, he felt it. The tiny rivet now had magical weight.

Then he released it.

With a ping like a spoon striking the bottom of a pan, the rivet shot off. It was so fast that Arthur didn't even see it move.

The pillow twitched, and feathers puffed out of a new hole on the surface.

Brixaby and Joy both let out roars of approval.

Cressida turned to him, hands on her hips. "Did you just put a hole through your brand-new down-feather pillow?"

"Uh . . ." The answer was yes, but Arthur wasn't an idiot.

Or maybe he sort of was, because he liked that pillow.

Then he saw Cressida's top lip twitch. She was holding back a smile.

"That's a nice card," she said. "Let's see how it does against my mana shield."

Despite Arthur's initial reservations, Cressida didn't have a wish to put herself in danger twice in one day. Her shield bubbled about her in a sphere, but she had Arthur fire at the edge of it just in case his rivet punched through.

It didn't, but it did ricochet off at an angle and strike the far wall hard enough to send rock chips flying.

Arthur lowered his arm. "I think we should practice outside."

"I agree," Brixaby said, which surprised Arthur. Then he turned to Joy. "Did you exterminate all the rabbits in that warren, or are there a few left for me to shoot at?"

"I think it would be better to find a new warren. All that's left are the baby bunnies," Joy said, then turned to Cressida. "Oh! I forgot. Brixaby and I were talking, and we decided you should have a new card, so you can be sneaky."

She looked meaningfully at Brixaby who only reluctantly pulled the Stealth Class card from his Personal Space.

Arthur was shocked his dragon hadn't eaten it already.

"Brix, are you sure?"

"You can't give me that card," Cressida said in the same breath.

"What is with you humans and not accepting cards?" Irritated, Brixaby flicked the card at Cressida, who caught it out of reflex. "It is a skill card, so of course I don't need to add it to my secondary core, but I would *very much* like to eat it, so you should hurry up and add it to your deck." He eyed the card mean-ingfully. "Before I change my mind."

"But . . ." She looked at Joy, who extended her neck and nudged the card back at her with the tip of her muzzle.

"My venom claws protect me, but I need to know you're safe, too."

Blinking back tears, Cressida nodded and pulled down the collar of her shirt to push the card into her heart.

She closed her eyes, and a moment later . . . she became harder to look at.

Though Arthur stared straight at her, it was as if his eyes wanted to slide to the side and focus on something else. Strange. He had never seen multiple **Stealth** skills work from the outside before.

"This is amazing," Cressida whispered. She deactivated her new card because suddenly she was front and center in Arthur's view again. Her eyes were full of tears. "Thank you, Joy, and . . . thank you, Brixaby."

"Yay!" Joy wrapped her wings around her rider in an enthusiastic hug—being very sure to keep her deadly arm away from her.

Brixaby let out a long, wistful sigh. It was clear he still wanted to eat that card.

And, likely, many of the shards that had gone into Arthur's too.

The next words slipped from Arthur without his thinking about it, but he knew it was right.

"Don't worry, Brix. You'll have more soon."

"What do you mean?" Brixaby asked.

Arthur took a breath. "We need to test our new cards out. Most of us have Stealth, and now we all have ways to defend ourselves. It's time we find out where the council stashes their combat cards."

CHAPTER 23

The big question was: Where would the Mesa Free Hive hide a stash of stolen combat cards?

Arthur had a pretty good guess.

It would have to be a place that was fairly inaccessible to the hive civilians and yet reachable by the council. A place nowhere else would go, and unlikely to have someone stumble upon it. Most importantly, it would have to be somewhere protected.

Arthur would bet money—and indeed he was about to bet his safety—that this location would be either in or near the underground prison complex.

He hadn't been back there since that initial visit with the would-be assassin, but he'd made a point of mentally marking where the entrance had been on top of the mesa.

The only problem? It was underground. That meant it needed to be accessed using earth powers.

None of which anyone had.

Luckily, both Arthur and Brixaby had the solution in their heart decks.

Over the last couple of months, both had kept an eye on who had the most interesting cards. Arthur, out of more scholarly curiosity, and Brixaby out of greed.

They both knew just the person they needed to visit for this task.

It was a green dragon who had muddy brown splotches covering the bottom of his belly and up his neck. It had the unfortunate side effect of making it look like a disease. He wasn't pretty, but he was pleasant enough to talk to. He was also one of the many dragons who had his own crafting booth, including several employees.

Since he was a green, his core card should be some kind of nature-based ability. But neither Arthur nor Brixaby knew what that could have been. Instead, this green was obsessed with pottery. And he had an Uncommon earth-manipulation card he used to make his wares.

It was a simple task to stroll down to the crafters cave in the evening, stand beside the open-air booth, and watch as the dragon smoothly crafted a vase made of expensive white clay on his pottery wheel. Two apprentices—both human— sweated as they ran round and round in a circular pit, pushing bars that linked up to the giant wheel above. They must have had endurance cards because they were able to maintain an even jog for hours at a time. Meanwhile, the dragon's claws seemed to coax thin walls to spring up out of the clay like magic.

New Counterfeit spell: Basic Earth Manipulation
Remaining Time: 11 Hours 59 Minutes 59 Seconds.

Arthur and Brixaby exchanged glances and then casually strolled away from the booth as if deciding to purchase elsewhere.

They now had a solid twelve hours to work.

That night was a quarter moon, waning. A few clouds scuttled across the sky, casting shadows on the silvery dark landscape.

They'd had to wait seven hours since getting the cards, but that still left them time to find the complex and explore. Everyone had taken care not to do anything out of the ordinary for that day, aside from looking at the crafter booths. Arthur was fairly certain they weren't being closely watched. He, Cressida, and the dragons had given every indication that they were settling into life at the Mesa Free Hive, and so far the council had left them alone. He rarely spotted Ghost following him—which might be the point. Arthur suspected they were waiting for the fury over the would-be assassination to die down before he was approached.

The only issue was Joy.

"I don't understand why I have to stay behind," she repeated, pacing anxiously around their small cave. She looked unhappily to Cressida, who was checking her dragon's saddle for signs of wear.

"You don't have a Stealth card," Cressida repeated.

"But I'm big and strong, and now I can poison anyone who threatens you! What if you get in trouble and I'm not there to help?"

"No one is going to attack us," Arthur said, hoping it was true. "If they have prisoners, they'll be behind bars. And the point of stealth capabilities is to make sure we aren't seen by anyone else."

"But—"

Brixaby made an odd rumble that Arthur had never heard from him before. It cut Joy's words short. Flapping his wings, Brixaby spoke.

"You can fight, which means you can protect us—from above. If this so-called council or anyone else tries to stop us or cut off our way of escape, you have my full permission to poison them."

She perked up. "Really?" Then she jerked in a familiar way, her bright eyes going slightly unfocused. "I just got a quest! Ohhh. It's a quest of protection!"

Cressida let out a breath. Arthur could tell she wasn't entirely thrilled with Joy's new bloodlust, but this was an aspect of who she was now.

I thought that would happen, Brixaby sent smugly into Arthur's mind.

Arthur gave him a surprised look, then shook his head and addressed them all. "Once we're outside, if you have to speak, whisper. If we get separated and you can't find your way back to the group, look for Joy. She'll be the beacon."

If anything, Joy looked even more pleased at this, though being visible on this mission wasn't a good thing.

Joy had now grown large enough that it was possible to carry Arthur and Cressida at the same time. But her wingbeats would be labored, and therefore loud, so she took Arthur and Cressida up to the top of the mesa in two trips. Cressida went first.

When Joy returned, Arthur swung himself up in the saddle and activated his **Stealth** skills. Brixaby did the same. Though Arthur could hear him buzzing right outside of Joy's slipstream she made in flight, it was as if his brain didn't want to acknowledge it.

Once leaving the cave, Joy flew through a series of tunnels that led to the main entrance. From there, she took to the clear dark sky and started climbing higher and higher, as if she intended to hunt out in the desert wilderness. Only when she was out of easy sight of the hive did she turn and head to the south. She'd turn again once she reached enough height and head straight back for the mesa. This wild flight path took time, but it was necessary. Going straight from the cave to the top would be too suspicious.

Joy landed near a small pile of rocks. Cressida seemed to emerge out of nowhere as she temporarily deactivated her Stealth card.

"While I was waiting, I saw a flight of dragons head off toward the sea," she said, pointing. "Might be night fishing."

Arthur frowned. He thought that the salt sea was too briny for any good fish. "Might be merchants . . . or scouts."

Either way, there was nothing much they could do about it other than to stay undetected. Their task was ahead.

Dismounting, he pulled a length of twine from his Personal Space. Through some brief experimentation in their cave home, they learned that it was very easy to lose track of one another while using Stealth, so they'd come up with this solution.

He wound twine around one wrist, gave it a few feet of cord for slack, and then handed it to Cressida to do the same before she passed the last of it to Joy. Brixaby refused the twine, electing to sit on Arthur's arm.

Tied together and under **Stealth**, they moved across the top of the mesa.

Every one of Joy's steps seemed to crunch incredibly loudly. If someone spied them from above, she would look strange . . . but less strange than a whole group moving together.

Arthur glanced around constantly, but the starry sky above was empty. No shadows fell over them except those caused by clouds crossing the moon.

It was strange here. Desolate. There weren't any sounds of crickets or night calls of birds in the distance. Just silence, with the loud crunches of dragon feet behind them.

Trying to shove the worry that something was off to the back of his mind, Arthur directed them toward the location he remembered of the prison.

It turned out he was a bit off. Before he hit his mark, his temporary Earth Manipulation skill transmitted a vague idea of a large space under their feet.

"Do you feel that?" Brixaby asked at the same moment. "It's here."

"I'm not sure." Arthur looked down at his feet and wished he had siphoned some sort of seeking skill. Unfortunately, neither he nor Brix had found anyone who both had one of those cards and used it often. "We're still pretty close to the mesa edge. I don't think this could be the prison."

"Well, we aren't looking for the prison, are we?" Brixaby asked. "That was only a starting point."

"What's going on?" Cressida's voice sounded distant, even though she was only a couple of feet behind Arthur. That was an effect of layered Stealth skills.

"We found an empty space below us," he answered.

"Well? Then what are we waiting for? The longer we're out here, the more chance Joy has of being discovered."

She had a point.

Arthur nodded, took a breath, and then pushed his arm out to the side. A portion of earth perhaps a foot wide and a few inches deep scooped itself out at his motion. At the same time, Arthur felt a drain from his mana reserve.

That helped explain why such a powerful earth-manipulation card was found at Uncommon rank. Lower cards could have higher abilities, but there was usually a downside. This card would need to be paired with some sort of mana-unlocking ability. Luckily, Arthur—and therefore Brixaby—had one.

From his shoulder, Brixaby made a similar gesture, and the trough widened.

Soon, between them, they had scooped a shallow pit out of the rocky mesa topsoil.

"That should be good enough," Arthur said. "Joy?"

"Are you sure?" she asked reluctantly. "My quest said I need to protect . . . not that I need to get all dirty."

Brixaby buzzed down to the edge of the pit. "Think of it as the best way to explode upward and surprise your enemies."

Joy turned to give a long, sorrowful look at Cressida. When her rider didn't relent, she sighed and shuffled over to crouch in the pit with her wings tucked tight, as if to ward herself from the dirt.

With a few more Earth Manipulation scoops, Arthur and Brixaby settled a thin amount of dirt over her, leaving her head free.

Arthur relaxed. In the black-and-white gloom, the soil obscured Joy's silhouette. Her head could easily be mistaken for a stone within any distance, and the red coloration in her pink scales made her that much harder to see in the dark. Joy was in place to watch and stay safely hidden. Now the hard part began.

Arthur stepped to the side, using the shadow of a nearby boulder to obscure the hole, and then he again used Earth Manipulation to dig down.

When Chablis had done this before, she had elegantly parted an opening that led to a downward staircase. However, Arthur and Brixaby were only working with temporary power—one not stamped on their heart and core like a real card would be—and had no experience working with earth.

The hole they dug was ugly, ragged, and Arthur felt his mana drain alarmingly whenever they had to lift boulders out of the way.

He wasn't sure if it was him or Brixaby who broke through first. But suddenly the soil at the bottom of their hole collapsed downward. He heard stones, pebbles, and dust falling on a hard floor below.

Everyone froze.

Joy shifted around in her shallow pit a few feet away, craning her head. "Is everything okay?"

"I think so." Arthur strained but didn't hear anything. No shouts of outrage or alarms being tripped. Whatever room they'd broken into was not protected.

Kneeling, he peered over the edge. He had a Night Vision enhancement, though he'd never put much effort into leveling it. Squinting, he picked out shapes through the gloom. Shelves?

Forgoing all caution, Brixaby buzzed down and then immediately up. "Pah. It's a storage space with cleaning items."

Arthur perked up. "Really?"

"Yes. Why are you happy about this?"

He shrugged. "Some of them might be joined to card anchors. I'm tired of leveling my Tidying skill."

And more importantly, they hadn't broken into an empty prison cell, which would have done them no good. They'd just have to find a way to break out of that next.

"How far down is it?" Arthur asked.

"Fifteen feet."

Cressida let out a breath. "I can make that if I use my mana shield but"—she cast a guilty glance at Arthur—"carrying two within the shield bubble will drain my mana."

"Save your mana. I have a better plan."

With that, he removed a ladder from his Personal Space.

Cressida stared. "Where did you find that?"

He eased the ladder in. It was one of the longer ones, about twenty feet, and the top poked out. "Oh, they have them all over where I work—they're used to go from cave to cave for those who don't have a movement card. I'll have to return it by morning. Hold the top, will you? I'll anchor the feet when I'm down."

Cressida nodded and held the ladder gingerly, as if she had never touched one before. Considering she grew up as a pampered noble and then a dragon rider . . . she might not have.

Arthur stepped around and started to descend, Brixaby buzzing at his side. His last view of the topside was of Joy sticking her good arm out from the ditch and waving.

He descended into the gloom, jumped the last two steps, and then looked around.

Brixaby had given him the impression that this was a cleaning closet, but the middle of the space was dominated by a giant wooden desk, finely carved and polished to a gleam. One wall had papers scrawled with writing, and the closest . . .

He stopped.

It had shelves filled with faintly glowing enchanted items.

CHAPTER 24

Arthur dearly wanted to run to the shelf and explore the plethora of enchanted items, but he forced himself to wait until Cressida safely descended the ladder. Then, he placed the ladder back into his Personal Space. But they weren't done yet.

There was still the issue of the gaping hole in the ground, which, from the right angle, would be visible from above. Yes, it was hidden within the shadow of a rock, but there was no reason to take undue chances.

Working together, he and Brixaby sealed the hole with a very thin, brittle sheet of stone—so brittle that he doubted it would hold weight if someone were unlucky enough to step on it.

A throbbing headache erupted behind his eyes as the last of it sealed away. Stepping back, he massaged his forehead. "I'm out of mana."

"I'm almost out as well," Brixaby said, unconcerned. "We have hours of the Earth Manipulation spell remaining, and time to refill our mana."

"If we don't get caught."

The dragon turned to look at him. There was no light in the room except for a few candle-flame-sized bears thanks to Cressida. The light played oddly off his scales, black one second, purple the next. "Then let us be sure not to get caught."

Flashing a smile, Arthur finally allowed himself to turn to the floor-to-ceiling shelf stacked with enchanted items.

The few minutes he'd taken—as well as the headache—had given him a moment to think. And to get a handle on his greed.

With chagrin, he realized that he had almost been an idiot. All he had seen were the objects, not the security surrounding them. Because, of course, there was. Glowing green and blue runes covered the shelving, etched into the vertical and horizontal slats. Additional runes were sprinkled around the wall that the shelving was anchored to. He didn't think they were decorative.

"Don't touch anything on that shelf," he said.

Both Cressida and Brixaby gave him looks as though that was completely obvious.

Cressida had spent the last couple of minutes inspecting the shelf while Arthur and Brixaby had worked. She shook her head. "These are a lot of weapons for people who claim to be above combat."

"They are likely selling them to other kingdoms at a large profit," Brixaby said.

Arthur stepped in for a closer look. Cressida was right. Most of the shelving space was taken up with knives, daggers, arrowheads, bows, arrow shafts, a glaive or two, as well as bats with vicious-looking spikes sticking out of the top, and various other weapons of war.

He wanted them, but . . .

"I don't suppose you have the skills to disengage these security runes," Cressida said, half resigned.

Arthur gave her a sheepish look. "Until you said something, I wasn't even sure they were security runes."

"Of course they are security runes," she said with a bit of impatience in her voice. "Haven't you seen them in your—" She stopped, and though the light was dim, Arthur spotted a blush crawl over her cheeks. She had forgotten he wasn't raised on some fancy noble's estate.

"They didn't have much need for security where I came from," he said easily, though somehow it stung at his pride. What if Cressida thought he wasn't good enough for her because of his birth? His blood was as good as hers—depending on how one counted that sort of thing, but . . . not his background.

He forced that thought away. It wasn't important.

"So, you're certain that these are booby traps?" he asked, turning back to the shelving.

His fingers *itched* to grab one of those daggers.

He didn't have a single active combat skill in regard to daggers, but properly enchanted weapons could substitute for a weapons or skill-based combat card. The main benefit was that anybody could use them.

If he had weapons, he wouldn't need combat cards.

"I'd say so, yes," she said. "I've seen this repeating pattern of three"—she pointed to several runes with indecipherable sigils on them—"in my father's study, locking away what he dearly didn't want us to look at."

With a frustrated sound, Arthur made himself turn away. Even if they weren't trap runes, they most certainly were alarm runes. They couldn't risk it.

Cressida's small flame bear acted as a candle, illuminating that side of the room in soft light.

Another shape stood out in the semi-gloom on the opposite wall. "What's this?" He started to walk toward it, and within a few steps, his mood brightened. "Books?"

Behind him, Brixaby made a dismissive sound, unimpressed. But Arthur was intrigued. "Cressida, bring your bears over here."

Cressida joined him, and the titles were illuminated—most written in gilded scripts on the spine.

"These are enchanting books . . ." Arthur said.

"What?" Brixaby zipped over so fast it was as if he had teleported there.

The dragon began to eagerly scan the bookshelf from top to bottom. Then, on the second shelf down, he pointed one claw at a book. "I simply must have this. Don't you dare say no."

Arthur hesitated, looking for more signs of rune security, but there were none. No glowing runes decorated the edges of the bookshelf. It seemed too easy.

"What is it?" he asked.

"Basic metal enchantments," Brixaby said.

Now it was Arthur's turn to take in a breath. He wanted to tell his dragon to take it, but . . . "Why aren't these books protected?"

"Pah. Craftmasters keep the best secrets for themselves," Brixaby said. "Passed from master to apprentice and within families. I know there are many things my chainmail master has kept from me." He seemed put out as he buzzed a little closer for a look, squinting. "Besides, this is an old edition."

Arthur's resistance was falling apart like a rotten bit of cloth. "Take it. But—"

Brixaby reached out and snatched the book before Arthur could add "Be careful."

No runes lit up. No alarms squealed into life. No threatening lights blazed, and the far door remained shut without any guards to come to see what was going on.

The only thing that happened was bits of the old cover flaked off in Brixaby's claws and drifted to the floor.

This was likely an edition so old it wasn't useful enough to keep under lock and key, but still too valuable to outright throw away. Likely this bookcase and its contents were for decoration.

Arthur stepped up and eagerly started to scan the rest of the titles. They'd come for richer prizes, but this trove shouldn't be ignored.

After a moment, he took a book: *Enchantment Basics: A Primer.* Then, on second thought: *Basics of Rune Security.*

Then he slid the books carefully together to fill in the holes. He turned to Cressida. "Do you want anything? We can't take them all—that would be too obvious. But I don't think they'd miss a couple here and there."

She gave him a look. "Why would I?"

"Because . . ." Then again, she didn't have a Personal Space with time-warp abilities or a card that enhanced skills. "Learning enchanting could be fun?"

She raised her eyebrows and then reached out to twist her flame-bear summon—which had been reduced to roughly the size of a stuffed toy, and indeed looked much chubbier and cuter than Wicker—to illuminate the third wall.

"I don't want anything to do with *that*," she said scornfully.

The wall was hung with slate and covered with complicated mathematical chalk equations. Arthur spent a few seconds trying to decipher it with his **Arithmetic** skills, but they were far beyond him. He looked down at the books in his hands.

"Maybe it's easier if I take it one step at a time." He put them in his Personal Space.

Brixaby had done the same. "Why would they keep their enchanters next to the prison?"

That . . . was a very good question. And it had ominous implications.

"It may not be what you're thinking," Cressida said. "This whole area underneath the mesa might be a secure complex for the elite. My father has some of his most valuable storerooms beside the holding cells, because it allowed him to save money on guards."

"Then this might be where they keep any card stashes. Let's take a look around." Arthur nodded to the door that, until now, no one else had touched. No runes barred the way out. He strode up, his hand hovering over the handle, then, steeling himself, opened it.

No alarms were tripped, and the door led out to a dim hallway. Arthur wasn't sure if he was disappointed or not. He half expected a prison barracks full of the hive's enchanters.

"Come on," he said, jerking his chin. They carefully explored the doors one by one, starting with the most impressive.

The largest set of double doors led to what was obviously an enchanter's workroom. Long tables were set up with tools, weapons, and other half-finished crafting projects.

Arthur's fingers twitched, and his Thief Class whispered that he could easily take a few more things here and there without being discovered. But he didn't want to take that chance. Plus, half-enchanted tools and weapons might be dangerous.

No, the real treasure was the knowledge in the books they'd already swiped.

They backed out of the workroom and searched the other rooms. These were mostly offices, and one resting area with comfy furniture and a plate of stale food on a counter, left over from a meal.

The final door at the end of the hall was locked with a circle of runes around the handle.

"I think I can open this . . . maybe," he said, looking it over with his rudimentary level 3 in **Rune Lockpicking**.

"If you can't," Cressida said, "will it raise an alarm?"

"Maybe," Arthur admitted. "But I can tilt the odds in our favor."

He retreated into his Personal Space, picked out *Basics of Rune Security*, and started to read.

At once, he realized why the book had been on the shelf. The language was odd. Some of the nouns and verbs were antiquated to the point where he wasn't entirely sure what it was meant to say. On others, the ink on the page had faded into illegible blotches. But as he flipped through the pages and continued reading, he added to his knowledge of the basics.

Roughly an hour later inside his Personal Space, he had raised his **Rune Lockpicking** skill by three levels. He was starting to feel the strain, however.

Reluctantly, he exited the space, blinking.

"Did you just do what I think you did?" Brixaby asked.

Arthur gave him a sardonic smile. "Three more levels."

"I would say that's unfair," Cressida teased, "but you are a Legendary card user. All of your power is ridiculously unfair."

Arthur wisely didn't tell her that the Personal Space was a Rare power.

Instead, he turned back to the lock. His approach wasn't perfect, and he didn't think that he could have shifted around the runes correctly without some prior practical knowledge. The enchanters would have been fools to keep a book filled with secrets used to unlock their own doors. But his prior knowledge, combined with a little luck, was enough to open the locked door.

It swung open, and Arthur half expected to finally come across the cache of combat cards.

What lay beyond was . . . an office. Arthur's shoulders slumped.

"Where are the cards?" Brixaby asked, clearly having hoped for the same thing.

"Now *that* is interesting," Cressida said, sweeping past him, as if unaware of his disappointment.

"What is it?" Arthur asked.

Cressida didn't answer right away. Her attention was on the wall with a large, odd picture in the frame.

For a moment, Arthur wasn't sure what he was looking at. The shapes were unfamiliar to the point he didn't recognize it as a map at first. Then he saw the shape of his familiar kingdom, which was right smack in the middle of a giant continent with only the bare edge touching an ocean. The rest of it was surrounded by deep gray. That was the typical designation of deadened, scourge-ridden lands.

There were several other large masses, different continents, similarly surrounded by gray, along with smaller green dots. Final strongholds against the scourglings. These were the other kingdoms and perhaps some of the larger free hives.

All three were silent, just looking at the map for a few minutes, taking it in.

Finally, Arthur spoke. "The scourglings own so much," he muttered. "Why can't they be satisfied?"

"Because they're the scourge of the world," Brixaby said.

With a shake of his head, Arthur turned away and looked to the desk, which was sitting prominently in the room. There were a few papers scattered here and there—inventory and materials requests for the enchanters. Nothing exciting, but this was clearly the office for somebody in charge. One of the drawers was filled with scrolls and loose paperwork.

"Let's go through these, Brix," he said, pushing half to the dragon.

Brixaby let out a sigh. "Do we have to?"

"There could be anything in these records." Arthur took out one of the purple apples, deftly cut it into two portions, and gave half to Brixaby. These apples helped prevent psychic damage, allowing them longer study in their Personal Spaces. It wasn't good to overuse them, which was why he hadn't eaten one before. "This is the last room, and there might be clues to where they keep the combat cards in here."

"Or it's a complete waste of time," Brixaby said. "I still say we wait in here, then ambush whoever owns this office and threaten to pluck out their cards if they don't tell us what we want to know."

"And what will we do about Joy?" Cressida asked. "Leave her up above all night to be discovered in the morning?"

Brixaby grumbled, but that was the argument that swayed him.

Arthur wasn't looking forward to this either, but he took his own half of the pile, shoved it in his Personal Space, then let his mind follow behind.

The next couple of hours made for very dry reading, and he wondered if Brixaby didn't have a point. Lots and lots of inventory and complex contract agreements with people he'd never heard of. Bleh.

Until, as these things went, he came to the second-to-the-last scroll. While reading the records, he'd learned that cards were as important in the enchanting process as in alchemy. Oddly though, not required in all cases. Many of the records were agreements to trade certain cards—usually elemental—between one free hive and another, because they augmented enchanting cards.

This last one was the most interesting. It was a requisition letter for a card. An unusually passionate one.

> *While I realize the cost is extraordinary, even for a Legendary-level card, I feel the benefits cannot be overstated. The incorporation of Call of the Heart*

would create an enchanted seeker tool unmatched by any other. I implore the council to reconsider . . .

Call of the Heart . . .?

Arthur didn't need to glance at the card he'd linked with Brixaby for confirmation. It wasn't his card, but he felt a pulse from Brixaby's Call of the Void.

This letter spoke of another card in Brixaby's set.

CHAPTER 25

Arthur was so excited he practically flung himself out of his Personal Space and back into real time.

"Brixaby! Look what I found! It's your card—"

But Brixaby had started speaking at the same time, equally excited. And his voice boomed over Arthur's. "I have located the hidden combat cards, and I will now receive your thanks!"

"Wait, what?" Arthur asked.

"What do you mean by 'my card'?" Brixaby demanded, again speaking over him.

Cressida slapped her hand on the desk between them. "Not all of us have time-warping storage abilities. One at a time, please. Arthur?" She gave him a look.

He was powerfully curious about what Brixaby had found, but Arthur continued. "I found a reference in this letter"—he plucked it out of his Personal Space to show them all—"of a Legendary-level card that sounds like it's part of Brixaby's deck."

"Is that so?" Brixaby buzzed around to hover over the letter and read. Arthur held it down so it didn't flutter away. A moment later, the dragon reared back in surprise. "Call of the Heart? What use is that? I can already take from the heart deck."

"That's a romantic-sounding card name." Cressida looked like she was trying not to smile at Brixaby's immediately disgusted snort.

"No, no, look." Arthur stabbed his finger down on the page, annoyed that neither one of them understood how important this was. "It says here, further down, that it might be enchanted to create a powerful seeking tool."

"That might be a concern," Cressida said.

"Why?"

She hesitated. "I don't know much about enchanting—well, hardly anyone does. Enchanters keep their craft secrets under lock and key. But there are always rumors." She paused again as if deciding if she wanted to say it but went on before Arthur could prompt her further. "The most potent enchanted weapons and tools require the destruction of the cards. It's a rather controversial process."

Brixaby reared back in shock, though a moment before he was acting as if he didn't care a whit about the card. One purple-black claw touched over his own heart.

"I've never heard that," Arthur said, but then had to admit, "though what I do know about enchanting could fill a thimble."

"We will soon learn more, thanks to the books," Brixaby rumbled. "But I doubt it's true. I smelled no scourge or rot in the workrooms we passed. Surely, if the enchanters were destroying cards . . ."

"No," Cressida said, "it's not the same as letting a card go to rot. The destruction is clean, at least. And it is only a rumor . . ."

"If it's true, it's still card destruction," Arthur said grimly. He felt a lot less excited about the prospect of learning enchanting now. It hit right up against the same moral quandary he had with Brixaby's Call of the Void—and the main reason he had never used it for himself.

Then he shook his head. Worrying like this was putting the cart before the donkey. "But if there is some truth to the rumor, then whoever has it is working with a Legendary to create a one-of-a-kind tool. If that's the case . . ."

"It will very likely be destroyed," Cressida said.

Brixaby huffed. "Oh no. Not my boring, romantic card."

Frowning, Arthur turned to him. "Brix, you know how powerful linked cards can become."

That gave Brixaby a pause. "Yes, yes, very well, then. But *my* information is still more interesting."

Then he plucked out a small hand-drawn map from his Personal Space and slapped it down on the desk in a way that would make any gambler with a royal flush proud. "The combat cards are not here. They're kept at this point: right at the end of the peninsula that extends out to the salt sea."

Eagerly, Arthur and Cressida both bent to look at it.

"You just . . . found it? Just like that?" Arthur turned the map his way and saw that, indeed, he recognized the shape of the salt sea. The Mesa Free Hive was marked out just to the southeast, and he'd seen that peninsula on clear days out to the salt sea before. The maker of the map had helpfully drawn out a tiny *X* at the tip and noted, combat stash.

It seemed much too easy for his taste.

"Is there a date on this map? Maybe it's not current?" he turned it this way and that way as if expecting a catch to reveal itself. "Any description of security?"

"No, the map fell out of a dusty, boring inventory scroll. I believe it was hidden there," Brixaby said, puffing himself up. "And I was the one to locate it. Yet I don't hear any thanks yet."

"Thanks," Arthur said dryly. Hearing that it was hidden helped ease his paranoia a little, but this still felt . . . off.

Surely in a place that was filled with security runes, there would be more security around a map than placing it in a scroll?

He wasn't the only one who felt that way. Cressida was frowning, too. "If this person knows where the combat cards are kept, why haven't they raided it?"

"Who says they haven't?" Brixaby asked. "I can't sense their heart. It might already be filled with delicious combat cards—they may have plucked the best out of the stash. We should hurry before any more are taken."

"Or they can't get to the peninsula for some reason," Arthur said, ignoring Brixaby's impatience. Though he keenly felt it himself. "I don't think they'd be able to walk to the spot without being seen, which means they'd have to get a ride on a dragon . . . and pay them with combat cards."

"That feels thin," Cressida said, then sighed, "but I don't have any other explanation. Unless this map is wrong."

"There's one way to find out," Brixaby said eagerly.

"Wouldn't it be nice," Cressida said with a smile, "if your Call of the Heart card was there with the combat cards . . . That's two scourglings, one stone."

"No chance of that," Arthur said. "The letter said it's with another free hive. The . . ." He trailed off, realizing he'd gotten so excited about learning of the card he hadn't read through the entire letter.

Quickly, he fixed that, scanning over the rest of the scrawled page. "The Island Free Hive."

"Island?" Cressida repeated, eyebrows furrowed. She stepped around the desk and back to the wall with the large map, scanning over it. "Here it is. This archipelago." Her well-shaped fingernail hovered over a spot in the ocean, bare except for a crescent of islands. "In fact, it looks like there are two free hives. The Free Hive of the Waves and the Island Free Hive."

Brixaby growled low in his throat. "The Free Hive of the Waves is where the assassin came from."

Both whirled around to stare at him.

"How do you know—" Arthur started.

In answer, Brixaby plucked out one of the scrolls from his Personal Space. "They had the enchanters look over his weapons to see if they could find an origin. They all agree: Free Hive of the Waves."

Which meant that was likely where the Mind Singer had made her home.

. . . Which also meant that the Call of the Heart was within her grasp.

If she didn't have it already.

Cressida and Arthur exchanged a look. He saw the same dark realization echo in her eyes.

"We *need* those combat cards," Arthur said.

Brixaby held up his claws in exasperation. "That's what I've been saying. We must secure them immediately."

"Yes," Arthur said. "Tonight."

"Why?" Cressida asked, startled.

"Because," Arthur said, "if the Mind Singer has access to a card in Brixaby's deck, we need all the help we can get. I'm taking all the enchantment books, and someone's sure to notice."

Of course, it wasn't that easy. After Arthur and Brixaby emptied the bookshelf of all the books, Arthur retrieved the ladder, and they climbed back up. He considered leaving the hole there, but why make it any easier for investigators to know how they were burglarized?

There was the chance someone would assume the books had simply been moved to another location. No need to make it look like a crime.

He and Brixaby's mana reserves had somewhat refilled—at least enough to seal up the hole with a rock plug and then kick some dirt over it. That wouldn't fool anyone with a higher-ranked earth-sense card, but the spot didn't look visually different.

As the two of them worked, Cressida walked over to speak to Joy.

Arthur was too far away to understand the words, but he caught Joy's excited tone. He suspected she was happy to get out of the dirt.

Finally, the hole was as good as they could make it. Which . . . wasn't that great. They might have borrowed the **Earthen Manipulation** skill, but neither were practiced or leveled in it.

"That's not going to last if someone walks over it," Arthur said.

Brixaby shrugged a wing. "Someone may discover this breach, but it would be difficult to link it back to us."

He had a point.

Arthur turned to Cressida and Joy. "Any problems, Joy?"

"I kept a real close eye out for the scouts, but I didn't see them return. I was so bored. And dirty," Joy added. "But then it said my quest was done, and linked to an upgraded quest if I wanted to continue. A really, really good one. But . . . I don't understand it."

"Oh?" Immediately, Brixaby hovered closer. Arthur suspected he was trying to barge into her aura and perhaps pick up on the quest himself. As with most meta powers, that was hit or miss.

"What don't you understand, dear?" Cressida asked. "What is your quest?"

"It's offering me the chance to raid a dungeon." She practically bounced in place. "And the reward is my pick of combat cards! But . . . what's a dungeon?"

CHAPTER 26

A dungeon," Arthur repeated with a nod. "That means the prison we saw at the top of the mesa was more of . . . a holding facility?" He turned to look out over the top of the mesa, silvered in the setting moonlight. "Then the 'dungeon' must be the true place meant to hold criminals with longer sentences . . ." He trailed off when he caught the odd expression on Cressida's face. Why did she look like she was trying not to laugh at him?

"Yes," Brixaby agreed, not noticing Cressida's look. "After all, they cannot very well send people to that horribly boring borderland village like they did with your father."

"That's . . . not what a dungeon is," Cressida said, sounding slightly strangled. "Dungeons are . . . well, they're a bit difficult to explain if you've never seen one before."

Joy sat up straight, her scaly lips peeled back to show her two green-tinged canine teeth. "Who locked you up in a dungeon?"

"No one, dear," she said with a laugh. "Dungeons are the names for specialized places nobles use to train proficiencies with their cards. They're made by special card users called dungeoneers—usually Rare or Legendary ranks. Though the dungeon I visited was made by an Uncommon and was somewhat lacking." She shook her head, remembering. "It's an extra-dimensional space—I suspect it's like your Personal Space, Arthur. But a dungeoneer has the ability to design and adapt the area to personal needs."

"Why would they train noble kids in a dungeon?" Arthur asked. "Why not out in the real world with tutors?"

Though even as he asked, he had an inkling. It was one thing to put a card in your heart deck, but quite another to become truly proficient with that card. Case in point, he was still discovering new aspects of his Master of Skills card, which he'd had for the longest time.

"Oh, there are many reasons. Foremost is privacy. To keep any word of your card from leaking out. Secondly . . . again, the dungeon space inside can be adjusted according to the dungeoneer's power and control. The one I visited was quite humid and warm, which was good because my family's land is in a far northerly climate, which means going outside to train wasn't always possible without risking frostbite. And the humid air helped me learn to control my bear summons without setting everything on fire."

Brixaby stroked his chin with two of his claws. "So, this may be a crafting training area?"

She shook her head. "It can be *anything*. A dungeoneer can create a dungeon in multiple ways. If I were hiding something, I would request a vault where only one person has a key, or a room full of deadly traps. It can even be an endless drop where someone needs to go in with a dragon or else fall to their deaths. Really," she added, "it's a wonderful way to hide a stash of combat cards. I just hadn't thought of it as a possibility because hiring dungeoneers is quite expensive."

Arthur turned to Joy. "What exactly did your quest tell you?"

"Just that I'm supposed to complete a dungeon and that the rewards are variable, but in the combat class."

"The correct terminology is 'run the dungeon,'" Cressida said.

Joy blinked and then nodded. "My quest just updated. Now I have to 'run' the dungeon. The rewards are still variable, though."

That was one of the issues with meta-dragon powers. They could be easily influenced by perception, but Arthur had hoped her quest description would offer some clues.

It also didn't escape him that the dungeon system was just another opportunity nobles had that regular people didn't. Not only did they have access to higher-level cards from the moment their heart deck developed, but they also had enhanced opportunities to *train* those cards.

Arthur had been lucky in so many ways in his life. Yes, he never had access to a dungeon or the library of cards that should have come from being a Rowantree. But he had been taken in and sheltered by the Wolf Moon Hive. If he hadn't . . . there was no way he would have gained the power and opportunity that he had. It was hard enough standing shoulder to shoulder with nobles now. If it hadn't been for the hive . . .

And despite his mixed feelings over his training at Wolf Moon Hive, he felt a twinge of homesickness.

Shaking his head, he dismissed it. "All right, time isn't on our side. We need to get in and complete—uh, *run*—this dungeon. Anything else you can tell us about them?" he asked Cressida.

"Other than the entrances being notoriously difficult to find?" She smiled sardonically. "I just want to emphasize that we can encounter *anything* in there, so we must be on our toes. There are so many different types of dungeons: some you can leave if you feel it's too dangerous to forge ahead. Others . . . others don't give you that chance. It all depends on the settings the dungeoneer decided upon."

And Arthur suspected a dungeon created to hide a stash of combat cards wouldn't be the gentle type.

He hesitated for a long moment—not because he was thinking twice about going. He wasn't. But because he wasn't sure if he should take anyone with him.

He looked at them all, one by one. "Only Brixaby and I really need to enter this dungeon." Because he knew there was absolutely zero chance that Brixaby would ever pass up the opportunity to find a stash of combat cards. "But Cressida . . . you and Joy already have some good combat abilities. You don't need to go."

"Of course we're going," Joy said. "I want to complete this quest."

"We're going, Arthur," Cressida said, her tone leaving no room for argument. "I'm your retinue rider, which means that we fly with you."

He knew he should probably try to talk her out of it, but he found that he couldn't. He *wanted* Cressida to come along. He wanted her and Joy's company, their abilities, and Cressida's friendship. And he wanted them both to share in the bounty of cards.

"All right," he said decisively, "let's go."

Before, they'd had Joy fly them up one by one to the top of the mesa. But now, with dawn only a few hours away, time was not on their side.

Arthur sat behind Cressida on the pink dragon's back. He was larger and heavier, but when it came to riding a dragon, the linked rider always sat in front.

The moon was starting to set, diminishing the last of the light. This was a good thing for them, because it made it easier not to be seen. But just in case, Cressida, Arthur, and Brixaby all used their stealth capabilities. They also kept an eye on the stars to watch for any dragon shapes obscuring the starlight. They still hadn't spotted the return of that scouting group from before.

Nobody spotted a thing, but the other scouts might have been using some sort of stealth skills or abilities, too.

They weren't stopped, and soon the salt sea loomed ahead of them. Joy followed its edge to a narrow, finger-like peninsula that extended into the water.

Arthur searched for any buildings, doors, footprints, or any sign at all that people visited this place.

There was nothing. The landscape was more desolate than it had been on top of the mesa. The gently lapping water was so briny with salt that it collected in crystals right by the edge. Nothing could live out there except for thick flocks of flies that fed on the salt. But even then, they were quiet at night, represented by black swoops of sleeping insects settled across the landscape.

"The dungeon is supposed to be at the very tip of the peninsula," Arthur called, just loud enough to let his voice carry over the wind.

Joy nodded and continued doggedly forward. However, her head hung low out of exertion. Carrying two people at once for a length of time had been difficult for her.

Arthur tried not to think about the fact that if they found a stash of combat cards, and if Brixaby ate enough of them . . . he might grow large enough to carry Arthur on the return journey.

He didn't want to get his hopes up.

The peninsula curled like a clawed finger back toward the east. Joy came into land, and Brixaby buzzed in a wide circle to scout the area. There was absolutely no life on this final strip of land. The flies were nowhere to be seen. Even the bare rocks were no larger than an apple.

Dismounting, Arthur stood and looked around. "Where is it?"

"They are hard to spot." Cressida didn't seem concerned at all. She simply summoned three different flame teddy bears that galloped out in different directions. Their light was no stronger than a candle, but would be terribly visible at night from afar.

But they had already decided to take this risk. They were committed.

Arthur looked at Cressida. "Let me guess. The entrances of dungeons all look different, too?"

She smiled at him in agreement. "You'll feel it when you get close. The only thing to do is to search around."

They spread out. The area at the very edge of the peninsula was no more than fifty feet across. As Arthur walked, he concentrated on the Earth Manipulation spell, though it told him nothing, and the twelve-hour timer was quickly counting down.

"Here it is," Cressida called out. She stood at the water's edge, so close that the tips of her boots crunched on salt crystals.

At first, Arthur couldn't tell what she was looking at, but as he got closer . . . the air felt off. Thicker, somehow, as if there was an invisible force pressing directly on his skin, yet not rustling the fabric of his clothing.

Confused, he looked around and studied the ground but saw nothing.

Cressida helpfully pointed. "Stand right here and look out toward the water."

He did and finally saw a thin, hairline crack hanging in the air about chest height. It would have been impossible to spot at night if not for the fact that one of her flame bears stood directly behind it.

It was a crack in the world.

"How are we supposed to get into that thing?" Brixaby demanded, buzzing around it.

"You just step forward," Cressida said.

Then she looked at Arthur. Everybody did. They were waiting for him to give the go-ahead.

Do I want to do this? Arthur thought.

But of course he did.

"Let's go." He took a last step to the line.

As he did, the air thickened, and though the hairline crack didn't move, it seemed to expand. Not from side to side, but it became deeper.

And though Arthur was much too wide, he still easily fit his shoulders in. It didn't make any sense at all, and yet, it did.

His next step took him to a completely new world.

He stood on bright green grass on top of a rolling hill. The briny salt sea was gone, and a hot sun blazed overhead on a bright spring day.

Stunned, Arthur stood for a second and was bumped from behind as Joy made her way through the entrance behind him. Brixaby soon followed and flew right over his head, turning abruptly around in shock as he found himself in the daylight. Arthur quickly moved aside before Cressida ran into him.

"Well," Cressida said, blinking and shielding her eyes from the bright sun, "at least this isn't an impossible drop."

"I would have caught you," Joy said.

Arthur turned in place. At the bottom of the hill stood a deep forest. The trees were so thick that he couldn't see past the first few trunks. And though he could not pinpoint why, it radiated menace.

He pointed. "I'm guessing that's where we search for the cards."

"Yes," Cressida agreed. "This hill is likely the safe zone. I'm guessing that forest is where the actual challenge is."

"But what kind of challenge?" Joy asked.

"It could be anything, dear. Traps, elemental guardians . . . real people who were sent to guard this place. Anything."

As if her words were an omen, a shrill whistle cut the air. Every hair on Arthur's neck stood up on end. He knew that whistle. That was the call of a scourgling.

Instantly, the dragons were alert, lips peeled back in instinctive snarls.

"It is to be a challenge!" Brixaby said, and a moment later, he was covered in gleaming chainmail he'd taken from his Personal Space. The effect was impressive, as the new metal caught the gleaming sunlight.

The foliage below rustled, and the first of the scourglings stepped out of the dark forest.

The body shape was sort of like a horse . . . only covered in gleaming black chitin. It had four powerful legs and a thick neck. The head, however, was more like an ant than a horse, complete with pincers each as long as Arthur's arm.

Four of them stepped out in total.

One for each of us, Arthur thought, then reached into his own Personal Space for something to defend himself with: a butcher knife that was enhanced thanks to his **Knife Work** skills and **Butchering** skill, and . . . a decent-sized shovel which was enhanced thanks to his **Shovel Proficiency** skill.

Cressida called Wicker, who stood eight feet tall.

And Joy just smiled at the scourglings with gleaming green canines. The covering over her venomous arm was gone, and she flexed green claws.

The scourglings charged.

CHAPTER 27

Oh boy, oh boy!" Joy practically bounced from foot to foot in excitement, green-tinged canine teeth poking out from below her lips. "We get to fight scourglings? Oh boy!"

Was it Arthur's imagination, or were those teeth longer and sharper than before?

He didn't have time to think about it, nor did he share in her excitement. His hands were sweaty on the hilt of the knife and shovel handle. As the scourglings advanced, all he could think was: I'm not prepared for this.

He was a dragon rider. When he fought scourglings, it was supposed to be on the back of a dragon—his dragon. One that was currently too small to carry him, but still roared out a challenge as if it were hungry and scourglings were the only thing on the menu.

The scourglings moved forward in a motion more like a skitter than a gallop. Though their bodies were shaped roughly like that of a horse, the joints were wrongly proportioned. They scuttled up the hill right toward them. The front pincers on their mouths clicked in anticipation.

But they were traveling uphill to meet them, and that put them at a disadvantage.

Cressida's flame bear, Wicker, let out a crackling roar and barreled toward them. It met the leading scourgling halfway down the hill and swept one large paw out.

Wicker, a being made of flame, didn't have any physical momentum. But when his paw struck the chest of the scourgling, a blast of fire shot out. The scourgling was blown backward, singed, and rolling down the hill with a high-pitched, piercing whistle.

Joy followed a few moments later, crashing down on the scourgling to the right, trying to dig green-tinged claws into flesh.

The scourgling reared back on two of its legs and menaced Joy with its clicking pincers. But it hadn't drawn back far enough. One of Joy's claws caught a scale and dug in, leaving a shallow groove behind. Joy snapped her teeth at another one who had wheeled around to try to engage with her.

That's when Brixaby darted in, using his **Flying Sprint** skill.

When he hatched, there had been some debate about whether Brixaby was an extremely dark purple dragon or something new entirely. At times like this, Arthur was certain he was purple because his four wings, along with his dexterous flying skills, gave him supernatural dexterity in the air.

Brixaby's claws raked down the front of the head, where the face would normally be. But unlike Joy, he didn't leave a mark behind.

The two terrible pincers snapped together around him, like a trap closing over prey. Brixaby was in the middle. However, the pincers seemed to flow through the little dragon's body and closed together on empty air.

With a quick buzz of his wings, Brixaby shot straight upward. He had used Arthur's Phase In, Phase Out card to escape.

"Their eyes are shielded!" Brixaby boomed out, frustrated.

"I was afraid of that," Arthur muttered but had no more time to think before the remaining scourgling—which hadn't been slowed by the dragons' or flame bear's attack—was almost upon them.

"Arthur!" Cressida yelled, stepping toward him.

He saw the intent in her eyes so clearly it was as if she had spoken them aloud. She planned to encase Arthur in one of her bubble shields.

"No," Arthur snapped, ignoring her to meet the scourgling directly. He dropped the knife back into his Personal Space because, up close, he saw the plate scale protection over the scourgling's body was at least half an inch thick. No surprise that Brixaby wasn't able to penetrate it. He had no idea how Joy had.

Blunt force would have to do. Taking a grip on his shovel, he swung forward with all his might. His strength attributes were a little higher than average. But as he swung, his **Shovel Tool Proficiency** kicked in. He landed a perfect strike against the creature's throat with the flat of the spade side.

It was enough to put a dent into one of the dark chitin scales and halt the thing's momentum. But not good enough to stop it.

So Arthur grabbed a small sack of flour from his Personal Space, along with a burning brand.

One of the many useful things about his Personal Space: since time stopped there, things that went in burning remained burning.

He threw the flour and the brand at the same time, letting his **Throwing** skill guide his accuracy.

The flour puffed out of the cheesecloth he had previously poked full of holes just for this occasion. And the fire caught.

The explosion was as intense as it was hot. Arthur quickly used his Phase In, Phase Out card to keep from getting caught in the blooming fire.

His mana consumption sank like a stone—thousands of little particles flying through where his body should have been took a lot.

That was why he had his Mana Amendment card. Linked with Phase In, Phase Out, it boosted the amount of phasing time he had. Originally, it had been ten seconds in a rolling hour. Now, it was thirty. Plenty of time for the quick flash explosion to pass through him.

He expected the scourgling to be badly burned at a minimum. At best, perhaps dead.

He didn't expect a dark, whistling form to charge right out of the explosion, half obscured by lingering flour and smoke. Arthur had only phased back for a bare second before he found himself phasing again just to step aside and through the scourgling charge.

The creature was badly singed but still on its feet—and whistling in high-pitched rage.

Arthur heard Cressida yell something from behind but couldn't focus on it.

Time for something else from his bag of tricks. He'd wanted to try this in a more controlled environment, but . . . oh well.

His Metal Shot card was part of his heart deck, and was available to him on an instinctive level. Lifting one chainmail-clad arm, he pointed it at the creature. In his mind's eye, he had perfect control over the rivets, just as if they were an extension of himself. It took a moment of thought to unlink the already-loose rivets from each other. Another precious second as the creature wheeled around to face him to charge a handful of rivets with mana.

The rivets shot off with plink-plink-plink sounds and struck the scourgling full on where its face should be. This close, Arthur saw only horizontal slits for eyes, and two more vertical slits for nostrils. There was no mouth at all, likely just as shielded for some reason.

Arthur leaned on his **Throwing Accuracy** skill to enhance his shot. That, and the fact that he was dangerously close to the scourgling, allowed one of the five rivets to strike the sweet spot just within the horizontal slit.

The creature must have had an eye under there somewhere because it reared back with a whistle that sounded like a shriek, and Arthur once again had to use his Phase In, Phase Out skill to keep from being trampled.

Unfortunately, he misjudged his timing and phased back in just as the creature whipped around a second time. Its hind end crashed into Arthur and sent him tumbling.

"Arthur!" Cressida yelled again.

A moment later, Wicker the flame bear was there, summoned out of nowhere, and struck the creature on its singed, scaly hide.

Arthur wheezed, sitting up and clutching his ribs. He took a look around the battlefield for the first time, realizing that three of the scourglings were down and dead. His was the only one left standing.

Cressida came to his side, her expression full of worry. "Are you okay?"

"I'm fine. I have Blunt Force Damage Resistance."

Which was a good thing, or else he might be looking at cracked ribs.

Arthur stood, ignoring a twinge from his side anyway—and readied himself to pepper the creature with more rivets.

It might not be fatal—he doubted he could punch through that thick chitin covering, but it might distract and enrage the scourgling enough to cause it to make a mistake.

He didn't get that chance because Joy came in like an avenging, venomous force of nature—Wicker ducked just in time to keep from burning her, Cressida's power acting in sync with her dragon so smoothly it was as if they practiced it.

Joy raked her claws over the scourgling's back before flapping away. This cut, unlike the others, was deep, and the necrotic lesion spread rapidly. It wasn't long before the scourgling succumbed to its injuries.

Arthur looked on eagerly as it fell, then frowned when he didn't see the characteristic glow around the scourgling's chest. No cards or even card shards to harvest.

Ignoring Cressida trying to fuss at him, he went to the edge of the hill and looked down. The remains of the other three scourglings lay in different spots on the side of the slope.

And, thanks to Joy's brand of poison . . . "remains" was the appropriate word.

"Hunks of rotting flesh" was more accurate. There was barely anything recognizable remaining, and no telltale glow.

Brixaby came in for a landing on Arthur's shoulder. He looked disgruntled, too.

"Did Joy's poison destroy the cards and shards inside the scourglings?" Arthur asked. That would be inconvenient during scourge-eruptions.

"No," the dragon said sourly. "There was nothing to harvest."

"What?"

But Arthur didn't get out another word before Cressida broke in, her voice high with stress. "Brixaby, are you just ignoring the fact that your rider put himself in danger? You could have lost him! Arthur, how could you?"

Both swung around to stare at her.

Joy just looked between them all, troubled.

"What do you mean?" Arthur asked.

"You just went after a scourgling with a shovel!" she said. "Why didn't you let me protect you with my mana shield?"

"Cressida, I'm fine," Arthur said. "I was safe. You know that I have—" He stopped and took another look at the stressed, fearful expression on Cressida's face. He came to a realization. "Wait. Wait, you don't know about my resistances, do you? I mean, you know I'm a tester for Flossie, but were you aware I *keep* most of those resistances?"

He had always meant to tell her everything. The full extent of his powers. Not only was she one of his retinue riders, she was probably his best friend. But . . . things had become strained and awkward between them right after she learned the truth of his history. And afterward . . . well, there was never any telling when they were being watched by the Free Hive Council.

"Cressida," he said, "I have several skills to help me out. Toughened Skin and Blunt Force Damage Resistance." He ticked stuff off his fingers. "I even have some esoteric things like Crystal Resistance, Saltwater Drowning Resistance, Smoke, some Lightning Resistance, and a whole host of others. Plus, you've seen me use Phase In, Phase Out—"

"Yes, for a second or two at a time. But if the fight went long . . . Arthur, you have no true combat card."

"I just took the eye out of a scourgling," Arthur said, feeling slightly miffed. "And I have a moderate healing card just in case."

"You sure do have a lot of cards for someone who just got his first combat card ever," Joy observed.

Brixaby snorted. "You should have seen the duel against his annoying cousin. Granted, I was in the egg at the time, but Arthur told me enough about it, and I met the man." His dark muzzle wrinkled up in disgust. "He has a combat-focused card, and Arthur still beat him at his own game. He is imaginative and uses his skills in unexpected ways. Didn't you see his flour bomb?"

Cressida hesitated. "Yes, but—"

"Oh, was that what that explosion was?" Joy said. "Do you have another one?"

"I have a bucketful, but not that many burning brands," Arthur admitted. He looked at Cressida. "I can take care of myself."

"That shouldn't be your job," she insisted, though her denial sounded a bit weak to his ears. "It's supposed to be mine and Joy's duty to protect the Legendary rider. Especially for these skirmishes. You have to save yourself for the big fight, and that's probably what's to come."

That got his attention. "What do you mean?"

Cressida waved toward the beasts. "These are the first challenges, the manifestations, that the dungeoneer put into place. The battles always start out small, but then they grow in strength and power."

Arthur opened his mouth to ask if she was sure, but then he took a second glance at the nearest scourgling. The one he had helped down.

A dark mist was starting to roll off the thing, as if it were slowly disintegrating in midair.

"What's wrong with it? No, Brix, get away from that thing," he barked, as the little dragon buzzed over to have a closer look.

"I am a dragon." Brixaby threw a disgusted look over his shoulder. "There's nothing from this scourgling that can harm me."

Joy cocked her head to the side. "I think what Cressida means is it's not a scourgling at all."

"It might have been, or something very similar to it that was used as a blueprint," Cressida confirmed. "The dungeoneer has full authority over what he puts inside this place."

It finally clicked for Arthur, and he glanced back to the body of the scourgling, which was disintegrating more and more by the second, the motes floating up into the air and disappearing. He'd thought that the others were featureless lumps due to Joy's poison. He'd been mistaken. "So they aren't real." He rubbed his chest. "They felt real."

"The danger *is* real," she said with emphasis. Then she scowled. "Which is why I was so concerned when you strode in there with no regard for your safety."

"I'm fine," Arthur said. "I'm not going to be the type of Legendary rider who will sit back and let others fight for him."

Cressida looked like she was about to argue again, but Brixaby made a disgusted sound. "If there is nothing to harvest from the scourgling, then what is the point? Where are the combat cards kept?"

All eyes went to Cressida.

She shrugged. "I can only guess."

"Then guess," Arthur said. "You're the only one with dungeon experience."

She chewed on her lower lip and said, "We'll know for certain soon, but . . . well, you know how I said there are different kinds of dungeons? Some are protected by tricks and traps. Some have a pathway you walk where you're ambushed by enemies and must fight your way through. I think that this one is one of the third types. The wave types. It would make sense if we're given a zone on higher ground, and I don't think that we're meant to go through that forest." She nodded to the dark forest, which looked thick enough to need someone with a **Machete Proficiency** skill to cut through. Arthur had no idea how the large scourglings had walked from that foliage.

"Wave types?" Joy asked, looking around. "Like an ocean wave?"

"No, dearest. Waves of enemies. If I'm right, these will disperse and will be replaced by more enemies. Harder ones to kill . . . and probably more numerous."

Her words struck through them, and everybody went still.

"What happens at the end?" Arthur asked Cressida. "How many waves are there?"

"I don't know. It depends on—"

"The dungeoneer?" Arthur asked, and she gave a sickly smile.

"The usual number is ten waves. And my guess is the survivors will be rewarded with access to the dungeon rewards. In this case, that means the combat cards. I hope."

Arthur hesitated for a painful second. He didn't want to ask the next question, but he would never forgive himself if he didn't and something . . . catastrophic happened.

"So, what do you say?" he asked, looking from one to another. "Do we press on?"

"We must," Cressida said quietly. "I checked, first thing. There's no exit."

A sinking sensation, like a heavy stone, gathered in his stomach, but Arthur kept his face calm and nodded. He didn't want to leave anyway.

"Joy, Brixaby, form up in front of us. Let's get ready for the next wave."

The last of the scourglings disintegrated. And as the final motes dissipated, new whistles sounded through the forest.

This time, six of the horse-sized scourglings stepped out.

At least I have more tricks up my sleeve, Arthur thought. *Because I might need them all before we're done.*

CHAPTER 28

Despite the fact that they fought more scourglings, the second wave went far better than the first. They knew what to expect now, and none was surprised by the heavy shielding over their body and eyes. Joy took out two in swift succession before turning to help the others with their battle.

The third wave increased the number of scourglings yet again, this time to ten. It was more difficult, yet still manageable. However, Arthur had to use his Phase In, Phase Out ability more than he liked. It renewed itself on a rolling one-hour basis, but if he didn't cut back, he was on pace to run out the timer.

This forced him to rely more on his newest card: Nice (Metal) Shot.

It proved to be a great distraction, and actually dangerous when he was able to hit one of the scourgling's eyes.

As he grew used to shooting instead of ducking away, he became more comfortable with the card as a whole.

When the second-to-last scourgling fell—blinded thanks to an excellent double shot, he received a new notification:

New skill gained: Metal Manipulation (Blacksmith Class)
Due to your card's bonus traits, you automatically start this skill at level 3.

In the middle of battle, he hadn't had much time to think about it. Though . . . it seemed odd.

A few minutes later, as the last scourgling of this wave lay dying, he glanced back through the notification to make sure he hadn't misread.

He hadn't. It . . . just didn't make sense.

His Master of Skills and Master of Body Enhancement cards didn't give skills for spells or combat.

But . . . metal manipulation wasn't combat or a spell, was it?

One could manipulate metal in forging, for example, using tools or even bare fingers if the metal was thin and pliable enough.

And this did belong to a Blacksmith Class.

Time to experiment.

"Brix?" Arthur said, looking up at his dragon. "Do you have any thin pieces of metal in your Personal Space? Any wire?"

The dragon flashed him a toothy, knowing smile. "You've received a skill to accompany your card? Good. This opens up many other avenues."

"Something like this hasn't happened before," Arthur said. Except . . . it had, hadn't it? His **Mental Shielding** skills were even more of a borderline situation between magic and skill.

Brixaby had a different take. "You've barely begun to push the boundaries of your cards in combat." He shrugged a wing and then pulled out a thick coil of wire from his Personal Space. It was so heavy that holding it made Brixaby dip in midair. He managed to heave it over to Arthur.

The moment the wire came within an inch of his skin, he felt it as if it were an extension of himself. He suspected if he pushed more metal skills—perhaps even got a Metal Forging Class in the future—he might be able to easily perceive imperfections in the metal.

As it was, he was a long way from that. He didn't even know what the wire was made of. Steel? Iron? Something like that.

But Brixaby was right. He hadn't pushed himself in combat. He had to be more imaginative.

He'd been caught up on the idea of the second half of the card: charging pieces with mana and flinging them at his enemies. But he also had control of the metal, didn't he?

He started winding the wire around his left wrist.

The fourth wave was even harder, with fifteen scourglings whistling for their blood.

Arthur used his Phase In, Phase Out card to loop a bit of the wire onto the base of a pincer. Phasing in, he stepped back and yanked a scourgling's head to the side, then quickly swept around to the side of another creature that was just rearing back—staggering from a one-on-one encounter with Cressida's flame bear. The wire coiled and looped any way that he wanted it as long as it was within an inch of his body, making it easy for him to manipulate and tangle up the creature. With his other hand, he continued peppering chainmail rivets to create space.

Then he got the brilliant idea to crimp one side of the rivet out to make a pointed arrow shape. They flew through the air with deadly ease and made that much more of an impact. They hit like arrowheads and sank deep.

Leaning hard on his card, he managed to take down three scourglings by himself, then helped with a fourth.

Brixaby was no slouch either. He used his mental ability to roar into a scourgling's mind, briefly shocking it. His claws were too small to truly penetrate the chitin scales, so Arthur had gifted him a small razor-thin knife from his Personal Space.

Not only did Brixaby have speed in the air as well as natural and skill-based dexterity, but he also had an uncanny sense of when he was about to be in danger. This was thanks to the danger sense he'd gained when he briefly consumed Prince Marion's time card.

And if all else failed, he had his own chainmail workings and a link to Arthur's Phase In, Phase Out card.

Between Cressida's flame-bear summon and her mana shield, she could both do a good deal of damage to the scourglings and keep herself safe.

The real powerhouse was Joy. One scratch from her venom claws or bite from her green fangs was eventual death to any opponent. Unfortunately, she didn't receive a further quest to kill scourglings, but she certainly fought like she did.

Working together, the fourth wave was exhausting but manageable.

The fifth wave, with twenty scourglings, was almost a disaster.

Arthur's Phase In, Phase Out had finally run out. The last second expired at exactly the wrong time, and he was forced to duck into Cressida's mana shield to avoid snapping pincers.

Each wave had taken longer and longer to complete. Arthur sensed he would soon have five seconds of phase time returned to him . . . but he wasn't sure he would make it that long.

A group of scourglings had gathered to batter at the mana shield. Each hit was a direct strike to Cressida's mana pool. From her pale face, her mana was running low.

For a few minutes, it was a question of which would happen first: Cressida's shield falling or the hour to roll over and allow Arthur five precious seconds of phase time.

Brixaby and Joy were the ones who bought them the minutes that they needed. Brixaby pulled every trick of aerial dexterity he had to buzz and harass the creatures to keep them away from the shield. And when they presented a target, he plunged his knife into the spine from above. If he managed enough power behind it, he'd literally cut the legs out of every scourgling.

To fight Joy meant to fight death, but she couldn't handle so many on her own.

Finally, Arthur gained his precious seconds. He stuck his arm out of the shield, not disrupting it because he was phased, and pelted several of the still-attacking scourglings in their eye slits. Blinded, they staggered away, which made them easy prey for Joy and Brix to pick off.

Finally, the last scourgling staggered and fell, bleeding and poisoned.

With a triumphant roar, Brixaby descended on it, knife gleaming.

"No!" Arthur barked. "Don't kill it!"

It was a testament to Brixaby's trust in Arthur that he pulled up short to hover above the creature. Though he didn't look happy about it.

"Why not? Don't tell me you're taking pity on it?"

"No."

Cressida's shield fell. She sat on the ground, exhausted. Meanwhile, Arthur bent over, hands on his knees to gulp air. "No," he said again. "It's going to die anyway, and once it does, it'll start disintegrating. We need . . . a few minutes."

That had been too close.

Cressida had a mana card that allowed her to quickly regain her mana, though not at the rate she was losing it in combat.

Everyone was exhausted. Even Joy settled on the ground, flexing her green arm as if the claws were cramping.

"Arthur," Cressida said, low. "I don't know how many more waves we can take."

Arthur nodded and glanced at the dragons, who were chatting to each other, oblivious.

Now that he had a moment to breathe, he looked into his Personal Space to see if there was some hidden tool, something else that could give him an advantage.

He could throw the remainder of his flour bombs. He'd been saving those, knowing they would be more effective with grouped-up opponents.

But other than that, nothing struck him as useful.

"Ideas?" he asked.

The dragons turned to him, and Cressida bit her lip. No one suggested anything.

"We should be fighting these like proper dragon riders, from up in the air," Arthur said. "Joy, do you think you could take me and Cressida up?"

"Yes!" she said immediately, but then paused. "But that will make me really heavy when I have to swoop down and poison the scourglings."

"No," Cressida said. "That's too much weight on you, dear. You have to be nimble to get away in time. If you fly us, you can't fight."

"Then how do we kill them? I can't keep flying forever, especially with two people. No offense, but Arthur is kinda heavy."

Brixaby growled. "I should be strong enough to carry my own rider. Why don't these useless scourglings have card shards?"

"We can't change that," Arthur said. "Focus on what we have control of."

Several dozen yards away, the final scourgling fully collapsed, on the verge of death. Soon after, it would start disintegrating. Once that was done, the next wave would begin.

"Do you have anything in your Personal Space that will help?" Arthur asked his dragon, a bit desperately.

"Yes," Brixaby said, "I have simply been holding it back until the optimal moment."

Joy brightened. "Really?"

"No!"

Arthur cast one final glance into his own Personal Space and then stopped. "The enchantment books," he breathed.

Then, without another thought, he flung himself mentally into his own Personal Space.

CHAPTER 29

The first thing Arthur did once he got into his Personal Space was to take a big bite out of one of his purple apples. He knew that this was going to be a strain. Mental fatigue was already threatening to creep up on him from his last study session . . . what? Two hours ago in real time? Less? He wasn't sure, and that was a little alarming, too.

Fighting for his life against waves of scourglings hadn't exactly been relaxing, either.

He didn't have a choice. This was their one, best shot at gaining an edge. He only hoped that it wouldn't take too long to go through the enchantment books.

Grabbing the first one, he started reading through it greedily. Like the others had been, the language was . . . odd. Antiquated. Trying to figure out some of the words through context clues slowed his speed.

But he pushed on, focusing on getting through one page after another as quickly as possible. His Eidetic Imagery card helped pick up the slack. And though he felt like he was skimming through the text, when he took a spare second to think back on what he'd just read, he had a pretty good recollection. It was as easy as going to a bookcase and flipping open a book to the exact right page.

It was nice to be able to simply sit and read—even though his body wasn't actually there. Arthur wasn't used to fighting, and this gave him a moment to breathe.

He remembered Prince Marion. He'd wanted nothing better than to read a good book without already knowing what it was, thanks to his troublesome time card.

Arthur spared a second to wonder what had happened to Marion. But only a second. Though this space was timeless, he still didn't have time to spare.

Finally, he got through the first antiquated tome, which gave him a good grasp on the basics of enchanting. Or at least, enchanting as it had been understood at the time the book was written. Which, judging by the cover, was hundreds of years ago.

He didn't receive a skill for it, but he suspected that he was on the cusp. It would only take a few attempts of physically trying. Likely, he'd receive it at a higher level than starting level 3, thanks to the books.

Setting the first book aside, he picked up the next and started to read.

He was halfway through it before he felt . . . if not competent, at least as if he had a solid grasp of the basics. The new knowledge hovered at the edge of his perception, ready to consolidate into a true skill once he started to apply it.

But he was starting to feel the strain of shoving so much information into his brain. The Psychic Resistance apple had helped, but it was a bandage over a rapidly worsening strain.

Gathering both books, he returned to the real world.

Hours had passed for him, less than an eye blink for everybody else. Cressida's mouth was half open as if she was in the middle of saying something, though for the life of him, Arthur couldn't remember the thread of conversation.

Shaking his head, he turned and tossed the books to Brixaby, who barely caught them in his claws. The dragon's wings buzzed angrily to keep himself in the air with the added weight.

"Read through those and tell me what you think," Arthur said.

Brixaby seemed to flicker before his eyes. One second barely holding up the books and looking annoyed. The next second, the books were gone, stored in his Personal Space, and Brixaby looked . . . contemplative. And also slightly disgruntled.

"We need more cards," Brixaby said.

"I know." Arthur sighed. "Don't we always need more cards?"

Cressida looked from one to another. "Wait, what just happened?"

"We learned the basics of enchanting," Brixaby said. "Try to keep up."

Arthur threw him a quelling look. "These books are old, and I suspect . . . antiquated. I don't think that they left the best, most up-to-date books on the shelf for anyone to grab."

Joy perked up. "So you're enchanters now? Wait, don't you need enchanting cards to be enchanters? Like how you need to have a woodworking card to be a woodworker?"

"What do you know about woodworking?" Brixaby asked curiously.

Arthur cut in before they could go down that rabbit hole. They didn't have much time. "Yes and no. You don't actually *need* a card to learn a skill. But . . . it does help. And someone with a woodworking card, for example, will almost always outdo someone who doesn't have a card. Enchanting works like that. *Technically*, anybody can enchant. It's a working of runes. It's not like alchemy, which actively needs a card to activate the ingredients."

If anything, Joy looked more enthusiastic. "Great! Then you can enchant one of those nets. Then we can stuff the scourglings deep down and they'll go away. Then the next few waves will be super simple—"

"Those nets were masterworks," Arthur said. "Brixaby and I only got the basics from the books."

"I feel confident I can enchant simple items," Brixaby said, "though it won't do us much good."

"Why not?" Cressida asked.

Arthur sighed. "These were books for beginners that included some basic enchanting runes meant to tie an item to a card's power."

"Like a card anchor," Cressida said impatiently, glancing toward the dying scourgling.

"Exactly." Arthur nodded. "Only, since Brixaby and I are very new to this, I think we'd only be able to tie a *portion* of the card's aspect to an object. For example, if I used my Phase In, Phase Out card—"

"Absolutely not," Brixaby roared loud enough to make Cressida and Arthur wince.

Joy just blinked at the dark dragon in surprise.

Arthur waved him down. "It's only an example. But if I used that card, we'd probably only manage to enchant one aspect of it. Like phasing out. And it would definitely come with the same limitations that the base card has. Meaning, only ten seconds in an hour."

"What good would that do?" Joy asked.

Arthur shrugged. "You phase the sword out, stick it in the enemy, then cancel the enchantment, which is effectively phasing it in again. Then your enemy has a sword stuck in their chest. It's not quite as damaging as being stabbed in the first place, but if it goes through anything vital . . ."

"Like the head!" Joy said enthusiastically. "I like that one. Let's do that."

"It doesn't matter." Brixaby tried to cross his arms over his chest, likely copying a stance he'd seen Arthur and Cressida use. Unfortunately for him, dragon elbows were a little stiffer than a human's, and his chest was too wide to allow for wing muscles. It just looked like he was hugging himself. "It is out of the question for Arthur to use that card."

"There's a catch you haven't told us about, isn't there?" Cressida asked.

Arthur nodded. "Brixaby and I haven't done this before, and the books emphasize again and again that there is a high chance sloppy enchanting destroys the card. Especially for new enchanters."

"And you and Brixaby are connected through every card in your heart deck, aren't you?" Cressida said. It wasn't a question.

"Yes," Brixaby confirmed. A devious look crossed his face. "But you and Joy aren't, are you?"

"You're not taking anything from her heart!" Joy snapped, unexpectedly fierce.

Cressida added, on the heels of her words, "Joy's cores are still too unstable to have anything removed. But . . . Joy and I are only linked through her Quest card and our linked card. We never linked to my flame summon card or my shield card."

"Cressida . . ." Joy whined.

Cressida held up a hand. "Dear, we need a card."

Arthur didn't like this idea either. "Cressida, you can hide out in my Personal Space for a bit. Time won't move for you there, so you won't gain any more mana or rest, but it would at least put you out of danger and reduce the weight on Joy if she carries me around."

"I'm not sitting out of the fight," Cressida said, "or leaving Joy to fight alone. So, which would be better? My flame summon card? Or my shield card?"

Arthur wanted to protest. He knew he should. He just . . . didn't have any other idea. She was the only one of them who could sacrifice a card.

The dragons were too young, their cores still too unstable. And Arthur's one and only combat card was in his heart . . . which was linked to Brixaby.

It had to be Cressida.

"Not the shield card," Brixaby said. "This is to be used as a weapon. Not something defensive."

"Yes, but her flame-bear card isn't ideal," Arthur said. "Is it something that will just . . . summon a whole bunch of flame bears? I know it's powerful because it's a Rare card, but I can't get my head around how it will work." All he could think of was Cressida's lesser version of her summons, the cute, warming teddy bears. Those would be less than helpful.

"You can't?" Brixaby snorted. "Well, you haven't spent the last few weeks in intensive crafting." He jammed his paw against his chest. "I have. Let me do this."

They were frighteningly close to a solution, though it was anything but perfect.

Arthur looked to Cressida. "Are you sure? There's every chance that this could destroy your card."

Cressida hesitated, and Joy said in a horrified whisper, "That card is from your heart . . ."

Cressida straightened her shoulders and visibly seemed to find her nerve. "I can handle it." Then she pulled down her collar a few inches and reached to withdraw the card.

This was good timing because the dying scourgling had just breathed its last and was starting to disintegrate. They didn't have much longer until the next wave started.

Cressida grimaced as the card came free. Some people wept when they lost a heart card. Some people collapsed. Some handled it stoically.

With a look of resolution on her face, she handed the card over to Brixaby.

Brixaby seemed to flicker as he entered his Personal Space. He returned but a moment later, his scales looking washed out with tinges of gray from pending exhaustion. But his expression was triumphant.

In his claws, he held four metal bars the length of Arthur's forearm, etched with glowing orange enchanted runes.

"You did it," Arthur breathed.

"Of course I did," Brixaby said, puffing up in pride. "Did you doubt me?"

Wisely, Arthur shook his head. "And the card?"

Everyone seemed to hold their breath as Brixaby produced Cressida's card. It was whole and unmarked. Cressida snatched it back, and with a groan of relief, returned it to her heart deck.

"Good as new," she said.

"Of course it is," Brixaby said, but then he hesitated, "but some of the results were . . . uneven."

"Hey, guys," Joy said, "I think that scourgling is disintegrating faster than it was before. It's almost gone now."

Everyone turned to look. Arthur's stomach dropped as he realized she was right. The last wisps of the final scourglings were dissipating into the air.

And right on cue, terrible whistles sounded from the forest.

The sixth wave was beginning.

CHAPTER 30

Quickly!" Brixaby handed out the bars of metal. They were about the length of Arthur's forearm and roughly an inch thick. Taking his, Arthur spared a moment to wonder what other kinds of crafting materials Brixaby had hidden in his Personal Space. Also, these were likely stolen. He should probably ask where his dragon kept getting his crafting supplies.

That thought was wiped away as his fingers brushed over the metal bar. It was warm, almost uncomfortably so. As if it were heated from within.

Joy waved hers around like a sword, though in her large hand, it looked more like a baton. "I like it. What does it do?"

Brixaby hesitated for a moment, and Arthur caught a flash of embarrassment from the dragon. "It should work best with Cressida, seeing as she has a fire-type card in her heart deck. I was able to transfer the element of fire and the concept of fire from your card to this object. Chances are, it will act differently for each person. I tried to make them all summon flame bears, but I think, with testing, it reflects on your own cards instead. Observe." With visible effort, he pushed a trickle of mana into the metal bar. Pure orange flame raced up from the handle to the blunt end, and as they got closer to the end, the fire took on a black quality. As if it were some kind of void fire.

"It should work off your existing mana, even if you don't have a fire-type card," Brixaby said. "Though I can't speak for its efficiency."

"You did great, Brixaby," Arthur said.

The dark dragon huffed. "Of course I did! Wait, why do you people keep saying that? Was there any doubt?"

"Not from me," Joy said. "I never doubted that you couldn't do it. Well . . . I was a little worried that you might destroy Cressida's heart card, and then I would have been angry at you. And I hate being angry at my friends—"

"You would have been angry with me?" Brixaby sounded shocked. "But naturally, you would have forgiven me in time."

"Of course," Joy said reassuringly. "But not until you replaced her card."

"Watch the trees," Cressida broke in. She had been turned to the forest. Many of the dark, haunted-looking trees were shaking as if large animals were passing through them and not caring too much about bumping into the foliage along the way. Or, more likely, there were so many that they simply couldn't help themselves.

Arthur clenched his jaw.

This is worth it, he reminded himself. A library full of combat cards was waiting for them at the end.

Besides, it wasn't like they had a choice.

Cressida was the next to push mana into her enchanted weapon. It lit up brilliantly, shining so bright that it was hard to look at. "This doesn't use much mana at all! But . . . Brixaby, why didn't you enchant us swords?" she asked.

"Because I didn't have swords in my Personal Space."

"You could have asked me," Arthur said. "I have a couple of sharp scrap pieces that might have acted as swords in a pinch. Or daggers."

"Arthur, you are such a pack rat," Cressida said with fond exasperation.

Arthur turned to her. "No, I'm not." He paused. "Am I?"

"You sure are." Joy nodded happily. "Have you *seen* your side of the cave? There's all sorts of bits and bobs in there."

"I see nothing wrong with that," Brixaby said.

"Thank you, Brix—" Arthur started.

"You should see his Personal Space. It is many times worse."

Arthur threw a glance at his dragon, the traitor.

But the little side conversation helped ease his nerves. He realized that he had been clutching the bar of metal so hard his knuckles were white.

No more hesitating. Arthur pushed mana into the metal bar. Brixaby had mentioned that the bar tailored itself to the user, so naturally, he was unsure how—or if—a fire-type enchantment would complement him. As he pushed mana into the roughly made weapon, he felt something push back. Right into his heart deck.

Arthur flinched spiritually and physically, but he didn't let up for a moment. It felt like the power was combing through his heart deck, trying to find the perfect match. This was much more advanced than he thought was possible. Especially for a beginning enchanter.

With a flash of shame, he realized he hadn't given Brixaby enough credit. The dragon had been working diligently over the last few weeks with his crafting. Yes, it had been at making chainmail shirts and whatnot, but he had been both focused and dedicated. Some of that skill had obviously translated here.

Naturally, Arthur assumed that the enchantment would find a partnership with his Metal Shot card, since it was his only combat ability. Maybe even Phase In, Phase Out. That would be interesting. So he was completely taken aback when it latched on to his Master of Body Enhancement card.

Flames erupted up and down Arthur's arms. He cried out in surprise, waving them around to put out the fire. It took a few seconds to realize there was no pain.

"Arthur!" Cressida yelled. Brixaby and Joy roared in shock.

"I'm okay! It doesn't hurt," Arthur said, slowing and staring at his arm. "The flames are above my skin."

Indeed, the base of the flames danced half an inch over his chainmail shirt. It wasn't even hot. Just a pleasant warmth that would be nice on a chilly fall day.

"Huh." He flexed his arm and waved it around, watching the flames burn merrily.

"Here they come," Joy called out, having kept an eye on the dark forest. Sure enough, with the sounds of shrieking whistles, the scourglings emerged, clacked their pincers, and charged.

Grimly, Arthur did a swift head count and came up with thirty.

His **Arithmetic** skill helpfully informed him that it was seven and a half scourglings for each person. A tall order.

We don't have a choice, he reminded himself yet again. *It's kill or be killed.*

With that in mind, he had seconds left to get ready.

Through the connection of the enchantment, he knew that the flames would work as long as he was touching the metal bar. But it was kind of a bad weapon. Arthur reached into his Personal Space and grabbed a bandage that he kept in his first-aid kit. Then he kneeled, rolled up his pants leg, and wrapped the metal bar so it lay flat against his calf.

The fire wanted to travel to his legs, but with an effort of will, he kept it to his arms.

"What are you doing?" Cressida asked, glancing at him.

He shrugged. "I have a better weapon." Then he grabbed his shovel from his Personal Space. It was a little battered from the last several waves, but it still functioned as a good bludgeoning tool. Unfortunately, the spade didn't light on fire. That would have been a nice effect.

Everybody else reactivated their enchantments. As they had different cards, the effects varied widely. Cressida's was the most straightforward. Three flame bears, each identical to Wicker, encircled her.

Brixaby's menacingly black flames coated his enchanted metal bar.

Joy didn't have a visible effect, not until Arthur noticed that all of her claws on her front and back limbs, even her green poisoning arm, were now fire-bright orange.

The charging scourglings hit the bottom of the hill and started climbing.

Cressida's three bears roared out crackling challenges and galloped down to meet them.

"Why do you have three Wickers?" Arthur asked. He knew that they would shortly be in battle, but he just couldn't help himself. "If the flame enchantment reinforces your fire card . . . Shouldn't you only have *two* bears? One for your card, one from the enchantment?"

"I don't know," she said. "It just happened. And my mana consumption is way down."

"Franklin's law," Brixaby said.

Arthur turned to him. "What?"

His dragon gave him a disparaging look. "You did read through the books, yes?"

"I read through one and halfway through the second," Arthur said. "I didn't want to get hit with mental strain."

Brixaby snorted. "You are my rider. You must finish what you start. When you *do* read through it, pay attention to how elemental enchantments reinforce cards. There is an echoing effect that gives an additional boost to similar elements. That is Franklin's law."

Arthur had no time to be embarrassed by getting shown up by his own dragon. The first of the scourglings had crested the hill.

Clutching his shovel in one hand, his arms still aflame, Arthur raised his other arm and focused on unlinking the chainmail rivets on the sleeve. Bathed in fire, they glowed red hot. Arthur shot one in experimentation, and the sizzle and whistling scream he heard from the scourgling he hit was satisfying.

Meanwhile, Joy had dropped down on the first of the scourglings. Her bite didn't only poison it—now it burned. And all of her claws left cauterized wounds behind. It was as if the protective chitin was not there. Some of her slashes cleaved right through to the bone.

Brixaby was finally finding real success, too. Only his black fire was odd. Instead of burning, it seemed to remove whatever it touched.

"Void fire!" Arthur heard Brixaby roar in triumph.

Shortly thereafter, more scourglings crested the hill, and Arthur found that whatever he touched with his hands also burned.

This next wave was . . . well, not easy, but they weren't on the back foot as they had been during the fifth wave. Instead of being almost bowled over by the sheer amount of scourglings, the new addition of fire enchantments let them hold their ground.

The one exception was Cressida, whose only power-up was to increase the number of bears. But the decrease in the cost of mana meant that the three Wickers could fight longer. The bears fought as an effective team, circling one scourgling and ripping it apart with claws of flame before heading to the next.

In the end, Arthur and Brixaby struck the same last scourgling standing at the same time. Arthur smacked it in the ribs with his shovel hard enough to send it reeling backward before he pelted it with more burning rivets. Before the scourgling could recover, Brixaby landed directly on top of its head and pressed the metal bar to its skull. The void fire burned away the top of the skull within moments, and the scourgling's body fell to the side, already starting to disintegrate before it hit the ground.

Panting, they all looked at each other, identical, almost manic grins on their faces. "I think we have this," Arthur said. "Only three more waves to go."

Then, finally, they'd have their prize.

Granted, Cressida was scraping the bottom of the barrel in terms of raw mana, and he was getting low, too. But he had hope. Judging by everyone else's expressions, they did too.

The seventh wave started.

Arthur expected forty-five, perhaps fifty scourglings since that had been the pattern of increase so far.

They got seventy.

And that was only an estimate because once the wave started, the true number began to make itself clear. It was a frantic race to begin killing them from a distance before the mob could reach them on top of the hill and swamp them all. No one had time to count.

Arthur put his Metal Shot card to maximum use. His chainmail sleeves were looking ragged, but he didn't have a moment to spare for vanity. Only the fact that he could heat the small pointed rivets gave him an edge. His **Throwing Accuracy** had gained several more levels, and that allowed him to hit the vulnerable eye and nose slits, too.

Cressida scraped together the last of her fading mana, and her three bears bowled down the hill and into the mass of scourglings, leaving bodies in their wake.

Joy and Brixaby were both terrors from above, but the fight was close. Too close, especially when Cressida's mana shield fell at the end with ten more scourglings to go.

In desperation, Arthur stood in front of her and deployed his flour bombs on the scourglings, which gave the dragons a few extra seconds to reach them.

"Take her into the sky," Arthur yelled at Joy.

Cressida objected, but Joy hooked her arms under her rider—being careful that her claws didn't touch skin—and heaved upward, flapping to gain height.

Brixaby let out a mighty roar and buzzed around in a dizzying pattern, his black flames burning merrily. No scourgling could touch him without losing parts of themselves. They might have still overwhelmed Arthur and Brixaby if not for their Phase In, Phase Out ability, which allowed them to duck out at a moment's notice.

But it was close. So close that neither one of them thought about saving one last scourgling for a break between the waves. When it was over, Arthur looked down in despair at the disintegrating scourglings in front of him, knowing that they had won, but Cressida was effectively out of the fight. And the next wave, the eighth, would surely be worse.

And that was when a bright light erupted at the top of the hill: a line that stretched from the grass twenty feet up.

It flashed, and when the light dimmed, Laird and Shadow stood there, looking around.

Laird spotted Arthur.

"Oh. You're all still alive. I didn't expect that."

CHAPTER 31

Arthur blinked at the two dragons. Their arrival had been so unexpected that, for a moment, he thought that they might be some sort of hallucination born out of either exhaustion or hope for rescue.

He immediately rejected that. He didn't *want* a rescue. He wanted to see this through.

Of course, Brixaby saw things in a completely different manner. "How dare you intrude on *our* fight! We have matters well in hand, and we will be the ones to win the prize. Go away!"

"By the looks of things, you should be thanking us for our swift arrival," Laird said.

"Which wave is this?" Shadow asked, looking around at the mounds of rapidly disintegrating scourglings.

Arthur exchanged a worried glance with Cressida. "We're about to start our eighth."

Now that the shock had worn off, he was growing concerned. If Laird was here, that meant that the council likely knew what they'd done. That wasn't good.

Though, drained of mana and weighed down by fatigue, Arthur wasn't sure there was anything he could do to stop them if Laird and Shadow had a way to drag them out of here.

He gritted his teeth, frustrated by his weakness.

"Oh, look! We have a little time before the next wave," Joy said casually. She pointed to a scourgling lying on the edge of the hill. There had been so many that Arthur hadn't taken notice of it. Unlike the rest, it wasn't rapidly disintegrating. It hadn't truly died yet, which meant they had a bit of a breather.

He would take any time he could get.

He turned to Laird and Shadow, who were exchanging surprised glances.

"What do you want?" Arthur asked. "Why are you here?"

Shadow half extended his wings in a shrug to Laird as if deferring to the other dragon.

Laird looked at Arthur. "Isn't it obvious? We want the same thing you do: combat cards."

Arthur heard Cressida take in a sharp breath of surprise.

His face remained stony. "Explain," Arthur demanded, glancing at the scourgling, which was still not disintegrating but didn't seem far off from death. "And do it quickly."

Brixaby buzzed over and landed heavily on Arthur's shoulder as if to provide silent reinforcement.

Laird nodded and spoke. "The same cards that I and my wing of dragons fight and bleed for are often sent right back to the hives and kings and queens as bribes to leave our community alone." His scaly lips ticked up over his teeth in an unconscious grimace. "I have personally seen the same cards liberated from one noble library only to be sold back to a kingdom to be sold again to the nobles. It's an endless cycle, and I've grown weary of it. Especially when part of the agreement means that *we* are not allowed to keep any of them."

"Why don't you keep them anyway?" Brixaby asked. "Who would stop you? Who would know?"

"There are many dragons who believe in what the council tells them. They think that because we have not been attacked so far by scourglings or by kingdom hives, we never can be."

"They're fools," Shadow added. "I've fought scourglings my entire life. They don't stop. Anyone who's heard rumors of our king knows he changes his mind on a whim. I've grown to like this place, but the council keeps its people like defenseless lambs, ready for the slaughter."

Arthur's eyebrows rose. He felt Brixaby's weight shift subtly on his shoulder—his only outward sign of unease. He knew that his dragon was thinking about the Mind Singer and the threat it posed. Laird and Shadow needed combat cards more than even they knew.

But at least the dragons had all but confirmed that this was where the council locked away their combat card library. Fighting through these waves wouldn't be for nothing.

"So, you want access to the combat cards, but you don't want to tip the rest of the council off about what you're doing," Arthur guessed.

Laird nodded. "You should have come to me first before trying this stunt. I would have been able to gather several more interested dragons." He looked sour. "And we all could have properly shared in the reward."

Joy cut in. "Okay, but how did you know we were here—wait, how did get in here in the first place? I thought nobody could come in and out? Not that I'm unhappy to see you here." She heaved a sigh. "These waves are getting *really* tiring. The boys don't want to say it, but we could use some help."

Laird shrugged. "This dungeon is meant as a death trap for those who don't have the key. In short, that means those who wish to test the dungeon can come in. But they can never leave until the waves are complete."

"You didn't answer her first question," Cressida said. "How did you know we were here?"

Laird gave her a flat look. "You didn't think the council would allow a Legendary and a Rare complete free rein did you? Ghost has been following you under stealth. He reported to me the moment you broke into the enchanter's complex. I brought Shadow in hopes of shaming you into good behavior again before things spun out of control. By then, you'd already entered the dungeon."

"I knew I wanted that Uncommon in my retinue," Brixaby said to Arthur.

"I don't get it," Arthur said, speaking aloud a thought that had been nagging at him since he first learned of the dungeon. "Why would the council even allow the risk? It just takes one group to complete the waves, and then they'll have access to the combat cards."

"That's where you're wrong," Laird snorted. "No one within memory has completed this dungeon without the key."

His words hit like a blow. Brixaby snapped open all of his wings. Arthur stepped back, and Cressida put a hand to her mouth.

"That is absurd," Brixaby said. "We have fought through the waves just fine."

But they hadn't. They had been on their last legs. They still were, Arthur thought, glancing over to the final scourgling. It still wasn't disintegrating, but it wouldn't be long now.

"No one?" Cressida asked in a horrified whisper.

"The only ones who have survived were those who were rescued by somebody with the key before they were swamped in the final waves," Laird said. "I've accessed the notes from the original dungeoneer, over fifty years ago. The waves begin sharply accelerating in difficulty starting from the seventh."

Arthur's spike of fear turned immediately into irritation. "Then why are you here? Are you looking to die?"

Shadow snorted. "That's the problem with you Legendary riders. You're never grateful for any help from the lower ranks."

That was hardly fair, and Arthur opened his mouth to say so, but Laird beat him to the punch. "You are lucky that we arrived at all. The dungeon only allows new participants to enter between waves, and we couldn't linger near the entrance for long or else risk being seen by spies. We are cutting it close."

Then the dragon reached to the side, there was a brief flash of light, and he withdrew a net gleaming with runes. Laird must have some sort of Personal Space ability of his own.

But that wasn't all, because he began withdrawing items from the rune-etched net. One was a green-tinged sword and shield he handed to Shadow. Another was a giant, dragon-sized bowl filled with steaming . . . oatmeal?

Arthur briefly wondered if this was a hallucination after all. Things had just turned too strange. But in the next blink, he realized what that oatmeal had to be. He took an eager step forward. "Those oats were grown in the experimental caverns, aren't they?"

Laird glanced at him. "You know about those?"

"I worked down there for a time. What does it do?"

"These oats rapidly regenerate mana," Laird said. Then he paused. "Soaking and cooking it makes it go down easier," he added, as if it was shameful that he didn't want to eat raw oats.

Arthur didn't care. He gestured for Cressida and Joy to approach. When Laird didn't object and indeed seemed expectant, Arthur grabbed a ladle from his own Personal Space. Dipping it in, they took turns sipping.

It was exactly as bland as oats boiled in water could be, without a hint of spice or salt. But immediately, he felt his mana reserves start to refill. It wasn't an instant process, but he had a feeling he'd be mostly full within a few minutes. Tipping the bowl back, Laird finished the rest.

"What other weapons do you have?" Brixaby asked, eyeing the net with interest. "I will accept a sword as well."

Laird looked slightly embarrassed. "If I'd had time to prepare, I would have brought more. These are my personal items." Then he straightened in pride. "But you have two more dragons at your aid."

Arthur still had questions for the dragon, some of which had been hovering since the first day he was brought to the Mesa Free Hive. But that had to wait. They weren't in the position to be choosy. The final scourgling of the last wave had fallen and was starting to disintegrate. They were nearly out of time.

"I've seen what you can do," Arthur said. "You're welcome to fight along with us and share the cards at the end. How many more scourglings should we expect for the next wave?"

"Two hundred," Laird said easily, as if this wasn't a devastating number.

Two *hundred?*

Arthur wanted to blanch, but that would not be helpful. He felt everyone's eyes on him. He was the Legendary rider. He was the leader.

"Then your place will be up in the air. The scourglings will slow right before they start climbing the hill. Hit them with all the fire you can while they're bunched up. That goes for everybody." He looked at the others, one by one, and saw that their expressions were grim . . . but not despairing. "Hit them with everything we have. No holding back."

As he spoke his last few words, the terrible whistles started again.

* * *

Now that Arthur had gotten a broader view of how this dungeon was supposed to work, he saw how it made such an effective trap. By the eighth wave, people would be exhausted. Their mana levels run low.

Any help that came from the outside would be chancy at best—the one-way door opened only between the waves. And once someone was in here, they were committed to either win or die. And they'd be coming in blind, not knowing what shape their friends were already in.

However, if there was a team loyal enough, or desperate enough, it seemed like this dungeon should have been conquered before.

It still felt like he was missing a vital piece of information.

His first worry that the scourglings in the last wave would not only be more numerous but significantly stronger didn't play out. They were still the same type of scourglings as before. It seemed that the dungeoneer only had a blueprint for one. But numbers were on their side.

Laird's fighting made the biggest impact.

He was fresh to the battle, full up not only on mana but on strength. Corrosive purple candle-top flames drifted down from the sky like evil snowflakes. Wherever they touched the scourglings, they burned. And they continued to burn right through the body and out the other side without either spreading or stopping.

Arthur suspected Laird had quite a few aspects to his flame powers, as this was subtly different from the ones he had seen before as a child. But he wasn't complaining.

Using the enchanted metal bar, Arthur heated his own metal rivets and sent them flying at the scourglings that escaped Laird's wrath.

Meanwhile, Shadow used his teleport power to pop right in front of the dark forest. His jade sword flashed—he wielded it more like an expert swordsman than a dragon, so it was either enchanted or he had a card power to help. He popped out again to another location down the line of trees before the scourglings could properly turn and swamp him. Each teleport was a mere blink of time—hopefully not enough for the monsters that lived in the shadow space to find him.

Meanwhile, Joy and Brixaby continued their hit-and-run attacks with poisoned claws and void fire, respectively. Cressida's three bears, empowered by a renewal of her mana, rolled down the side of the hill like unstoppable forces, burning paths through the scourglings.

They were an effective team. So effective that the two hundred scourglings were whittled down to less than forty that managed to crest the top of the hill. Arthur was forced to take shelter in Cressida's shield bubble a couple of times. The mana renewal oatmeal didn't affect his Phase In, Phase Out card. He once again ran out of time.

But forty scourglings were much more manageable, especially when Shadow and Laird came to assist.

Before Arthur knew it, the last of the scourglings was disintegrating.

Laird pulled a second bowl of oatmeal out of his rune net.

"How does that not tip over and spill everywhere?" Joy asked, cocking her head to the side.

He shrugged. "I don't know much about enchantments. I just know that it doesn't."

"I would *very* much like to examine the runes on that net after this is done," Brixaby said, again eyeing it. Arthur had originally thought it was because he wanted the treasures inside. It turned out, he just wanted to study the runes.

The other dragon gave him a bland look. "We'll see." Then he pointedly tucked it away before Brixaby could get too close. As before, he shared the bowl.

"Two more waves," Arthur said. "We can do this. We're almost done."

"I thought you said . . ." Shadow trailed off and looked at Laird in confusion.

Laird grimaced. "One more wave, technically. One thousand scourglings."

Cressida, who had been taking a delicate bite of the oatmeal, nearly coughed it back out. "One thousand?"

Arthur felt the same.

"Yes," Laird said. "This requires a dragon's assistance, which is a reason human teams have failed in the past. I suggest we fight them from the air."

Brixaby grumbled at that, but he didn't outright object.

Cressida and Joy went up as a pair, and Arthur sat on Laird. There was a little bit of irony there. He never thought that he would be able to ride the dragon that had given him his first big break in life. For the sake of Brixaby's feelings, he didn't make a big deal of it.

Instead, he looked to his dark dragon. "If we can get you enough cards, we might be able to fly together soon."

Brixaby looked slightly mollified.

The ninth and final wave was . . . immense. So many scourglings came out of the forest that they toppled the trees. The weight of them—the physical effect of so many clustered together—killed the grass underfoot, leaving blackened rot behind. The shrieks were so loud that Arthur had to resist clapping his hands over his ears.

Instead, he grimly got on with the work, pelting the things from above. His once finely crafted chainmail shirt was in tatters from using all of the rivets.

When he ran out of those, he started pulling heavy objects out of his Personal Space and just tossing them down. He had one sturdily built chair and several large rocks that were sacrificed to the cause.

And when he ran out of that, he copied the spells Laird was using:

New Counterfeit spell obtained: Candle-flake Fall
Remaining Time: 59 Minutes 59 Seconds

New Counterfeit spell obtained: Ever-flame
Remaining Time: 11 Hours 59 Minutes 59 Seconds

New Counterfeit spell obtained: Corrosive Flame
Remaining Time: 59 Minutes, 59 Seconds

The last wave wasn't exactly dangerous, but it was a pure slog. Laird and Arthur could only rain down so many flames at a time, and Joy's movements were restricted when she had to worry about the safety of her rider on her back.

They did what they could, and slowly but surely, the scourglings were whittled down.

It was Brixaby who killed the last one. On a hill now blackened of life and covered with so many disintegrating scourglings that they didn't realize it was over until the whistling finally, *finally* stopped.

Laird landed, and everybody else followed. All stared around at each other as if they couldn't quite believe that they'd done it.

"What happens now?" Arthur asked, looking around. He half expected trumpets to blare out of triumph, and combat cards to rain down from the sky. But there was nothing.

Again, Laird and Shadow exchanged a look. This one was grim.

"The tenth wave," Laird said.

Brixaby let out a sound suspiciously like an undignified squawk. "You said there were nine!"

"The last wave is not a fight, but a test."

As soon as he said that, a bright line split the air and then expanded, resolving itself into a gleaming golden doorway.

Laird continued. "By design, only one is allowed access to the reward—the library. We either decide here who among us goes in, or we fight one another for the privilege."

CHAPTER 32

Shadow immediately lunged for Joy.

Standing on top of an open hill and not near any large shadows was surely what had kept him from teleporting and then attacking. Still, he was a fully grown dragon, and she had only recently become large enough to fly with her rider in the air. It wasn't a fair match-up.

Out of all of them, her venomous claws presented the most immediate offensive threat. That had to be why Shadow wanted to take her out first.

All of this flashed in and out of Arthur's head in a second of horror as he watched his former allies turn on them. Just as the dungeon was designed to do.

Arthur's arm snapped out, but he had used the last of the chainmail rivets during the final wave. They likely littered the grassy field, but he only had control if he was within an inch of them.

He was too far away to stop Shadow and Joy, to do anything but to yell, "No! Stop!"

The sound of his voice was drowned out by Cressida screaming Joy's name in horror.

Thankfully, Brixaby was closer.

He must have used every bit of his **Quick Sprint Flying** skill to get between the dragons—the lunging Shadow and Joy, who was no coward or a fool and was bringing up her claws to defend.

"STOP!"

Brixaby had a ridiculously deep voice for a dragon so tiny, and no concept of what being quiet was. His "whispers" could be heard across a room. So when he roared out the word at the top of his voice, Arthur felt it in his chest.

For a moment in time, Brixaby was a Legendary dragon, and he had just given a Legendary order.

Of course, Joy and Shadow had no choice but to stop, shocked still in place.

It lasted for only a moment, but that was all Arthur needed.

He wheeled around on Laird, who hadn't moved yet. Likely, the plan had been to capture or incapacitate Joy and then use her as leverage.

"We don't have to do this," Arthur said. "I have a way to get you all into the library."

Laird leveled an unimpressed look his way.

It was Shadow who replied, swinging his head around. "Lies. You just learned of this restriction a few moments ago."

"And you've been planning on turning on us from the start!" Cressida snapped. She ran to stand by Joy's side, and though Arthur knew she'd used up every bit of mana in the last wave, thinking it was the last, her hands were out as if she were about to try to summon her flame bear anyway. She'd probably burn through her life force to do it if she had to.

"Only with the deepest regret," Laird confirmed. "You have no idea how long I have waited for the chance to freely access the combat library, how many under my command—dragons and humans—have died in various attempts. If we had any warning you were going to try, we could have planned more properly. You could have been told what to expect."

"We need those combat cards," Arthur said.

"So do my people."

"No," Arthur repeated, "you don't understand. *We* need the cards. Us"—he gestured around the group to indicate them all—"and everybody out there. Anybody who's willing to take one. Two of them, if we can."

That took the dragon by surprise. He narrowed his eyes. "You intend to completely strip the council of all of its wealth? Return it to the hive? The people? Hmm. I've heard of governments like that. They tend to work well on paper, but within a generation—"

"No," Arthur said, "the council is working fine, but they're being shortsighted. They're not just giving wealth back to the hives and kingdoms. They're giving away our one source of protection, and if I'm right . . . we may need that protection."

He glanced at Brixaby, who nodded back.

"Protection? From who? The kingdom hives?" Shadow barked. "What do you know?"

"I believe that a scourgling known as the Mind Singer is out there gaining power right now. You remember the last demi-scourge-eruption?" Arthur said. "That was organized, in part, by her."

"And she is the same one we believe sent an assassin after Arthur," Brixaby said.

Laird rumbled deep in his throat. Outwardly, it sounded a lot like a growl, but Arthur recognized it as a pensive sound of thought. "The council investigated that.

I told you that particular free hive that man originally hailed from has been acting odd. Not returning messages. We are all independent, and that is not too unusual. Especially if there is internal strife. We aren't the kingdoms, and we can't compel other hives to trade or return inquiries. But you believe there's something more?"

"I think that there's a creature out there that has mind magic powers and has already shown that it can control a large number of people." Arthur added, "And since she sent an assassin after me, she likely knows this hive has Legendary cards within it."

He carefully kept out the fact that he and the Mind Singer had a history.

"And unlike the kingdom hives," Cressida added, "you don't have a large dedicated fighting force to repel an invader."

Shadow snarled. "If you're so concerned, why didn't you leave?"

"Other than the fact that we're essentially prisoners here?" Arthur asked.

Laird scoffed. "It is mostly bluster, you know. You likely could have left if you put your mind to it. But the council wanted to dangle the carrot first and leave the stick for an emergency. We wanted you loyal to this hive. As you said, you're Legendary."

"I don't see *you* leaving this hive," Brixaby said, pointedly to Shadow.

The other dragon shrugged. "I have nothing back at Wolf Moon, but I don't want to stick around any place that cannot defend itself. I am a dragon, not a sitting duck."

"Which is another flaw in your plan, Arthur," Laird said. "Most in this hive would not take a combat card if offered. They do not wish to fight."

"They might take a combat card if mind-controlled thralls were beating at their door," Arthur said. "But the point is, our goals aren't mutually exclusive. We all have reasons to get as many cards out of that library as possible."

"Agreed," Laird said, but then he leered at Arthur, all teeth, "Then you won't have any objection to *me* entering the library." He held up his rune net. "I will bring out as many cards as I can fit."

"I told you, I have a better solution," Arthur said.

"And what would that be?"

He hesitated. "Only one person can walk through the entrance into that library, yes? But you've read the parameters of this dungeon. Are there rules excluding anyone from bringing a personal storage space inside? Or a restriction from taking anything out from a personal storage space, once inside?"

Laird hesitated, and Joy made an "ooh" sound. She understood.

Shadow just looked slightly confused, and Brixaby, smug.

Instead of answering, Laird reached into his rune net and withdrew a sheaf of papers. Since they were meant for a dragon to handle, each page was at least three feet wide. However, the handwriting scrawled upon it was pin neat and ridiculously tiny. Laird must have practiced writing small.

"These are the notes based on the original design for the dungeon," Laird said, laying the papers down and flipping through them one by one. The tiny writing covered both sides of each page.

"Why is there so much?" Joy asked, craning her neck over.

Laird spoke absently as he read. "There's more to a dungeon than simply willing it into existence. Everything from how the clouds pass through the sky to the blades of grass exists on a blueprint. But the dungeoneer must still incorporate all aspects, including reactions to every conceivable encounter with the scourglings. For example, how they behave with a ten-person team versus a single person. The disintegration time, and the rules of the waves themselves. I'm told it's very complicated—ah, here." He tapped a claw at the middle of the page, and Arthur came over to look down at it. He had no problem reading upside down, but on top of everything else, the words were in shorthand and didn't make sense at first glance.

"There was a limit imposed on how many people may actively cross the threshold to the library: just one individual," Laird said. "And there is an allowance for dimensional storage, which makes sense. I know that Chablis uses a high-quality rune net to transfer cards due to their magical weight."

"That's fine, then," Arthur said.

Laird glanced up, and Arthur saw a frank assessment in his eyes. "What is your plan?"

"I can transport you all in my Personal Storage." Arthur hesitated for a moment, then added, "Well, there is a size limit, but I assume since you brought us to this hive in those nets, they'll fit you and Shadow? Then we can put the net in my storage."

"A storage within a storage," Laird mused.

Shadow was unimpressed. "Laird, this is ridiculous. You can go in and bring out all the cards using the net. Then he can do whatever he wants with his portion and give them away to crafters to his heart's content."

"No," Laird said softly, "that will not work."

"Why not?" Shadow asked.

"For the same reason you cannot simply stuff a card anchor full of cards. There is a magical weight to each card—especially the higher-ranked cards." Laird held up his rune net. "This could fit perhaps thirty Common, ten Uncommon, or three Rare cards for the dragons I wish to gift the combat cards to. Tell me, Arthur, how many cards can you fit in your Personal Space?"

"I don't know," he said. "It was made by a Rare card. I've held both a Rare and a Legendary card within it without any strain."

Laird nodded. "One benefit of cards over mere enchantments. The only question is: How can I trust that you will do as you say?"

That was easy. "Because I owe you," Arthur said. "There was no reason for you to give a random child a Legendary card, and I know you did not expect anything to come out of it."

The dragon looked away. "That is . . . perhaps not all of it."

"What do you mean?" Arthur asked, but he had phrased his last few words deliberately. He still remembered, when he first arrived at the free hive, Laird mentioning a "profit" from giving him his card.

Laird didn't answer for a moment. "*Officially*, the free hives do not have Legendary cards. The kingdoms would surely want them. But in reality . . ." He tilted his head. "There have been rumors of a Legendary card—some call it foresight. Others, prophecy. Some believe it's all a ruse. But just before I attacked Baron Kane's security cart, I was contacted through . . . means." He snorted. "I won't tell you how. But the words led me to believe that if I gave away the card I found, that gift would be returned tenfold. Also," he added, "had I brought that card back here years ago, I'm certain there would be no Mesa Free Hive left today. Unclaimed Legendary cards draw every greedy eye. They are a curse."

Arthur wasn't sure how he felt. He'd wondered so many times why Laird had given him the card back then. Opaque revenge on Baron Kane felt like a thin excuse, but his thinking he'd be rewarded later felt more . . . draconic. More real.

It also gave Arthur the exact opening he needed.

"You still put me on the path I'm on now. I *want* to do this for you, Laird. I want to help you, and I want to help everybody else gain the combat cards they need. You spoke about being rewarded tenfold. This is it."

And I can't be sure you won't betray me, he thought but did not add. *You're not going into that library alone.*

He could almost feel Cressida cringing off to the side. The trained noblewoman in her likely hated the fact that he openly admitted he owed the dragon, but it was the simple truth. Besides, it wasn't like their goals weren't somewhat aligned.

"It wasn't like I could use a Legendary card without poisoning my core," Laird muttered, "and I honestly didn't expect you to survive. You were so . . . tiny."

He tapped one claw on the ground, considering.

Arthur already knew what he was going to say. A human being might refuse out of further suspicion, or more likely, a sense of pride. If he were a man, his ego would be telling him to take on the library himself. He wouldn't be able to let himself trust Arthur.

Dragons were a bit more straightforward and practical.

"But if you betray us, naturally, I will kill you, Legendary rider or not. Then

I'll simply take back that card that I gave to you," Laird said, ignoring Brixaby's outraged growl.

But Brixaby didn't put up too much of a stink, either. He knew that the battle was all but won.

Laird sighed. "How does this Personal Space of yours work?"

CHAPTER 33

Arthur walked into the door made of light.

Despite Laird's assurances that the dungeon's trials were over, he still braced himself with a light thought on his Phase In, Phase Out card. He half expected to come face-to-face with a never-ending horde of scourglings, their pincers clacking.

Those scourglings would be showing up in his nightmares.

But there was no final "gotcha" from the dungeon. That had been in deciding who would claim the card library.

Instead, Arthur stepped into a cool white marble room. Completely bare of furniture, it was large enough to easily fit Laird and Shadow, with much room to spare for the rest of them.

The only feature was at the farthest wall from the door: thin shelving meant to house cards.

Those shelves were half empty.

Considering they stretched from floor to ceiling, this wasn't a disappointment.

Arthur longed to rush over there and start perusing the cards. But he had promises to keep.

He'd given his word up, down, and sideways that the first thing he would do would be to release the others so they could all approach the cards together.

Arthur removed Brixaby from his Personal Space.

The little dragon erupted into the air, claws already out. He'd been thinking along the same lines as Arthur.

He looped around in the air to take in the room in a flash. Then he looked back at Arthur.

"Naturally, this means we're taking our picks of the cards first?"

"And cards for Cressida and Joy," Arthur confirmed. He felt only a twinge of guilt about breaking a word he'd just given. "If there's anything especially suited for them."

"Yes, as my retinue riders, they should have the top choice." Brixaby started to buzz to the far wall and then stopped. "I believe Joy's cores are still too unstable to accept another card right away."

"If that's the case, we'll have to pick something to fit her as she grows." With great dignity, Arthur walked to the wall. Unlike what he actually wanted to do, which was to sprint over there like a madman and tear into the cards. He'd worked hard for this moment, and he wanted to savor it.

Glancing at Brixaby, he asked, "How is your core?"

An arrogant snort was his only response.

The two looked at each other, and then their patience snapped. Arthur ran flat out the rest of the way for the wall of cards. Brixaby, of course, got there first.

The dark dragon started examining the shelves from the top down. Arthur began from the bottom up.

If there was an order to the cards, he couldn't find it. They weren't sorted alphabetically but grouped together by type, even if the ranks were mixed up. The vast majority were Common with a few Uncommon and a couple Rares mixed in.

But each and every one had combat applications, which made them hugely valuable.

Arthur quickly scanned the titles.

Fog Veil, Water Vortex (which was an Uncommon but only worked when both parties were submerged in a large body of water), Ice Sword, Shocking Finale . . .

The next few cards in the row were earth elemental, which didn't interest Arthur.

The next, however . . .

Ember Rain
Uncommon
Elemental Combat

The wielder of this card will be able to conjure a shower of hot embers from twenty feet above their heads. They will be immune to any heat or impact-based damage, though allies and enemies will not be. This is a skill-based effect.

"How is that a skill?" Arthur's fingers itched to grab the card, stuff it in his card anchor, and see if his Master of Skills or Body Enhancement would pick it up.

But he knew it would be pointless. Master of Skills wouldn't permanently add anything combat or magic-related, and Ember Rain was both.

That was the reason he hadn't automatically scanned for weapon-based combat skill cards. While he would still consider them, he'd have to keep any card like that in his anchor. He wouldn't be able to pull the same trick he had with the Stealth Class card.

Shame, really. But not enough of one to make him hesitate more than a moment.

"This one would be good for Cressida." He reached for Ember Rain, then hesitated, glancing to the side.

The next card read:

Supernova Unleashed
Common
Elemental
The wielder of this card will gain the ability to release a massive explosion of fire and kinetic energy in a 360-degree ring. This release will not damage allies or the wielder's existing card effects.
Cooldown: 30 Minutes

"I think she'd like this even better," he breathed.

On the face of it, Ember Rain was the stronger card. Especially if it was leveled up. But the last sentence about the Supernova not damaging existing card effects made it the winner. He could easily see Cressida unleashing it while safe inside her mana bubble. There was no warning that it used mana, either, only the cooldown effect to balance it out.

This was an excellent card to use in a dire situation, and he wanted Cressida to have it.

"Why not both?" Brixaby asked, clearly seeing Arthur's dilemma. "We'll pick one for them now, and then they'll pick one for themselves later, remember?"

"Right." Feeling foolish, Arthur grabbed up the Supernova card and stuck it in his Personal Space.

It was . . . mighty tight in there, but luckily a card was thin, and as it was a Common, the magical weight was nothing at all.

"Have you found anything for Joy?"

In answer, Brixaby casually flicked a card down to Arthur.

Sharp as Nails
Common
Body Enhancement
This card grants the wielder the ability to lengthen finger and toenails to sharp knife points using mana. Higher mana costs will result in sharper nails. Advanced levels allow the user more control over this body enhancement.

Arthur stared. "I've seen this card before."

Immediately Brixaby zipped down to hover behind his shoulder, looking over the card with more interest. "Oh?"

"Years ago. How in the world did it end up here?" Letting out a breathy chuckle, Arthur flipped the card back and forth. The basic image was exactly as he remembered it, as was the description. "I was just a kid. It came from—well, it doesn't matter. He wasn't a good man. He actually plucked it out of his heart like it was nothing. I didn't even realize what that meant at the time." He shook his head. "I guess he never got it back."

"It will complement Joy's claws nicely when she's ready for it," Brixaby said.

Arthur agreed and added it to his Personal Space.

Now came the big questions. Arthur grinned at his dragon. "Find anything for yourself yet?"

He half expected Brixaby to produce a handful of cards. And he fully expected the argument to come—they had to be careful on their first picks not to take too many and tip Shadow and Laird off about what they'd done.

But Brixaby only said, "No, but I am still looking."

Then he buzzed back to the shelves.

Arthur returned to the same. The next section he saw had some weapons-based cards.

Now that would be useful. Brixaby was nowhere near large enough to carry Arthur. Until he had the might of a dragon under him, he'd be defending himself.

Most of the cards were Common and focused on a single sword aspect or skill.

Quick Draw Sword: Instantly conjure a sword made of mana.
Cross Guard Punch: Strike out using the cross guard of one's sword in a surprise strike up to 2X the wielder's strength.
Insta-Stab with a Sword: Skill-based. Guaranteed pinpoint accurate thrust with a sword. Does not work with daggers or other bladed objects.

As the last was a skill-based card, it was too good to pass up. Arthur plucked it out and briefly added it to his card anchor. He waited a moment for the notification that the skill had been added, starting at level 3. Then he removed it again and replaced it on the shelf.

Instantly, the skill grayed out and went dormant. Arthur couldn't use it without the card, but if he were ever able to get something like Penn's Master of Combat card . . . there was every chance he would have access to that skill.

"Aha!" Brixaby cried out, nearly startling Arthur into knocking against a shelf.

In the next instant, the little dragon flew down with a pair of cards clutched in his claws.

From the simple design on the back, Arthur knew their rank. "You're . . . trying to choose between Uncommon cards?" he asked.

"Hardly! This one shall be mine. And this one, yours." He pushed one of the cards to Arthur. "They are of the same set and complement each other nicely. I'm certain you'll agree."

Makeshift Weaponry

Uncommon

Combat

This card grants its wielder the intuitive ability to perceive ordinary objects
as potential weapons, and to wield them effectively to attack and defend.
This card does not grant the improvised weapons additional strength or
durability.

Arthur was not excited about that last line, but it did explain why the card was only an Uncommon. Still, it had possibilities. Especially paired with his skills in various tool proficiencies.

"I'm surprised you want an Uncommon," Arthur said, glancing up at Brixaby. "I never thought you'd settle for less than a Rare."

"Pah, a Rare would likely add a mana requirement, and you have too many mana-hungry cards as it is." Though Brixaby was hovering in the air, he still extended a pair of wings in the approximation of a shrug. "And you're not seeing the full picture."

"What do you—" Arthur stopped as he realized he had indeed been focusing on the wrong thing. "These are from the same set, and you're linked to all the cards in my heart deck. But wait, will I be able to link to your secondary core?"

Brixaby hesitated. "I don't know." Then, just as quickly, he regained his confidence. "But I don't see why not! Think of how powerful we will be if our cards can be separate, but whole!" He let out a booming laugh that came out somewhat maniacal.

Arthur's eyes narrowed. "You still haven't shown me your card."

"I am merely saving the best for last." Brixaby turned his card around for Arthur to read.

Combat Weaponsmith

Uncommon

Crafting

The wielder of this card possesses an innate understanding of the physics and
mechanics of weapons crafting. As a weaponsmith, the wielder receives a

25% bonus in strength and durability while using any weapons they created while wielding this card.

There was no doubt they were of the same set. The wording was similar, and the simple Uncommon designs on the back of the cards looked as if drawn from the same artist. One was a forge crossed by a sword. The other, Arthur's, had various tools like a hammer, scissors, and sewing needle also crossed by a martial-looking asword. Put the two together, however . . .

"So, if I improvise a weapon, will I get a bonus from the secondary card? Since, by using the first card, I officially 'made' it a weapon?" Arthur wondered.

Again, Brixaby shrugged. "Perhaps. Do you wish to find out?"

Obviously, the answer was yes.

Arthur added it to his heart deck. One advantage of using an Uncommon card was that the weight in his heart felt negligible.

He watched with anxiety as Brixaby added his to his newly formed secondary core.

Brixaby had said he was ready, but he couldn't help but remember what Joy had gone through—and how it had changed her on a fundamental level.

But Brixaby's secondary core was formed—newly so, but it counted. The little dragon shuddered from the tip of his nose to the point of his tail.

Alert: A card you have linked with shares a set synergy with your existing card.
Combat Weaponsmith to Makeshift Weaponry
These two cards have been combined into a pair.

Alert: Due to this Uncommon find, your basic Luck stat has been temporarily increased by +1.

"Huh," Arthur said. "That's the second time I've gotten a temporary luck boost."

"I received one as well," Brixaby said. "Luckily."

Arthur swatted at the dragon, who easily buzzed away in a dodge.

"Also," Brixaby added, buzzing to a lower shelf and plucking another card. "I wish to consume this Common Zephyr's Fury card."

Consuming a card was different than adding one to the core. For one, it was less risky, and for another, it would allow Brixaby to grow.

. . . Some. It was only a Common.

"What does it do?" Arthur asked.

"It's a combat movement enhancement used to allow the wielder a flying strike," Brixaby said. "Consuming it will strip most of the power, but I feel like I will add swiftness to my flying. Also, there is an earth card—"

"Choose one," Arthur said firmly. "And don't eat it yet. Everyone will figure out what happened if you're suddenly larger."

Brixaby grumbled under his breath but tucked the Zephyr's Fury card into his Personal Space.

Arthur spent a few moments tidying up the shelves and arranging the cards to cover any perceived gaps.

Then he nodded to Brixaby to walk with him back to the front of the room, where they'd first entered.

Arthur took in a breath. "Okay. We just got here, remember?"

"I don't know what you mean," Brixaby answered. "I certainly haven't added any new cards to my secondary core."

Arthur flashed him a grin. Then he reached into his Personal Space and mentally unstored Laird.

CHAPTER 34

Arthur let himself feel a little gratification when Laird popped out of his Personal Space, immediately bared his teeth, and summoned a lick of purple flame dancing at the end of each of his claws.

Despite his reassurances to Arthur that the library was safe, he, too, had been ready for a fight.

The dragon whipped around so quickly that Arthur had to duck to keep his head from getting knocked off by his large tail.

It only took a moment for Laird to see that there was no threat—the final room was indeed empty except for the cards along the wall.

Then he turned to Arthur, eyes narrowed in displeasure.

"You said that I was to be the first out of your Personal Space." He eyed Brixaby meaningfully.

Ah . . . whoops. In all the excitement, Arthur had forgotten about that little detail.

Brixaby swelled up in indignation. Before Arthur could get a word in, the little dragon buzzed right up in Laird's face, above the muzzle and between his eyes. "Arthur is *my* rider. Of course he sought me out instantly on arrival. We are a partnership, and half his cards wouldn't even work correctly without me!"

"Not half my cards . . ." Arthur started, feeling a little sidelined.

Laird, however, coughed out a laugh that had a burst of hot air behind it. The sudden change in air pressure sent Brixaby tumbling back, but with a blur of wings, he regained his spot, looking murderous.

"I suppose I should just take it on good faith you two didn't . . . peruse the combat cards before setting me free." Laird's voice practically dripped with sarcasm.

Arthur kept his expression as bland as he could, though he let a little exasperation leak into his voice. "I'm a man of my word."

"Man? You are still a pup, half grown. Though . . ." Laird took another look around the room, then at the shelves, which didn't look picked clean. "I suppose your little trick to get us in here has worked."

"I've held up my half of the bargain," Arthur lied. "It's time to hold up yours."

The dragon turned a hard glare at him. But it only lasted a moment.

"Spoken like a true Legendary rider. Even if"—he glanced at Brixaby—"you're still one with much learning to do."

Then he pulled out his rune net from his extra-dimensional space.

Laird's space wasn't nearly as large as Arthur and Brixaby's. But the addition of the net made all the difference.

He made a motion of dipping his clawed hand in and out, as if he were scooping out water from a bucket. But with each motion, Cressida and Joy appeared.

That had been the final terms that had won Laird over—Arthur and Brixaby wouldn't get Cressida and Joy back until Laird was released from Arthur's Personal Space first. Aside from Brixaby, they were the smallest persons and only just able to fit in his net. Seeing them, Arthur removed Shadow from his Personal Space. The two dragons had been a tight fit.

"It worked." Shadow looked around, seeming stunned. "I didn't allow myself to think it would . . ."

"Because you're a pessimist, my friend," Laird rumbled.

"But where are the cards?" Joy stretched her neck to look around, then made a loud gasp when she spotted the far wall. "Oh! I didn't see over your back. There they are. Let's take a look. Why are we all standing here? Let's get our cards."

"All the cards," Brixaby said, eager and enthusiastic, as if he hadn't seen them before.

The two dragons took off to the shelves.

"Wait." Laird slammed a large foot in front of Joy. It was effectively like planting a tree in front of her. She skittered to a stop.

The old Joy might have looked shocked, or more likely, tried to instantly make better friends with Laird. As she was now, Joy went from excited to angry, lips pulled back over green-tinged fangs. She flexed her still-unsheathed green forearm, but at Cressida's quiet word, she didn't attack.

For his part, Laird looked at Joy with interest but not overall concern. Arthur got the impression that this was a test for her as much as it was Laird throwing his weight around.

"I will not allow a free-for-all where we stuff in the first combat card that we see," Laird said.

"You aren't in charge," Brixaby snapped, but then added, "But yes, we will choose our new cards carefully. Then Arthur and I will give away the rest to those willing to fight, as we all agreed."

"I don't see any problems, then," Laird said, with a smile full of fangs.

Tired of watching the dragons fight for the top of the hierarchy, Arthur pushed past them all and strode, deliberately, to the far wall of cards.

Cressida gave him a concerned look but quickly matched her stride to join him. With a smug glance Laird's way, Brixaby flew beside Arthur.

Leaning on his **Acting** Skill, Arthur carefully controlled his expression to look alert and very interested in the cards, as if this were the first time he was setting eyes on them. Thankfully, the wall was rather wide—built on the scale of dragons, no doubt, and it allowed everybody to get a good place for viewing.

"Oh, there are so many," Joy burbled happily. "I was worried when I only saw this one wall's worth of shelves, but there are *so many* types of cards. Cressida, how do we decide?"

"I would suggest carefully," Laird rumbled. "Choose something that would complement your existing cards."

Joy thought about it for a moment, then she shook her head. "No way. It would be super boring if everything revolved around my poison claws or my quest powers—not that I know how that would happen—but I think it would be more fun to be like a bag of random tricks. Don't you?"

Laird gave her a dismissive look, and without an answer, plucked a card from the top shelf. One Arthur hadn't seen before.

"What's that?" he asked.

Laird glanced at him, and Arthur wondered if he was going to answer at all. Then the dragon said, "A Common card meant to help me control the temperature of the flame." He glanced at Joy. "It will complement my existing cards nicely."

Arthur tried—and failed—to keep a sense of dismay off his face. Had he seen that before, he would have considered it a top contender for Cressida's powerset.

"Arthur," Cressida said, turning to him with a card in her hands. "What do you think of this?"

She held up the card that he had been hoping she would pick: Ember Rain. He tried not to feel too smug.

"I think that would be perfect for you," he said honestly. "You're not going for, uh, a random bag of tricks like Joy?"

"Someone has to be the traditionalist here," she said with a light laugh.

"No way, Cressida. Don't pick that. I found the perfect card for you." Abruptly, Joy barged in, practically dancing from foot to foot in excitement. "And it's one of the few Rare cards, too." She paused. "One of the rare Rare cards?"

Cressida ignored the wordplay. "What is it?"

Proudly, Joy displayed the card. It was an intricately etched card with the outline of elegant cranes flitting around the back of the card, some spearing fish in inky water and others dueling with pointed beaks. As this was a Rare card, the movement of the pictures was intricate and beautiful. One crane stabbed the other, and the second exploded into . . . were those water droplets?

"Water Cranes?" Cressida asked.

"Yes," Joy said, nodding. "The ability to summon cranes made of water. That goes perfectly with your flame bears! Ohh, can I name one? Like how you named Wicker?"

"Is this card in the same set as your flame-bear summons?" Arthur asked.

It would be an incredible stroke of good luck, though . . . maybe not considering Arthur and Brixaby had just gained a point to their temporary luck stat. Maybe Cressida would be the one to benefit, considering she was their retinue rider.

But his hopes were dashed a moment later as she shook her head. "No, the cards in my flame-bear set are well documented. They're all different flame summons. This is just a similar card, except it's water."

Brixaby buzzed to Arthur's shoulder to get a closer look. "Cranes? Why aren't they sharks? Sharks are much fiercer."

"Sharks can't swim through the air, silly," Joy said. "Cranes can fly."

"Yes, but cranes are not made of water—"

Ignoring the dragons' bickering, Arthur watched Cressida. She held each card in her hand, biting her lower lip. He wished dearly he could tell her that he'd already picked out a card—and a good one at that. But not now with Laird and Shadow so close.

Finally, Cressida said, "I'll take the Cranes."

"Yay!" Joy cried.

Brixaby groaned.

"It'll complement your flame bears well," Arthur said. "Brix? Joy? Have you found one for yourself yet?"

"Sure have!" Joy said.

"Wait, really?" Arthur was a little taken aback, surprised that she was able to find two cards in such a short period.

Brixaby looked startled too and quickly flitted back to the shelves.

Joy proudly showed her card:

Strike Where They're Going to Be . . .
Common

Meta

The wielder of this card will intuitively grasp the flow of a single combatant while in battle. This passive ability will enable the wielder to anticipate movements and intentions and strike at the optimal time.

"I can't use it *now*, of course," Joy said easily, "but I think it will be nifty when my core stabilizes. I'll be able to poison scourglings so much more easily!" She held up her green claws as if in triumph.

"Not exactly a surprise—a meta dragon choosing a meta card," Laird said around a yawn.

In answer, Joy turned and stuck out her forked tongue at the other dragon. He chuffed.

Brixaby, meanwhile, roared out, "I have found the perfect match!"

He buzzed down, a card clutched in his claws. He pushed it at Arthur.

Night-Mare Fire
Uncommon
Illusion

Upon activation, an illusion of flames will grow outward from the length of the spine. While the illusionary night-mare effect is active, any sentient being the wielder touches will experience a vision of their deepest terror. This card uses mana.

"You . . . really want this card?" Arthur asked, unsure. He'd seen a dozen or so other cards with more potential than this. Also, while it didn't say so, he had a feeling that the mana cost would be high. That was usually the case with illusion-type cards.

Finally, he wasn't impressed with the horse-type name play and was surprised that Brixaby would lower himself to that kind of joke.

But Brixaby's red eyes glinted. "I'm certain."

His dragon had something in mind. Deciding to trust him, Arthur gave him the card.

"It seems, Arthur, you are the last to choose," Laird said.

"What about Shadow?"

The riderless dragon had slunk back away from the library so smoothly that Arthur hadn't realized he'd stepped away until that moment.

"I've chosen," Shadow said and didn't volunteer anything else.

"I'm surprised you haven't picked a card—or two—by now." Laird watched Arthur closely as if seeking a deception.

Arthur shrugged easily. "I wanted to get my dragon and retinue rider settled first."

"Hmm. Well, if you allow me to make a suggestion . . ." Laird reached to the top shelf, which was much higher than Arthur could view without a ladder.

If Arthur wasn't focused on his own deception and watching Laird for signs he'd figured it out, he might not have caught the sleight of hand.

Laird acted like he pulled a card from the shelf, but for a split second, the tips of his claws disappeared in thin air.

He withdrew a card.

"This might synergize well with your current deck," Laird continued.

20-Point Spree
Uncommon
Body Enhancement
*The wielder of this card can use a once-a-day boon to temporarily
increase their base attribute by twenty points. This effect lasts ten minutes.
Afterward, the chosen attribute is reduced by 50% for one hour.*

Several things occurred to Arthur at the same time. The first was that he was now *convinced* he had seen Laird pluck the card out of his own Personal Space. This was not a combat card, and there was no way Brixaby would have missed it while perusing the shelves. This also meant that while Arthur had been discussing cards with Cressida and Joy, Laird could have easily been plucking ideal cards for his own dragons from the shelf and shoving them into his Personal Space.

Arthur and Brixaby hadn't exactly counted the cards before letting everybody out.

And the last thing, of course, was that Arthur very, very much wanted this card. Yes, it had some significant drawbacks once used, but that was the nature of a high-quality but low-ranked card. They tended to be double-edged swords.

Best of all, he could add it to his card anchor and not his heart deck, saving himself valuable space.

Arthur hoped he didn't let any of the greed he felt cross his face.

"Yes," he said calmly, as if his heart wasn't beating rapidly in his chest, "I think that this card will work nicely."

"I suspected as much," Laird said, which brought Arthur to the last point. If Laird was giving Arthur a card out of his own personal stash . . . why? What did he think he could gain?

He set that question aside for now. Slipping the new card into his card anchor, he dismissed the notification that asked which attribute he wanted to add twenty points to. He could only use that feature once a day. Best to save it.

"Now that that's all settled, let's divide up the remaining cards," Arthur said. "I intend to bring out as many as I can—I don't think that the council will give us a second try at this dungeon."

Laird's dark chuckle told him he was correct.

"Everybody, go through the cards and set aside anything minimally or completely useless," Arthur continued.

These were all combat cards, but it didn't mean that they were all *great* combat cards. For example, he saw a card that turned chicken feathers into . . . chicken-feather-shaped swords. The conjured swords were incredibly sharp, but it wasn't practical. He'd only bring cards like that out if he had room to spare.

"Hey, I have a question," Joy said, "how do we get out of here?"

Arthur looked around, and so did everybody else. He hadn't realized it until now, but there was no door leading to the outside.

For a moment, Arthur was flummoxed.

Shadow spoke up. "I sense a dark mass of shadow beyond that wall." He used his tail to point back to the direction where they had entered the room. "I suspect it's a false wall. Probably one last trap to keep in those the council didn't want entering in the first place."

"Pretty sneaky," Joy said, "but after a while, anybody trapped in here would try everything to get out. So it wouldn't stop us for long."

Shadow merely shrugged and then looked away, keeping his thoughts to himself.

"What do you think the council will do once they discover our theft?" Cressida asked.

"Likely launch an investigation," Laird said. "Thankfully, we don't have card users who specialize in forensics. That's been a problem when we have occasional crimes committed with no firm suspects."

Arthur remembered Doshi, one of the first dragons he had ever met. Between his and his rider's linked cards, he could look back through time and project an illusion showing what had happened at the point of a crime. It wasn't a powerset useful at hunting scourglings, so he had been sent around to different towns on the outskirts of the kingdom to solve problems and build up goodwill for the hives. He certainly made an impression on Arthur as a young boy.

"And," Laird continued, with distinct satisfaction in his tone, "the council will likely put me in charge."

"The fox guarding the hen house?" Cressida asked in surprise. "Won't they be suspicious when your dragons appear with new combat abilities?"

"Child," Laird said heavily, "I'm not like you, who plans to give out cards willy-nilly. My wing riders will be carefully chosen for discretion."

"You might be glad we did," Arthur said quietly. "Combat cards will be needed soon."

Laird gave him a hard look. "Are you certain about that?"

Arthur nodded. "As certain as I can be."

He just wished that he wasn't.

Arthur had previously emptied the contents of his Personal Space back in the final wave of the dungeon to fit Laird in there. He didn't think that he was essentially hoarding junk like Cressida and Joy had joked, but he did have a lot of items he hadn't touched since he originally stored them.

The only things that he kept were small, light, and important. The purple apples, as well as a host of other herbs and magical components he had managed to scrape together, along with a few choice weapons and tools, including some empty leather satchels in case he found more. Oh, and the chicks and turkey poults. A few books, of course. An extra set of clothing including a thick coat, a few emergency meals and some skins of water, his basic first-aid, a length of rope, and his spare bedroll. And a few other—minor!—items here and there. That was all.

So, his Personal Space was about as empty as it could be. Even so, he was able to fit almost two hundred cards in there.

Unlike storing Laird and Shadow, the problem wasn't size. It was the magical weight of each card. Eventually, Arthur started to feel like he had eaten an overly large meal. The feeling of discomfort—of being overly full—only grew more acute as he added card after card. Eventually, he could only add the Commons, and then it became too much to do even that.

"I'm done," he said, bending down to rest his weight on his knees and panting.

"My turn," Brixaby said. He started to shove a card into his Personal Space, but then stopped, wincing, and then looked at the card—an Uncommon—as if it had betrayed him.

"Full?" Arthur asked.

"It appears so. I access my Personal Space through your card, but it seems like there is a limit."

Arthur let out a breath. "I was hoping it wouldn't be like that. We both have our own Personal Spaces . . ."

"Yes, but your magical weight is a different thing entirely," Laird said. "If I shoved fifty cards into this rune net, it would unravel as if I had shoved in a ton of brickwork and then tried to fly around with it. Or more than one Rare pair," he added, looking at Joy. "You are both heavy."

Joy ignored that. "So how did you steal that noble's library?" she asked, cocking her head. "I'm pretty sure that's what you guys did right before you kidnapped us, remember?"

"Those were specialized nets." Laird flicked his tongue out in distaste. "And obviously well-guarded by the rest of the council. I couldn't very well take off with one of those nets without raising suspicion."

Arthur frowned at the shelves still full of cards. He hated to leave so many behind, but he couldn't think of another solution.

"Okay, Cressida, if you have any room in your card anchor, grab a card or two, otherwise . . . I think we're done here." He looked around and didn't see any objections. It was time to go. If people noticed their absence, it would raise the suspicions of the council.

Arthur had no idea how much time had passed on the outside. A search might have been launched for them already.

Well, at least I get to try out my new stealth skills, he thought dryly. *Getting back to the hive without raising suspicion will be fun.*

But if they managed it . . . he was looking forward to experimenting with his new cards. For the first time, he had some solid ways to defend himself. While he still wasn't entirely combat focused, it made for a nice change.

And he couldn't wait to see the looks on Cressida and Joy's faces when he surprised them with the other cards he and Brix had picked out.

As Shadow had said, the back wall was not real. Joy easily tore through it with her claws to expose another few feet of space beyond, and a brightly lit exit.

While it seemed there was a restriction on more than one person coming in, nobody had bothered to create one upon leaving.

Without thinking, Arthur strode forward through the exit first.

He fully expected to be half blinded by bright desert light. Instead, he was greeted by darkness and a star-filled sky. It was still night. Could it be that all the fighting had only taken a few hours? Or had time passed differently inside the dungeon?

But he couldn't dwell on it for long. He wasn't alone.

Several large dragons stood sentinel around the dungeon entrance. Arthur didn't recognize any of them.

PART 4
DRAGON (RIDER)

CHAPTER 35

Arthur's first worry was that these were dragons from the Mesa Free Hive's council. Maybe they had some sort of enforcement group that didn't include Laird.

Except . . . there weren't any insignia visible. Some of the crafter dragons wore elaborate collars to show off their skills with their craft. Woodworkers had intricate pieces made of wood, for example. Metalsmiths and jewelry makers had much the same.

These dragons didn't have a thing that set them apart from the rest of the hive's population.

In addition, they looked down at Arthur with expressions completely devoid of anger, worry, or even triumph that they had caught their prey. There was practically nothing in their eyes. It was as if they had all come to meet Arthur on a random lovely night out on the shores of the lake.

The largest of the four was a female yellow nearly as large as Horatio's dragon, Sams. However, she carried many more wrinkles about her eyes and nostrils, indicating she was older. She was the first to speak.

"So, you are the dungeon survivor."

The survivor. They knew he'd come from the dungeon.

Arthur didn't bother to answer her. Instead, he stepped to the side of the dungeon's entrance.

A moment later, Brixaby erupted into the air. He took a split second to look around at his surroundings. Then up at the dragons.

Immediately, he flared his top two wings menacingly while the bottom two continued to buzz to keep him aloft.

"And who do you think you are?" he demanded. "Don't bother trying to raid the dungeon after us. We have just cleaned it out. Ha!"

Well, there went Arthur's half-baked idea to pretend he didn't know what they could possibly mean by "dungeon."

Again, the yellow spoke. Though her expression remained oddly blank, her voice dripped with menace. "You ask who we are? I will tell you. We are the—"

Another bright flash of light from behind Arthur. Joy appeared.

"Oh, it's still nighttime!" she exclaimed before looking up at the other dragons. "Hello! Who are you?"

"We are—"

Another flash and Cressida was there. She took a startled breath upon seeing the four dragons. Immediately, her political mind went to work. "I suppose you're from the council? No." She corrected herself with a shake of her head, "You aren't wearing the proper insignia. What is this about? Who are you?" She glanced at Arthur for an explanation, and he shrugged.

The yellow dragon spoke. "We are the—"

Another two flashes, one followed quickly by the other. Laird and Shadow had arrived.

Now we outnumber them, Arthur thought smugly. *Assuming I ever find out who they actually are.*

"Who, by the card who spawned you, are you?" Laird barked, going instantly into aggressive mode. He was smaller than the yellow dragon, but when he flared his wings in anger, he cut quite the figure.

Arthur couldn't help himself. "They've been trying to tell us."

Despite the many interruptions, the yellow dragon didn't seem perturbed. No exasperation or annoyance crossed her features. The same with the others. It was as if they were completely accepting of the circumstances and only vaguely interested in whatever happened next.

And there was something else. One of the dragons, the smallest, kept catching Arthur's attention. By his size, he was perhaps only six months old and vividly scarlet red. Even his claws were colored like blood. Outwardly, he looked just as passive as the others. But there was something else that Arthur couldn't put his finger on. Something was *wrong* with the dragon. Whatever it was put Arthur on edge.

He caught Brixaby glancing repeatedly at the dragon, too, with his muzzle wrinkled in distaste. It looked like he wanted to snarl or sneeze, but couldn't decide on which.

The yellow dragon waited an extra moment, as if to make sure no one else was about to pop out of the dungeon before speaking. "We are the—"

"Oh, I do know you!" Joy cried. "You're the scouts I saw flying overhead earlier. I'm sorry to say you didn't do a very good job. You missed us completely when we were over by the mesa." Joy looked like she wanted to pat the other dragon's paw in sympathy. "I'm sorry. Maybe you'll do better next time."

"Joy, let them talk," Cressida said.

The yellow dragon, who still had not shown a hint of impatience, was finally able to complete a full sentence. "We are the chosen emissaries sent to deliver a message to Arthur Rowantree."

"Emissaries?" Immediately, Arthur's mind flashed to Wolf Moon Hive. Had he been discovered at last? He dismissed that worry a moment later. These dragons didn't look familiar to him at all, and Wolf Moon was a smaller hive.

"Yes," the yellow said, finally showing some emotion: a curled lip over a fang. "We have been sent to express Our Lady's displeasure to Arthur the Liar."

The second dragon, a blue, added, "Arthur the Deceiver."

The third, a brown, intoned, "Arthur the Betrayer."

Arthur glanced at the scarlet dragon, but she remained silent.

"So you're from the Mind Singer," Arthur said flatly. He reached for bravado that was easy to fake, considering he had just come from multiple life-and-death battles. Was this night ever going to end?

Or maybe it wasn't false bravado but a sense of relief. The Mind Singer was the best one to find them from a lot of bad choices.

If Wolf Moon had discovered he and Brixaby were at Mesa Free Hive, the king would be told at the very least. He might choose to move against the entire hive. Considering the unstable man was partnered with a Mythic, that was the last thing Arthur wanted.

Assassins paid by his uncle's side of the family were an equally unappealing choice. Arthur didn't give a damn about Lional Rowantree, but his feelings around his cousin, Penn, were complex. It didn't help that Penn had a combat card within the same set as Arthur's own. Those future implications weren't something he felt comfortable thinking about, much less sharing with Brixaby, who hated Penn with a passion.

One cousin would have to kill the other.

So yes, being confronted by the Mind Singer's minions was the lesser of those evils. Also, Arthur had a growing list of enemies. He should do something about that.

"Have you come to try to assassinate me?" Arthur added. He figured the answer was yes, but it was worth asking. "Again?"

"No," the yellow said. "We have come to raze everything you love and hold dear to the ground. Then we will bring you pain as you have never known before, until you give up your cards, including the ones you just stole from the dungeon—yes, Our Lady knows of that, as she knows of all things—to make the pain cease. Only then will we grant you your wish and put you to death like the animal you are—"

With an outraged roar, Brixaby flew in front of Arthur. "You have come too late. We have plundered the dungeon of all its treasures. Now we are stronger than you could possibly imagine. Move aside, Uncommons, and perhaps I will let you live."

Arthur knew Brix was tired down to his core, but one would never know based on his attitude.

Half grinning, Arthur opened his mouth to snark something like "You'd better listen to him," but something Brixaby had said caught his attention.

Uncommon.

Yes, the four dragons were Uncommons, weren't they?

But the scarlet didn't feel like one.

That sense of oddness pinged in Arthur's mind, and he finally realized what had been bugging him about the dragon. She felt magically heavier. Though the outside was Uncommon, the inside was . . . different.

Mind Singer, what have you done?

As one, the four dragons rose onto their hind legs, their wings spread wide. It wasn't the best pose for battle since that move exposed a dragon's more vulnerable underbelly. But doing it in perfect unison, wingtip to wingtip, made for an impressive sight.

Joy's whispered "What are they doing?" was drowned out by the dragon's speech.

The yellow was first. "We are no mere Uncommons."

The blue piped up next. "Our Lady has granted us purpose."

"And she has granted us vision," added the deep voice of the brown.

For the first time, the scarlet spoke. Her voice was as young as Arthur thought. "And she has granted us power."

It hit Arthur and Brixaby at the same moment. Arthur, because he had come to a terrible realization. Brixaby, likely, because of his danger sense.

That Uncommon had a higher card in her core.

Arthur only had time to yell, "Cressida! Shield!"

CHAPTER 36

The scarlet dragon opened her mouth and unleashed a Legendary power.

What blasted from between her jaws was more of a force than a sound. It seemed to vibrate the seawater, the earth, and the very air around them. Yet notes hung in the air like snippets of a forgotten song. It was beautiful. But mostly, it was terrible.

Cressida's bubble shield snapped up.

Rocks the size of Arthur's head were thrown in all directions by the force of the blast. Most bounced off the shield. Those that hit the shield dead on stayed in place as if glued. They seemed to vibrate in place. Then they crumbled into gravel before Arthur's eyes.

The sound was almost impossible to describe. All-encompassing. A bone-deep pain that struck everywhere at once. Arthur clapped his hands over his ears, but it didn't make much of a difference. He glanced over at Brixaby just in time to make sure he had made it inside the bubble, too.

The dark dragon had made it in. He buzzed to land on Joy, who was cowering, nearly flattened on the ground. She vanished into his Personal Space.

Joy being Joy must have granted him permission without him needing to ask. Or maybe she had just longed to get away.

Instinctively, Arthur used his Phase In, Phase Out card so that the terrible force went through him.

And he saw from the transparent quality of Brixaby's scales that he had done the same.

He couldn't extend that protection to Cressida. Her hands were also clapped over her ears, her mouth open in a silent scream.

Arthur wished that he could throw her into his Personal Space, too. But she was the only one who could keep the mana shield up—which was a thin, imperfect Rare barrier between them and the destruction outside.

Arthur's gaze flicked out beyond the boundaries of the bubble.

Laird had dived behind the shield, curled up as tight and small as the dragon could reasonably get to keep every part of him behind Cressida's bubble. His head was practically buried in the rocky soil. Arthur had no idea how much protection that would give him, but at least he was doing better than Shadow.

He had been caught completely out in the open and seemed to be trying to use his teleport powers to get away. Darkness passed over his scales once or twice, right before it was shattered by the sound wave.

He collapsed in place, blood gushing from his eyes, mouth, and dimples dragons had on the sides of their head in place of external ears.

Then his scales started peeling away as if ripped off by the force of a hurricane.

Arthur looked away.

Shadow wasn't the only dragon in trouble.

The scarlet Uncommon was dying.

Only a few seconds had passed since the dragon had opened her mouth, but a growing blackness had started mid-chest—where dragons kept their cores—and was rapidly expanding. It looked like how Joy's poison affected the body. Only this was not just a rot Arthur could see, but one he could also somehow *feel.* It was as if the power of the card was leaking outward, tearing and destroying the dragon as it did so.

He'd always been told that a lower-rank dragon taking on a higher-rank card would poison them. He thought it was a slow process, but apparently using the card quickened it.

Less than ten breaths of space after the dragon first activated the card, the blackness had extended down all her limbs and finally up her throat.

The force/sound cut off abruptly, and the dragon staggered to the side, her eyes wide and somehow clear and startled.

Then she fell to the side.

The three other Mind Singer dragons had not been affected by the blast—no doubt protecting allies was part of the card's power. The moment the scarlet dragon collapsed, the blue dragon pounced on her body.

"No!" Arthur saw what was about to happen. "Cressida, drop the shield!"

Still staggering, breathing heavily as if she had just run a mile, Cressida only stared at him. She looked like she was in shock.

Arthur turned and used his Phase In, Phase Out to pass through the barrier. He pointed. "Stop that dragon!"

The blue was above the scarlet's body, beckoning the core cards out so that he could take them. He'd surely insert the Legendary card in himself, which would be a suicidal act. But one that would likely kill Arthur and the others.

Cressida's Rare shield had barely held on. One more blast . . .

Brixaby had seen what was about to happen, too. He used Arthur's Phase In, Phase Out and buzzed up and around the shield, back toward Laird. Arthur didn't know what he was planning, but he hoped it was good because he had almost no idea how he was going to stand up to three dragons and survive.

But almost no idea was better than none at all.

Dexterity or Luck? he thought, but the choice was obvious. He activated his 20-Point Spree card and threw all twenty points into his Luck.

Another one of the enemy dragons, a brown, lunged for him first.

Arthur pulled out a length of rope.

It was rope was only about fifteen feet long and coiled neatly together. Much too short to tie up a dragon.

He concentrated on his Makeshift Weaponry card and felt an idea spring to his mind as if by pure inspiration.

The dragon arched downward as if to bite him in half. Arthur suspected this was a ruse, the Mind Singer would want him alive at least long enough to see the rest of his friends and allies die. Her thralls had as much. But it would stall him.

Arthur flicked out the rope and snapped it back. The motion was clumsy, but the dragon's head was close, and he had a large target. Plus, Arthur was feeling lucky.

The end of the rope flicked right against the dragon's eye.

The brown let out a shriek of surprise as dust erupted around its feet. It pulsed its card in instinctive surprise.

That gave Arthur the second he needed to slip by it.

But the brown had at least succeeded in stalling him for a few heartbeats. That was all the blue dragon needed to take the Legendary card from the dead scarlet.

Arthur caught a flash of the card. The brilliance and flowing inky images told him this was indeed a Legendary card.

Then it was gone as the blue shoved it into his own chest.

Oh no.

Arthur took a breath, about to call for everyone to retreat. He wasn't worried about himself, but Brixaby, Cressida, Joy, and Laird. If the card could choose who was impacted, surely they would die before Arthur.

Before he had the chance, a dark, Brixaby-shaped streak shot to the blue dragon.

. . . And up his nose.

The sound the blue made was a part snort, part squeal. That squeal got louder when smoke started billowing out of his nostrils. Then the blue dragon flung himself to the side, desperately pawing at his muzzle.

Apparently he had trouble concentrating enough to activate the card with his sinuses literally burning. Brixaby must have activated the enchanted metal bar.

Arthur turned at a roar to see that Laird was alive and bringing down a whirl-wind of purple candle-top flames on the yellow dragon.

The yellow countered with a shield not too dissimilar from Cressida's, only one made of pure light. Unfortunately, it was an Uncommon facing a Rare power. It had only limited effectiveness. Some of the candle-top flames penetrated the shield and the yellow screamed as they burned her scales.

Meanwhile, the blue was flinging its head back and forth. He dislodged Brix-aby, who shot out, end over end, clutching his fire-enchanted metal bar.

Arthur darted to the side to catch him, but with quick beats of his wings, Brixaby regained control.

The blue had suffered horribly. Half of one nostril was burned away, leaving a hole in its face.

Not that it mattered. He'd soon be dead from the card poisoning his core anyway. He looked down at Arthur with triumph in his eyes. For a moment, it was like locking eyes with the Mind Singer.

Arthur heard the snippet of a song ringing in the back of his mind: lyrics of command.

The blue opened his mouth.

So much for luck, Arthur thought.

At that moment, Joy, with Cressida sitting on her back, erupted from his shadow.

Cressida had used Shadow's teleport power, which meant . . .

"No, you don't!" Joy cried, leaping up and slamming her venomous claws into the base of the blue's throat to stop the noise before it could start. For good measure, she bit his face to pump more poison in.

The blue died without uttering so much as a peep.

CHAPTER 37

The yellow dragon died moments later, burned alive by Laird's candle-top flames.

The only one of their enemies left alive was the brown dragon.

"Give me the card," he sang, pushing through a new storm of purple candle-top flames to lunge at the dead blue dragon. The flames sizzled on his scales, but he didn't react at all. Looking closer, Arthur saw his scales were reinforced with either hard-packed dirt or stone.

The brown's focus was absolute, his yellow eyes open and manic as he ran toward the blue.

"Stop him!" Arthur yelled.

Joy spun around to face him, teeth and claws bared.

Brixaby got there first. He swooped over to the brown's chest. The brown was so focused on retrieving the other dragon's card that he didn't even glance down at the Legendary dragon.

Big mistake. Brixaby plucked a card right out of his core.

That got the brown's attention.

He spun around with a wheeze. "Give me my card! My card . . . my card . . . Give me my card . . . My rider's card," he said still in that odd lyrical cadence.

Joy lunged, but Arthur had sensed Brixaby's plan and changed his mind. "No, wait! Joy, stop! We need him alive."

All the other dragons were dead, and at the very least, they needed somebody to be able to answer questions.

"What card? This card?" Brixaby waved the brown's card in front of him and deftly avoided a snap of the dragon's teeth.

The brown was in bad shape. Laird's candle-top flames had still made an impact. Several clusters of scales were burned through to the skin, leaving red welts. He was clumsy, and with every other step, he kept looking back toward the blue dragon, as if fighting a compulsion: the desire for his rider's card and what the Mind Singer was telling him. He staggered over every step, one foot going one way, the other pointing in a different direction.

All in all, he made a pathetic sight for such a large, stolid dragon.

Joy came to stand between Cressida, Arthur, and the brown dragon, her wings spread in defiance in case he turned his anger toward them.

But Brixaby was doing his best to keep the brown's attention, waving the card in front of his snout and generally working the other dragon into a froth of anger.

"What kind of dragon lets their rider's card fall into the claws of another?" Brixaby said pitilessly. Then he openly stuck it into his Personal Space. "You want it? Come in here and retrieve it."

With a roar, the brown dragon closed in on Brixaby.

For a heart-stopping second, Brixaby let him.

The moment the brown dragon touched him, however, he disappeared.

"Wait . . ." Cressida swung around to look at Arthur in accusation, as if he had just pulled that trick. "Didn't you say you needed permission to put someone sentient inside your Personal Space?"

Arthur nodded, eyebrows raised. He was impressed. "He must have wanted to go in there after his rider's card—Brix!"

Brixaby dropped like a stone, hitting the ground and groaning, holding his head.

Arthur rushed to his side. The little dragon waved him off.

"There's too much in my Personal Space. Between that dragon and the cards . . . I'm full." He rubbed his stomach, looking like he was ready to burst.

"Will you be okay?"

The dark dragon looked at him, his bloodred eyes full of defiance. "I am Brixaby! Of course I can handle a mere Uncommon in my Personal Space." He flapped his four wings a little feebly and barely managed to lift himself into the air.

Arthur reached down and picked him up. "Why don't you take a break?" he suggested.

Brixaby grumbled but climbed onto Arthur's shoulder.

He returned to see Laird standing over Shadow's body. The dragon stared down, a bleak look on his face.

"He was one of *my* dragons," he said as Arthur, Brixaby, Cressida, and Joy joined him. "I am only a Rare; our bonds are not the same as it is between a Legendary and their retinue, but . . . He had sworn himself to follow me."

"I didn't know that," Arthur said. Then he asked the question that had been bothering him since seeing Shadow arrive with Laird in the dungeon. "Has he *always* been one of your dragons?"

"Do you mean, was Shadow a spy at Wolf Moon Hive?" Laird asked. "No. But he quickly saw the value of joining the cause." He looked to Cressida. "You have inherited his cards, then?"

Arthur stiffened, wondering if they were about to fight. After all, Laird had just said that Shadow was his friend. Arthur hadn't had time to process what he'd seen: Cressida had harvested Shadow's teleport card.

Cressida faced the large dragon. Standing at her side, Joy bared her teeth in an unsubtle threat.

"Only because of a great need," Cressida said, and from her anchor, which looked like a tiny jeweled purse, she pulled out seven other cards. "I was pressed for time," she said, a tactful way of mentioning they were in the midst of a battle, "and was forced to take one, but as his friend and leader, you should have the rest of his deck. I'm certain that's what he would have wanted."

Brixaby sat up straight on Arthur's shoulder. "You're giving back the Shadow Teleport?"

Cressida steadily held out the other cards—several of them were Rare from what Arthur could discern, though he couldn't read the titles. "Unfortunately, the teleportation card had to go into my heart to use it."

Arthur was certain that was a lie, but he admired her steely resolve.

Laird's eyes narrowed, and Arthur wondered if he was going to contest this or if he would let it go. The Shadow Teleport was a valuable power—Arthur should know; he and Brixaby's powers had copied that card's power on several occasions.

But Cressida was offering a deck of cards as a gesture of goodwill. That wasn't insignificant. She held Shadow's lifetime of wealth in her fingers.

With a delicate shifting of his claws, Laird took the cards and looked them over.

"I didn't know Shadow for long," he said, "but anybody with eyes could see that the death of his rider broke something inside him. It was why he did not mind so much coming to our free hive. With that said, I think he would be angry if the linked card that he and his rider created together were separated."

Brixaby shuddered on Arthur's shoulder as if disturbed by the thought.

Laird plucked one card out and returned it to Cressida. "And of course, as the lead investigator for the council, I will be *required* to look at the cards of our attackers." He turned to gaze around at the dead dragons meaningfully, eyes lingering on the scarlet, which would likely have a natural card to match his flame power. Then his gaze focused on Brixaby. "Can that brown escape your Personal Space?"

"No, it's timeless in there. He is my prisoner," Brixaby said, standing proudly. Only Arthur knew how much that, along with all the other combat cards, was straining him.

Laird snorted. "Then we have another issue to discuss, Arthur Rowantree."

"The Legendary card," Arthur said.

"Yes. Interestingly, I have run across the same issue, both times in your presence. As I've told you, a Legendary card in a free hive represents an imbalance. Every scruple around not having a combat card will grow wings and fly away if the humans hear there is a Legendary up for grabs. And I suspect, you would fight me for it," Laird added wryly.

"I would never fight an ally," Arthur responded, albeit not entirely truthfully, "but I understand as a Rare dragon you can't have it."

"Stop being so diplomatic, Arthur," Brixaby said. "He saw Uncommons become core-poisoned. That's the only reason he didn't keep Master of Skills. He won't keep the Legendary card now. *I* will take care of it."

Brixaby attempted to rise into the air as if to retrieve the card himself, but he quickly dropped to the ground again, panting.

"Is he okay?" Laird asked.

Once again, Arthur picked up his now-disheveled-looking dragon. "He has a lot in his Personal Space, and we're sharing the card," he explained, and carried Brixaby to the blue dragon.

Since the dragon was dead, with its cards ready for harvest, they didn't need Brixaby's ability to extract cards from decks. Once they were some distance away from the others, Arthur took the opportunity to activate his Stealth Class skills and ask quietly, "Why didn't you take out his card in the first place? You went for the nose, not his core."

"I intended to," Brixaby grumbled. "But my danger sense warned me away."

Arthur hesitated. "Is it going off now?"

He cocked his head as if consulting an inner voice. "No."

"Let me pull the cards, just in case," Arthur said.

He harvested them without any issue. The blue had two additional Uncommon cards besides the Legendary.

Naturally, Arthur read the Legendary first.

Full of Sound and Fury
Legendary
Combat (Elemental – Sound/Force)

The wielder of this card will be able to emit a sonic blast that vibrates molecules in air, water, solid matter, and living flesh. This sonic blast will vibrate molecules at increasing speeds, and at its most potent, may tear apart molecular bonds. In such cases, this card will provide a 50% damage reduction due to any backlash. This power travels out in a cone-shaped attack, though the wielder may be able to choose allies to be immune to the power. Objects may be damaged up to one mile away.

This card both uses and unlocks mana. The mana pool for this card is set

*apart from a secondary pool, so that the user may always have access to this
card even if all other mana is drained. With practice, the user may be able
to extend or refine their attack range.
Seek cards within the same set for additional elemental powers.*

That was terrifying. Arthur wasn't sure what a molecule was, but he understood that tearing it apart would not be a good thing. He guessed that these molecules, whatever they were, likely existed in living beings like Shadow. The poor dragon had been torn apart from the inside out.

Off balance and unthinking, Arthur shoved the Uncommon cards Brixaby's way. "Can you hold these cards?"

Brixaby's dark complexion somehow managed to look green. "I . . . would rather not." He looked like he was so full he wanted to throw up.

"Oh. Of course." Arthur's Personal Space was so full he couldn't even fit in one of the Uncommon cards, let alone bear the magical weight of the Legendary card, so he retrieved an empty leather satchel from his Personal Space—one of the few items he had kept there because of its compactness. The satchel was simple with a drawstring top. No one would ever guess there was a Legendary card inside.

Out of curiosity, he glanced at the Uncommon cards.

The first was likely the blue's core card. Humidity into a Cup was an Uncommon power to condense the air's humidity into an ice glass filled with fresh water.

It might seem like a trivial power, but in a dry desert place like the Mesa Free Hive, it would be extremely valuable.

The second Uncommon card, however, made Arthur pause.

A Sword Cuts Both Ways
Uncommon

Trap

*On the occasion this trap card is ever stolen or forcefully taken from a heart
deck, it will release a pulse of pure death energy, instantly killing both
the thief and the wielder. This card becomes inactive upon the death of a
wielder and may be harvested normally.*

Arthur's face went pale. He resisted the urge to grab Brixaby from his shoulder and wrap him tightly in his arms. If he'd used his card-plucking power . . .

Thankfully, Brixaby's danger sense had steered him clear.

A shiver of cold fear down his spine, immediately followed by hot rage. The trap had been intentional, with a set target. The Mind Singer was aware of Brixaby's abilities, and she had anticipated their next move once they saw the effect of the Legendary card. Only Brixaby's danger sense—and a good deal of luck—had spared his dragon.

And at that moment, Arthur's timer on his bonus luck ran out.

If he hadn't picked that attribute to boost . . .

He didn't want to think about it. Instead, he turned his thoughts to the Mind Singer. She'd tried to kill Arthur, which he could accept. But now she'd turned her attention to Brixaby.

He already hated her.

Now, she *had* to die.

CHAPTER 38

Laird looked around at the bodies of three enemy dragons and one ally. He heaved a sigh.

"I will take care of this."

The last of the adrenaline that had carried Arthur this far was fading, and he wanted nothing more than to find a bed and sleep. Pure will and a healthy dose of his Exhaustion Resistance helped him continue to stand.

Cressida, meanwhile, was visibly wilting with one hand on Joy to keep standing up. Brixaby still perched proudly on Arthur's shoulder, but his head was drooping.

"Are you sure?" Arthur made himself ask. After all, if the council discovered the theft of the combat cards, all of this might be for nothing.

"I came in on a later wave and haven't been fighting as long as you," Laird reminded him simply. "Besides, I need to get ahead of the investigation. Shadow's death, unfortunately, will lend weight to my story."

"What story will that be?" Arthur asked.

"What else?" Laird let out another long sigh, and abruptly Arthur wondered how old the dragon was. Under the harsh moonlit sky, he seemed positively ancient. "I'll report that these were kingdom hive dragons—probably not your kingdom. I'm sure I'll find a mark on their hides or identifying trinkets, or I'll claim there's one on the report. While they haven't moved to wipe us off the map, it's not unheard of for a hive to take an occasional sideswipe."

"All the more reason why you should defend yourselves," Arthur said, thinking of the combat cards.

Laird gave a single nod and turned away in obvious dismissal.

Arthur glanced at Brix to see if he was about to take exception to that—a Legendary being dismissed by a Rare. But it was a mark of how tired Brixaby was that he didn't comment.

Besides, Laird had a good point. Reluctantly, Arthur turned to leave.

The hive lay on the other side of the large mesa to the north. They had gotten here by flying on Joy. But, seeing as the pink dragon was so exhausted that her normally vivid scales were dull, Arthur knew he couldn't ask her to fly them back.

They would have to walk it. And judging by the way the moon and the stars wheeled in the sky, they only had a couple of short hours before sunrise.

"Well," he said, "let's get going."

Cressida pushed off of Joy and, gesturing for her dragon to follow, walked up to him. "I have a better idea."

Then she placed one delicate hand on Arthur's shoulder—the one without Brixaby on it. Her second hand pressed to Joy's scales.

A moment later, they were enveloped in darkness.

No, not darkness, *shadow*. And those shadows were boiling with monsters . . . though they seemed far away.

They erupted at the base of the mesa at the deepest point of shadow.

Arthur had no time to exclaim in surprise or mentally slap himself for forgetting so fast she had a new teleport power.

Cressida's knees started to buckle, and Arthur caught her right before she hit the ground.

"That was the last of my mana," Cressida gasped. Judging by the harsh way she breathed, that little stunt had likely cut into her life force, too.

It wasn't a permanent problem, but she would need a good, rich meal and a long night of sleep to recover what she had just spent.

"Take your time," Arthur said, "you just saved us a long walk."

And likely discovery. He doubted they would have been able to travel back across the desert without being seen.

Turning, he looked back the way they came. They were so far from the tip of the peninsula that Laird wasn't visible, and he couldn't pick out the bodies of the dragons among the boulders.

"Poor Shadow," Joy said mournfully. "He deserved so much better than to die like that."

Arthur looked back at her and realized that her scales weren't dull from exhaustion—at least, not *only* from exhaustion. She looked to be honestly grieving for the other dragon.

"I'm sorry," he said awkwardly. "I didn't know you two were friends."

"Oh, we weren't. I don't think he liked us very much." But she still sounded sad enough that she might as well have said that they had been the best of friends. "That's fine. I still liked him, and I thought he would have been a very good addition to Brixaby's retinue. But maybe Cressida having his card is the best way to honor him."

"I would still rather have Ghost in my retinue," Brixaby said. "Although"—he gave a speculative look to Cressida—"your stealth and new teleport card may mean Ghost isn't needed. I chose well when I accepted you into my retinue."

Cressida let out a breathless chuckle and tipped her head to the dragon in a surprisingly elegant gesture. "Thank you, sir," she said with only the slightest sarcasm.

Brixaby flipped his wings in satisfaction, clearly not picking up on it.

Arthur took a few moments to look around. His **Night Vision** was rather good—a benefit of his Master of Body Enhancement, though he was still at the minimum level 3.

They were in a hollow scooped out by the wind and blowing sand. He didn't see anybody around him, but he knew that dragons, and sometimes people, used different exterior hollows of the mesa to curl up and fall asleep in during the relatively cooler night.

"Brixaby," he said, "take a quick look around and see if there's anybody close enough to eavesdrop?"

Brixaby might be tired and overly full, but he was always up for showing off his flying skills. Buzzing straight up into the air from Arthur's shoulder, he flew out and then around. Everybody stayed silent; the only sound in the still night air was the droning of Brixaby's wings. There weren't even any crickets in this desert landscape.

Weirdly, for a second, Arthur felt intensely homesick for the Wolf Moon Hive—its winding canals, the city that always had something going on outside the hive, and the general sense of life and purpose.

He had gained much by being here in the Mesa Hive, but he didn't want to stay forever.

Brixaby returned shortly, landing back on Arthur's shoulder. "Two dragons are asleep fifty feet above, but they're only Commons," he said dismissively. "And they're snoring."

Arthur nodded. "We'll keep our voices down."

Joy managed to perk up. "Secrets?"

"I wanted to know about that other card that Laird gave you," Arthur said to Cressida. "If you feel comfortable, of course."

He added that part because it was true that Cressida and Joy were part of his retinue, but they were also his friends. A card deck was an intensely personal thing.

Joy perked up. "Oh yeah," she said, shedding her grief for Shadow in an instant. "I kind of wanted to know too. What did he give you, Cressida?"

Cressida pulled it out of her card-anchor purse. "It is a Rare card, but not nearly as exciting as you're likely imagining."

The back of the card was interesting. The illustrations moved, as all Rare cards did, but they didn't just move, they slithered and twined and twisted around. Were those . . . snakes?

Cressida flipped the card over to show them.

Slithering Shadow Sender
Rare
Utility
The wielder of this card will be able to conjure snakes and serpents made of shadow and deliver a message to any individual. There is no restriction on distance. The wielder must be able to clearly visualize this individual and be able to speak his or her message out loud. The messenger serpent will be able to carry back a reply message on its return. Sending the message does not require any mana; however, a donation of mana is required by the recipient to send a reply. The amount required depends on the distance from the sender.

It was easy to see why this was a Rare card. If there was no limit on distance for the sending, Cressida could send a message to Wolf Moon Hive—to anybody—without the cost of mana. Yes, it wasn't a combat or a craft spell, but it was very useful.

"Oh, good," Joy said. "Another spell in the form of an animal. Cressida, I like your theme."

"It's not a theme, dearest," Cressida said, perhaps sounding a little more prim than usual. "These are merely coincidences."

"She has a point," Brixaby said, stroking his chin. "I wonder if they are from the same set?"

"I don't think that they are," Cressida said, then looked around at all of them, visibly surprised. "So you think that I should add it to my card deck?"

"Why not?" Arthur asked.

"It's not exactly useful. Brixaby can speak into our minds."

"Only for a short distance, and you can't speak back. Though that makes sending orders easier," Brixaby said.

"Oh, Cressida," Joy gasped, clearly alarmed that Cressida thought otherwise. "You *have* to add it to your deck. You heard Laird before. This was poor Shadow's card. This was the card that they created together through their link. You *have* to reunite them. You just have to!"

That made Arthur wonder what Shadow's rider's card had been. Something with snakes, perhaps, to create this linked card?

"Cressida, those things you see when you teleport . . ."

She gave him a wan smile. "They're mentioned in the card description, as a warning. I'm able to teleport myself and others at a 90% reduced mana rate, but we're 'Trespassing where mortal beings dare not tread.' That's the risk for every teleport."

"Shadow mentioned something like that once. He said they caught his scent."

She shivered. "I get the feeling I shouldn't use it too often. And though the linked card doesn't have that warning, I fear there will be some other drawback."

"It is a useful utility," Brixaby agreed. Then he glanced at Arthur. "But you may want to save space in your deck. We have other cards to choose from."

"What do you mean? Wait . . . Oh, Arthur," Cressida said, her voice heavy. "Did you do what I think you did?"

He looked directly at her. He wasn't going to apologize. "I didn't want to take any chances that Laird or Shadow would betray us or fight us for the best cards."

She nodded, and while she didn't exactly smile at him, she didn't seem upset, either.

Cressida was from a minor noble house. She knew how to play the politics game, but he was still relieved she didn't seem angry.

Joy seemed too tired to bounce up and down, but she still weaved from side to side. "Well? Well?! What did you get us? What did you get us?"

Arthur produced the cards that they had held back.

Supernova Unleashed
Common
Elemental
The wielder of this card will gain the ability to release a massive explosion of fire and kinetic energy in a 360-degree ring. This release will not damage allies or the wielder's existing card effects.
Cooldown: 30 minutes

Sharp as Nails
Common
Body Enhancement
This card grants the wielder the ability to lengthen finger and toenails to sharp knife points using mana. Higher mana costs will result in sharper nails. Advanced levels allow the user more control over this body enhancement.

"This is good," Cressida said. "Really good. Also, no animals. Arthur . . . it's perfect. Thank you."

"Oh, I like this," Joy said, looking over her card with equal enthusiasm. "This will let me poison people so much easier! Thank you." She looked at Cressida, then at Arthur and Brixaby. "I think that I'd like to try it now."

"Wait, Joy, your core—" Cressida started.

"I've been thinking a lot about my cores, and even if the second one isn't super solid, I think it's good enough. It's ready for a card."

"But are you sure?"

"She is the dragon," Brixaby said. "She's the one who knows if she is sure. Not us."

"There is no rush," Cressida said.

Arthur winced, but said, "Actually . . . there is."

Cressida swung around to glare at him, but he wasn't going to back down.

"This is the second time that the Mind Singer has attacked us. Maybe the third if the boiler room explosion wasn't an accident. This time it was with a Legendary card. What do you think will happen next time?"

"She'll attack us with two Legendary cards?" Joy asked.

Brixaby looked briefly excited about that but then, with a shake of his head, he said, "No. She won't give us the pleasure of possibly obtaining two more Legendary cards from her."

"No," Arthur agreed. "I think next time, she'll send all of her troops—or thralls, or whatever you want to call it—and try to overwhelm us en masse. It may not work, especially with the cards we just received . . . But if we're here in the Mesa Hive, that means that a lot of people and dragons will be in the way."

Joy looked properly horrified at this. "Then I *have* to have this combat card."

"What about the one you picked earlier?" Cressida asked. "Strike Where They're Going to Be?"

"I like that one too," Joy said, "but it's mostly focused on my ability as a meta dragon. This one will enhance my poison ability. I think . . . I think that I'd better only try poison, first."

Arthur watched Cressida visibly struggle with herself. She loved her dragon and felt protective over her. But she couldn't argue with this logic either.

"If you feel anything is wrong, you take the card out immediately. It's not your primary core the card will be going into, it's your secondary deck, so that won't be a problem."

"I know. That's the whole point of a secondary deck." Joy sounded so positive and matter-of-fact that it didn't come out sarcastic at all. She leaned forward and rubbed the bottom of her jaw against the top of Cressida's head in a parody of a head pat.

And she immediately stuck the card into her core.

Joy's eyes went very wide, and everybody stared at her for a few seconds.

Brixaby crouched on Arthur's shoulder, half poised, as if ready to snatch that card out of her core at a moment's notice.

But then Joy relaxed. "Oh, it's no problem at all. But . . . there *is* only room for one for now."

Cressida breathed out something that Arthur was fairly sure was a northern city swear word, and sagged in relief.

"Well, that's all very well and good. You are even more useful to us now as retinue riders. I am very pleased," Brixaby said, "Now, Arthur, while we're here, we might as well address what we're all *really* thinking about."

Everyone looked at him. Arthur decided to take the bait. "What's that?"

"The Legendary card, of course," Brixaby said, "and when will be the most optimal time for me to eat it."

CHAPTER 39

Brixaby waited for a beat. "Just kidding, of course. I'm going to consume the card now!"

"Hold on there," Arthur said, slightly alarmed. "Let's wait until we get back to our room. We don't know what will be waiting for us." Or how Brixaby would react after consuming a Legendary, especially since his Personal Space was practically popping at the seams.

He looked around at the dark, still landscape. It was so quiet and peaceful that it was easy to let himself believe they had gotten away with their theft. But that was an illusion.

"I don't even know what day it is," he admitted, and with those words, the weight of exhaustion once again settled on his shoulders. They'd faced too many battles in too short of a time: first the dungeon waves and then the four dragons, one of which was still alive and needed interrogation. It felt overwhelming to think about what he still needed to do. "Let's just . . . get to our room first," he said on a sigh, dreading the long walk ahead.

"I can take us," Cressida said. "I can sense the shadows, and there are a lot back in that room."

"Are you sure? What about those monsters? Your mana?" She might have regained some mana in the last few minutes, but it wouldn't be enough to completely replenish her.

"Well, I won't be good for much after," she said, "but neither will any of you if we spend the next couple hours walking. As for those shadow monsters . . ." She shrugged. "Like I said, I wouldn't want to teleport multiple times within a few minutes, but they seemed far enough away the last time."

"Cressida, I don't think—"

She cut off his argument by placing one hand on his shoulder and the other on Joy's. A second later, they were enveloped in shadow. Shadow that seemed to last and last.

From the corner of his eye, shapes turned to look their way. They started moving closer.

"Cressida?" Arthur wanted to say, though no sound came out. His alarm grew. What if this was too much for her? What if they were stuck in this place?

Well, he had combat cards now. He'd fight their way out if he had to.

But then they emerged in a room that was nearly as pitch dark as the shadows, save for a couple of vague outlines.

Then Cressida collapsed into Arthur's arms.

"Cressida!" Joy shrieked.

"Brixaby, get the light," Arthur instructed. His arms supported Cressida's legs and back, holding her close. Despite being unconscious, she wasn't very heavy. Cressida was petite, but her personality always made her seem larger than life.

Brixaby acted fast and buzzed to the front of the room to pull back the curtain to the balcony. The scattered anchor lights from other balconies and walkways provided a soft illumination. It was enough for Arthur to make his way to Cressida's cot and lay her down.

"Will she be okay?" Joy asked, coming over and knocking over a few pieces of furniture along the way. "Will she? Will she?"

Before Arthur answered, Joy halfway climbed up on the cot—but she was too heavy. Rope lines that held up the mattress frame snapped, as did some wood. The right side dipped alarmingly.

"Joy, get back! She's fine. She's breathing. I need you to give me some space," he said, pushing back her head, which was about twice the size of a horse's.

The pink dragon did fall back but still managed to hover. "But she's not waking up. She's not saying anything!"

"That last jump must have drained her vital energy, but it's not permanent. It can be replenished with rest," he explained. Joy was intelligent and familiar with mana replenishment, but she was also panicked and not thinking straight. "You haven't received a quest to save her or anything, right?"

"No, I haven't gotten a quest for some time," she replied. "I think I might've skewed the reward system a bit by getting so many great cards all at once."

No doubt, he thought with a sigh. Then he remembered his healing card.

Without another thought, he withdrew it from his card-anchor tattoo.

Moderate Self-Repair

Uncommon

Healing

The wielder of this card will be granted the ability to repair minor to

moderate wounds and injuries. Severe, crippling, complex, or mortal
wounds may be only partially healed. This is an active effect and requires
the use of mana.

He scowled at that last line. Cressida's lack of mana had caused the Shadow Teleport effect to eat into her vital energy. Adding any card—even a healing card—wouldn't help at this point. Besides, it wasn't like she needed the healing.

Reluctantly, he tucked it back into his anchor tattoo.

"She needs time. Joy, watch her for a bit while I talk to Brix."

"Yes, yes! Of course." Nodding frantically, Joy tucked herself up against the side of the cot, her neck stretched up to lay right beside Cressida, one sky-blue eye fixed on her face.

Knowing the dragon would watch her like a hawk, Arthur got up and walked to the front of the room. He paused and glanced back. Joy had really grown recently. It had been easy to miss over the last few weeks, but he suspected she would be on the larger side for a pink dragon when all was said and done.

Arthur continued out to the balcony where he found his dragon perched on the rail, staring at the card in his claws.

"I've flown a circuit to scout," Brixaby said as Arthur walked up. "Nothing seems amiss, and my danger sense hasn't been triggered."

Arthur nodded. Typically, he tried avoiding discussing important matters outside where anyone could hear. But he wanted Cressida to rest. Besides, it was so dark and still out, he had a hard time believing there were any watchers.

Still, he lowered his voice. "So what's your plan with the card? You want to consume it? Not add it to your core?"

For the first time, Brixaby seemed hesitant. "I need to become stronger."

"You can do that by adding it to a secondary core."

"A *Legendary* card in my secondary core?" Brixaby sounded taken aback. "Why would I add the best of cards to a lesser core?"

Yet, there was a hint of uncertainty in Brixaby's eyes—an unfamiliar expression on his usually confident face.

Reluctantly, Brixaby held out the card to Arthur. "Shouldn'tyoutakeit?" he said so quickly that Arthur almost didn't catch his words.

"Me?" Arthur began, then took a moment to truly think about it.

A Legendary was too magically heavy to add to his card-anchor deck. But what if he added it to his heart deck?

He took a moment to mentally review his deck.

Master of Skills and Master of Body Enhancement were his current Legendary cards. Because they were a pair, they counted as one slot. Skills in his spirit slot and Body in his body slot, of course.

Personal Space, Mental Bookshelf, and Eidetic Imagery also counted as one slot as they were three-of-a-kind. Those were all linked to his mind.

His other heart deck slots included: Nullify Card; Charming Gentle-Person; Return to Start; Phase In, Phase Out; Nice (Metal) Shot; Makeshift Weaponry; and 20-Point Spree.

Eight slots were taken out of ten in his heart deck.

Counterfeit Siphon was a linked card he shared with Brixaby. It existed somewhat outside his heart deck in a special space only reserved for him and his dragon.

Even his card anchor, however, felt a little strained with Moderate Self-Repair, Mana Amendment, and Mana Vault. He'd needed to get it upgraded for some time.

He could slot the Legendary card into his heart deck, but . . .

"No." The word was painful to say, and even Brixaby appeared taken aback.

"No," Arthur reiterated, with more determination this time. "You know I like having a variety of cards in my deck, but most of them are utility-based. This card . . . just wouldn't fit."

"It would give you the element of surprise," Brixaby pointed out.

Arthur shook his head. "Legendary cards carry more weight than any others. They're the foundation of a deck. I don't want a deck of sonic cards. It's not me."

Yet, Arthur recognized his hypocrisy. If he didn't take it, Brixaby would consume it, which meant destroying that card. Forever.

He wasn't thrilled with the idea, but he wasn't to stop Brixaby from growing stronger.

With the same hesitation Brixaby had shown earlier, Arthur returned the card to his dragon. "No," he said for the third time, "this belongs to you. You should consume it."

Relief washed over Brixaby's face, followed by excitement and naked greed.

"This will greatly empower me!" Brixaby declared. Without further ado, he swallowed it down.

The card, bigger than Brixaby's head, looked oddly small as it seemed to shrink upon entering his mouth, drawn in by his Call of the Void.

"I was going to ask if you wanted to remove that dragon from your Personal Space first," Arthur said, amused.

"That is my Personal Space. This will add strength to my card, not take up room in my core. I wonder what ability I'll gain—" he began, but was interrupted by a burp that sparkled with mana breaking down. Then he burped again. And again. The last burp was big enough to knock him off the railing, where he caught himself with his wings.

"Are you okay, Brixaby?" Arthur asked.

"I feel . . . very, *very* full," Brixaby replied, pressing his now-bulging stomach.

Arthur remembered Brixaby's hatching day, how the dragon had tried to consume several Legendary cards at once and had nearly gone mad with the attempt.

Brixaby buzzed back to his perch on the railing, but he was visibly drooping. He looked like he was ready for a good nap.

"Let's get you back onto a cot, too," Arthur said, lifting the weakening dragon into his arms. Brixaby didn't even try to protest.

As he walked back, Arthur wondered if this was the last time he'd be able to carry Brixaby like this.

He found Joy where he left her, but asleep. Cressida's breathing was still even, her skin a little more pale than usual, but not bloodless. Arthur laid Brix on his own cot and lay down next to him.

Resting his hand on Brixaby's back, he closed his eyes, intending just to rest them for a moment.

He was jolted awake by the sound of alarms echoing throughout the hive.

CHAPTER 40

Arthur experienced a second shock when he realized his body lay on a bare sliver edge of the cot's mattress. A hard bulk pressed into his back.

Joy climbed into my cot again, he thought irritably.

Arthur shoved his arm back. His elbow hit hard, unyielding scales.

"What's that noise?" came Cressida's thick voice from somewhere on the other side of the room, from her bed. She sounded about as bad as Arthur felt.

He could have sworn he had just closed his eyes to sleep a moment ago, but when he forced his eyelids open, he saw light peeking out from around the balcony curtain. It was daytime. He'd been asleep for hours, at least.

And still, that shrill alarm was going off. *Ugh.*

Arthur didn't even have room to turn around without falling off the cot. So, reluctantly, he slid off in a controlled fall to the floor. Then he finally looked back.

It hadn't been Joy pushing him off the mattress after all.

"Brix?" he breathed.

His dragon was *huge*.

Well, not huge for even a purple. But the bulk of his body was about the size of a small donkey—the same ones that used to pull Red's cart when Arthur rode with them on the caravan. His tail was so long that it flopped off the other end of the cot.

It wasn't just that he had grown. He had also visibly matured, with matte-black plates of hard scales like armor down the length of his spine and over his elbow, wrist, knee, and ankle joints. The rest of the scales covering his body were a shimmery black with an iridescent purple sheen to them. There were flashes of true royal purple between the larger scales, as if the dark covered his purple skin.

"Brix," Arthur breathed. "Look at you. You've grown! Brix, wake up."

But the dragon didn't so much as stir. Not even when Arthur reached to shake him.

He felt the weight of him now—he easily weighed as much as Arthur himself. Considering dragons usually remained lighter than they looked to get up in the air, that was substantial.

"What? Brixaby?" came Cressida's voice from the other side of the room. She sat up and stared.

Joy's head popped up from behind her rider. She looked equally as shocked.

"He's not waking up." Arthur reached for the link between himself and his dragon but found it strong, sure, and steady. No sign of sickness or distress.

"Wow, he's big now," Joy said, adding, "Not as big as me. But still really big. Half the size of a normal purple, maybe? So not pink big but—"

"What happened?" Cressida asked.

"Brix ate the Legendary card." Arthur frowned and stroked a hand down his dragon's back. "He's breathing fine, and his temperature isn't up."

"He's probably digesting the magic," Joy said. "You know how if you eat a really big meal and then you feel really, really sleepy and—"

"But what's that noise?" Cressida asked. "Are those alarms?" She seemed groggy still. Arthur finally peeled his eyes away from Brixaby to take a good look at her. Dark circles ringed under her eyes. She looked like she hadn't slept for a week rather than having just woken up. And, more unusually, she was a beat or two behind Arthur.

He saw the moment the realization clicked. Her eyes widened and she hissed, "Do you think the alarms could be—do you think the council's discovered what we've done?"

"At least that the combat cards are missing," Arthur confirmed grimly. "They'd have guards at our door if they thought it was us."

"Then we must act as normal as possible." Cressida started to get up but wavered on her feet.

Joy squawked in alarm and pushed her head and neck forward to brace her.

"You haven't recovered yet," Arthur said. "Sit back down and stay with Brix." He glanced down again at his dragon. Despite his anxiety, he got the strong impression that he wasn't in danger. Just processing the magic. Considering it was a Legendary card, that meant a *lot* of magic.

But it was inconvenient. If his suspicions were correct, this was going to be awkward timing.

Cressida sat but still protested. "Arthur, no—"

"I'm the Legendary rider, which means I can speak for us. I'll just say Brixaby is out crafting or something—"

"I'll go with you," Joy offered.

Arthur shook his head. "No, I need you to protect Brixaby while he's sleeping. He's too vulnerable right now. In fact . . ."

Arthur reached into his card anchor, pulled out his 20-Point Boost card, and shoved it at the still-protesting Cressida. "Put this in your card anchor. If the worst happens, use it."

He rose and turned to the balcony.

Halfway there, he felt something different in the room. It wasn't something he could put his finger on. His eyes told him nothing had changed. His ears didn't catch a sound.

But the difference, the dissonance in the air, resonated with his Stealth Class.

On instinct, Arthur looked at the curtain that had been drawn across the mouth of the cave. The one he now knew was an illusion.

"Hello, Ghost."

Abruptly, the dragon flickered into view.

He had stuck his head under the curtain and was looking around. From his expression, Arthur guessed he hadn't heard much of the previous conversation. If they were lucky, he'd just arrived.

"How did you know I was here?" Ghost demanded and then looked past Arthur, grumpy expression blanking in shock. "Is that Brixaby? What's wrong with him? Is he sick?"

"He ate too much," Joy said.

That gave Arthur a seed of an idea. "He fed on the card shards we've been collecting over the last few weeks. It's taking a while for him to digest them."

Ghost gave him a flatly disbelieving look. Only then did Arthur remember Laird said Ghost was the one who tipped them off. Had he followed them under stealth? Whose side was he on? The council? Laird?

The dragon seemed to be on the verge of calling out his lie. Or perhaps he had reported to Laird last night and not followed up. Either way, he glanced again at Brixaby and scowled.

"He ate shards? And that's what's made him grow? Well, he can sleep it off some other time. Chablis and the rest of the council need him. And you," he added, as an afterthought.

"Why?" Arthur asked. "Does it have to do with that racket outside?"

"Those are alarms, foolish boy. And I don't ask questions of the council—"

Another deep dragon voice echoed from outside. "There's been an attack on our hive."

Ghost withdrew his head to look out. Arthur followed him past the curtain. Sure enough, Laird stood outside, claws half dug into the stony wall to keep balance. There wasn't enough room on the balcony for two full-grown dragons.

"So, the rumors are true, then?" Ghost asked Laird, flicking his tongue out in distaste.

Laird didn't look at him. His yellow eyes were fixed intently on Arthur. "There was an attack last night," he said heavily. "We believe from another hive. The dragon you arrived with, Shadow, was unfortunately killed."

Joy let out an overly dramatic gasp from back inside the cave. "What? Shadow! Oh no, not him. I'm *so* surprised—"

Cressida hushed her.

Thankfully, Ghost didn't seem to be paying much attention. His attention was fixed on Laird. "Which hive? Which kingdom?"

"Another free hive," Laird said.

Ghost rocked back. "That can't be possible—"

"They've sent an emissary to take responsibility for the killing," Laird said, still looking intently at Arthur, "and have come to negotiate our surrender."

"What makes them think we'll accept that?" Arthur asked.

"They seem to be under the impression," Laird said, still staring hard at Arthur, "that the dragon they killed was a Legendary."

CHAPTER 41

Arthur's emotions were in a whirlwind. Confusion over how the Mind Singer could possibly think that she had killed Brixaby mixed with worry he'd gotten himself in too far over his head. Deep in his mind, Arthur still saw himself as a kid from the border village. Less than nobody. Now he was involved in high politics and had sentient scourglings threatening entire hives because of him.

But the most prominent emotion was seething anger.

The Mind Singer had known Brixaby's abilities well enough to lay a trap card. Then she had been so convinced it would work that she had made major moves because of it.

Arthur sensed that more of this plot lay under the surface—this was the type of thing Cressida excelled at, not him—but all he could focus on as he accepted a ride from Laird to the council's mesa was that the Mind Singer was a threat. She had to be eliminated.

Despite his seething rage, he wasn't completely blind to what was going on around him. He'd expected Mesa Hive to be in a state of minor uproar. The alarms had been blaring nonstop for minutes now with no sign of abating.

Arthur expected people to be evacuating. Maybe gearing up to defend themselves.

Instead, he saw shops and booths shuttering up, people darting into larger caves, and others clustering in worried knots. All talking and glancing worriedly up at the tall bubbled ceilings, as if wondering if the stone would fall down on their heads at any moment.

No one was preparing for battle. They looked to be just waiting for the shoe to drop. Some even looked slightly annoyed that their day had been interrupted.

And they have no combat cards, he thought and had to resist the urge to reach into his Personal Space, withdraw a handful, and toss them down like confetti.

He might have done it if Ghost weren't flying beside Laird. *That* might be hard to explain.

Patience, he told himself and leaned forward to call out to Laird. The dragon was large, and because Arthur sat at the base of his neck, he had to yell to be heard over snapping wings and the rush of wind.

"I'm going to activate my stealth skills. Try not to forget I'm here."

Sometimes the stealth skills could work oddly on the mind.

Laird snorted. "You may have matured, but you are still a bitty thing and easily overlooked. I don't think the scourgling is concerned with you. Only your dragon."

That was a very dragonish attitude to have. He was also, Arthur was sure, dead wrong. The scourgling had a vendetta, and Arthur would be a fool to ignore it.

But Arthur wasn't asking for permission. Only giving a heads-up.

He focused on his Stealth Class and activated every skill in it: **Silent Movement**, **Heightened Awareness**, **Camouflage**, **Evasion**, **Deception**, **Concealment**, and of **course** Stealth. The overall class also gave him a boost of +5 to Perception and +3 to Luck.

Luck would be vitally important because he had the feeling he would need all he could get.

Nothing changed from his point of view, though he did see Ghost throwing him some odd glances his way. As a Stealth card specialist, he likely wasn't fooled by Arthur's skills.

Arthur threw a sarcastic wave at him.

With a scowl, the dragon turned his head away.

He smirked, but then, as an afterthought, focused on activating his mental-blocking skills as well. *Never hurts to be prepared.*

Laird, of course, knew all the shortcuts and aerial byways in the hive. They erupted into the bright sunshine moments later.

Too bright.

Arthur covered his eyes with a wince. That movement let him mask a long glance back over to the salt sea and the peninsula.

There was no sign of the dragons they'd fought last night, or of Shadow's body. It was only bleak gray and bleached white stone out there. All the bodies had been removed.

He wanted to ask Laird what exactly he'd done, but again, not when Ghost was near. He was lucky the silver dragon wasn't asking him pointed questions about what had happened last night.

Both adult dragons curved their wings and beat swiftly upward to crest the top of the mesa.

Again, Arthur was surprised. He fully expected an enemy army waiting for him, considering the alarms. Maybe the Mind Singer herself with her sisters.

Instead, he saw the humans of the council gathered together in a loose circle near to where the entrance of the prison had been. Meanwhile, four unfamiliar dragons flew high overhead in tight, perfect circles like circling vultures. They didn't come close enough to identify.

As Laird came in to land, Arthur took a swift glance around for signs of their break-in last night—was it only last night? It felt so long ago. He saw nothing. The hasty patch job he and Brixaby had made still held up.

He wished his dragon were here now.

Chablis pushed to the front, her eyes slipping over Arthur as she frowned at Laird. "What took so long? Where is the Legendary pair? Is it true?"

"I knew it," one of the councilmen grumbled. "They're dead or fled. Your plan didn't work, Chablis."

Chablis turned and opened her mouth to retort. Before she could say anything, notes drifted down from the circling dragons above.

Whispers on the mesa, shadows on the wall.
Your Legendary defender's fallen, woe to you all.
We demand your surrender, lay your weapons down.
Hand over your combat cards, or in the fight you'll drown . . .

Drown?

Arthur glanced up. The dragons were so high in the sky that they looked smaller than the top joint of his thumb.

One of them must have had a communication card to send that . . . *song* to them, then.

Which meant they could likely hear what was being spoken.

Arthur hopped off the dragon's neck and landed lightly. No one so much as gave him a second glance.

It was as close to being invisible as he could get. Though he suspected that if he spoke or made a spectacle of himself, people would notice him.

He glanced up at the circling dragons. Hopefully, his stealth worked on them too.

Then again, had the Mind Singer ever laid eyes on him? Possibly during the demi-scourge-eruption. Though he thought he might have been fighting her sisters rather than the Mind Singer herself. She might have caught a glimpse of him when she first escaped the scholars' library. He didn't want to risk it.

Sliding one hand over Laird's scales as he walked to let the dragon know where he was, he ducked under his chest. Laird was tall, but Arthur couldn't quite stand up straight. Crouching, he dropped his stealth skills.

Laird glanced down at him, and then, within moments, ushered Chablis closer.

The woman was visibly startled when she saw Arthur, her eyes wide. She didn't say anything, however. Her eyes flicked upward, and Arthur nodded. They had to keep quiet.

Shushing the council members—several of whom had spotted Arthur and started to speak—Chablis ducked under Laird to join him. It was an odd meeting place, but perfectly hidden from above.

She spoke in a whisper. "If the worst happens, will you help us?"

Will you fight for us? was the unspoken question.

Arthur nodded.

Chablis turned and ducked back out. She'd only risked a moment, knowing they were being watched—and probably listened to—from above.

"Council members," she said, "it appears we have no choice. We should treat this group like any other kingdom hive: Get this over with and pay them off. I propose the standard pricing."

"I disagree. This is no kingdom hive," Laird snapped. "This is a hive run by a scourgling. It cannot be reasoned with—it's already admitting to attacking us once! Of killing a Legendary dragon under our care!"

One of the council members spoke up, his voice creaky with age. "The kingdom hives will not allow a powerful scourgling—if that is truly what this is—to exist for long. I say we shoo the thing off our doorstep before it brings its war to us."

Arthur looked on in confusion. Were they saying what he thought they were saying?

Chablis turned to Laird. "Scourglings cannot live here—we barely can with all our utility cards. It's a wasteland. It would be pointless to attack us," she added, a touch louder and clearly aimed at the listening dragons, "but in the spirit of efficiency and goodwill—"

And cowardness, Arthur thought.

"—we could deliver a payment of combat cards. As we do with all kingdom hives," she finished.

"Aye," said the creaky councilman.

Three more ayes followed, with Laird being the pointed nay.

With a satisfied nod, Chablis stepped away from the others and directed her voice upward. "Our payment of peace is twenty Common cards, ten Uncommon, and three Rare. All guaranteed combat focused."

Arthur felt a little sick. Not only with the suggestion, but the knowledge that Chablis was offering something she didn't have. And she didn't know it.

Well . . . on second thought, there were perhaps twenty semi-useless Common cards and possibly ten Uncommon. Possibly. They hadn't left any Rares behind, however.

The circling dragons didn't hesitate a moment.

We agree, our hearts convey,
But as a warning, act fast and do not delay.

"That's a yes." Chablis glanced at Laird, saw he was still sheltering Arthur, and then nodded to Ghost, who stood nearby waiting. "If you could convey us to the peninsula? Laird, please stay with our . . . guests." She nodded upward.

"This is a mistake," Laird growled. "A scourgling's greed will never be satisfied."

"That's your opinion. You were outvoted."

With that, Chablis made her way to the silver dragon. The other council members followed.

Arthur watched them go, fighting with himself all the while on if he should call out. If he had Brixaby by his side, he would have. Together, they had taken on four dragons last night. They might be able to at least drive these off if they made a stand.

Assuming the council members had combat cards hidden up their sleeves and were willing to use them.

But he didn't have Brixaby or Cressida or Joy by his side. And Laird stayed just as silent, which was telling. Arthur wondered if he had a plan or if he was just as frustrated.

Ghost flew off, his wingbeats labored with four people on his back.

How long would it take to get to the library and discover it had been looted?

It turned out it didn't matter, because the moment they disappeared into the dungeon, Laird let out a bitter bark of laughter.

"So whatever this is really about begins. I tried to warn them, but as you saw, I was *outvoted*."

Arthur saw he was looking up. Carefully, he stepped out from under the dragon to peer upward, though he kept within his shadow.

The singing emissaries had stopped circling in place and were now flying in a different, complex pattern. All of them were figure eights that met in the middle and expanded out again.

It was odd, almost ritualistic.

"What are they . . ." Arthur started.

He trailed off. There was something different about the air. It was tingly. It was different, thinner, and tingly at the same time.

For some reason, it affected his Mana Vault. It was as if someone were knocking at its door. Arthur kept it firmly shut.

Whatever they were doing, it was a spell. A powerful one.

With a sound like tearing paper, the sky seemed to rip in two. Two of the dragons—they looked dark green, though he couldn't tell for sure—broke off from the figure eights and grabbed each side, then they pulled the rip open wide enough to let dragons through.

"That's a portal," Arthur gasped, and before he could think otherwise, he turned and leaped onto Laird's neck. "Back to the hive. We need to close the entrances. We need to defend it."

As Laird lifted into the air, the first dragons from the Mind Singer's hive poured out of the rip in the sky.

CHAPTER 42

As Laird climbed into the air, he opened his mouth and roared.

Arthur half expected a whirlwind of candle-top flames to come out and wreak destruction.

But this wasn't a spell. It was a command.

Three dozen dragons all scattered around the top of the mesa suddenly came out of camouflage. There had been zero indication they had been there at all.

Arthur had been proud of his stealth skills, but those paled when magic spells were involved.

With roars of their own, the dragons took to the air and headed straight up toward the portal.

"Who are they?" Arthur asked.

Laird glanced over his shoulder at him. Though dragons didn't exactly smile like human beings did, there was no doubt: the dragon was grinning like a fool. "They are the ones I collected the combat cards for, of course. These are my dragons. *My* retinue." He looked up at the portal, which had been torn open to a wide rip in the sky.

Enemy dragons poured out. Laird roared louder. "It is good to fight scourglings again, as real dragons ought!"

His other dragons roared out their agreement. They passed Laird and Arthur on their way to the portal—some already had spells clutched in their claws. Each and every one looked eager.

Though they had left their home hives and kingdoms, it appeared not all of them were happy to be only crafters.

Laird didn't head for the portal. Instead, he folded his wings and dropped down the other side of the vertical wall toward the hive's mesa entrance.

Falling with his stomach in his throat, Arthur still didn't focus on the ground. He trusted Laird not to bash him into the hard-packed soil below.

Instead, he craned his head up to watch the first of Laird's dragons reach the portal.

The initial momentum went to the defenders. They had fury, speed, and righteousness on their side, and they met the emerging dragons with a flurry of spells, skills, and charms. The magic was so thick in the air that from a distance, it looked like a flurry of colored sparks.

The barely heard notes from the Mind Singer's dragons faltered, then turned sour and discordant as the dragons and riders were knocked aside. Some fell from the air, others were briefly stymied by spells or by force, regrouped, and came back for an attack.

And more and more dragons poured out of the portal.

Shortly, the initial shock passed. The Mind Singer's dragons had a distinctive advantage, and it was plain to Arthur as to the reason why:

The attacking dragons had riders on their backs, and Laird's dragons were unpartnered.

That meant the defenders were fighting a double-card deck as well as the linked card that the rider and dragon shared.

Not to mention that a seasoned dragon and rider pair knew each other's powers and trusted one another. They fought more effectively as a unit.

Arthur watched one of Laird's blue dragons spit mist at a silver and its rider. A bubble of mana immediately encased the silver. It was more than a shield, however, as the mist turned back on the blue to cover it. The blue let out a shriek that was cut off as its wings seemed to freeze in place, frozen or paralyzed.

It started to fall, but the silver rider held out her hand and yelled something, and the frozen blue simply splintered into thousands of bloodless bits, which rained down to the ground. The cards that had been in its cores fluttered down after.

Other fights were happening all around the portal as more and more of the Mind Singer's dragons poured in. Meanwhile, only a few more Mesa Free Hive dragons had joined after the initial rush.

Laird spread his wings to land, and Arthur tore his gaze away to focus on the wide hive entrance. A small crowd had gathered there, attracted by the sounds of battle. Most, upon seeing the battle above, backed up in fear and confusion. A few dragons flew up to join and defend. Some of the humans ran out to send long-range spells or attacks up into the air.

It wasn't enough. They needed so much more.

They needed combat cards.

Laird landed right in front of the entrance. As he did, a flat serpentine shape separated itself from his shadow and slithered into the air. Finding Arthur, it rose with a cobra hood extended. Then it spoke in Cressida's voice.

"Joy and I are hearing loud explosions out there. Brixaby is still asleep. Please tell us what's going on. Do you need help?"

Remembering the terms of the card, Arthur mentally reached for his Mana Vault card and aimed a trickle of mana at the shadow serpent. To his surprise, the mana connected quite easily.

"We're under attack by the Mind Singer's forces. Try to wake Brix, but if he can't get up, stay with him and protect him at all costs." He cut off the mana after the last word, and the snake immediately turned and dove back into Laird's shadow, returning to Cressida.

Meanwhile, Laird had been trying—and failing—to field questions thrown at him from the crowd gathered at the entrance. Most looked from him to the portal in the sky with wide eyes but did nothing to help.

Arthur took a deep breath. He didn't feel ready for this, but it was his burden to bear. "Let me talk to them."

Laird stood up tall, extended his red wings to their full length, and roared.

The crowd fell briefly silent. Arthur felt the gazes of the Commons, Uncommons, and a sprinkling of Rares staring at him—likely hoping he'd find a way to save them.

But he couldn't. He could only give them the tools to save themselves.

No doubt a seasoned leader would have pretty words. Arthur only had blunt ones.

"We're under attack from a hive led by a scourgling who has mind powers—"

A brief uproar had him pause.

Swallowing, Arthur continued, leaning on his **Leadership** skills to project his voice louder. "You must either defend yourselves or flee."

Another uproar, humans and dragons yelling, "I can't fight!" and "There's nowhere to go!"

"Then you must fight!" Laird snapped at the last of them.

Arthur agreed. He reached into his Personal Space and drew out a stack of thirty cards and held them up.

It was only a portion of what he had stored, but the hush that fell over the group was more effective than Laird's roar. Arthur held unimaginable wealth in his hands.

"These are combat cards. We don't have time to be picky. So if you're willing to fight—it's first come, first serve."

Then he threw that wealth out into the wind.

Some held back either out of shock or fear. But many more rushed forward. The dragons and people who already had a speed-type card were the first to reach the pile.

Being magic cards, they didn't flutter very far before landing on the ground. Laird was smart enough to jump into the sky before the first people reached the cards. He flapped low, closer to the entrance. Arthur took out a second stack of ten cards and cast the cards to the wind.

Then again and again.

Choosing a card was traditionally done with deliberation and care. Combat cards in the wrong hands could be equally as dangerous to use to the wielder as to the opponent.

But they didn't have time.

The dragons, especially, only glanced at the card long enough to make sure it was their rank or lower, before shoving it into one of their cores. Arthur saw some hasty swapping between different dragons.

The important thing was, after the cards were added to a heart deck or core, that person was ready to fight.

Some flat-out fled without taking a card. Dragons and humans, running or flying out into the bleak, sun-bleached desert. Or skulking back into the walls of the hive as if that could protect them.

Those were relatively few in number. Most were more than willing to defend their home.

Several of the dragons immediately flew upward to help Laird's defenders. But their backs were bare of riders.

"Partner up!" Arthur called, after tossing out another small stack of five to the ground. "Dragons and humans. You're stronger together than apart."

One of the dragons roared in protest. "We're not a kingdom hive!"

"But you are a *hive*," Arthur countered, "and you're going up against scourge—"

"Down!" Laird roared.

Arthur activated his Phase In, Phase Out just as Laird shifted under him. The dragon was fast enough to save himself, but a spear the width of Arthur's arm and as long as a tree flashed through his incorporeal body. It struck the dirt with a thump and burst into splinters that made people cry out.

Canceling his Phase In, Phase Out, Arthur looked up. The aerial fight had been pushed downward by more dragons exiting the portal. The fresh fighters going to join them would help, but the Mesa Hive wasn't highly populated. They could easily get overwhelmed.

"We need to close that portal."

He wished Brixaby was here, but though he kept casting glances toward the entrance, there was no sign of him, Cressida, or Joy. It was left to Arthur and Laird to do the job.

"Agreed," the dragon growled. "Cast out the rest of the cards." He turned to yell at the ones still below. "Fighters and those with cards that can affect a large area, follow me! We must close that portal! I'll punch a hole through!"

With strong beats of his wings, Laird flew upward.

Arthur held on tight with one hand, the other throwing out the rest of the cards. His Personal Space felt empty without all that magical weight.

That meant he had room to put more stuff in.

"Laird!" He pounded on the dragon's neck to get his attention. When the dragon cast him an annoyed glance, Arthur pointed. "Him! I need that chainmail."

An enemy orange flew close by, trying to harass a blue that was spitting water bullets at him. However, the bullets curved in midair. Instead of landing true, they hit the long tail-to-neck chainmail suit the orange wore. It didn't look enchanted—likely, it was an effect of the orange's core card. He was also one of the few fighters without a rider.

"But don't kill—" Arthur started.

The rest of his words were swallowed by the wind as Laird rushed forward in a burst that had to have been card-powered.

He didn't activate his disintegrating candle-top flames as Arthur feared. Instead, he came in from the orange's blind spot and bowled into him from above, claws out.

Though Laird aimed for the neck, those claws were drawn, magically, to the chainmail collar instead.

That was fine, because it was the chainmail that Arthur really wanted.

Laird didn't have a saddle or straps to hang on to.

Holding his breath, Arthur let himself slip off Laird's neck and tumble onto the enemy orange's back.

CHAPTER 43

In the moment of clarity between when Arthur left Laird's back and right before he landed on the enemy orange, he experienced a moment of harsh clarity: *Am I insane?*

Then in the next moment, he struck with a force that knocked his air from his lungs. He didn't have time to recover from that before he started to slide down the chainmail armor. It was well made, buttery soft, and without any easy seams or gaps for him to grip on to.

Arthur focused on his Metal Shot card.

With a will of mana, he made the chain rivets stick to the arms of his outer jacket, his sleeves, and the fabric covering his knees.

His slide off the side of the dragon halted, and he was able to take a proper breath to refill his lungs. But he was still in trouble. The wind whipped around him like a hurricane—a combination of their forward movement and the turbulence from many frantically beating dragon wings.

Most importantly, the orange hadn't failed to notice him.

He whipped his head around, his eyes the exact color of his scales—wide and staring, and yet oddly blank. There was no light inside. Nobody home.

When he opened his mouth, he screamed a sound that was half a melody. He was within the Mind Singer's clutches. He might even be alerting the Mind Singer to Arthur's presence right now for all he knew.

Meanwhile, Laird hadn't simply flown away. He continued to harass the orange by beating at his head with his overly large wings. It was an attempt to take the orange's attention off of Arthur. It wasn't entirely working, but the orange hadn't tried to shake him off yet.

He had only seconds.

Concentrating, Arthur ran a finger down the length of the chainmail rivets, concentrating all his mana on the effort of fine control. The rivets unlinked from one another in a line. Then he repeated the process a foot to the right, capping it off with a line on the top and bottom to complete the strip.

He pulled off the armor in a swath, wrapping it awkwardly around himself. But as the rivets were only a couple inches from his body, he was able to make them relink in a thick sash.

Or what he preferred to think of as: ammunition.

It only took a few moments, and in that time the orange managed to duck Laird's beating wings and twist around to see what Arthur was up to again. This time something like recognition flashed in his eyes.

And Arthur felt something brush up against his mental skills in a way they hadn't during the fight with the Singer's dragons last night.

It felt like something was probing and being nudged away by his **Mental Blocking** skills. It was curious, not angry. Not yet.

Probably because it didn't know if it was Arthur or not.

Arthur's eyes flicked up to the portal that was still spitting out dragons fresh to the fight.

But it was more than that, wasn't it? It was also a direct link to the Mind Singer.

Arthur focused on his area-of-effect **Mental Shield** skill.

He wished he was strong enough to bathe the entire sky with it, but his Mana Vault had taken a hit thanks to grabbing the chainmail. The best he could do was to focus the Mental Shield around himself—and Laird to keep him safe just in case—and extend it over the orange's head, past his nose.

The effect was immediate. The orange stopped in place so abruptly that Laird overshot the other dragon and had to quickly flap to circle back around.

But the orange wasn't fighting him. He looked around, confused.

"What?" he asked in a surprisingly high voice that was devoid of all melody. "What happened? Where am I? Is there an eruption?" He looked around and down, politely puzzled to see no scourglings in the sky.

"Mind magic," Arthur gasped, taking the opportunity to rip a second swath of chainmail away. He wrapped this around his waist like a thick belt. "You were under a spell."

The orange's head twisted around to Arthur. He looked aghast at the patchwork his fine chainmail had become.

"Hey, I hope you intend to pay for that . . ."

"I just snapped you out of having your mind taken over." With a heave, Arthur pulled himself directly up onto the dragon's back and stood. Then he pointed downward. "Go take shelter in that hive. You'll be safe there. Don't come back up until the battle's over. She might ensnare you again."

"She?" the orange asked, still seeming bemused. Then he visibly focused. "And who do you think you are to give me orders?"

Above, Laird chuckled darkly. "The Legendary rider of the Mesa Free Hive. Reach out and feel his power for yourself."

Dragons were much better at instantly determining internal card rank than humans.

The orange froze, his eyes going even wider. "Yes, sir," he said, and very helpfully stayed still while Arthur jumped back onto Laird.

As soon as Arthur was safely aboard, the orange dragon folded his wings and dove.

Arthur watched carefully, but there was no indication that the Mind Singer had re-ensnared the orange again once he left Arthur's skill zone. It made sense, or else their own dragons would be actively being ensnared. He guessed that she had to be close to initially take over a mind.

All in all, getting himself his chainmail armor/ammunition had only taken a few spare minutes. That delay had allowed the Mesa dragons with their new combat cards time to catch up to Laird. Half of them had peeled off to help with the general battle. The other half circled close by, waiting for instructions. Most of those had human partners on them—not linked, but friends or people who were willing to fight and defend the dragon they rode on.

"Follow me!" Laird roared. "To the portal!"

The dragons roared alongside him. Together, they rose in a ragged formation, spells and elemental long-range attacks firing ahead. Arthur even caught glimpses of conjured arrows.

The enemy dragons clustered closest to where they emerged from the portal. They fell upon the rising defenders eagerly, as if they were hungry.

Gripping Laird's neck with just his legs, Arthur grabbed a swath of chainmail, raised both hands, and started peppering the dragons in front of him with unlinked rivets.

He'd learned from the battles last night and aimed for the dragon's sensitive spots: their faces, eyes, nostrils, throat, and stomach.

None of it was deadly to them, but it did provide a stinging distraction.

Laird opened his mouth, and his deadly candle-top flames spewed forward. These were different from the ones Arthur had seen before—they cycled from purple to a blazing toxic yellow and back again at random.

The candle-top flames danced merrily ahead, and where they brushed other dragons, the flames clung on and didn't seem to want to extinguish, even when one dragon covered himself with a bubble of water.

The aftermath was . . . gruesome.

"Hold back if you can, Laird," Arthur said. "These are victims, too. They're under the Mind Singer's spell."

"They're also enemies!" Laird roared, unsympathetic. Then to the other dragons, "Punch through!"

Arthur didn't have time—and he knew he didn't have the place—to complain. There were more attackers than defenders. After all, dragons fell from the sky on their side just as often as the Singer's. It took time to become truly proficient with a new card and tease out all the helpful nuances. Even combat cards.

But they were getting close to the portal.

Either the Mind Singer hadn't figured out what their goal was yet or was distracted by managing so many minds.

Arthur tried to break her hold over enemy dragons as they flew upward past them, but his skill needed at least a few seconds to take effect. Touching them with the area of effect wasn't enough, and it was too much of a mana drain to keep it up. Reluctantly, he focused more on fighting rather than saving.

Arthur peppered a path of stinging rivets in front of Laird.

Twice, Arthur caught sight of Ghost—just a flickering outline out of the corner of his eye that he could never fully focus on.

The other dragon worked as a silent assassin, sneaking up and then physically attacking dragons who were in the middle of setting up complex spells. One time, he interrupted a dragon to great effect. Whatever spell it was weaving with bright strings of mana collapsed and then blew up in its face.

Laird bolted past a yellow dragon who was reflecting flashes of pure sunlight into the eyes of the hive's attackers.

Then, briefly, there was a straight shot to the portal.

Two dark-green dragons were on either side of the rip in the sky, holding the edges open as if reality itself were heavy fabric. A silver visibly fed mana into the greens to help them keep up their strength.

"Get me close!" Arthur yelled, but Laird was already powering ahead.

He sent a burst of flames—a gout of traditional red-and-orange fire—straight to the mana-wielding silver.

The silver's rider reacted immediately by casting a semitranslucent shield over himself and his dragon. Laird's flames splashed over the top and the sides. It didn't blast through, but that interruption gave Laird the second he needed to close in.

And once they were within the spell's aura, Arthur was able to copy it.

New Counterfeit spell obtained: Mana Springwell
Remaining Time: 11 Hours 59 Minutes 59 Seconds

Arthur immediately activated Mana Springwell and slapped Laird on the neck, pumping him with fresh mana. His own Mana Vault benefited as well, steadily climbing upward from a quarter full.

Laird shuddered in relief.

Arthur caught a flicker of movement he couldn't focus on. Ghost was with them.

"Ghost, take out one of the greens—"

The flicker moved, and one of the greens screamed as a gash appeared on her side.

Immediately, her rider moved to heal her, but the cut provided a distraction. Something in the depth of the unnerving rip in the sky flickered.

Arthur reached for the two spells he felt from the greens.

New Counterfeit spell obtained: Portalus Creatus
Remaining Time: 59 Minutes 58 Seconds

New Counterfeit spell obtained: Temporal Tatter
Remaining Time: 59 Minutes 58 Seconds

He could only temporarily copy the spells, and they wouldn't be as powerful as if he had the whole cards. But destruction was always easier than creation.

And the dragons were *physically* holding the rip open.

"Laird! Attack the other green!"

He waited a beat until Laird closed in and then jumped off the dragon's back, concentrating all his might and mana on the two portal spells. As he fell, he reached to grab the rip in the sky.

Up close, his eyes didn't want to concentrate on it. He felt himself being pulled in—in danger of being spit out on the Mind Singer's side.

When using the spell, however, the rip became less of a hole in the sky and more like a very, very dense fabric.

His hand closed around the sky like it was heavy cloth, and the weight of his falling body ripped it out of the surprised green's claws a moment before Laird struck it.

Arthur concentrated on tearing down the spell as he fell, and the rip closed along with him.

The other green shrieked and tried to reach out to regain control, but the construction of a portal was a delicate thing, and Arthur had just upset the balance.

He felt with a sense he didn't have a few moments before that emerging dragons were being tossed back out the other side as this end closed off.

And as he glanced through the closing portal, he swore he saw a bat-shaped scourgling glaring through the other side.

Arthur's head exploded with pain. He wasn't sure if it was rapidly dwindling mana, a mental attack battering his skills, or both.

As he fell, the rip closed, and the fabric of reality slipped from his fingers.

Arthur kept falling.

But only for a few seconds.

Something slammed into his back as sharp claws gripped his arms. His chainmail tore under the strain, then recombined a few seconds later.

"Laird!" came a familiar boom in Arthur's ear. "Why aren't you taking better care of my rider?"

Arthur jerked to a painful stop. He was . . . hovering in place.

Brixaby had caught him.

CHAPTER 44

Arthur twisted to get a better look at his dragon.

"Brix! You're—"

"Magnificent?" Smugness practically dripped off the end of his very pointed muzzle. "Impressive? *Gargantuan?*"

"You're awake," Arthur said and grinned at his dragon's offended look.

But, as a matter of fact, Brixaby did look very impressive in the light of day. He was still the size of a decent cart donkey, which could handle the weight of a man without armor on. But his features had developed and appeared more refined from when Arthur had last seen him.

Brixaby's scales were at the same time a deeper black and yet showed off an iridescent purple shimmer when the light caught him at just the right angle. Occasional flashes of the deep purple skin in gaps in the scales reinforced his true color, as were his wings when the sun shined through the thin membrane.

His barrel was wide with a deep chest and visible muscles meant to support four rapidly beating wings. His tail, however, was long and whiplike which indicated that there was more growth coming.

Brixaby's head and muzzle had lengthened subtly in proportion to the rest of his body, with his muzzle curving downward ever so slightly. It reminded Arthur of a farmer's scythe—elegant and very deadly.

Aside from his size, the biggest change to his silhouette was the spikes that ran down his spine. They were thin and curved backward to a wicked point. He had similarly elongated scales on his knees, wrists, and elbows. Any dragon that tried to tangle with Brixaby in the air would receive a spiky surprise.

His dragon glowered down at him. Now that he was larger, his expression was that much more fearsome. "What are you doing? You don't have wings yet. You can't fly."

"Yet?" Arthur let out a laugh. It shouldn't be funny—they were in the middle of a battle—but with his limbs buzzing from adrenaline thanks to his fall, he couldn't be in a better mood. "Find me a body-enhancement card that gives me wings and we'll talk about it."

Though chances were, even with a card like that and his Master of Body Enhancement boost, Brixaby could probably still outfly him.

In the last few seconds, Brixaby had easily buzzed away from the worst of the fighting.

That was another change: What had been a hummingbird hum from his wings was now a deeper drone that Arthur could feel in his breastbone. He imagined that could become a terrifying sound to their enemies.

"Hurry, climb up," Brixaby said. "You closed the portal, but there's still a fight to be had." His bloodred eyes glittered. "And I'm looking forward to showing you the benefits of my new power. No peeking! I want it to be a surprise."

Arthur rolled his eyes but didn't look into Brixaby's deck. Instead, he swung around and gripped his dragon's scaly elbow. He had a moment where he mentally tried to reach for his 20-Point Spree card to give himself a boost of strength, then remembered that Cressida had it.

He had to do this himself.

Legs kicking in the air, Arthur pulled himself up bit by bit. Brixaby grabbed his foot to help stabilize him, and using the leverage, Arthur reached to grab one of the spiky ridges that went down Brixaby's spine.

That was going to be interesting to sit on.

But as he pulled himself up and then swung his leg over, he realized his dragon was, more or less, made for him.

The neck ridges were viciously pointed backward, but they also flattened out at the base of his neck and for a foot or so behind his spine before spiking out again. That allowed Brixaby to have full flexibility of his neck without his ridges clashing with one another. And, conveniently enough, it gave Arthur a place to sit.

Though if he leaned forward, he might get stabbed.

For the first time, he truly experienced what it was like to fly on his dragon.

His seat was comfortable. Not narrow or bony like some courier purples he'd flown with. Also, he was able to grip his dragon easily using his legs, instead of feeling like he was trying to straddle a wide platform, like some of the larger dragons he'd flown on.

Though Brixaby could dart in all directions, including nearly straight up and down, his body remained completely level in the air.

But just in case, Arthur grabbed a length of rope from his Personal Space and lashed his own legs down. He'd seen Brixaby's acrobatics, and there was no way Arthur could hang on if the dragon did a loop-the-loop.

The second he was ready, Brixaby buzzed forward, straight into battle. Arthur, on his back, whooped.

The portal might have been closed, but the fighting continued.

Arthur had half hoped that cutting off the connection would end the Mind Singer's influence over the dragons. But it seemed, just like the team they'd fought last night, that the Mind Singer had sunk her claws into her thralls and made it hard for them to shake loose.

Her dragons were likely left with some instructions in case they found themselves alone.

Worse, one of the remaining green dragons was trying to reopen the portal. Arthur didn't know if he could do it, but he had the help of the silver mana user.

"Brix," he said, leaning close across his dragon's narrow neck to call out his command, "whatever you're about to do, make sure it stops them." He pointed to the portal.

"Hold on!" Brixaby said, and the angle of his rapidly beating wings changed as he shot nearly straight upward, while managing to keep Arthur's seat absolutely stable.

Through their bond, Arthur sensed that Brixaby was showing off. It would have been easier to tilt vertically, but the rope Arthur used on his legs was for emergencies only.

"Definitely getting a riding saddle," he muttered. "One with a lot of wide straps."

"Make them black," Brixaby said. "It will go nicely with my scales."

When he was level with the portal, he stopped. Then he opened his mouth and roared.

From the moment he hatched, Brixaby had a naturally loud voice.

This new roar went beyond that.

He had stripped a portion of the power away from the Legendary Sonic Attack card. How much, Arthur wasn't sure, because he had followed Brixaby's request and had not actually looked yet.

He observed instead.

Brixaby's open mouth, of course, was pointed away from him, so Arthur only caught a bare sliver of the blast. It was still deafening.

The sound was somehow . . . shallower than the card last night had been. A single deep note of nothing, of void, instead of a full chorus of destruction. And it didn't quite shake the air in the same way the card had.

But the effect still had an impact.

The green and silver opened their mouths in what Arthur assumed were squeals of pain. It couldn't be heard over Brixaby's low nothing-blast.

The rider on the silver clapped his hands over his ears before slumping boneless across his beast's back.

The two dragons struggled for a moment, and if they had been caught on the edge of the blast, they might have been able to move away. Now, there was no escape. They didn't fall apart in the same way Shadow had. Instead, they slumped in the air and fell with blood streaming from their ear holes.

"Follow them down," Arthur demanded, feeling cold. He hated the killing, but what was done was done. "I want their cards."

"Sure," Brixaby said. "But they aren't dead."

That shocked him. He stopped Brixaby's gather for a dive with a squeeze from his knee. "Then wait."

He looked again at the falling dragons and realized that while they were in bad shape, they seemed to be halfway stunned. The dragons were making a token effort to control their fall. As Arthur watched, one managed to straighten his wings out and turned his plunge into a downward spiral. The silver's rider seemed to be coming around too and was waving his arms in a casting pose. The silver's fall began to slow.

They'd live, but they were out of the fight.

"I call it my Stunning Shout," Brixaby said.

Finally, Arthur looked at Brixaby's core card.

Call of the Void
Legendary
Nullify
The wielder of this card has the ability to take another card of the same rank or lower from any deck. Once placed in a temporary deck, the new card's aspects are slowly consumed and added to a list of ten removable/adjustable slots to grow the wielder's strength.
This list is not transferable and will dissolve upon the wielder's death or removal from the core.
This card is part of the Call set. Search out other cards in this set to add to your power.
Card Effects:
4/10
Attribute: Charm +5
Spell: Magic Nullification, Level 5
Instant Danger Sense (2-second warning)
Stunning Shout, Level 3

The skill was indeed called Stunning Shout.

"Huh."

A lot of the power had been stripped from the Legendary card. Brixaby didn't seem to have the ability to exclude allies from the cone of destruction, or much control over the effect except for "loud" and "less loud." But what was left was still powerful and acted like a skill. Arthur didn't have any complaints. It meant the shout could be powered up.

His attention was drawn by an alert from above. Laird had gone off to skirmish with several other dragons after Brixaby had caught Arthur. Now the red dragon roared for everyone's attention.

Arthur was too far away, but he saw the red dragon point and followed his gaze.

Sometime in the last few minutes, a contingent of the Mind Singer's dragons had broken off from the main battle to fly over the salt sea.

"What are they doing?" Arthur asked, though a sinking sensation had settled in his stomach.

"They must be after the dungeon. Ha!" Brixaby laughed. "Little do they know it's been cleaned out."

"No, they're far over the water. They're—"

He stopped, seeing a pattern begin to form among the faraway dragons. Some separated from the rest to dive toward the water at a steep angle, only to pull up sharply just before hitting. The wind of their wings made the waves choppy.

No . . . It shouldn't be possible to see the waves out from this far. They were bigger than they looked.

"That song," Arthur breathed.

Brixaby looked back at him. "What song?"

Laird must have already made the connection because he was roaring for the defenders to gather together. Meanwhile, more and more of the Mind Singer's attacking dragons broke off from their own fights or finished their own, only to turn and fly out to the sea. They were like moths to a flame.

And now that Arthur was seeing them all at once, he noted there were a lot of blue, green, and silver dragons in the bunch. Water, nature, and magic.

Some of the diving blues began to bring up big globs of water with them on the way up, only to release the water at the high apex of their climb. It crashed back down, magically coaxed into a sticky glob that could be carried, or a chunk of ice. That in turn created more waves, which were growing higher and higher.

"I thought it was just a bad rhyming scheme," Arthur said. "It was a warning. They mean to 'drown us'—swamp the land or the mesa. That's a brine sea! That amount of salt will sterilize the land. Brix, fly. We have to stop them!"

CHAPTER 45

W hy fly out that way?" Brixaby asked. He pointed his muzzle down, toward the still-spiraling, bleeding green dragon—the one who had been holding the portal open. It was nearly at the ground now. "All we need to transport everybody over there is right in front of us."

He sounded eager to steal a brand-new spell. A portal type, at that.

Only the lessons on dignity he had been forced to take at Wolf Moon Hive kept Arthur from slapping his forehead. "No need. I already have a couple of spells." And thanks to the mana silver, he was topped up on power.

Just in case, he placed his hand on Brixaby's neck and let the mana flow into him as well. It was an incredibly useful spell.

Brixaby and Joy loved to talk about getting others into their retinue, but Arthur wanted that silver in his, whoever he was.

That was a problem for later.

Meanwhile, Laird was bellowing orders, pulling everybody's attention toward the dragons out to the salt sea. Unfortunately, they were miles away—a ten-minute flying sprint at best.

Arthur had the spell to get them there in a blink.

"Brixaby, fly me up high. We want to portal down over them—Ooph."

Brixaby did what he asked almost before Arthur had finished talking, coming to a stop so fast that Arthur was thrown forward, catching himself right before he hit one of those backward-facing spines. Then Brixaby spun around, and Arthur got a view of the battlefield below.

There were fewer of the Mind Singer's dragons than he'd thought there had been before. Many had fallen, though most of those were injured instead of dead, and they'd managed to land in a controlled fall. Several ground-based skirmishes were occurring right now.

Others lay broken on the ground. Including tiny broken bodies of humans, looking like dolls scattered in the dust. Arthur could not tell at a glance who were the attackers or the defenders.

They all went up on my orders, he thought, then shook himself. Now was not the time for self-recrimination. Now was the time for action.

As if reading his mind, Brixaby bellowed, putting a hint of his Stunning Shout into it. That had the effect of mentally slapping people and dragons alike. The few skirmishes left stopped. And the moment the defenders were distracted, the Mind Singer's dragons tore off straight to the sea to help the rest.

Arthur gestured to the sea, which had waves now cresting over twenty feet high. Some of them crashed against the peninsula, flooding over it. And still, the waves built higher and higher.

The sea was shallow but vast, and Arthur did not doubt that if they got those waves up high enough, they could get it to wash over the mesa. Not only would that be a danger to the people hiding inside, but the toxic salt water would destroy all their crops and almost ensure nothing could be grown afterward without the aid of some serious magic.

"Earth dragons—anybody with rock, soil, or metal powers—head down to the mesa and seal it up. The rest of you, follow me through the portal."

Turning, Arthur activated one of the portal spells in his mind. Then he scraped his fingers down into the fabric that was the sky.

It wasn't easy. He wasn't working with a full-blown spell card, just a copied spell. He didn't have the details of it like he would with a normal spell card. He was forced to go by instinct and feel.

And this spell practically *gushed* mana.

He felt mana flow out of his fingertips even before there was a visible sign of a rip in the sky. His fingers caught something, and he clamped on and dragged his hand down. A dark line appeared, but the space beyond it was so cold that it felt almost hot.

Arthur grimaced but kept on, knowing that his healing card could handle a little bit of frostbite.

He tried not to think that it usually took two greens to hold open a portal during a scourge-eruption. Arthur was going to have to do this all by himself.

As Arthur worked, Brixaby sank, allowing Arthur to lengthen the rip. But there was only that freezing blackness beyond. What was he doing wrong? What—

Oh. The destination.

He held an image of the sea in his mind. Instantly, the darkness snapped into blue sky again. Blue sky that was almost indistinguishable from his own because it was only a couple of miles away.

The mana still flooded out of him, but at a slightly more reasonable pace now that the portal had a connection.

"Brixaby, have you gotten a copy of the spell, too?" Arthur asked, his voice strained.

"No. I can't copy your copy," Brixaby replied, annoyed.

Arthur sighed, but he had suspected as much.

"Okay, let's rip this open."

Brixaby knew what he meant immediately, and flew diagonal and straight up, allowing Arthur to peel back the sky as if it were a curtain.

His mana dropped like a stone, and Arthur yelled, "Stop!"

This was his limit. The portal was perhaps fifteen feet long and ten feet wide. If he made it any larger, he would lose his hold. His arms trembled with the weight of holding the fabric of reality open.

"Through the portal," Brixaby yelled at the awaiting dragons. And one by one, they darted in.

At least, the smaller and medium-sized ones did, who were able to fold their wings and dive through. The humans on their backs pressed low to keep from being scraped off.

Laird bellowed again. He was too large for the portal, but within moments, he had a contingent of other larger dragons heading out the long way. They would be there in a few minutes, and hopefully, act as support for the battle to come.

Meanwhile, Arthur's mana was already two-thirds gone and dropping fast.

He tried to activate the mana refill spell, but that split his mind in too many directions. His hold on the portal grew slippery, and he started to feel the fabric of space slipping through his fingers.

"Hurry them up. I can't last too much longer."

He focused solely on the portal, allowing Brixaby to yell and hurry the rest along. Finally, when he was only a few percentages from empty, the second-to-last dragon—a yellow—dove in. The very last was a cheerful pink dragon.

It was Joy, with Cressida on her back.

Joy's claws were stained red, but her expression was triumphant. "Hi, Arthur! Any way we could help?"

"Get through the portal!" he yelled, sweating.

"Sure thing," Joy said.

Cressida added something as well, but her voice was lost to the wind.

The moment Joy's tail disappeared through the portal, Arthur gasped out, "Brixaby, now!"

Brixaby completed a turn so sharp that he practically spun in the air. Then, as he dove through the portal, Arthur let go of the edge.

The sky folded back into place within a few seconds, just like a piece of cloth. That gave Brixaby just enough time to dart through and out the other side.

They made it . . . straight into the chaos of battle.

Arthur glanced back and saw that Laird and his larger dragon contingent were still a few minutes out, at the very least.

The water had gathered into one large wave, which rolled ominously back and forth, with blue dragons shaping other, smaller waves to add to it. Each one increased its mass and overall energy. Meanwhile, the rest of the Mind Singer's dragons acted as a vanguard, protecting those blues and throwing themselves in front of anybody who tried to stop them.

Judging by the dragons who floated down below, they had paid ruinously for it, but with each moment, the giant wave was building.

Arthur immediately activated the mana spell to refill his supply. "Brixaby, target the blues."

Brixaby obediently opened his mouth, inhaled so deeply that his sides stretched out, and dove.

Arthur's mana had only recovered a few percent, but it was enough to start peppering enemy dragons on the way down with more rivets.

The second Brixaby was in range, he targeted a blue, who was shepherding along a smaller wave, with his Stunning Shout.

The blue staggered in the air, shaking its head and looking confused. The small wave collapsed without joining the larger one.

Arthur caught a flash of orange out of the corner of his eye. A large dragon was headed right for them, his claws physically lengthening.

Oranges were materials experts, and this one seemed to have some kind of body modification. His frame had lengthened, and now he was like a knife darting through the air, claws extended too straight, just like swords.

But he wasn't the only one with claw-based power.

Joy, who had taken her position as a guard and was flying behind and just to the side of Brixaby, peeled off and hit the orange first. Her claws were much smaller but loaded with deadly poison.

Meanwhile, Cressida yelled something, and Arthur was suddenly surrounded by a flock of water cranes that dive-bombed past him into the dragons below. One even landed in a building wave, breaking the spell and dispersing it.

Arthur and Brixaby's charge had punched a hole through the Mind Singer's dragons' defensive line. Others followed, and many of them targeted the dragons shepherding the massive great wave.

The one in charge of the largest wave was a blue shimmer dragon—so high quality that his scales caught the light and flickered with the sun.

"Attack the shimmer blue!" Brixaby yelled, both out loud and in several minds.

The shimmer blue was instantly targeted by a whole host of spells. Most were Common spells. Nothing extraordinary. But the sheer volume all targeted at one dragon was more effective than Brixaby diving in and doing the work himself.

This is what it means to be a leader, Arthur thought. There was a time and a place to make the final blow, but sometimes it was equally, if not more, important to direct others to do the same thing.

The shimmer blue fell, stunned. And the great building wave collapsed on itself with a huge ploosh that sent water up over the banks of the shallow sea and rolling far out into the desert. The mesa was several miles off, and Arthur suspected it would only be hit by gentle waves.

The salt that the water left behind would be a problem if anyone ever wanted to plant outside, but it was better than flooding the entire Mesa complex.

Speaking of . . .

He glanced at the mesa, then frowned. Dust rolled up off the top of it, and he saw a V of dragons flying away rapidly.

Were those more crafters who didn't want to fight? He didn't know for sure, and he didn't have the luxury of finding out because, despite the waves collapsing, there was still a battle to win.

He and Brixaby directed the defenders to attack the remaining enemy dragons.

"Brixaby, order everybody to stun if at all possible. And only kill if they have to."

Brixaby grumbled, but with bellowing shouts, he passed the word along. Unfortunately, too many broken dragons and people landed in the briny salt water and drowned.

Arthur tried not to look. But now they had momentum on their side, and they were reinforced when Laird's dragons finally reached the battle.

Soon, it was all but over. They'd won.

Arthur was readying himself to tell Brixaby to land among the stunned Mind Singer dragons. If he could break her hold on them one by one, he might be able to gather some information. But first, he had to find some healers to tend to the injured. Arthur was looking around for a courier purple when he spotted one conveniently heading right toward him.

It was a young purple, only a little smaller than Brixaby. She must have had a speed-enhancement card because even though she beat her wings at a normal speed, she seemed to effortlessly fly faster than Brixaby.

Brixaby didn't like this and flew around the purple, who then twirled around to face him. The result was that the two dragons began whirling in the air.

Arthur was in danger of being sick. "Brixaby, stop that."

"Oh! Oh! You're Brixaby! I wasn't sure. They said to find the black dragon, but you are purple too," the young dragon said in a high, childish voice.

"What do you want?" Brixaby demanded.

"I have a message for your rider. Oh! There you are!" The purple turned wide eyes on Arthur as if she hadn't spotted him before now. "Chablis says the eggs have been stolen, and you're to come back to the mesa *right now*. You're in big, big trouble, I think. Sorry," she added.

"Eggs?" Brixaby demanded. "What eggs?"

It wasn't very often that a purple looked at somebody else like they were an idiot, but that's exactly what this one did.

"The dragon eggs. *Our* dragon eggs. Well, not mine," she added, "but all the rest. Stolen to the last shell. Everybody's really angry. Come on." She flipped her tail and immediately flew back to the mesa.

Arthur and Brixaby glanced at each other.

"Wait," Arthur said, "they have a hatching ground here?"

"I'm glad you said it and not me," Brixaby muttered. "Also, I do not like being summoned so rudely by somebody who owes *us* a debt for just saving them."

Arthur hesitated, knowing the eggs were important, but then he nodded.

"Land," he told Brixaby. "Let's see what we can do to break the Mind Singer's spell over those dragons."

The missing eggs would have to wait.

CHAPTER 46

Something isn't right about this," Arthur muttered to Brixaby.

His dragon sank fast, without any of the grace that the older dragons with larger wings possessed. Brixaby didn't glide; he simply buzzed downward, leveling off only when he felt like it—but not before jinking right and left to avoid other dragons passing by.

"What's wrong? We won and sent the enemy back with their tails between their legs." Brixaby blithely ignored the fact that there were several final ongoing skirmishes on the ground by Mind Singer thralls that had been forced to land. But they were being subdued by the hive dragons and a few of the humans who had come in to help.

That was one area where the crafters excelled, especially those who had cards that dealt with textiles. More than one dragon was snarling and struggling, bound up in cloth ropes that shouldn't have been as strong as they were. Another was draped so thickly in chains that Arthur couldn't tell if it was male or female. A third had her head sticking up out of a giant, dragon-sized roll of carpet.

It was a goofy solution. Arthur imagined the kingdom hives would have called it undignified, but if little tricks like that kept the enemy dragons contained, Arthur couldn't fault them.

He pointed to the dragon rolled up in the giant carpet. "Let's start there."

Brixaby buzzed over in a moment and came to such an abrupt stop that Arthur was nearly thrown over his neck. At the last moment, he locked his knees and held on.

New skill level: Dragon Riding (Animal Husbandry/Dragon Rider
Class)
Level 15

Huh. It had been a while since he had leveled that skill up.

Dismounting, he walked over to the still-struggling yellow dragon and the man watching over her. He was an older fellow with a completely bald head and a nose that could have been better described as a beak. But what really set him apart from the others was the look of deep satisfaction on his face as he gazed at the yellow dragon. It wasn't cruelty or malice. It was accomplishment.

He glanced over at Arthur as he walked up and nodded with a bob of his head. "So, I suppose you're the Legendary rider everybody's been talking about?"

Arthur had a moment to contrast the stiff formality—even fear—of Wolf Moon Hive folk versus what he experienced regularly here.

"Yes, I'm Arthur, and this is Brixaby. I assume this is your work?" He gestured to the carpet.

"Indeed it is," came the reply, that look of satisfaction crossing his face again. "Though, I'll say that Kloy here doesn't seem to be in the right mind to appreciate it."

In response, Kloy, the yellow dragon, howled in rage—though strangely with a musical note behind it—and bit down on the roll of carpet that imprisoned her. She managed to tear through it with her teeth. At a gesture from the man, the carpet repaired itself instantly.

"Kloy?" Brixaby asked. "You know her?"

"She's my sister's dragon, from another hive," the man answered. "Though I don't know where my sister is. And Kloy isn't telling me."

"Let's ask her, then." Arthur stepped up to the still-bound dragon and concentrated on his area-of-effect Mental Shield skill.

He felt the skill cast out into a wide, invisible bubble. Instantly, the yellow dragon's howling ceased. She blinked and looked around.

Then, in a high, but surprisingly clear voice, she asked, "Where am I?"

The man stepped forward. "You're at the Mesa Free Hive, Kloy."

"Georgie? Is that you?" She squinted down at the man in shock, then at herself, all bundled up. "Is this supposed to be a prank? Where is Perita?"

Brixaby flew up to hover practically nose to nose with the other dragon. "You attacked my hive, and now *you* will answer my questions. What can you tell me of the Mind Singer?"

"Who?"

"The scourgling that took over your mind! What are her plans? What were her orders?"

"A scourgling? I assure you, I don't know what you're talking about. I was going to get a snack, and Perita, my rider, was to watch my eggs—my eggs!" She gasped, then wiggled more fiercely than ever before. "Georgie, let me out of here. This isn't funny. Where is my clutch? Where are my eggs?" She looked around, worried. "What's going on? Why am I in your hive, Georgie?"

The man, Georgie, glanced at Arthur for permission. At Arthur's nod, he gestured, and the large, intricate carpet unrolled itself, dumping out the yellow dragon. The carpet instantly snapped several times in the air, ridding itself of all dust before it wrapped itself into a neat bundle again. That, Arthur suspected, was likely his card power—a power over rug and carpet cleaning. But with enough time and skill, Georgie had adjusted it to do his bidding.

The yellow dragon leaped to her feet, a frantic look in her eyes.

"Where are my eggs? Where is my rider?" She might have taken to the sky, but Brixaby hovered above her and gave a deep growl.

Kloy, finally seeming to sense Brixaby's rank, quailed.

"We're trying to find out what happened," Arthur said, feeling a twinge of sympathy for her. "Your hive was taken over with mind magic. And the one responsible sent you to attack our hive."

Kloy's gasp of horror did not sound fake. "But what happened to my clutch and my rider?"

Brixaby was . . . less than empathetic. "Why don't you tell us? I command you to tell me the last thing you remember."

She straightened. "I told you. I needed to eat. I had freshly laid my eggs only three days ago, and I left my rider behind to go grab a lamb from the pens. I flew out of the hatching ground and I heard . . . a song?" She cocked her head, the scales over her muzzle crinkling as if she wasn't sure of her own memory. "And the next thing I know, I woke up here."

"Nothing else?" Arthur asked. "No orders? You don't remember the scourgling? Or how many others she had with her?"

"I don't remember anything at all. I just woke up here." She gave Arthur an annoyed look but then glanced around. Seeing the other dragons, many of whom she likely recognized, Kloy slumped. "I don't know what's going on. Please, sir, may I return to my clutch?"

Arthur exchanged a glance with Brixaby, who shrugged his wings. "I don't know if it's safe yet," Arthur said. "For now, stay here with your rider's brother."

"But what about my eggs? I trust my rider, but she is human. Only a dragon knows how to take care of her eggs."

"Kloy, it sounds like it may be dangerous to return right now," Georgie said. "You know how devoted Perita is. She'll keep your eggs safe."

The yellow dragon looked less than certain but also so lost that she didn't have much of an argument. After glancing again at Brixaby and seeing his stern expression, she nodded.

Arthur gestured to Brixaby, and the two of them stepped away to speak in private. Arthur lowered his voice.

"Do you think it's a coincidence that she's a nesting mother, and the Mind Singer's other dragons just took off with the Mesa Hive's eggs?"

"What would a scourgling want with *eggs*?" Brixaby demanded. "Eggs are useless until they hatch, and then baby dragons are useless for months afterward. Unless, of course, they are Legendary," he added. "But Kloy is only a Common."

"You came from a Common," Arthur reminded him. But then he shook his head. "It may be a coincidence, but I don't like this. Where are Joy and Cressida?" He'd lost track of them during the fighting and only caught a glimpse of the two helping to put down the last of the skirmishes. Glancing around, he caught a flash of Joy's bright hide wheeling in the sky to the north. They weren't in a fight—it seemed she was keeping a lookout.

"Brixaby, send a message: I want them to go back to the hive and tell me what's happening there."

Brixaby nodded, and his bloodred eyes focused for a moment as he mentally sent along the order. "Done."

Meanwhile, Arthur turned to the rest of the subdued dragons.

Now that the tide of battle had turned, more and more reinforcements had come from the hive to see how they could help. Many brought along healers on their backs.

Brixaby grumbled at their late arrival, but Arthur decided to be generous and assume the latecomers hadn't received any of the combat cards. They were crafters and couldn't fight outright. But they could help now.

However, once this was over, he intended to speak to the council and get a list of who exactly could fight, and their general capabilities.

They were lucky that the Mind Singer had only sent a couple hundred dragons this time. Had it been a whole hive's worth . . . Well, he doubted the battle would have gone their way.

Was it luck? Or something else? And why did the Mind Singer go after the *eggs*?

He set those worries aside for now and concentrated on visiting the groups of subdued enemy dragons and freeing them from the Mind Singer's control. He had to work at a methodical pace to allow his mana to recharge. The spell helped, but after a few hours, his insides—his spirit—felt sore. Like he was exercising a muscle that didn't normally get a lot of use.

It was a discomfort he could set aside. The dragons and the people were more important.

It was satisfying to see blank eyes become focused again. Though, like yellow Kloy, none of them seemed to have a memory of falling under the Mind Singer's control. They had gone about their day, then woke up and found themselves confused in a brand-new place. Some of them were rightfully upset to find that they were injured during their "missing time."

More than once, Brixaby had to flex his Legendary-dragon authority to keep squabbles from breaking out.

The more dragons who woke up from their spell and claimed not to know anything, the more Brixaby became frustrated. "You mean to say that you let a scourgling all the way into your hive, take over your dragons and riders, and you didn't even put up a defense? You didn't *notice*?" he demanded while buzzing around the head of a sheepish-looking pink dragon.

Brixaby was harder on this one than the others because the pink was one of the few Rares that had come through the portal.

"I don't know what happened," the pink dragon said as he gingerly flexed a wing. Unlike Joy, there was no shimmer quality to his hide at all. His color was a washed-out pale red. "I was taking a break from work—my card specializes in logistics, and we just had a meeting planning out the best crop rotations, you see. It was midday, and the rocks were nice and warm. I went up for a nap. Then I woke up . . . here."

Brixaby snorted in disgust.

"How do we know that you didn't kidnap us?" piped up a young green Common dragon. "How do we know it was a scourgling at all? Maybe you're the one with mind magic!"

Brixaby turned a withering glare at her, and she shrank back.

"I protect the dragons under my care," Brixaby said coldly, turning his angry eyes back on the pink. "As any higher-ranked dragon should. No scourgling would ever creep up on me."

The pink dragon gulped but got the hint and extended a wing over the young Common green as if to cover her.

Brixaby snorted again and turned away.

Meanwhile, Arthur wasn't having luck with the human contingent.

"There wasn't any warning at all," one woman said. "I was washing some clothes—I'm on laundry duty today, and I thought I heard a song on the wind. Sort of far away. I was wondering if there was a festival about to break out. And the next thing I know"—she shrugged—"I'm here."

Arthur nodded, then directed her to join the rest of the abled-bodied on the trek back to the hive, where they could get shelter and something to eat. Then he went on to the next group.

This one contained the silver with the mana card.

Brixaby buzzed down to join him. For a horrified moment, Arthur thought he was going to try to land on his shoulder. But Brixaby seemed to remember his new size at the last second and instead landed on the ground to walk beside Arthur. On the ground, the slight arch of his spine reached Arthur's ribs. Arthur slung an arm over Brixaby's back, just because he could. He still hadn't gotten over how much his dragon had grown.

"You did good today during the battle," he said.

"Of course I did," Brixaby said, his head lifting in pride. "And it was much more convenient to have you flying with me than riding on someone else.

Though the first thing we do once we reach the hive is to commission a riding saddle for you. I will *not* have my rider falling off in battle."

"I'd rather not fall off in battle too," Arthur agreed.

Then he paused for a moment and looked around. While there were people everywhere, everyone seemed busy. There was so much chaos he was almost certain they weren't being watched.

Arthur took a chance.

"Brix, I don't like this. Is your Return to Start anchor still keyed to Wolf Moon Hive?"

His dragon looked surprised. "Yes, but we cannot go back. That would be leaving Joy and her rider—"

"No." He shook his head. "I think we should key it here. Not at the Mesa Free Hive. Right here." He tapped several pebbles with his foot. "The council may turn on us for the combat cards or try to pin the missing eggs on us somehow. Or maybe the Mind Singer will open up a new portal late in the night and attack the hive. I don't want to be trapped in there."

Brixaby made a pensive growling sound under his breath. "I suppose one escape route is as good as another. And if I must use that card, I would rather not find myself back at Wolf Moon at this point."

He reached down and plucked a pebble. It glowed brightly as he keyed into it. Then he dropped it on the ground. Arthur repeated the process with a pebble of his own.

Return to Start was an escape hatch—one they hadn't had to take yet. Arthur hoped that they wouldn't need it, but it was good to have.

With a mutual nod, they continued toward the group of dragons.

Brixaby looked ahead to the silver and his rider, who were standing sullenly beside some healers. The silver seemed to be focused on the rider more than the dragon, though there were still streaks of dried blood that ran down the dragon's ears. A result of Brixaby's Stunning Shout.

The look he turned on Brixaby was murderous, and Arthur thought he caught a little bit of distortion in the air around him, as if he were readying a spell.

Arthur cut that off immediately by extending his Mental Blocking shield.

It took a few more seconds than usual—likely some interaction between the silver's natural magic and his own. Then the silver blinked pale blue eyes and looked around. "Where am I? My rider? Hershel!" He nearly shoved the healers aside to check on his rider. "What happened to him? Will he be okay?"

"I grow weary of explaining this over and over." Brixaby sighed but trotted forward to do just that—in a blunt, unfriendly way.

Arthur stepped close to the healers to exchange a word. "Will he recover?"

"Yes, sir, in time. Though he may have headaches for the next week or two. It's almost like he was bludgeoned upside the head, though we don't see any impact . . ."

"It's a sonic injury," Arthur said, nodding toward Brixaby.

The healer blanched. "From a Legendary? Then he's lucky to be alive."

Nodding, Arthur turned to Brixaby, who was giving the silver the most insulting offer to join his retinue ever.

"And of course, I already have a reliable second hand, but I shall require you at my side to serve me."

"I'll . . . think about it," the silver said.

"It's a shame that very useful mana card is your core card—pity. I would very much like to have it." Brixaby gave a long lingering look at the silver's chest.

Arthur thought it was time to step in. "We haven't had time to introduce ourselves. I'm Arthur, and this is Brixaby. When your rider wakes up, have him contact me."

"Yes . . . yes, of course," the silver said, though he sounded doubtful. And after a beat, he added, "My name is Tannai, and my rider is Hershel."

Arthur quickly pulled Brixaby away.

"He will make a fine addition to my retinue," Brixaby said, loud enough for Tannai to turn his head and stare at them as they walked away.

"Maybe he would join—if you toned down looking like you want to eat his cards," Arthur suggested.

Brixaby gave him an offended look. "I would very *much* like to ingest his cards . . . upon his, uh, *natural* death, of course," he added.

"See, talking like that doesn't help," Arthur said, but dropped it as they came to the next group, and the next.

Unfortunately, none of the rest had much more information to add about how their hive was taken over. Arthur suspected there might be some memory alteration at play, which was disturbing because that meant the Singer had access to more mind cards.

Either that, or she truly had been able to creep into a hive and take over without anyone knowing.

He waited to share his fears until he and Brixaby had finished with the last group.

"If the Mind Singer could just take over a hive like that"—Arthur snapped his fingers—"why didn't she do it here?"

"Because of us," Brixaby said.

Arthur looked at him.

The dragon looked back, completely serious. "Didn't you once tell me you were able to shake off her power before?"

"It wasn't easy," Arthur said, "and it was only because of my skills—"

"Which have gotten stronger, no doubt, and that was *before* you linked cards with me," Brixaby said, shifting all four of his wings up and down in the approximation of a shrug. "I would like to see her try to take over *me*."

"You might have a point," Arthur said. "Also, she might have a limit to how many minds she could handle at one time. I just wish I knew why she had her dragons take off with the eggs."

Brixaby shrugged again. "We haven't interrogated everybody."

"We haven't?" Arthur looked around. He couldn't see any other groups of dragons being actively subdued. Most that were able to fly had left for the hive, leaving a few scattered groups that were being visited by healers. They'd visited them all. "Who did we miss?"

In answer, Brixaby stepped back and then removed the brown dragon they'd fought last night from his storage space.

CHAPTER 47

Brix! What—"

Arthur was cut off as the newly released brown dragon roared in rage and took a swipe at Brixaby. He had, Arthur noted, extremely long claws.

Also, it said something about how singularly angry the brown was that he didn't even hesitate after instantly—from his point of view—going from night to day, and facing a dragon roughly the size of a cat to one the size of a small horse.

"My card . . . give me my rider's card . . ." the brown growled, yet managed it in a lyrical cadence.

Brixaby might be larger than he had been before, but he still had amazing, almost supernatural maneuverability. A quick buzz of his wings took him into the air and kept him just out of reach of the angry brown's claws.

"What are you waiting for?" Brixaby yelled back down at Arthur. "Use your Mental Shield skill!"

Oh. Of course.

Chiding himself for being too stunned to react, Arthur reached for the skill. It was easy—he'd done it dozens of times that day already.

Unfortunately, it made no immediate difference to the brown. He was still very much trying to kill Brixaby, sing-screaming, "Give me back my rider's card . . . his card . . . his card . . ."

What was going on? Why was this dragon still under the Mind Singer's influence?

Maybe he was so angry about the card that he was trying to kill Brixaby anyway. Dragons were protective over their riders.

"Brix! Give him back—" Arthur had to quickly duck as the brown whipped around, its tail swiping over his head with the force of a whip. "Give him back the card! He might be more reasonable!"

"Or he might attack me with earth magic," Brixaby yelled back, still effort-lessly ducking swipes. "I should just consume the card and *then* fight back."

That caused a bellow of rage and despair from the other dragon.

Arthur straightened. This had gone on long enough. "Don't be cruel. Do you even want an earth power?"

Brixaby gave a put-upon sigh as if he wasn't currently dodging back and forth with claws missing him by inches. "I suppose not."

"Give the card to me," Arthur said.

Brixaby glanced back over his shoulder at him dubiously, but with a loop that took him over the brown's next swipe, he doubled back and bolted over to Arthur using a Sprint skill.

Arthur extended his arm, and the Uncommon card dropped from Brixaby to land neatly in his grasp.

"I hope you know what you're doing," Brixaby muttered as he flew over him.

Honestly, so did Arthur. The only thing he knew for sure was that either the Mind Singer had her metaphorical claws dug in so deep that his skill couldn't break the brown out, or she had used a different technique for him and his group instead of the main battle group. The latter seemed more likely.

That meant Arthur needed another way to reach the true dragon inside.

But he wasn't going to be stupid about it.

The brown dragon let out a roar that literally shook the ground and made the pebbles dance around Arthur's feet. He charged forward, giving every indication he was about to squish Arthur and take the card back.

So Arthur grabbed a pair of scissors from his Personal Space and shoved the card between the blades, ready to snap down.

The brown skidded to a stop, horror writ large on his face.

"I've never cut a card in half before," Arthur said, almost conversationally. "I don't think it will be easy—they are magic. But I happen to have advanced levels in a tailoring skill, including one called the Perfect Snip. I think I can manage."

The brown said something so garbled that Arthur couldn't understand. White froth had collected on the corners of his mouth and dribbled down his jaw. His eyes were rolling and looked insane, but all of his focus was on Arthur.

Finally, he managed to collect himself a little and muttered, "My card . . . Return my rider's card . . ."

"I will," Arthur said. "But first you have to answer some questions. Where is your rider?" Part of him wanted to ask about the Mind Singer—not that any-body had been able to answer that so far. He had to start small.

The brown dragon made a frustrated sound. "He's at home—at the hive—he's—" The dragon trailed off, then briefly looked confused before anger once again reasserted itself in his gaze.

"If he's at your hive, then why do we have his card?" Arthur asked.

"*You* took it from me," the brown growled. His words were fierce and deep, but for once, there wasn't any hint of a lyrical cadence in it.

A sudden hunch made him try another tactic. "Tell me about him. Tell me about your rider."

Brixaby, who was hovering nearby, snorted. "Why do you want to know about an Uncommon rider? He can't join our retinues."

Irritably, Arthur waved him off. That wasn't helpful.

"Mine is the *best* rider," the brown said defensively to Brixaby. "He loves the earth just as much as I do. He doesn't care that I'm only an Uncommon with a basic card. He picked me out from my hive's nursery out of dozens of browns, and I would do *anything* for him. And when *she* came . . ." He stopped, cocking his head as if puzzled.

"She?" Arthur asked. "The Mind Singer?"

Mentioning her name was a mistake. The brown's eyes clouded again, and he looked at Brixaby with pure hatred. "We have to kill you, or else she . . . she . . . she will . . ." But again, he stumbled to a stop.

"What did she tell you?" Arthur asked.

"To kill the dark dragon. Keep his rider alive," the brown snarled. "Our lives would be forfeit, but our riders . . . Our riders would be free . . ."

Brixaby hovered lower. He didn't say anything, but he watched the brown dragon, his expression troubled.

"Then why," Arthur asked, "do *you* have his card?"

"Stefan gave it to me—straight from his heart. He told me to use it to do what she said. Then I could come back to him . . ."

Arthur felt his heart clench at the story, but Brixaby had another take.

He puffed up, daring to fly right in front of the other dragon's nose. "Well, you failed to kill me, so what are you going to do to save your rider? Surely you don't intend to serve the one who captured him? A scourgling?"

"I . . . if I bring her your core cards, I . . ." The light in the brown's eyes briefly flared, but he didn't finish. The brown dragon shook his head ponderously back and forth as if confused. "I don't want to serve a scourgling. She . . . she's a scourgling?"

"The antithesis of dragonkind," Brixaby confirmed. "And you're helping her."

"She put you and your friends under a spell. Do you remember attacking us last night?" Arthur asked, stepping forward. "Do you think that you would normally attack another hive—attack a Legendary dragon if you were in your right mind?"

"I don't even fight normally," the brown said, looking at his long claws. He seemed at that moment very lost. "I move the earth."

Arthur felt that they were on the verge of a breakthrough. "What's your name?"

"Digger."

That was the most stereotypical brown dragon name Arthur had ever heard of, but it fit this dragon completely. He had an unusually short neck and powerful limbs—just the type one would think would be at home close to the ground.

"And your friends? The other dragons last night?" Arthur asked, taking a chance. "Who were they?"

Sure enough, the brown picked up on his wording. "Were?"

"You remember last night," Arthur repeated calmly.

New skill gained: Deprogramming (Mind Healing Class)
Due to the Master of Body Enhancement's bonuses, you automatically
start this skill at level 3.

Arthur blinked in surprise. Deprogramming? What an odd phrase, and yet he understood its meaning completely: To break the hold or sway of someone who had been charmed. And the class was interesting. He felt that it was a borderline skill, as close to mind magic as his Mental Shield skill was.

The brown shuddered from the tip of his nose all the way down to the tip of his tail. "Their names are—were—Blood Dew, Vivi, and Charling. They came with me. They . . . we attacked you," he said, in dawning realization, blinking and looking at Arthur and Brixaby. "You killed them." Then, with a flash of teeth and a bit more anger, he repeated, "You *killed* them."

Brixaby snorted without any pity. "The little red dragon poisoned herself with a Legendary-level card, but not before killing one of *my* dragons. On the orders of a scourgling." If he were human, he would have spit to the side.

Suddenly, Digger's eyes were clear. He snarled, flexing his claws. "A scourgling has my rider!" Then he looked at Arthur. "And you still have his card."

"I was just keeping it for you, until you felt more like yourself." Out of sheer politeness, Arthur hadn't read the card. But as he extended his hand to return it, he just so happened to flip the face of it his way.

Stone Skin
Uncommon
Body Enhancement
*The wielder of this card will have access to the Stone Skin body
enhancement, which will harden the outer layer of skin to that of the
consistency of basic granite. However, this will not impact the wielder's
flexibility or agility. This card may be used for one hour per 24-hour rolling
basis. There is no mana cost.*

Arthur wished that there was some way he could keep the card for himself, but he didn't think Digger would appreciate that.

Digger plucked the card out of Arthur's hand with surprising dexterity, considering the length of his claws. He let out a sigh as he added it back to his secondary core.

"Tell me what you remember," Arthur said.

Again, the dragon shuddered.

"Stefan and I were out preparing a new field for planting. He'd built his card deck around farming. I don't like vegetables much, but the animals that eat the vegetables are tasty." Now that he wasn't murderously angry or under the Mind Singer's spell, Digger spoke in a slow, rolling cadence. It was easy to imagine this dragon linked to a farmer. "I heard the music on the wind and thought it was kind of pretty at first. We paused to listen. We thought there might be a festival soon. But then the music started to speak to me, and I had no choice—I *had* to listen. I had to obey." Another shudder. "I don't know why she picked me for the job to attack you. Some people were able to sort of fight it—I think Stefan was one. I don't know why. He didn't have a mind card."

"Arthur once fought off the Mind Singer, back when I was in an egg," Brixaby added proudly.

Digger eyed him for a moment, but then nodded.

"Did she say what her plans are?" Arthur asked.

"No, she didn't share her thoughts with us. Only orders." He paused. "But there was something funny going on with the hatching grounds. I remember she kept all the nesting mothers close. Had to keep an eye on them. Some were able to fight her. As you know, dragon mothers can be vicious." His lip curled upward to show teeth in the dragon version of an appreciative smile. Though, like Brixaby, he didn't seem too concerned about the eggs.

"Her dragons went after the hatching grounds here," Arthur said. He looked at Brixaby. "Do you think that could be related?"

Brixaby shrugged. So did Digger.

"I may be only an Uncommon," Digger said, "but my rider needs me. If you plan to go after this scourgling, I want to join you. And if you don't—I'm going to go after her anyway."

"Well, I hope you're ready to fight soon," Brixaby said, unconcerned. He had turned back to look at the hive. "My second-in-command, Joy, has returned. And she looks angry enough to kill."

CHAPTER 48

For once, Joy did not live up to her name. When she landed, she was nearly vibrating with rage. Cressida, sitting on her back, had an equally stormy expression.

"What happened—"

But before Arthur could finish, Joy exploded. "Every single egg has been taken by those . . . those mean nasty monsters! I hate them! Egg-nappers are mean, and evil, and . . . and no one was able to stop them!"

"Many of the nesting mothers are gone, too," Cressida said, voice tight. "Chablis and the rest of the council believe they followed the kidnappers. A search party from the hive was sent out—we waited until word came to report back. I would've sent a message by shadow, but my mana is almost out."

"Just the eggs?" Brixaby asked. "Was anything of value stolen as well?"

Joy's head snapped around to Brixaby, and for the first time in their friendship, she pulled her scaled lips back from her teeth and hissed at him. "The eggs *are* important—more important than your stupid head!"

Brixaby reeled back as if he had been slapped.

"Whoa there." Digger stepped forward and placed a large brown stumpy leg between the two of them. He looked like a teacher who was separating children just before a schoolyard fight. "Young pink, that is a Legendary you're challenging."

"I'm his second-in-command, so I get to call him a stupid head anytime I want!"

For his part, Brixaby looked more confused by her anger than offended.

Arthur decided to redirect the conversation. "What did the search party find?"

Cressida still looked angry but was frowning at the bickering dragons too. She turned her attention back to Arthur and shook her head. "They're gone.

One of the silvers detected magic up in the sky—we think that they had another portal user with them."

Arthur felt the particular swooping sensation in his gut that came when he knew he had overlooked something. He didn't remember releasing one of the shiny green portal users from the Mind Singer's influence. There had been a lot to do, and in the back of his mind he assumed that perhaps the dragon had died. But he still should have checked—or sent somebody to check for him.

If I had a full retinue, I would've had more subordinates I could trust, he thought with an inner wince.

"The greens who opened the original portal needed that mana silver to help power it. But maybe they had enough personal mana to keep it going for a small party," he said.

"What would a scourgling want with dragon eggs?" Joy practically wailed. She looked distraught enough to cry, had she been human.

"She had an interest in our hive's dragon eggs, too," Digger said reluctantly. "But I don't know why."

Cressida turned back to Arthur. "One more thing: Chablis demanded that you report to the council immediately. By which, she means her," she added, unusually acidic.

"We do not jump to the council's orders," Brixaby snarled. "They should be on their knees thanking us for saving their hive."

She shook her head. "You made them look incompetent today. They won't be thanking you."

Privately, Arthur agreed with Cressida's assessment. But his feelings were more in line with Brixaby's. Arthur took a deliberately slow look around, just in case they were being spied on by someone with a divination card.

The last few minutes had seen the final dragons from the battle mostly clear out. Healers and sympathetic folk were still working with the grievously wounded and overlooking the fallen. But all the living had been broken out of the Mind Singer's hold. That was the important thing.

There wasn't much left to do here.

Still, Arthur made no attempt to jump to Chablis's command. He found a couple of rivets that had been knocked out of place in the chainmail he wore and spent a few extra seconds using his Metal Shot card to smooth them down.

Then, casually, he looked up to see everybody was staring at him. Brixaby, smugly. Joy and Digger with open curiosity, and Cressida with amusement. She knew what he was doing.

That reminded him.

"Cressida, Joy, this is Digger. His rider is currently being held hostage back in his hive. He'll be joining us to fight the Mind Singer until we can get him back."

Joy perked up. "Nice to meet you, Digger, now that you're not mind-scrambled. So that's the plan? We're going to save the eggs and rescue your rider? That's so sad, Digger. I'm sorry about him. I'm Joy, and this is Cressida, and we're happy to have you join our retinue. What's your power? Oh, I bet it has to do with earth because you're brown. Wait, is that rude to say? I'm sorry if it is, I'm just really excited—"

Thankfully, Brixaby cut her off.

"Yes, the dragon out for revenge will be quite a potent addition to my retinue. Welcome, Digger. What other interesting cards do you have? You mentioned moving earth?"

Chablis, Laird, and three of her council members were gathered on top of the mesa, arguing with each other, with some glancing up sour-faced as Arthur and his small retinue descended.

Arthur was past caring about what they thought. He was too busy relishing the feeling of flying on his own dragon. That wasn't going to get old anytime soon.

Also, Brixaby was always good for an impressive entrance. He buzzed straight down, managing to keep his body level the whole way. He made it look effortless, but he must have been working hard not to unseat Arthur because Arthur received a Dragon Riding skill-up from that maneuver.

Meanwhile, Digger and Joy came in to land the traditional way, by sailing in and dumping altitude.

Laird gave Digger a considering look, obviously recognizing the other dragon, but he said nothing.

"It's about time," Chablis snapped. "Explain yourself."

Arthur didn't bother to dismount Brixaby. The dragon only stood as high as a donkey, anyway, and Arthur liked looking down on her, just a little. "You asked for me to defend the hive, and I did. Successfully."

"That's not what I'm talking about. You raided our card library—our wealth! After we took you in, sheltered you—"

"After your dragons kidnapped us by force," Cressida said. "Were we ever free to leave?"

Chablis ignored her and glared at Arthur, who stared steadily back.

So, she had put two and two together. And judging by the fact that Laird was still welcome among the rest of the council, he hadn't been implicated.

Arthur briefly thought about throwing him under the wheel cart, but there wasn't a point. If all went according to his plan, he would need Laird on his side.

"The Mind Singer's forces attacked the moment you went into the dungeon," he said. "I assume she thought that the council would have kept the most potent cards for themselves, and she wanted you out of the way. And I didn't keep your wealth. I gave it back to the hive. Anybody who took a combat card is welcome to give it back. Have you asked?" he added pointedly.

One of the councilors made a blustering, angry sound and stepped forward. "We are a peaceful hive, focused on crafting, building, and creating. We have no need for war—"

"Yet war came for you anyway," Arthur said, exasperated. "I'm not saying what you're doing is not noble, but the whole world is in the fight of their life against the scourglings. You can't hide forever. Nowhere is truly safe."

"That's why we have a select few to fight for us." Chablis indicated Laird, who growled.

"And yet you don't give us the tools that we need when we request them."

"Come off it, dragon," one of the councilors snapped. "You don't mean tools. You want more cards that will give you power over us. We've seen other hives fall to coups before—"

"Enough," Arthur said, putting several skills including **Voice Projection** and **Leadership** behind the word. It came out before he had even thought about what he was doing, but they couldn't get bogged down in old arguments. "We don't have *time* for this. I understand that the hive's eggs have been stolen, and it seems a group managed to escape through a portal?"

He glanced at Laird as he said that and noted that the big red seemed only mildly concerned.

Joy, however, bristled again.

It did seem that there was a difference between male and female dragons when it came to their outlook on eggs.

"That's not all," Chablis said, "they also raided our experimental gardens, and one of them had a poison card. I'm afraid the soil won't be capable of growing anything until we get some specialized card users to rake over it. Even then, rations may need to be cut."

Arthur had some idea of what was growing in those experimental caves. He wasn't allowed access to all of them, but he shuddered at the thought of the Mind Singer getting those potent plants. What would she do with them? Start her own farming operation?

Farming . . . *Oh no.*

"The last time this scourgling tried to gain power, it fed card users to a growing demi-scourge. Do you think it could be doing something like that, but with the eggs?" Arthur blurted.

Joy gasped.

"Interesting theory, but why bother?" Laird asked. "Pardon me for saying, Joy, but eggs are not interesting to anyone but dragon mothers. It's when they hatch that they have potential."

Digger nodded. Brixaby simply looked bored.

"And when they hatch, they have brand-new cards. That's how most new cards are brought into the world, isn't it? Through dragon cores," Arthur said grimly. "It's much easier to hatch new dragons than it is to collect separate shards, especially for the higher-tier cards."

"Interesting theory," Chablis said. "But the majority of the eggs laid here were Common."

"The nesting mothers went too, and remember Commons can lay higher-tier eggs. Brixaby is proof of that," Arthur said. "His egg was laid by a Common purple."

Brixaby stood up proudly, as if challenging anybody to make a joke. Of course, no one did.

Chablis looked less than impressed. "That might be true, but the chances of producing a Legendary dragon—"

"Rares are laid much more frequently than Legendary eggs," Laird broke in. He regarded Arthur in a new light, and with a disturbed expression. "And from what I understand, this scourgling is at Rare rank."

"It is," Arthur confirmed. "Which means that it could use any Rare card that came from . . . from farming hatchling dragons," he added with an apologetic look to Joy, who had put her head under her wing in sheer horror. Cressida had dismounted and stood by her side, comforting her.

A shadow darkened the sky.

Everyone looked up, and Arthur automatically raised a hand, accessing his Metal Shot card.

But it wasn't an enemy from above. It was the same purple dragon who had delivered a message to Arthur before.

Brixaby bristled. "What are you doing here, interrupting *my* meeting?"

The purple gave Brixaby a wary look but then silently passed a scroll off to Chablis. Then with a flip of a tail in Brixaby's direction, which looked more flirtatious than dismissive, the purple took to the air.

"What is it?" one of the other councilors asked.

Chablis held up a hand for patience as she quickly unrolled and read the scroll. Then, with a sigh, she lowered it. "After we were attacked, I sent word through certain channels." She glanced at Arthur. "I'm sure it won't surprise you to learn we have communication with other free hives."

Arthur nodded.

"And?" Laird asked.

"Three other free hives have been hit within the last twenty-four hours. Hives of the Meadows, Red Earth, and Sky. Until I sent word, it was assumed that these were all isolated incidents or perhaps raids from jealous kingdom hives. It's happened before. But like us, all lost their eggs from their hatching grounds. It seems," she said with another sigh, "Arthur's dragon-farming theory . . . has merit."

"Of course it does. I wouldn't link with an idiot," Brixaby growled.

But his growl was not nearly as fierce as Joy's. "We have to get those eggs back! We can't let her do this!"

"We won't," Arthur said. He took a breath. This wasn't going to be easy. "But we need to contact the kingdom hives."

CHAPTER 49

Arthur expected some reaction from his proclamation, and he wasn't disappointed.

The three council members immediately exploded into instant denial.

"Absolutely not!"

"Us? Bow to the kingdom? Never!"

The third man looked at Arthur with a tinge of disgust and suspicion in his eyes. "This has been your plan all along, hasn't it? Bring us back under the thumb of your kingdom?"

Arthur ignored the three of them. They weren't the most important ones here—they didn't have the power. They were simply mouthpieces, and from what he could tell so far, they would end up voting however Chablis wanted them to.

His true attention was on Chablis and Laird. The two of them were exchanging glances, and considering one was a dragon, it wasn't subtle.

"There is more, isn't there?" Arthur asked flatly. "In the scroll."

Chablis shook her head and started to hand it over. However, Cressida intercepted the message, and with a sniff toward the head councilwoman, made a show of opening the scroll and reading through it herself.

Arthur suspected it was a noble thing. The leader didn't bother reading the main message. That was for the second-in-command to do, and then to report accurately.

He would've been slightly annoyed at the interruption, except that it was clearly meant to tweak Chablis's nose.

After a moment, Cressida looked up. "That's all the scroll says."

"But that is not all it *means*," Laird rumbled. "How did that abomination learn where the nests are located?"

"What do you mean?" Arthur asked, then remembered that he had never come across the dragon nests in the hive, either. And he had been here for months.

"The Mind Singer has powers over minds," Cressida answered impatiently. "She could direct other dragons to show her dragons where the nests are—"

"Nesting mothers would never reveal the location of their eggs." Joy was so upset by the thought that she raised up on her hind legs, wings extended in mild threat.

Laird nodded. "Nesting mothers are fierce, and often conceal their eggs where they shouldn't. Yet every single one of our nests were found and raided."

"Because the Mind Singer has powers over *minds*," Cressida repeated, but then stopped. An odd look came over her face.

Arthur realized it too.

"Except none of our dragons were taken over by her. She only brought over other dragons she had subjugated." He looked to Cressida, and then to Brixaby, who shrugged but looked disturbed. "Maybe she was saving her power for the nesting mothers?"

Laird rumbled in amusement. "If she had the power to take over the mind of a nesting mother dragon from a long distance, she could have taken over *all* of us the moment that portal was open. I said the instincts of a nesting dragon are strong, but I spoke too lightly. Look at her." He nodded down to Joy, who now looked nothing like her namesake. Her face was scrunched in a half growl, with her wings still extended. Cressida had moved back to her side, but Joy was ignoring her rider and looked ready to spring up into the air and fight the first person she saw.

Laird continued. "She's not old enough to have laid her first egg. Now imagine the ferocity of a dragon protecting her own nest." He nodded to Brixaby, who was looking on in mild confusion. "The smartest thing a male dragon can do is stay out of the way until the shells are cracked and the inner cards are formed. Then the hatchlings become our problem."

"We don't know what the Mind Singer's true powers are," Chablis started, but a sinking realization had come over Arthur. He groaned.

"She found all the nests—including the ones that were hidden. That means she has a seeking card, and a strong one." He looked to Chablis, who stared back with dawning horror in her own eyes. "Maybe even a Legendary one."

The moment the word *Legendary* was uttered, it was as if shutters were drawn over Chablis's expression. She went utterly neutral to try to hide her dismay, but since Arthur was watching for it, it was as good as a confirmation.

Two of her three councilors were not so good at hiding their reactions.

One gasped. The second, the one who had accused Arthur of having an ulterior motive to bring in the kingdom hives all along, narrowed his eyes. "And how exactly would you know of a Legendary seeking card, young man?"

Arthur wasn't about to explain he had read it in notes while sneaking into the council chambers. Instead, he reached for his **Acting** skill and turned a dismissive look on the man. "How do you think? It's—"

"It is a card in my set!" Brixaby all but roared. And since he had increased in size several times over, his roar *echoed*. One of the councilors slapped hands over his ears. Even Laird winced. "Why wouldn't we know about it?" Brixaby continued. "Brother to my own card? It's a Legendary seeking card—the ultimate power—" He practically licked his lips.

"The Mind Singer wouldn't need to take over several hundred very fierce dragon mothers," Arthur cut in before Brixaby overdramatically gave something away. "She would only need to use one Legendary card and have her minions swarm over the nests. Most of the females followed after their eggs, right? They'll want to ensure that they hatch . . . and so does the Mind Singer."

Joy growled at that.

Chablis looked at Arthur. She wasn't a fool, and clearly guessed that Arthur still hadn't explained how they knew about the card. He considered it a good sign she wasn't bringing it up. "You said this scourgling is a Rare? And yet you believe she has the power of a Legendary?"

Arthur shook his head. "No, she has thralls willing to poison themselves . . . I don't think that she would give it to a human. He or she might be able to fight back with a Legendary card in their heart. But a lower-ranked dragon would only last a few minutes before the card poisoned its core. Maybe just long enough to reveal a few pieces of information. But it would be enough."

What he didn't add was that it also helped explain how the Mind Singer had located him and Brixaby long enough to send a team of assassins with a Legendary card and a truly evil trap card, but likely why she didn't know they had survived. There might be some restrictions on even a Legendary seeker card . . . Or she just needed dragons for the upcoming fight and wasn't able to wring out the correct information.

He'd find out when he got his hands on that card.

He glanced over at Brixaby and saw his bloodred eyes practically burning.

Arthur had a pair of Legendaries in his heart, and it was about time his dragon had the same.

Just as his resolve hardened, one of Chablis's councilors broke in. "Assuming all of this . . . this *guesswork* is correct, your solution is completely out of proportion to our problems. We have won the day. Now is the time to rebuild, and yes, mourn the ones who were lost." He shot a feigned look of sorrow toward Joy, who raised her lips in a snarl. "Our dragons will have more eggs to love and care for."

"Whoa, there!" Cressida jumped right in front of the man just as Joy struck at him with her fangs bared. Thankfully, Joy's love for her rider overrode her rage at a man who was writing off somebody else's eggs. She jerked her neck to the side just in time, and her teeth snapped on empty air less than a foot from his body. Flecks of spittle and green venom caught the sunlight before hitting the ground.

The man jumped back in a delayed reaction, clutching at his robe as if that would've given him any protection. "Why, you little . . . You little monster!"

"Joy," Cressida said. "The man is allowed to have his opinions . . ." She shot him a disgusted look. "Even if they are cowardly and wrong."

Arthur half expected Brixaby to jump in with a reprimand of his own, but the black dragon just sat on his haunches, looking pleased with her intensity.

Above, Laird chuckled. "I don't know how to make it any more clear. You would do well to remember to be careful when talking about the death of eggs in front of a female dragon."

Arthur decided to step in before things grew out of control. "Yes, the females that are left can always have more eggs." He held up his hand to forestall Joy's reaction. It was a mark of how much the pink dragon respected him that she didn't snarl his way. "But what's to keep the Mind Singer from raiding us again? And she'll be stronger next time. She might even have whatever it is she's using the seeker card to find."

"If your guesses are even right," the council member snapped.

"He may be," Chablis said with a sigh. Then she looked at Arthur. "But that doesn't mean I will willingly give over this hive to the kingdoms."

Arthur met her gaze. "I wasn't asking."

She drew in a sharp breath, and again Arthur held up his hand. "But I don't think that will be necessary."

Inside, he could barely believe his own bravado, but keeping a firm grip on his **Acting** skill, he didn't allow any doubt to show on his face. "Brixaby, send a message out to the hive. Anybody willing to fight may keep the combat cards they were given. Anyone who wishes to go back to crafting must relinquish their card to somebody else."

"And what if they put the cards into their heart?" Chablis asked.

Again, Arthur met her gaze. "I happen to have a dragon who excels at stealing cards."

Brixaby's chuckle was downright evil.

PART 5
(BATTLE) LEADER

CHAPTER 50

Ten minutes were left on Arthur's copied portal spells. It would have to be enough.

Arthur looked down at the dragons arrayed below him in the air and gulped.

Brixaby had taken him high up in altitude, to a point where he had to rapidly beat his wings to stay steady against high winds. A constant whistle of air blew past his ears, and he was in danger of not feeling his nose soon. That meant his conversation would remain relatively private. At least to anybody who didn't have an eavesdropping card.

Arthur leaned over his dragon's neck and asked, "Are we doing the right thing?"

Brixaby's answer was dismissive. "As opposed to what? Letting the Mind Singer win?"

"No." He shook his head. "We could return to Wolf Moon Hive quietly. Send the message to them. Let them know that we're alive and that there is danger out here."

"We *are* sending a message to them," Brixaby said. "And that message is we're a Legendary pair with an army of dragons behind us, and they better listen."

Arthur couldn't explain his reticence to his dragon—that until Brixaby had cracked his shell, he had lived his life in the shadows. That he didn't mind facing his enemies, but he'd always done it as sneakily as possible.

It was easy to be bold when facing down Chablis and the rest of the council. Arthur had known that if he let any weakness show, that if he even hesitated and didn't put their plan into action right away, things would fall apart.

But they were small fry compared to what he faced in the hive.

Though he supposed he had come too far to back down now.

At his request, Brixaby had used his ability to send messages straight into others' minds to pass the word along: those who wanted to keep their combat cards would fight with Arthur and Brixaby. Those who didn't would relinquish their cards or have Brixaby forcefully remove them.

That message being transmitted straight into people's minds had a nice effect. Many had relinquished their cards. But many others had joined with Arthur, under the assumption they were there to fight and not join the kingdom hives. The real surprise came when other dragons asked to join up, too. Most of those who hadn't been given combat cards had received the ones that had been given up by those staying behind.

A large portion of the newcomers were female dragons, enraged at the thought of a scourgling farming dragon eggs.

In hindsight, Arthur should have asked Joy to keep that little theory to herself.

But the moment the meeting had broken up, they found a gathering of worried people waiting below the mesa.

Joy, still spitting fury, had flapped down to speak to a few of the other waiting dragons.

The word had spread, and they soon had more volunteers than combat cards.

Arthur was just glad for the visible show of support. It kept the council from delaying and undermining their plans. That was reinforced by Cressida coming to him in a quiet moment and telling him to move fast. The more they dawdled, the more time he gave people to think twice.

Like it or not, the lives of a small army of dragons and people were now his.

I'm not ready for this, Arthur thought for perhaps the hundredth time.

Then he shoved that thought down, straightened, and nodded to his core retinue.

Joy and Cressida flew at his flank on the right side. Joy had recovered her good mood now that they were on the move, though she flexed her green venom arm as if readying it for war.

Laird was a steady presence on his left, though somewhat behind. Joy flew beside Digger and the mana silver, Tannai. His rider had stayed behind, but Tannai had not been hard to convince to join this fight.

Tannai had two clutches of eggs with two Uncommon females back at his home hive. While he wasn't as crazed about the eggs as a nesting mother dragon, he was fond of his mates and didn't want to see them under the sway of a scourgling.

Arthur nodded back to him, and both rider and dragon flew forward.

It was time.

When the silver got within a dozen feet of Arthur, he cast simultaneous spells: Mana Springwell and Mana Redoubling. Right after they hit, Brixaby copied the spell and recast it on Arthur.

The double boost increased the capacity of Arthur's Mana Vault to four times its usual size.

With this many dragons behind him, he needed every scrap.

He checked his current counter: eight minutes left.

"Pass the message along. No one is to use combat abilities on the other side until I say so."

He felt Brixaby's grumble, but also heard in his mind as the dragon passed it along.

Then Arthur took a deep breath and accessed his portal abilities.

And he tore a rip into the fabric of the world large enough to let his dragons through.

There was a raging blizzard in full effect over Wolf Moon Hive.

This wasn't an uncommon occurrence, as it was one of the most northern hives.

But it had also been high summer when Arthur and Cressida left. So coming back to winter, two months later, was a shock.

Doubly so since Valentina's dragon specialized in weather manipulation.

Arthur had lived at the hive since he was twelve years old, and the only time he remembered a harsh blizzard was when the dragons had gone to fight the scourge-eruption.

Arthur was the last to come through the portal and promptly held on tight as Brixaby was flung to the side by a freezing gust.

"We can't stay out here!" Arthur yelled, but the wind whipped the words away so fast he couldn't even hear them. Driving snow stung at his face and hands, and he knew if they didn't land and find cover soon, his limbs would become numb. He didn't have a proper dragon saddle yet.

Arthur leaned over Brixaby's neck and bellowed at the top of his lungs. "Tell them to land—tenth floor!"

He remembered an open area on the tenth floor meant for the higher-ranking dragons. It was large, spacious, and temperature-controlled thanks to a variety of card-anchor magics.

Brixaby repeated his orders in the minds of their followers. Then the world fell out from under Arthur as Brixaby buzzed downward.

The wind, snow, and clouds were so thick that Arthur couldn't see more than a few feet in front of him. Turning, he couldn't even spot the end of Brixaby's tail, and his head and muzzle on the other end were partially obscured by haze.

Arthur couldn't direct the flight, couldn't brace himself or anticipate when he was going to land. He was utterly dependent on his dragon—helpless in a way he had rarely felt since he'd received the Master of Skills card.

He had to trust Brixaby to guide him to safety. And though he didn't always agree with his dragon's aggressive, proud, and often selfish outlook on the world, he found he wholeheartedly trusted him to keep him safe.

Brixaby buzzed downward into the storm, falling faster than the snowflakes that spun and danced around them until Arthur had to close his eyes or else would feel sick.

And suddenly, it all ended.

They crossed an invisible barrier where the influence of a card took over.

The wind went from a howl to a gentle breeze, dry enough to evaporate the fog. The air grew instantly warmer—not comfortable by any means, but enough to melt the falling snow. Arthur and Brixaby now descended in a gentle rain.

The dragons who had joined them through the portal broke through as well. Joy's shimmery pink hide caught the light from the torches hanging off the slopes of the hive.

Arthur glanced around for the markers on the slopes and saw they were already at level seventeen. They'd had to descend far to get out of the weather.

For whatever reason, Valentina's dragon was not blunting the worst of the storm.

The pair was old. What if . . .

His thoughts were cut short as an alarm rang from the hive slopes. Not the usual alarm of a scourge-eruption.

Arthur's portal had been noticed.

Several dragons with riders already aboard cast themselves aloft. Card powers gathered between jaws and in the air around them. Guards. And judging by the feel, there was at least a Rare in there.

In fact . . . did he recognize that yellow dragon?

"Sams!" Arthur yelled, and the yellow dragon with the deepening purple belly pulled up short. He had been one of the few gathering a spell between his claws—likely a sunlight mirror, though Arthur didn't know what he planned to do with it since it was pitch black outside.

His rider was so covered against the elements that Arthur hadn't recognized him on sight. But his voice was all Horatio's.

"Arthur? You're alive?"

CHAPTER 51

The foul weather had given Arthur one advantage: He was able to keep secret how many dragons he'd brought with him. Only his retinue was close by and visible in the gloom.

Thinking quickly, Arthur directed Brixaby to send a message directly into the minds of his followers: *Land safely, get under shelter, and above all else, stay quiet.*

Brixaby's stated range was "within shouting distance." Out in the open, even in a storm . . . that meant he could easily reach most minds he wanted.

Meanwhile, Arthur's retinue followed Sams and the rest back down to land on the newest level.

On the ledge, the temperature was artificially warmed thanks to environmental card magic. Even the outcropping the dragons landed on was dry, the rain evaporating inches above the surface.

Arthur took in a breath of fresh air that smelled familiar in a way that the Mesa Free Hive never had.

We're back, he thought to himself.

But he only allowed himself a moment to relish it.

Horatio had dismounted his dragon the moment Sams's claws hit firm rock. He came striding up to Arthur, boggling not only at him but at Brixaby as well.

"Rumor had it your dragon hadn't been growing," he said. "Seems you figured out what was wrong."

"Nothing was wrong!" Brixaby boomed. "This hive simply did not afford me the right opportunity to grow!"

In more ways than one, Arthur thought.

"Horatio, how are you here? Why aren't you at Buck Moon Hive?"

His friend shook his head impatiently. "Never mind that. How are *you* even alive? News came in that you died during a scourge-eruption. I didn't want to believe it at first, but then it seemed to be true because my *friend* would have sent me a message." He glowered at Arthur, just in case he didn't get the point.

Arthur didn't have time to let the guilt soak in. Several of Horatio's other riders had dismounted and come striding up to listen. But a few of their dragons had slid off to speak to purple messengers clinging to crags off to the side. Those purples quickly buzzed away.

No doubt word of their arrival—and miraculous survival—back to Wolf Moon Hive would quickly spread.

Arthur glanced over his shoulder long enough to ensure the rest of his personal retinue of Cressida, Digger, Laird, and Tannai had landed safely behind him.

Turning back, he stepped forward to grip Horatio's upper arm. "We don't have much time. Tell me what's going on. Why is there a storm beating down on the hive? Is Valentina . . . is her dragon . . ." He trailed off, unsure how to finish.

He would never say he'd been friendly with the other two Legendary riders—especially after they'd failed to prepare him for his visit with the king. But out of the two, he much preferred Valentina over Whitaker.

Horatio's expression went from shocked and offended to grim.

"No one official has said anything. Sams and I are Rares, but we're still low on the totem pole. Valentina and her dragon haven't died," he added quickly, "but the general gossip is that their strength is failing."

"Then why do I sense three Legendries?" Brixaby asked in a dangerous voice.

Arthur winced. If Brixaby could sense three of his kind, they could likely sense him soon . . . if they hadn't already.

Horatio shrugged at the dragon's question. "Politics. It's part of why I'm here, too."

"The other hive leaders thought we were dead and took the opportunity to try to take over the leadership of Wolf Moon?" Arthur guessed.

Horatio nodded once in affirmation. "Buck Moon has been leading the charge—and you never answered my question, Art. *How* are you still alive?"

"It's a long story . . ." Arthur began.

"Oh! Oh!" Behind them, Joy jumped up and down. "We were kidnapped by a hive that's outside of our kingdom, but now we get to save one of their sister hives instead. Maybe them, too. I don't know. It's very twisty. Hi, I'm Joy," she added to Sams, who was looking down at the pink in puzzlement.

Horatio sputtered. "What do you mean, a hive outside the kingdom? There's nothing outside the kingdom!"

"Turns out," Arthur said, "not only is there livable land outside our kingdom, there are other kingdoms. I'll explain later," he added, "But I have to speak to the leadership. I'd like an escort through the storm to back up top, but we'll get there on our own if we have to."

One of the Uncommon riders who stood near Sams objected. "That's not a good idea, sir. We don't know if these people are who they say they are. They could be using an illusion or body mod card to impersonate someone. We should wait to get them checked out by one of the mind-mages."

"That isn't going to happen," Arthur said. He wasn't about to let anyone go shifting around his or Brixaby's mind.

Beside him, Brixaby flared two of his wings in a threat. "I dare any white dragon to shuffle through my mind and come out the other side!"

Which was a good point. As a Legendary rank, Brixaby could likely over-power any Rare or Uncommon the hive could throw at them.

From the shuffling of feet and uncomfortable looks, others knew it too.

Arthur turned back to Horatio. "You and I were roommates at the orphan-age. We both worked at a restaurant, scraping card shards together—"

But Horatio shook his head. "That's common knowledge for anyone who does a little research." He considered for a moment, and then his dark eyes nar-rowed. "When we were kids, I snuck out and went to the festival—one of the first you'd seen, if I remember right. You remember what else happened that night?"

Arthur felt a grin stretch his face. "Yeah, except *I* was the one who snuck out, and you followed. And you took me to see card duels. I'd never seen anything like it."

Horatio stared at him for a moment as if trying to weigh his answer, but Arthur knew he had spoken true.

Finally, he nodded and looked to Sams. "It's him."

"I can feel the weight of their Legendary cards," Sams added. "Assuming that is not some sort of trick."

"It's not, but we need to speak to leadership, and we need someone to light the way." Arthur looked at Sams who, as a yellow, was a dragon with natural light-based magic. "Didn't you once ask to be part of my retinue?"

Instantly, the troubled look on Horatio's face faded, and he grinned. Arthur had just won him over.

For all the commotion on the lower levels, word had not yet spread up to the top of the hive.

The storm was every bit as bitterly fierce as it had been before, but this time Arthur and the rest of his retinue were prepared for it.

And most importantly, they had Sams to light the way.

The big yellow dragon glowed like a miniature sun ahead of them.

Through the driving blizzard, Arthur lost track of where his position was in the sky, and most importantly, the stone-hard sides of the hive. One gust of wind could dash them all against the rocks.

But the dragons seemed to know where they were, and so Arthur was forced to put his faith in Brixaby.

Life was so much easier now that he could ride his own dragon.

So instead of worrying about what could happen, Arthur let himself focus on the rapid beating of Brixaby's four wings.

Odd. He'd always thought of it as a droning buzz, but now he realized that there was a pattern to his wingbeats. The bottom pair beat a little less rapidly than the top pair. They were broader and stretched to cup more air with every stroke. The top two were faster but bent more with the wind.

He realized that the bottom pair focused on stability and power. The top was for directional control.

Arthur's revelation was rewarded with not one but two additional levels in his Dragon Riding skill.

The moment the notifications came, Arthur gained the wisdom to shift his seat slightly back toward Brixaby's center of gravity.

The dragon grunted something in surprise. Arthur couldn't catch the words but thought they were positive. And he didn't think he imagined that Brixaby powered through the air faster than ever.

However, the wind got worse as they rose in altitude, and the temperature plunged. If this continued, Arthur worried he'd get frostbite on his exposed fingers and nose.

Just when he wondered if he should direct the retinue back into the hive and climb to the top from the inside, the glowing beacon that was Sams went in for a landing upon a platform wide enough to hold a Legendary dragon.

Or in this case, three of them, if Brixaby was right.

Brixaby landed with Joy right behind him. Cressida, on her neck, yelled something that was lost to the winds.

In front of them, something gigantic moved.

It took Arthur too long to understand what his eyes were trying to tell him. He hadn't forgotten the size of Elissa, Valentina's old Legendary dragon, but she was a cloudy blue color, and the lines of her shape were obscured by the storm.

He thought it was clouds from the storm moving until a massive dragon head resolved itself out of nowhere and stared down at Arthur and Brixaby with the stern expression of a disappointed grandmother.

"You." Elissa's voice was even louder than Brixaby's but still quivered with age. "You have arrived at last."

Arthur felt a force of mana pulse out of Elissa.

Instantly, every flake of driving snow, the bitter wind, and even the freezing fog that he had not been fully aware of, melted away. It was as if Arthur and the others behind him stood in a bubble of pleasantly warm early summer air. Even the mist that should have come up from the wet rock underfoot evaporated instantly.

It was the mark of a Legendary dragon's power. And also a mark of how weak Elissa was that she could only flex this power to the tip of the ledge.

In the suddenly clear air, Arthur saw how diminished the dragon had become. She was much skinnier than she'd been before. Cloudy blue scales and flesh practically hung off her bones.

He had to swallow the urge to ask if she was all right. She clearly wasn't.

Even Brixaby remained silent, which said a lot, because he wasn't a subtle dragon.

"As always," Elissa said with a weary sigh, "you have a dramatic sense of timing. Come, join the meeting."

"Meeting?" Arthur repeated.

In answer, she swung her giant head to the side, opening the way to a large stone arch that led into the hive itself.

Time to face the music.

Arthur nodded and stepped forward. So did Cressida, but Elissa swung her head back, barring her way.

"You may leave your retinue on the ledge," the Legendary dragon said to Arthur, not bothering to speak directly to those of lower rank.

Brixaby bristled, but Arthur put a hand on his shoulder. He suspected the "meeting" was a gathering of leaders. If that was the case, they wouldn't appreciate or include lower-ranked cardholders. Besides, he wanted someone outside to watch his back.

"Cressida, Joy, take care of my retinue while I'm gone," he said.

Cressida nodded and walked over to speak to Horatio and Sams privately.

Arthur and Brixaby moved forward.

Elissa's power ended as they crossed under the arch. At that point, the internal weather control of the hive took over. It was notably warm inside the cavern, and though Arthur's view was obscured by a curved stone hallway, he heard voices raised in argument.

The first voice belonged to Whitaker, blustering and angry. "You have no right, no standing!"

"I assure you," said a second, unfamiliar male voice, "this decree has been signed by every leader of the eleven other hives. It was unanimous."

The third voice was querulous and weak, but the words were stone. "You're forgetting one important signature, Vonby: the king."

There was a dangerous pause.

"Do you truly want to get the king involved in this? Or his beast?"

Whitaker again, shouting. "If you think we're going to hand over our hive to the likes of you—!"

It was at that point that Arthur crossed into the main room, Brixaby by his side.

They found three of the most powerful people within a hundred miles all gathered in one room, squaring off.

Whitaker stood with hands clenched at his sides with his chest puffed out. Valentina, in contrast, lay reclined on a fluffy cloud—an aspect of the card's power she shared with her dragon.

The third person was someone new. He'd had some exposure to other Legendary riders in the kingdom's hives, but he was certain he had not met this man before. And he was so distinctive that Arthur would have remembered him.

The man was in his late forties to early fifties with a sheet of steel-gray hair that fell straight to his waist. If not for his broad shoulders and muscled physique, Arthur might have mistaken him for a woman.

When he turned at Arthur's arrival, he saw a badge of a stag on his right breast: Buck Moon Hive.

But most of Arthur's attention fell to the other two hive leaders.

Valentina was too self-contained to gasp at Arthur's appearance. She looked just as sickly as her dragon, if not worse. Her suddenly hard expression made her face skeletal.

Whitaker, by contrast, let out a half shout of surprise and stepped toward Arthur. His expression was so fierce that Arthur wasn't sure if the man wasn't feeling relief or rage—if he wanted to punch Arthur or embrace him like a long-lost colleague returned.

"Who are you?" the stranger said, then did a double take at Arthur, perhaps sensing the weight of card power in his heart.

"Well, it seems all your schemes have been for nothing. The missing rider has returned," Valentina said briskly.

The new man's face went sheet white with rage. "Is this a joke?"

"I've returned," Arthur confirmed and then gestured to the side. Brixaby, who had been hanging back to obscure himself in the shadows, stepped forward. His bloodred eyes glinted in the firelight. "And with my dragon."

The gray-haired man flicked his hand in their direction. The air around Arthur suddenly dried out and prickled with an uncomfortable heat.

Brixaby snarled a warning. Just as abruptly, the temperature dropped down to normal.

"It's no illusion. I feel the heat of their circulatory system," the man said. He turned back to Whitaker and Valentina. "Is this some kind of a test? A ploy to test your better's resolve?"

Whitaker ignored the man and strode toward Arthur. "Where have you been?" he all but growled out.

Arthur kept his face and voice calm, unworried. "I was a guest at a free hive."

"Which free hive?" Whitaker snapped, which confirmed Arthur's theory that they weren't a secret to the leadership. Whitaker continued before Arthur could answer. "Those kingdom traitors! Have you become one, too? Huh? Tell me!"

"You will not speak to my rider that way!" Brixaby growled.

Arthur appreciated the backup, but he could already tell this was going to be an argument best handled by humans. "Brix, please go back out to the ledge. I can handle this." Deliberately, he turned his back on Whitaker as if he didn't see the other man as a threat. He added, low, "Make sure Joy speaks to Elissa."

He caught the exact moment Brixaby understood. His bloodred eyes glittering, he gave one last derisive snort at Whitaker and then turned back the way they'd come.

Arthur looked back at the other leaders. Whitaker was red in the face with anger, and the gray-haired man didn't look much better. Valentina's expression was still hard, but he thought he caught a bit of amusement in her eyes.

"I am not a traitor. My oath to the king remains unbroken," Arthur lied. "Brixaby and I weren't taken to the free hive voluntarily, but I'm not going to apologize for the time I spent—"

Whitaker spoke over him. "They kidnapped you? Then this means war—"

Ignoring him, Arthur continued. "And I've returned with a warning."

The gray-haired man laughed. "A warning? You're in no position to threaten us, child." He turned to the others. "I don't see how this changes anything. You two were so incompetent that you let a new rider with a Legendary card fall into an outsider's control. It's almost worse than his death."

"I take it the other hives wish to put their extra Legendary dragons into Wolf Moon?" Arthur asked.

"That is Vonby's plan," Valentina confirmed, meaning the gray-haired rider.

"It'll happen over my dead body," Whitaker growled.

Vonby puffed up as if to speak. Arthur cut across him.

"I don't care. Replace them or don't—it doesn't matter. I told you I came with a warning. I have direct evidence that a Rare-ranked scourgling has taken over at least one of the free hives . . ."

And he quickly outlined the basics of what he had guessed what the Mind Singer was up to, including dragon farming.

The leaders listened at first with incredulity, then disgust, and finally growing alarm.

As Arthur revealed what he knew about the raids on nests, Valentina sat up. "Who knows about this?" she demanded. "If the female dragons find out—"

And right on cue, there was an enraged bellow from Elissa. "THE EGGS?!"

Arthur carefully kept his grin to himself. Brixaby had understood his plan perfectly: Joy was very good at spilling secrets.

He managed a neutral "I believe that cat is out of the bag."

Valentina's expression became thunderous. "You must learn discretion if you ever intend to lead here."

"Sorry," Arthur said blandly, "that wasn't one of my lessons before I was taken to the other hive."

Inside, he also seethed that no one had asked—or seemed interested—in the fate of the other hatchlings and riders in his class. Nothing about Cressida and Joy, even though Joy was a high-grade shimmer Rare, or Len and Tamya.

That blue dragon and his rider were right to leave, he thought.

"If this intelligence is to be believed," Vonby said with a snide look in Arthur's direction, "I fail to see how this is our problem. The free hives exist outside the law of our kingdom. Let them deal with this issue themselves."

"Of course it's our problem!" The shout came from Whitaker, who had only looked more and more twitchy during Arthur's story. "It's the duty of all of the hives to fight the scourge. And from the boy's story, this one has been setting itself up nice and proper, gorging itself on cards."

Wow. Perhaps Arthur had underestimated Whitaker. Maybe he had more honor and compassion inside than he'd ever outwardly shown—

"And things have been so boring here. It's been, what, two weeks since the last eruption? If we don't fight soon, we're going to lose our edge."

Never mind, Arthur thought. But at least the man was on his side.

Valentina spoke up. "This isn't the first time a high-level scourgling has tried to gain a foothold in our world. They tend to burn themselves out like a wildfire that's grown too hot and too fast. But," she added with a weary look at Whitaker, "he's right. It cannot be allowed to stand. We must go."

"This isn't a scourge-eruption," Vonby said. "If Arthur is to be believed, it will be a raid on another hive. Dragon against dragon." He looked hard at Arthur. "Assuming, of course, this isn't a mistake or a convoluted trap."

Arthur stared back at him. He had nothing to prove, and if worse came to worse, he'd reveal something he'd kept left out of his story: there was a Legendary card in play.

"I take it that Buck Moon Hive won't be a part of this fight?" Valentina asked with a raised eyebrow.

Vonby gritted his teeth, and orange sparks briefly highlighted his lips. Some sort of flame power?

"No hive will be a part of this. We serve our kingdom, not outsiders."

"Excellent." Whitaker clapped his hands. "More cards for us to harvest." Turning, he clapped Arthur on the shoulder—hard enough to send him stumbling forward a step. "Glad to have you back, kid. I'll send word to sound the alarm. I assume you can give our portal card users the destination? Yes? Well, I'm off." He strode away at a fast clip, visibly excited for a fight to come.

Vonby stared after him with a lip curled in disgust. "You must be joking. You can't possibly take on an entire Rare-ranked scourgling nest with one small hive's worth of dragons."

Arthur didn't bother telling the man he'd brought dragons of his own to help with the numbers. He lifted his chin. "As Whitaker said: it's more cards for us."

The man looked back and forth between them, annoyance and concern warring on his face. He seemed to be on the urge of demanding they see reason, but in the end, he only shrugged. "If your hive is overrun, don't expect us to swoop in to help."

"Of course not," Valentina said. "Your help would lead to a leadership coup."

"We're on the same side, Valentina."

"So you say, Vonby."

The two stared at one another for a moment. Then, with a shake of his head, Vonby turned to stride out, all injured dignity.

"Finally," Valentina muttered under her breath. "Now Elissa can finally let that storm up."

Arthur looked at her, surprised. "She conjured the storm?"

"That annoying man has an extraordinarily powerful fire card." She smiled thinly. "He and his dragon hate the cold and the wet. Now," she added before Arthur could take that in, "don't think I didn't notice you left a lot out of your story, young man."

"I was at the Mesa Hive for months. I couldn't tell you everything in one go."

She leveled an unimpressed look at him. "I'm old and dying, not stupid. What has got you so riled up about this scourgling in particular? Why do we have to hit it now?"

Arthur was tempted to say, *I brought half a free hive's worth of dragons with me, and they're sure to be discovered before dawn. But I don't want to say anything because you may not let them leave, or you'll see those numbers as a threat to your power. They follow me, not you.*

So instead he told her his second-biggest secret.

"I believe the scourgling has a Legendary card—one that will pair very well with Brixaby."

She let out a long breath. "Making you each the wielders of two pairs. The king will not like that."

"Only if he finds out," Arthur said, feeling daring. "Are you really . . . Are you unwell?"

"The healers have given me weeks at best," Valentina said. "It's a growth, they say. It's been managed for years, but eventually, the healing magic wanes and the growth spreads. I plan on beating their expectations, but yes, Arthur, it will get the best of me. Elissa . . . isn't far behind, I fear." Her hard look softened, but it wasn't for her dragon. It was for Arthur. "And now that you've decided to return, my passing will make you a true leader of the hive."

Arthur wasn't sure why that hit him the way it did. Only that deep down, he wasn't sure he was ready.

Valentina continued ruthlessly. "I don't envy you the next few decades. We're a small hive, and while Whitaker is good in a fight, that's all he's good for. It will be your job to manage him, Arthur. This will help."

Her thin, birdlike fingers rose to her chest, and to Arthur's shock, she removed a card from her very heart.

She turned it to face Arthur.

It was a mind card.

CHAPTER 52

Arthur read the card. To his continued surprise, it was a Common.

Well. That likely explained how Valentina had managed to keep it under wraps.

Subtle Influence

Common

Mind

The wielder of this card will be granted the power to subtly influence direct conversations in which they are participating. The wielder will be able to push a subtle weight to all of their words, which will have the effect of nudging a conversation in the direction they wish. This is a minor influence and may be counteracted by a strong will. Conversely, this card will have a greater effect on an unsteady, weak, or compromised mind. This is an active skill that uses mana.

Seeing this card colored every conversation he'd ever had with Valentina. He couldn't pinpoint a specific incident he had been manipulated, but Valentina had always seemed like a larger than life person, as if she held an outsized presence in the room.

He thought it was the force of her personality. Now, he wondered.

Looking at her as she held the card out to him—what must have been the major source of her power—she seemed . . . diminished. And he didn't think it was only because she was dying.

"What are you waiting for?" she croaked, a thin smile on her lips. "Surely you have a card that has unlocked the use of mana?"

It was meant to be a joke, but it fell flat.

Mind cards were strictly regulated for good reasons.

Not that it had stopped Arthur. Brix's mind-messaging ability had come straight from one of the Mind Singer's "sisters."

No, Arthur was bothered by something else.

"Valentina, you *know* the cards that I have," he said carefully. "We talked about the cards I had back at Buck Moon Hive." Pause. "Remember?"

She stared at him for a moment, and then her gaze went vague. "No, we didn't. In . . . Buck Moon Hive? When was . . .?" She shook her head. "I'm afraid I can't recall. You are young, Arthur. As you get older, the days seem to fly by faster and faster. Memories pile up, they jumble together and . . . sometimes, I'm afraid I lose details. I'm not the only one." Her gaze sharpened to make her seem more like her usual self, and she speared him with a significant look.

"You're talking about the king."

Nodding, she finally dropped her outstretched hand, though the card still stayed in place, hovering between them on a small pillow of cloud.

"Of course I'm talking about the king." She raised a thin hand to rub at her temple. "That man is more gone than present most of the time, as you're now well aware." She let out a long sigh. "I am sorry."

Arthur's eyebrows went up. "About?"

"We should have prepared you on what to expect with the king. Well, *I* should have. Whitaker was supposed to at least advise you, but even when I ordered him to do it, I knew there would be little hope he'd follow through. Nevertheless, I understand you're still angry. From what I've gleaned, it was a close call, was it not?"

He kept his answer to a clipped "It was."

"I think I feared getting my hopes up over you," Valentina continued. "I was wrong and acted like a coward. I should have known that someone who managed to come from nothing and yet still beat out all those other brats to link with a Legendary dragon would have the gumption to succeed with the king. But I suppose that's part of growing old, too. It becomes easier and easier to fall into pessimism . . ."

She trailed off, and Arthur found himself at a loss of what to say. He didn't want to tell her that he forgave her, because he hadn't. He was still irritated over his incident with the king, and he knew that Brixaby was practically enraged. The dragon never forgave, and though Arthur tried to be a calming influence, this time, he agreed.

Again, Valentina's eyes had gone vague. "That is the push and pull of life—the great catch. The people who are most likely to have great power are rarely forced to forge the life skills to lead. Or worse, they wield the strength of their cards against every problem like a hammer. They think that gives them true power, but it makes them effectively useless as a leader."

Arthur watched her carefully. And he wondered if part of her fragile appearance wasn't an act because she had very neatly circled back around to her original point. "Now you're talking about Whitaker."

"Of course I am," she snapped, showing a bit of her usual feistiness. "The man should have *never* been given a Legendary card, much less gotten close to an unlinked dragon. Remember this in the future when a highly ranked egg is laid: Dragons choose on the compatibility and power of the cards in the heart, not on their rider's personality. And certainly not on capability."

But that wasn't entirely true, Arthur thought. Or else Brixaby would have chosen his cousin, Penn.

Well. Maybe not when Brixaby had first hatched. There were some issues with Brixaby's own core card being incomplete, and Arthur had a pair of Legendary cards in his heart to Penn's one. But later, when the king had given Brixaby the option to switch riders, take Arthur's cards for himself, and have access to Master of Combat to boot . . . Brixaby could have easily had all the power he wanted.

Instead, he'd rejected Penn completely.

Unaware of Arthur's thoughts, Valentina continued. "If life was fair and just, Whitaker would have remained a useless noble dilettante. He could have been placed comfortably on the outer portion of his father's lands while a more capable sibling took over management. By my own first card, he could have been happy, and he wouldn't have been put in a position to do anyone any damage. Instead, he was regulated to this small northern hive." She snorted. "The king's mind is lost, but he is still shrewd about personalities. He knows what Whitaker is."

Arthur couldn't help himself. "If that's the case, why are you in this hive?"

She smiled, exposing a good set of teeth that were nevertheless grayed with age. "He knew I was too much of a threat to his power to put me anywhere else." Her mirth faded. "But as you can see, my time is coming to an end. Soon, Whitaker will be in charge of everything here—in name. And it will be your job to manage him."

The mind card was still up for grabs and not in Valentina's heart. So there was no excuse for why her words hit him so hard—except that they were the simple truth.

Arthur saw his own life yawning out ahead of him. Decades and decades of managing Whitaker away from his worst impulses. All the while, the man wouldn't take him seriously because Arthur was younger and more junior to him.

Arthur would be left to do all the work to hold the hive together. Meanwhile, the wolves of the other hives would be ever circling, waiting to swoop in and take whatever Arthur didn't manage to keep safe.

And above them, the undying king would always be waiting for him to make a fatal misstep.

He was in for a life of deep frustration born out of stagnation, because if Arthur was stuck doing the actual work, when would he ever be able to grow stronger?

A voice that sounded a lot like Brixaby whispered they could always arrange a convenient "accident" for Whitaker.

But then, surely, the other hives would take the opportunity to pounce. If they took over Wolf Moon Hive completely, Arthur would be placed as a junior Legendary somewhere else—and carefully watched and untrusted because he had originally come from a different hive.

His job, his life, would be frustrating and largely thankless . . . and for what?

Looking at Valentina, he saw deep sympathy in her eyes. She knew what he was in for because she'd been carrying this load for the hive for a long time. But the difference between them was that she'd had seniority over Whitaker and therefore some influence over his worst impulses.

Arthur didn't.

"What even is the point?" Arthur blurted.

She shrugged her shoulders. "Someday, Whitaker will die and you will ascend to the high leader position. There may even be another Legendary egg laid in the interim. If you're clever enough to keep it here in this hive, you may be able to cultivate an ally—"

"No," he said sharply. "I'm not talking about this stupid power play. I'm talking about the war. What is the point? We're about to go up against a scourgling that has taken over one of the free hives and all the dragons in it . . . but what then? Never-ending fighting against endless eruptions while managing someone who can't be bothered to manage himself? I have better things to do with my time—with my *life*—than play babysitter and contribute to a perpetual war. Where do the scourglings even come from? Do you know? Does anyone?"

She didn't answer and, frustrated, he continued.

"Valentina, there has to be a better way than waiting around to act and then fighting. There's more to learn than what's inside this kingdom. I've seen beyond the borders—"

"What may or may not be out there isn't your concern," she said firmly. "Your duty is to Wolf Moon Hive. You made that agreement when you decided to link with your dragon. It's the price of power. Now," she added sharply when he opened his mouth. With a shooing motion, she pushed the tiny cloud carrying the card at him. "You know what kind of a card this is and why you must keep it secret. You're no idiot, Arthur. Take it."

Arthur snapped his mouth shut. Not because he had more to say, but because he knew whatever words he managed would fall on deaf ears. He gave no voice to the resentment boiling in his heart.

But he knew now that as much as he would be able to do—even if he dedicated his entire life to the hive—it wouldn't matter. He would be stuck mitigating the disaster that was Whitaker without truly being able to grow his own power. He'd have precious little time, if any, for concerns outside the hive. And even if he did, he'd be closely watched. That meant no more helping people like his father.

Arthur had become part of the system that had helped imprison his family. He was now powerful, but with responsibilities that weighed him down like chains.

At the same time, Arthur had some sense. He wasn't going to argue with a dying woman who had dedicated her entire life to the status quo.

But as Arthur took the Common mind card, he promised himself that her life was not going to be his.

The cycle ended here.

CHAPTER 53

As Arthur crossed the threshold out to the ledge, the hive-wide scourge-eruption alarms started to blare: a long tone followed by the deep ringing of bells, which were quickly picked up and repeated throughout the levels.

Arthur paused, frowned, and glanced around. Whitaker had seemed all gung-ho to go out and fight, which had been a help during the meeting. But Arthur had expected there would be a quick meeting or a conversation about tactics ahead of time. After all, this wasn't like a typical eruption. This would be dragons against other, mind-controlled dragons. They had to go in with a plan.

A bad feeling settled in the pit of his stomach. He wasn't a complete idiot—there was every chance Valentina had been playing her own game and trying to poison Arthur against Whitaker for her own ends. Though based on what Arthur had seen so far of the man, he hadn't doubted her.

Still, this was different.

He's not really going just to throw the hive at the Mind Singer, is he? he thought, the sense of dread increasing. No, Whitaker couldn't be that much of a fool.

Arthur cupped his hands around his mouth and called, "Brixaby!"

He spotted his dragon a few moments later, speaking with Elissa. Her massive head rested on her paws, her expression fierce as she seemed to lecture the younger dragon. It was a direct mirror to what had happened inside Valentina's room.

At Arthur's call, both dragons looked his way. Elissa nodded as if granting Brixaby permission to leave.

But Brixaby, being Brixaby, didn't bother waiting for her approval and quickly flew to Arthur's side.

"I need you to get in contact with the hive's white dragons," Arthur said before he had fully settled to land. "Tell them what we're about to face and that the hive needs protection against mind-to-mind intrusion."

After all, there was no point in sending people and dragons to fight only to have them get captured and turned against their friends.

"I'd like to see the Mind Singer *try* to ensnare me," Brixaby snarled.

"She probably couldn't," Arthur admitted. "And she might have to work hard to take over the Rares since she's one herself, but the Uncommons and Commons make up the bulk of our forces."

Brixaby's expression turned even more fearsome, which was his way of showing concern.

He buzzed off without another word.

He hadn't been gone a moment before Cressida jogged up to Arthur. "Joy's been talking with the other dragons—the females, mostly."

Arthur nodded. "I heard she was spreading the word about the eggs."

"Yes, well, they had some news of their own to share." Her expression was pinched with concern. "Whitaker has sent orders to absorb *all* of Valentina's retinue into his own. He took every one of her Rares and cut loose the lower ranks."

Arthur let out an annoyed breath but nodded. He wasn't surprised. "Valentina won't be fighting with us." It would be nice if she could rally herself one more time, but she hadn't shown any sign of doing so. She might really be dying.

Cressida gave him an impatient look. "Arthur, he's trying to undermine you before you even have time to establish yourself as a leader. He hasn't taken any dragon pairs that claim to be under your retinue *yet*, because that would be a direct challenge. But he's setting himself up to be the leader with the most power."

Again, Arthur felt the weight of responsibility and helpless frustration settle over his shoulders. What was the point of all this? Part of him wanted to say, *He can have the hive if he can figure out how to run it himself.*

Instead, he asked, "Horatio and Sams?"

"They managed to stay back after the Buck Moon Hive leader left. But Whitaker—"

"I know. I'll figure something out, Cress, but we have to stop the Mind Singer's plans." And with all luck, gain a powerful card to add to Brixaby's core. He didn't have time for Whitaker's power play.

He would have said more, but there was a sudden shift in the air. Below, all the dragons and their riders, alerted by the scourge-eruption alarms, were getting into position. Sleepy riders, jolted awake, were preparing their linked mounts with saddles and straps. They had a few minutes until everyone was properly ready.

I need to speak to Whitaker, Arthur thought, regretting his decision to send Brixaby away.

He had a whole retinue. He could have sent Cressida, Horatio, or even Laird on an errand instead of his own dragon. He needed to delegate better.

A sharp whistle cut through the air. Arthur's head whipped around in that direction so swiftly that he momentarily felt like his body wasn't under his own control. A bare moment later, as the impulse dissipated, he realized that it hadn't been.

Someone had just used a spell on him to yank all his focus and attention in a certain direction. And judging by the sudden silence from the hive below and all around, it had happened to everyone.

Likely, it had been a mind spell of some sort.

But he didn't have time to think about the implications of *that*, because at that very moment, Whitaker's new, strengthened retinue appeared.

An entire group of dragons nearly two dozen strong seemed to float down from the misty clouds. Their visibility in the fading storm was enhanced by several yellow light dragons that illuminated them all with a heroic glow.

It was an impressive display.

Together, they circled the hive in a wide V formation with Whitaker's orange dragon at the point.

Arthur felt the gaze of thousands upon them.

Despite his very mixed doubts about Whitaker's ability to lead, he had to admit they made a brave show. Each following dragon was a Rare, with scales and saddles polished to a shine. The riders sat straight back and proud, and the dragons themselves all looked healthy and eager. All ready to rush into battle.

One of them—probably Whitaker's dragon since, as an orange, he excelled at material manipulation—altered the last of the misty raindrops so that they glittered like actual jewels as they dropped past, picking up the color of each dragon's hide and reflecting it to the eyes of the watchers.

Arthur only realized he was gaping when his attention was drawn by a nearby flutter of wings. It was very similar to Brixaby's but subtly wrong enough to break the spell.

Glancing over, he saw a small purple courier dragon land. He wore a golden sash and puffed himself up officially.

"You're Arthur, rider of Brixaby?" The purple spoke more clearly than most of its kind, and Arthur got the impression that it was an Uncommon.

"I am."

"Leader Whitaker says to advise the portal dragons of the destination."

"But we're not ready yet. Most of the hive hasn't even had time to saddle their dragons. Go back to Whitaker and tell him we need to speak—"

"Sorry, sir, I don't change or explain the orders. I only relay them."

Arthur grit his teeth.

A moment later, Brixaby returned, landing next to Arthur and flaring his wings aggressively at the purple dragon. "The conclave of mind-mages hear and obey the hive leader," he said, smugly before peering at the purple. "What do you want?"

"Whitaker's setting himself up for a grand entrance through the portal," Arthur said, then called Laird over. "Inform the portal dragons of the location of Free Hive of the Waves, but make sure they understand that it's not to open until I give the say so."

"Hive politics?" Laird guessed, but he didn't argue with Arthur and took off anyway, flying up toward where the green shimmer dragons were circling in the brightening dawn sky.

"Hive politics," Arthur repeated on a mutter, and then addressed Cressida and Joy. "Go to Whitaker and ask him when would be the best time to coordinate and plan our attack."

That was as gentle of a message as he could make. A reminder that they needed to know what they were doing before they went charging off. Hopefully, Whitaker would be happy circling the hive and looking powerful for a few more minutes before he came down and they got down to real business.

Meanwhile, what Brixaby had called the conclave of mind-mages was now landing on the ledge. Arthur's retinue had to scoot off to the side to make room for them. There were five in total, ranging from a white so dull that it looked almost silver to a blank absence of color he'd only seen in expensive chicken eggs. Every one of them had a rider on board. All were unfamiliar except for one man, Devi, whom he had once met in Valentina's presence.

Devi stayed back while another man dismounted and approached. He had a gentle, soft face, but Arthur didn't trust it. He snapped all of his mental shields up.

As the man drew closer, Arthur saw that he carried . . . a stack of cards?

"Well met, Arthur." The man smiled. "My name is Bryce, and I'm sorry that we must meet for the first time under these circumstances. However, we bring good news."

"You bring us a tribute of cards?" Brixaby demanded, looking hungrily at the thick stack.

"Not quite," Bryce said, and held out the stack. Behind him, the other riders dismounted with their own stack of cards in hand. Each stack was nearly a hand span thick. "Your dragon explained what our hive will be facing, and we do have a solution. Part of our duties is to protect against mind magic during eruptions. One of our number has the ability to link his power to block minds using these card anchors."

Arthur reached out and grabbed one of the cards. They weren't magical at all—just slips of unusually thick paper cut into the shape of a rectangle. It simply had the words mind block stamped across the top along with a red bar that ran the length of the card. It was a simple card anchor.

"Unfortunately, this is a time-limited object," Bryce continued. "As the power of the anchor is used, the red bar shrinks. When it is gone, the strength has failed. These are activated by the touch of skin to the card—or scale, as they do protect dragons as well."

Arthur's own Counterfeit card did not react to it. Then again, it had never copied a spell from another card anchor before. Like, for instance, a lamp connected to a light card or environmental card.

Arthur accepted the stack from Bryce and turned to pass them to the closest person standing nearby. "Horatio, start distributing these." He glanced back at Bryce. "Can you make more?"

"We cannot," Bryce said. "By oath, our powers are restricted until we get the consensus of all hive leaders."

"Valentina will agree, and so will Whitaker," Arthur replied. "Once he comes down to plan out our attack."

After all, this couldn't be the first time Whitaker had fought a scourgling with a mind card. Yes, the Mind Singer was stronger than usual, being a Rare, but a Legendary dragon's main duty was to stand in reserve in case a demi-scourgling ever erupted. He knew the drill.

A part of Arthur winced even as he thought it, knowing he was jinxing himself with that thought.

He nearly kicked himself a second later because up high, twin portals activated.

Whitaker's voice, magically enhanced, boomed across the sky. "Wolf Moon Hive! Ascend with me to the portal! Today, we fight the scourglings without the interference of the other hives, which means more bounty for the rest of us. We will show the rest what we are made of. Follow me!"

Cursing, Arthur grabbed another stack of cards from the outstretched hands of a mind-mage, tossed it into his storage, and quickly mounted Brixaby.

"Stop him! They don't even know they're not heading for an eruption! Stop!"

Brixaby surged forward before Arthur was properly seated, throwing him back. But by leaning on his Dragon Riding skill, Arthur was able to hold on.

Brixaby was incredibly fast and ridiculously maneuverable, but Whitaker, who sat at the head of his retinue's V formation, had a massive head start.

Even as they raced to intercept, Arthur knew that they would be too late.

Whitaker, with his powerful retinue of dragons behind, was already heading toward the nearest portal. The rest of the hive streamed up after them.

They were heading into a fight that they were completely unprepared for. Whitaker was practically feeding new recruits to the Mind Singer.

Arthur saw a flash of pink as Cressida raced to join him. Joy flew at a flat sprint just to meet Brixaby halfway in the sky. Cressida cried out, "He said to follow his lead and then dismissed me. Arthur, I tried to stop him—"

At that moment, Whitaker disappeared into the portal.

"Brixaby," Arthur said, "send a message to the dragons, anybody who will listen. Tell them *not* to enter the portal until they take a mind-block card anchor!"

For one of the first times since Arthur had met Brixaby, he felt the dragon hesitate. "You want me to tell . . . everyone?"

"That's not too much for a Legendary, right?"

"Of course not!" Brixaby snarled. Then Arthur heard his own message relayed right into the middle of his mind as Brixaby used his messaging ability to blast it out. But his mental voice was more of a whisper than his usual boom—stretched out and thin—and he staggered in midair afterward. That action had cost him.

"I only ate a Rare card to gain that ability. There are thousands of minds," Brixaby said, much more subdued than usual. "I believe I reached them all, but the message is . . . faint."

Arthur patted his neck. "You did good."

But not good enough. Some dragons and riders who were right behind Whitaker stopped at Brixaby's message, looked around in confusion, and then continued on through the portal. Others took heart from seeing them pass through and followed as well.

However, a few of the more prudent dragon pairs peeled off and circled around in confusion. They were a minority, however. Perhaps one in four.

Looking down, Arthur noticed that the dragons who had followed him from Mesa Free Hive hadn't made a move toward the portal at all. Most were busily accepting the card anchors that Arthur's retinue was passing out. But that still left the Wolf Moon Hive dragons who were still flowing through the portal.

Arthur wanted to call out to them, but he couldn't project his voice across the vast expanse of the hive in the open air. Not even with any skill. He watched helplessly as more dragons followed Whitaker through the portal.

It was going to be a slaughter.

Finally, Brixaby said, "There are fewer minds now."

"Then I need you to relay this message: We will be fighting other dragons whose minds have been taken over by a scourgling. Use the card anchors we will pass out as a mental shield and watch the red bar. When it runs low, return to get another."

His retinue riders continued passing out cards, but the process was taking too long, and he knew that the ones who'd gone through the portal were fighting for their lives. They needed to hand out the cards faster.

He caught a flash of purple out of the corner of his eye. Arthur turned to see quite a few riderless purples had made their way to the top cone of the hive. Likely to watch the excitement.

"Brixaby, send a message to all the purple couriers. Here's what I need to have done . . ."

A few minutes later, purple couriers were gleefully passing out cards to anyone who would accept them. They were thrilled to assist, even if they couldn't fight.

Brixaby, meanwhile, had recovered his breath from that first message. "What are we waiting for?"

Knowing better than to say "*You*", Arthur looked up at the portal. No one had come back out from the other side yet.

Arthur looked up toward the portal. "All right, it's time. Retinue riders, with me."

Brixaby surged forward and was quickly followed by Joy, Sams, Laird, Digger, and Tannai.

There was a secondary roar as the dragons who had followed Arthur from Mesa Free Hive and the dragons who had heeded Brixaby's warning all gathered up behind him.

Brixaby aimed for the shimmering portal.

CHAPTER 54

With Arthur and Brixaby leading the front, the rest of his retinue shifted into a blade formation.

It was a formation Arthur had learned in class in his first months in Wolf Moon Hive but never had the opportunity to take part in. But with people he trusted, it felt seamless.

Arthur and Brixaby were in front. Joy and Cressida flew behind and just off center to the right. Sams and Horatio took the spot behind and just to the left.

As one of their most offensively based dragons with ranged magic, Laird took the spot directly behind Arthur.

Digger and Tannai flew to either side of Laird as his anchor.

The blade formation turned out to be the perfect choice, because they erupted from the other side of the portal into chaos.

Men and dragons screamed in a terrible cacophony. And along with that, Arthur was hit by hot, wet air—so viscerally different from the cold dry air of Wolf Moon that he gasped involuntarily and then regretted it because it felt like a wet rag had been shoved over his mouth.

The sky was filled with fog so dense and sporadic that Arthur couldn't easily count the numbers in the sky or much of the lay of the land below them.

Around him, men and dragons all fought in a free-for-all without any hint of a formation on either side.

Arthur caught chaotic glimpses of Wolf Moon Hive dragons fighting other dragons with their eyes blank, as if they moved in a dream. Yet most of the enemy fought with teeth and claws, not reaching for card powers.

And above that all, an invisible weight seemed to bear down on Arthur's head. It wasn't something he could put his finger on or truly identify, except that he felt his **Mental Shield** skills snap into place.

Glancing down at the mind-block card, he already saw a sliver shaved off of the top of the red bar. It was activated and working hard to keep him safe.

The Mind Singer had grown strong, and they were now in its territory.

He took all of this in within a few seconds. Then Brixaby flew into the thick of the fray. It was almost impossible to tell friendly dragons from foe. Heads snapped their way and dragons of all rank and color—wearing Wolf Moon insignia and not—moved to attack.

Sams let out a roar of challenge. A subtle brightness lit the air. It wasn't much—as if a cloud had moved away from the sun. Yet the slight increase still vaporized much of the surrounding fog.

The dragons that had turned toward them winced away, shrieking. Their riders threw hands over their eyes, and what card powers had been ready to launch went awry: fireballs, sharp shards of ice, and even a few conjured arrows flew off in the wrong direction.

Arthur remembered that Sams and Horatio had some sort of invisible light card. Horatio had explained it as a very bright shade of violet that the eyes could not quite see, but that the body could feel. Whatever that meant.

Laird added his powers. Within moments, they were surrounded by merry purple candle flames that looked deceptively delicate, but viciously burned whatever they touched. The dome of candle-top flames moved through the air at the same speed they did, creating a barrier between themselves and any attackers.

Cressida's largest flame bear galloped through the sky alongside Joy, and Arthur saw him swat away a small blue dragon that had managed to fly in under Laird's dome.

Brixaby brought out one of his enchanted metal bars, though he didn't light it yet.

Arthur briefly thought about asking Brixaby to activate his Night-Mare Fire, but as the fire would grow up from his spine, and Arthur was currently sitting there, that might be a bad idea. They had enough spell effects surrounding them for the moment.

Meanwhile, they were continuously refreshed by a wellspring of mana thanks to the silver.

With all these powers activated, and the pure speed that Brixaby set, they managed to blast past the first line of defenders.

Most importantly, behind them, others started to emerge from the portal. Like Arthur's retinue, they were protected by the mind-block card anchor.

The new wave of dragons clashed with the existing. The enemy numbers had been swelled by the dragons who'd followed Whitaker.

Where was Whitaker anyway?

Arthur looked for a large rust-orange hide but couldn't spot Whitaker's dragon anywhere.

The fog was patchy, yet incredibly dense. It was easy enough to lose a dragon, even one of Crag's size.

It didn't matter. They had to shave down the Mind Singer's numbers, and he knew exactly how to do it.

Arthur retreated into his Personal Space.

The quiet, though untidy, room was a shock to the system after the screaming chaos outside. He took a moment just to breathe.

But only a moment because even though this place was timeless, Arthur still couldn't shake the feeling he had no time to spare.

He grabbed the lengths of chainmail he had stored—most of it was looking rather ragged by now, though it didn't matter. Using his Metal Shot card, he started unlinking rivets and then twisting them into points at one end with jagged edges. They looked much like fish hooks with a loop at the end with a small gap before the circle was completed.

Then he started threading a corner of the mind-block card anchors through the open loops before relinking it again. When he had gone through the entire stack of mind-block cards—about fifty or so—he took a bracing breath and exited his Personal Space.

He grabbed one of the altered cards, and with his Metal Shot card, used the jagged rivet on the corner to fire it at the closest mind-controlled dragon.

It was a light-green dragon in a state Arthur never wanted to see again: It seemed the rider had been taken over by the Mind Singer, but the dragon was still fighting her control.

However, the rider had taken a conjured sword to the dragon's back. He was chopping away at hard scales while the dragon cried out and writhed, unwilling to throw his rider off. Vines laced out from under the dragon's scales to hold the rider's wrist, but the blank-faced man cut through them and slashed down at the back of his dragon's neck again.

Arthur shot two cards: one at the rider, the other at the dragon.

His Metal Shot card only gave him the ability to control the metal rivets an inch from his body. The card attached to it proved ungainly in the air and would have fluttered short due to drag.

Except Arthur's Makeshift Weaponry card had kicked in. And a portion of it dovetailed quite nicely with his Master of Skills card.

It happened quite naturally. Right before throwing it, he had received inspiration, and with several flicks, folded the thick card paper into a sleek arrow shape, which removed the drag. It took a second per card.

New skill gained: Paper Arrow (Origami Class)
Due to your card's bonus traits, you automatically start this skill at
level 3.

Arthur grinned. It wasn't exactly a combat skill, but he would take it.

The altered cards still went sideways, but the dragon was a big target.

One of the rivets stuck true, and the jagged fishhook points dug into the scales.

Immediately, some of the haze cleared from the dragon's eyes, and he yelled, "Mitchum, what are you doing?"

Mitchum didn't reply. The card Arthur aimed at him had flown awry, and he was still under the Mind Singer's control.

But Brixaby had seen what Arthur was doing. With a quick flick of his wings, he broke out of his formation, weaved between Laird's protective candle-flame dome, dove the thirty or so feet down, and slapped the man—literally—with a card to the back of the neck.

Michum staggered forward with the force of the blow. His conjured sword collapsed into sparkling mana.

As Brixaby flew away, Arthur saw the man sobbing out apologies and pressing on the cuts to slow his dragon's bleeding.

They would be okay, and there were hundreds of other pairs like them.

"If you have any more extra mind-block cards, give them to me," Brixaby said to his retinue.

Horatio and Digger had partial stacks, which they gave up gladly.

Arthur spent the next few minutes in his Personal Space making up more of them.

Then his retinue aimed for the thickest clusters of enemies, and he sent cards flying. There were more mind-controlled dragons than he had cards, however.

"These card anchors won't last forever," Laird warned. "We need to reach the Mind Singer."

"Right now, we're cutting her army out from under her," Arthur said. "That's just as important—"

He stopped as a cry boomed out across the air in Whitaker's voice.

"RETREAT. WOLF MOON HIVE. BACK TO THE PORTAL."

Arthur glanced up and to the side just as two clouds of fog parted, and finally spotted Whitaker.

He had taken up position above the fray, but it looked like that hadn't stopped some of his own retinue from turning on him. It seemed that the Mind Singer had been able to take over a Rare after all, though no doubt with some trouble.

Unfortunately, anyone who tried to attack a Legendary was about to have a very bad day.

Arthur saw one dragon pair twist in the air to come around and fly at Whitaker with claws outstretched. In a moment, the shading of the dragon went from summer blue to stark white as their flesh turned to marble. They dropped like a statue, forever frozen in an attack position.

"Wolf Hive, retreat!" Whitaker sounded again, and his beleaguered retinue turned back for the portal.

"Coward!" Brixaby boomed out, though for once his voice wasn't as loud as Whitaker's. It wasn't aided by a card. "Stand and fight the scourge!"

Other dragons—many of whom had just been saved by the mind-block cards—turned for the portal.

Unfortunately, like any retreat, it gave heart to the other side. Mind-controlled dragons threw themselves and their powers at those trying to get away. Many of them followed the escapers back through the portal to continue the fight over Wolf Moon Hive.

"Arthur!" Brixaby twisted his head around, bloodred eyes practically sparking with rage. "We must stop them."

"No, Laird is right. The mind-block card won't last forever, and once they are out of range and the portal is shut down, those dragons will be out of the Mind Singer's grasp. The white dragons can help with the rest."

Cressida turned to him, horrified. "We're not leaving?"

"No," Arthur said. "We're going straight for her." He pointed down.

Now that some of the dragon formations were breaking up, the sky was clearing of fog in the brightening sky, and Arthur got a clear view of the hive below them for the first time.

Like with Mesa Free Hive, this wasn't a traditionally shaped dragon hive. This was a massive cliff face, chalk white from some unfamiliar stone, which stood on the edge of a cold, dark sea.

Beyond, on the landward side, stood a fat volcano, its bright lava pulsing in the sun. In the miles between the two sat a low fog bank. It was a combination of the heat from the hot lava and the cold sea that caused the thick humidity.

"She's somewhere down in those cliffs. That's where the power is coming from."

Arthur glanced down at his mind-block card. The red bar was halfway gone, even though they'd only been fighting for a few minutes.

The Mind Singer had grown much, much stronger. That made it all the more important that they stop her now.

Arthur signaled his retinue.

"Dive!"

CHAPTER 55

Digger! It's time." Arthur couldn't hear himself over the scream of wind as they fell almost straight down, but Brixaby could, and must have relayed the message to the brown dragon.

Their dive was so fast—wings tucked and noses pointed down with the riders pressed against their dragon's necks—that none of the attacking dragons could reach them. And if they could, they would have surely been bowled out of the way.

No one bothered. To all outsiders, the dive looked entirely suicidal. Some hopefuls watched with partial attention, for when they hit the ground there would be cards to harvest.

However, before they'd even left the hive, Arthur had made sure to get an outline of Digger's general card powers aside from Stone Skin.

He had been named aptly.

Under them, the onrushing ground seemed to swell up and then part and reshape itself. It was an open maw that led to a tunnel—a pitch-black tunnel, until Sams's scales shone like a miniature sun and lit the way.

No doubt, all the true entrances to the hive would be guarded by mind-controlled dragons, and perhaps even scourglings—though there hadn't been any sign of them so far.

So Arthur had elected to make his own entrance straight into what he hoped was the heart of the underground hive.

As a brown dragon with natural earthen magic, and a local, he knew his hive inside and out.

The tunnel must have opened close to their target because despite the mind-block card and Arthur's Mental Shield, a slithering lyrical voice rang through his head. *Kill the pink, the brown, the silver, the yellow, the red. Leave the Legendaries to me!*

Don't worry, Arthur thought. *We're coming.*

A moment later, they entered the mouth of the tunnel.

The air stank in a way that immediately threw Arthur back to his childhood in his borderland village. This was the stink that the scourge brought. Only this was magnified because, unlike the deadened lands at the edge of the kingdom, the presence of the scourglings was actively rotting away all life down to the unseen nutrients that lived in the soil.

It was worse than the humidity, plugging up his nose and driving out every other scent.

Joy whined but held steady as they flew through the tunnel, though slowing from their dive.

"Opening ahead," Digger called.

Sure enough, the rocky soil parted into a large open space that must have been part of the hive proper.

Open, but not empty.

Below them, from wall to wall, sat clusters of dragon eggs. Some were patterned. Most were a flat matte color that ranged through the rainbow, though a few special eggs glimmered as if they held a particularly good secret within.

There were hundreds and hundreds of clusters, all containing two to five eggs with occasional singles placed here and there. The majority sat on the stone ground, completely bereft of a nest. Others had twigs or bits of sand swept up and piled around to cushion them. These were the ones that were guarded.

Mother dragons with blank gazes hissed and spread their wings in threat at the newcomers.

Arthur braced himself for an attack, knowing how fierce the females could be. But nothing came.

The answer came from Joy's agonized cry. "Scourge-touched. Oh . . . look, they're all scourge-touched, even with cards. We have to help them! Cressida? We can't leave them like this!"

For a moment, he didn't understand what she was saying. Dragon eyes were better than human eyes in many ways.

Brixaby shuddered under him.

"What—" Arthur started, but at that moment they flew over a blue who stood on her hind legs to hiss up at them, snaking her neck back and forth. Her color wasn't uniform: She had a pale white stomach, which was an indication she'd linked with two riders in her life. And one was a mind-mage.

To his horror, Arthur saw red and brown lesions on her pale belly and even more spots that looked like the start of mold . . . or rot.

"That shouldn't be possible," Arthur muttered. His hand landed on Brixaby's neck as he grew sharply concerned for his dragon.

Everyone knew that having a card protected against scourge-sickness and scourge-rot.

Except that Joy had been born scourge-touched. She'd had an unformed card in her core, and the Mind Singer's presence in a nearby guild had been enough to infect her, even through the egg. So it was possible in certain circumstances.

Had he just put Brixaby in additional danger? What about himself? Everyone who followed him? Sometimes the scourge-sickness took root in the lungs, and every breath reeked of the rot.

No, Arthur thought sharply. They all had whole cards, multiple cards. That had to provide even more protection than a hatchling with a half-formed, defective card.

And perhaps the nesting mothers had multiple cards, too, but they had been living in this enclosed tunnel with the scourge-rot in the air for some time. Furthermore, their minds had been taken over by a scourgling. The Mind Singer might have done something to suppress the strength of their cards.

Behind them, Laird muttered, "This whole blighted hive will have to be razed to the ground."

"What about the dragons trapped down here?" Joy snapped. "Their eggs?"

Arthur's hand clenched on Brix's neck ridge. "Brix, go down to the blue. Don't let her bite you." Who knew what would happen if he got an open wound here?

Brixaby immediately switched positions, buzzing diagonally in a way no other dragon but a purple could. He shot close to the blue-white dragon, who bit at them but missed by a wide shot.

Interestingly, she wasn't using her card's powers. Perhaps his guess about the Mind Singer weakening them had been right, or she was striking out with the anger of an animal with no higher thought at all.

It didn't matter. Arthur readied a riveted mind-block card and fired it. It shot out and struck her under her jaw.

Instantly, the dragon's eyes cleared. She blinked and looked around and in a hazy voice said, "What? Where . . . My eggs?"

"Collect your eggs and fly out of here!" Joy yelled, circling above her. "Others, too, if you can carry them. Go!"

"Use this." Digger gestured, and a dragon-sized bowl made of hard-packed earth rose from the ground.

The blue-and-white dragon wasted no time piling eggs into it. Arthur hoped she wasn't only going to save her own, but he didn't have time to stick around and see. He prepared another mind-block card anchor and fired it, this time at a green female.

Brixaby helped by getting them as close as possible with his pinpoint flying, neatly avoiding claw strikes and wild bites. Jinking right and left hard enough to make Arthur's teeth rattle in his skull, he nevertheless got Arthur close enough to practically be at point-blank range.

This was essential because Arthur didn't have many cards or rivets left, and he couldn't afford to miss.

Joy trailed as close behind as her flying abilities would allow, screaming instructions at the newly mind-freed female dragons. "Gather all the eggs around—no, not just yours, there's one right there. Now get out of here before that mind block wears off!"

Some of the female dragons had so many lesions and spots of rot that Arthur wasn't sure if they were capable of flight.

All were capable of escape, though, and took off in an awkward gallop on foot if they had to.

Digger surged forward to take the lead. "Here. The heart of the hive is this direction."

If it was, Arthur couldn't tell. All the twisting, turning, and weaving to get to the nesting mothers had made him completely lose his sense of direction. But this was Digger's home hive, and he had to trust that he knew the way.

Glancing down at his own mind-block card, Arthur saw that another slice had been carved from the top of the red bar. Perhaps a third remained.

They flew on, and the tunnel around them grew narrower. Soon they were forced to squeeze in and then fly single file.

"I feel earth manipulation all around us," Digger called back. He'd maintained his position at the front of the line, but his stubby brown wings were in danger of scraping the sides. "Don't touch the walls!"

As if the walls were listening in, they seemed to flex inward without moving at all. Digger grunted, and the walls shifted back.

Behind them, Laird groaned.

"What is going on?" Brixaby demanded.

The brown shook his head heavily from side to side. But he continued flying on, and everyone took the cue to keep flying after him. None dared stop. "Trying . . . to keep all the earth from caving in."

"You're what?!" Laird roared, and Arthur got the impression he would have turned tail at that moment—if not for the fact there was nowhere else to go. Flying away meant being out of Digger's sphere of influence over the earth. That would be deadly.

Laird wasn't the only one who was frightened. The light pouring out of Sams to guide their way briefly flickered as he lost his concentration.

"Let me give you a boost." That was the mana silver, Tannai, sounding entirely too chipper. With a show of agility Arthur didn't expect, the silver dragon blew on ahead under Brixaby and Digger.

He twisted so he was flying upside down in a feat that no two-winged dragon should have been able to accomplish except by card power. Tannai placed his claws on Digger's stomach, directly injecting mana into him.

Digger exhaled, and the tunnels seemed to breathe along with him, expanding into a wider, more comfortable size.

They had more room in the tunnel. But to Arthur's horror, this exposed very dusty eggs that had been previously covered.

Someone had been trying very hard to entrap them and didn't care much about the cost.

"Digger—" Arthur started to say, then stopped. He was about to ask if there were dragon mothers entombed in the soil as well. Though, unlike eggs, they would need to breathe, and . . . they were very likely behind help.

"Oh, hey," Joy piped up, "I just got a quest."

Laird growled. "Is that important right now?" He still sounded stressed.

Arthur glanced back at him. Though dragon faces were not the most expressive, their body language spoke volumes.

Laird flew with hunched shoulders and wide eyes. He'd gathered all his purple candle-top flames close to him, as if needing them for personal warmth. He was not having a good time in these small tunnels.

"Yes, it is important," Joy called back. "And I think it's a neat one."

"I got it too." Brixaby sounded beyond delighted, almost to giddiness. "Defeat the heart of the rot and receive . . . a Legendary card!"

"Hey, that's no fair. I only got a Rare, but the good news is, if we live, the rest of you will also receive complementary cards. Don't you think that's neat?" Turning her head, she stuck out her tongue at Laird.

Digger suddenly maneuvered to stop hard in the air. He wasn't one of those dragons who could hover in place, like Brixaby, and there wasn't room to turn. Instead, he had to quickly dive to spill forward momentum.

As he did, Arthur caught a glimpse of the reason why: a solid earthen wall had risen before them all.

Unfortunately, he only got that glimpse. Brixaby could stop. The others could not, and a pile-up ensued.

The light flickered dizzily as Sams shifted this way and that to lose his forward speed. Joy tried to dive like Digger. Unfortunately, so did Laird, but he'd been a touch too slow. He clipped Joy, sending her spiraling backward into the tunnel Digger had warned them not to touch.

"Cressida!" Arthur yelled and reached out. But he was much too far away and could only watch for a horrified second that seemed to stretch out, certain she was about to be crushed between the stone and her dragon.

Joy hit and half sank into the wall. It was as liquid as mud, but with a sucking power that immediately started to pull her in.

Though she was about to be smothered, and mud already coated her sides and up to her chest, the pink dragon yelled "Cressida!" with horrified, wide eyes, wiggling as if to see her rider.

Brixaby roared in protest but had the good sense not to dart to Joy and risk being sucked in as well. Instead, he flickered his wings and swooped to join Digger.

The brown had turned and was staring hard at the wall—clearly using his power to try to win Joy back.

As Brixaby entered the brown's aura, he too, picked up the spell. So did Arthur.

New Counterfeit spell obtained: General Earth Manipulation
Remaining Time: 11 Hours 59 Minutes 59 Seconds

This was Digger's power and what made him such a valuable dragon, even for an Uncommon. His power was broad enough to be useful in all areas of the earth.

If he'd had any specific power over rocks, over soil, or any single facet, he would have surely had been hatched with a rare shimmer quality to his scales. But he was a dull, matte brown. It fit him.

Arthur and Brixaby both added their strength to the spell. Though they didn't have the finesse Digger did, they at least had brute strength and determination.

And, of course, they were backed up by Tanai, who didn't lift a claw to help fight but ensured they were always topped up.

The mud wall seemed to flex, as if fighting them.

"Don't try to carve her out. You'll crush her that way," Digger advised through gritted teeth. His narrowed eyes never left the still-struggling Joy. The mud hadn't advanced, but Cressida was completely buried. "Just solidify the wall and harden the earth. I'll break her out."

That sounded counterintuitive to Arthur, but he had to trust Digger knew what he was talking about when it came to soil.

Though the spell they'd copied didn't have power over the water in the mud, he was able to feel the particles around the sloshing water. With Brixaby's help, he used those particles to push the foreign liquid out and away.

The soil around Joy suddenly dried out. Instead of entrapping her, it finally gave her leverage to put her front and back feet down and pull free.

Sams rose up on his hind legs and extended claws out to her, which Joy grabbed with her non-venomous arm.

With a yank and the sound of cracking mud, Joy was pulled free. Cressida, still strapped into her saddle, came with her.

She was covered from head to foot in chalk-white dust and coughing so hard her face shone red underneath.

Joy dropped to the ground, and so did Brixaby. Arthur slid from his neck and ran to her.

It was hard to reach her. Joy twisted this way and that, trying to flex her neck backward to see her rider. "Cressida! Are you okay? If you're coughing, that means you're breathing, which means you're going to be okay, right?"

"She'll be fine. Joy, stand still!" Arthur commanded. The moment the pink dragon paused, he leaped up, grabbed the dust-coated straps of the saddle, and hauled himself up the rest of the way.

Cressida was bent over, still coughing. It seemed the only clean parts of her were the inside of her mouth and her eyes, which stood out starkly against her chalky-white dusty skin.

He felt over her briskly, trying to be impersonal but aware every second of how close he was to losing her.

"I'll be fine," she croaked and gave him a half smile. Louder, she said, "Joy, I'm fine!"

"Do you need my healing card?" Arthur asked.

"No, but you . . . you got me out just in time."

Arthur's heart felt like it had frozen to stone. He stared at her, and if Brixaby were a larger dragon, if he was certain he could manage both their weights, he might have done something stupid like scoop her up and carry her to him. Brixaby could protect them both. He could protect *anyone*.

Behind them, Digger huffed. "I told you not to touch the walls." He swung his head back to the forward wall, which had halted their momentum. "This is not natural."

"I could blast through it," Laird declared then paused. "But the explosion may not be a good thing for us in such a small, confined area."

Digger shook his head. "No, this isn't something that can easily be blasted through. It's as thick as I am long from nose to tail, twice over. Someone wanted us to go no further. Maybe entrap us here."

Arthur made himself pull away from Cressida. She had straightened up and seemed to be breathing a little easier, though with a rasp. He looked at the wall and frowned. "No doubt another wall will be put up in front of us if we go back. The Mind Singer has every reason to keep us here breathing this rotten air."

"And it gives the thing more time to gather its forces, or just crush us between the walls," Horatio said, always ready to lend a gloomy prediction.

A horrified shudder went through Laird's body. "So we stay here and wait to die?"

"No, no, calm down." Digger eyed the stone wall again and then let out a heavy sigh. "I have a specialized drill card I share with my rider. It ought to do the trick, but once I use it, I'll be done."

"I can give you the mana you need—" the silver began.

Digger shook his head in a slow, ponderous way he had about him. "No, it takes stamina. I should have enough left to crawl out of here afterward, but I'll be exhausted. But there's more: if my sense of direction's right, there should be a large room beyond. We call it the Amphitheater. Can't say what the scourgling's hidden in there for you to find."

"We'll have to risk it," Arthur said.

"Wait, we can't just leave Digger behind," Joy exclaimed. "His mind-block card will wear out soon, then the Singer will have him again, and he'll just be back where he started. That's not fair!"

The brown didn't look surprised, just resigned. "Then you'd better do a dragon's duty and kill the scourgling before that happens. Besides, I haven't smelled a hint of my rider yet. Something tells me he's not ahead, but behind, and down. I want . . . I want to go back and look for him."

Laird looked like he was at war with himself. For a moment, Arthur was certain the red dragon was going to ask to accompany Digger, too. He was uncomfortable in the tunnels and would want to be paired with someone who could keep them from being buried alive.

At that moment, Arthur admitted to himself he wasn't sure he entirely trusted Laird. He was completely independent, had his own motivations, and had been the one to pass the message to the portal dragons not to open the way to this hive before Arthur gave the word. They had done so anyway. Was that because Whitaker overruled him, or had Laird backstabbed him?

So he was relieved when Laird pulled a rune net out of his Personal Space type storage and handed it to Digger.

"Stuff as many eggs that still look alive in here. I don't think every one of the nesting mothers will be able to get them out."

"I'll do that." Taking the net, Digger turned to the wall and narrowed his eyes. "Stand back."

Arthur quickly remounted Brixaby, and the dragon flew about halfway up in the tunnel and farther back.

Digger continued to stare at the wall, as if trying to burn a hole through it with his eyes. A moment later, that was almost exactly what happened.

A circular section of the wall simply evaporated and left a straight tunnel all the way through. It looked just big enough for Sams and Laird to crawl through if they tucked their wings in tight.

Laird groaned at the sight of it.

Digger sagged in exhaustion, but no one made a move to step forward.

"It's safe to touch this wall," Digger breathed through pants, guessing at their hesitation. "The drill charm effectively . . . destroyed the enchantment, but I'll have to watch it from . . . this side to be sure." He shook his head again. "Hurry."

"Forward!" Brixaby yelled and shot through the tunnel. Due to his size, there was plenty of room for him. Arthur didn't need to dismount. Neither did Cressida, which was good because she was still recovering.

Horatio unbuckled himself from his dragon's saddle and jogged alongside Sams, who had to practically crawl along on his belly to get through. Tannai was next, followed by Laird, who looked like every step cost him.

They made their way as quickly as possible, though Arthur gained some sympathy for Laird's fear. He got the impression the walls could snap shut at any moment—indeed, that they wanted to, but only Digger held them back.

As Digger had promised, the thick wall ended and opened into a massive open underground area. He suspected this had once been a meeting area, or perhaps a craft market. There was artwork on the walls and carvings in the stone. All of it had become faded and dusty, and like everything near the scourglings, spotted with a fine layer of growing mold.

And it was now a place of horror.

The first sign was the stink, which was worse than even scourge-rot. This was of active organic decay.

As Sams fully emerged, bringing the light with him, Arthur's eyes caught a glimpse of rainbow color. He turned to see . . . dragon bodies. Tiny bodies from the size of medium dogs to small horses, all piled up in a mound that rose to the height of a building. They'd been tossed away like unwanted scraps of clothing. Broken shells littered the area with blood spotting the white insides in a garish display.

The scourglings had indeed been farming the newly hatched dragons. And this was the harvesting area. It seemed as soon as the new dragons were hatched, they were . . . disposed of, and the cards from their cores taken.

It was horrific. Arthur turned away with a grimace.

Then his gaze landed on the middle of the room.

Sitting on a small clutch of eggs, like a queen on her throne, was a snow-white dragon.

Or at least, she would have been pure white if not for the weeping lesions on her head, neck, and body.

This white dragon—a mind-mage—was under the control of the scourgling.

She raised her head and stared at them.

Then, despite the mind-block card, Arthur felt a psychic attack go straight through his skull.

CHAPTER 56

Arthur's area-of-effect **Mental Shield** skill snapped up into place.

That was all that kept him, and everyone else, from keeling over.

The sharp drilling pain stopped. Arthur glanced at his mind-block anchor card and saw that the bar was rapidly running dry. Perhaps ten percent left.

As he watched, it dipped by another small notch.

If not for that and his skill . . .

He glanced back up at the white dragon. She sat in the middle of the room on a slightly raised platform surrounded by eggs. She was just as affected by scourge-rot as the other nesting mothers had been—especially her jaw, which was so diseased he saw yellow-white flashes of bone.

She hadn't moved other than to swing her head around and stare intently at Arthur. But he could feel the weight of that gaze pressing against his **Mental Shield** skill. It was as if she held both sides of his head within her claws and was steadily pressing in. If he slipped up for even a moment—

"Arthur, the ceiling," Brixaby said.

Keeping a firm hold on his skill—having a nearly unlimited source of mana behind him from the silver helped—he looked away.

His first impression of the space they'd stepped into was that it was vast, with a curved stone ceiling so high up it was lost in shadow. Following Brixaby's gaze, Arthur realized that it was dark with brown-black scourgling bodies. Most clung upside down like bats. Alive and wriggling, the entire ceiling seemed to pulsate with them.

Arthur saw flashes of long gangly limbs here and there. Not all were a batlike shape. Some had evolved.

It seemed the mother dragons weren't the only ones busy laying eggs . . . or however scourglings bred. He had no idea.

What had he led his retinue into?

At last . . . The Mind Singer's voice penetrated straight into his thoughts, despite the shield.

And so have I, he reminded himself.

With a snarl, Brixaby moved forward. "Reveal yourself, worm!"

"I am no worm. I am your host, and I have provided quite the welcome." Her lyrical cadence still managed to drip with sarcasm. "My children, kill them all but the Legendary boy. Harvest their cards and bring them to me."

The ceiling above seemed to pulse. Countless spells, effects, and card techniques rained down.

Arthur had no hope of counting them all. They represented all elements, almost every material from steel bolts to lightning, boulders of earth, nightmarish illusions he couldn't look away from until they were briefly obscured by a sheet of toxic yellow snowflakes. There were summoned creatures of all shapes and sizes, including a fiery horned dog that was rapidly consumed by rain . . .

The Mind Singer had been taking the cards from the farmed hatchlings and passing them to her children.

The only reason Arthur and his retinue were not evaporated from the hundreds of card effects was that all had been released at the same time. Most interfered with each other.

Untrained dragon formations had the same problem, and the final weeks of training were meant to address it. Arthur had never gotten that far, but he'd seen the schedule.

He saw the result now.

Forks of lightning went awry, not shooting down but striking metal spikes, which were blasted sharply to the side or else turned into shrapnel, which struck earthen boulders. Those boulders crumbled into dust, which soaked up much of the acid rain . . . when that rain wasn't eating into the summons, which went wild with rage. And dozens, maybe hundreds of other interactions and interferences.

That was their only saving grace. It bought them the extra second they needed for Cressida to snap her mana shield up. With Tannai aiding her, the shield was thicker than it had ever been before.

It wasn't large enough to cover Arthur and Brixaby. They'd taken that extra second to leap to the side. Then Brixaby plopped down on his hind end, his eyes half shut in concentration.

He opened his mouth and roared out his Stunning Shout for all that he was worth—the one ability they'd kept back for this fight, lest it tip the Mind Singer off.

His Stunning Shout, too, was aided by the extra influx of mana.

Arthur, who sat just behind the cone of destruction, felt nearly deafened by it.

Spell effects and debris that had been on the verge of raining down on them were blasted away. Most of it crashed into other debris and effects, to ruinous results. Even more interference.

The results would have been deafening all by itself, but compared to the force of Brixaby's shout, it happened in silence.

Then the shout reached the scourglings high above.

Swathes of the ceiling seemed to peel away and fall down—but it was only the densely clustered creatures losing their grip and falling off.

These, too, came to bad ends as their uncontrolled fall brought them into contact with card effects that had been lighter than gravity. Or else defensive measures that now worked against them.

Arthur wasn't sure what some of them hit—some kind of powerful explosive effect—because a soundless ball of flame blossomed from the middle of the ceiling and spread in secondary and tertiary explosions. These possibly took out more scourglings than Brixaby's initial shout had.

Still, Brixaby roared again and again. He targeted different dark points along the ceiling and several clusters that had outright panicked and tried to fly away.

Brixaby was not the only one attacking, either.

Cressida dropped her shield, which allowed Laird and Sams to step forward.

Laird sent out a rippling dome of purple candle-top flames that caught even more of the falling debris. This was not a normal fire. Some of the flames ate through spell effects as long as they took a visible form.

Meanwhile, Sams seemed to glow under the odd purplish effect that was his and Horatio's invisible light. Though there was no beam, suddenly everything up above was lit in garish display. Scourgling teeth and claws glowed as if from an inner source. It made them that much easier to target.

"Laird!" Tannai yelped. "Don't burn the bodies! The cards!"

Arthur didn't understand what he meant until Laird grunted in acknowledgment. His purple flames flickered, glowing briefly brighter, then dimmer again as he adjusted some quality within them.

The flames still vaporized anything that came falling down . . . except now for organic material. Scourgling bodies fell straight through.

There was an awkward moment where Cressida snapped her shield up again. A wave of stunned—and now broken—bodies struck against it like heavy rain.

Arthur and Brixaby were protected thanks to the Stunning Shout knocking everything aside.

Cressida let the shield down the moment the worst had passed.

As soon as she did, Laird and Tannai both jumped forward and started grabbing the scourgling bodies—no, they were *harvesting* them for the cards. So many cards, free for the taking, represented tremendous wealth.

"Stop!" Arthur ordered. "We're not done yet! We need to find the Mind Singer."

"Where is she?" Cressida asked. They had not started harvesting, though even Joy eyed the nearby scourgling bodies speculatively. Looking around, Cressida repeated, "Where is she? Did we kill her?"

No, it couldn't be that easy.

Arthur's gaze turned aside as if he had been compelled. The white dragon still stood in the middle of the room. Debris and scourgling bodies surrounded her— some had landed on the unhatched eggs. But nothing had touched her directly, as if the scourglings had done everything in their power to avoid her.

Or what was perched *on* her.

It was hard to tell at first. The white dragon's scales were peppered with rot and her jaw was particularly bad. One white cheek was gone, showing teeth underneath.

And there, tucked up against the base of her neck where a rider would sit, was a brown-black spot larger than the others.

It was a batlike scourgling. The Mind Singer.

Why is she still there? Arthur wondered. She was so still, it looked like she was waiting.

But for what?

Perhaps she was exhausted from controlling all her thralls in the hive. In that case, he had to act now.

"The white dragon!" Arthur yelled.

His mind-block card anchor had only a sliver of power left. They had to end this now.

Brixaby opened his mouth for his Stunning Shout.

CHAPTER 57

Just before Brixaby let his shout loose, the sounds of flapping wings brought Arthur's attention up. Several dragons—more of the Mind Singer's thralls—had just burst through the top of the stone room via an aerial tunnel. They must have been laying in wait for this moment, protected against Brixaby's previous shouts. There was one yellow, one blue, a silver, and a pink.

Their scales bounced back the last of Laird's candle-top flames. These were all shimmer-quality dragons. One, the blue, was definitely a high shimmer like Joy. He seemed to glimmer in the gloom.

Dismissing them, Brixaby turned back to the white dragon.

The shimmer yellow reacted just as Brixaby released his Stunning Shout. A shield, much like Cressida's mana bubble, fell between Brixaby and the Mind Singer. As the Stunning Shout struck, the surface of the shield turned entirely reflective.

And like a mirror, it bounced the spell back.

Brixaby flattened himself on the ground, and Arthur felt the shout roll over him. The shield was slightly curved and reflected the cone of destruction at an upward angle. While flattened, they'd caught the barest edge of the cone. So instead of knocking him out, it just felt like a punch to the head.

Arthur's mouth tasted like iron. He spat to one side and saw bright red blood.

The shield turned transparent again. The white dragon on the other side smirked at them. The smile dared Brixaby to try that again. The effect, however, was ruined by the sight of the Mind Singer squatting on the base of her neck.

"That shield cannot deflect everything!" Brixaby yelled and gathered himself up to spring at it with claws and teeth.

Arthur laid his hand on the side of Brixaby's neck. "It might. She's trying to waste our time, Brix." He glanced up at the circling shimmer dragons. These hadn't been brought out at random. He guessed every single one of them had a trick to tie them up. As soon as their mind blocks failed, the Mind Singer would pounce. "We need to take them out."

Following his gaze upward, Brixaby roared in a challenge. He sprang aloft, pulling his enchanted bar out of his Personal Space. It lit up with the strange dark void fire, which glimmered oddly in the cave.

Behind him, Joy echoed Brixaby's roar and flung herself into the air as well. So did Laird, though his wingbeats were heavy and struggling. They might have an unlimited mana supply right now thanks to Tannai's Mana Springwell, but this had been a long fight. Laird was tiring.

They only got a few dozen feet up before the shimmer blue dragon cast his spell.

Blues tended to be natural water-elemental users. But a fair fraction of them also sided with the element of air. That was why there were so many fog and mist card users among that color. Valentina's dragon, Elissa, took that to another level and could easily control all local weather patterns.

This shimmer blue also fell outside the norm. He didn't deal with water. His card focused on air.

Arthur saw the dragon cast the spell. Air whooshed around him as if he were in a tornado. From the corner of his eye, he noted Cressida once again using her own shield spell.

He and Brixaby had no choice but to manage the spell as it came.

They were Legendary users, and this would be one rank lower. There was every chance Brixaby would just plow through it, and his nullification magic would handle the rest.

The tornado-like spell hit. But it didn't impact them—it sucked the air away. Brixaby's wings continued to flap, but there was nothing to provide lift.

Brixaby's enchanted bar extinguished. They fell like a stone from twenty feet up. Arthur would have shouted in shock, but there was no air for him to shout in.

Dragons were flying creatures, and flying meant occasionally falling, too. He landed on all four feet—Arthur, however, fell right off his seat, hitting the hard ground. It hurt, but all that paled next to the fact that he couldn't breathe. His lungs were already burning with the need for air.

Next to him, Brixaby went mad, bucking and kicking and clawing at nothing, as if struggling to free himself of the spell. Arthur thought he might be trying to work his nullification magic. It probably would eat through the lesser-rank spell . . . eventually. Not before they suffocated.

Another flash of movement caught his eye. Cressida and Joy had managed to land more gracefully, but Cressida was out of her saddle seat, coming around to Joy's front. From her reddened face, her shield had failed against the blue's air spell.

Grabbing a knife from her belt, she jabbed the blade right into Joy's green forearm.

Had she been taken over? Was she a thrall, too?

But aside from a wince, Joy looked unworried. Her blue eyes were still alight with life—not deadened as if listening to a song no one else could hear.

Cressida staggered over to Arthur and shoved the dagger, handle first, into his hands. It was wet with Joy's blood.

He didn't understand. What did she want him to do? He couldn't think. He couldn't breathe, and the world was already starting to gray at the edges . . .

The dagger was coated with Joy's blood. Was her blood poison?

It clicked the moment the blade came within an inch of his body.

His Metal Shot card made him aware of the blade.

Of course.

Arthur started dumping mana into the blade. As much as it would hold. He looked up at the circling dragons, knowing he would only have one chance. He had to make this work. The gray tunnel in the corners of his vision had become dark, and the walls were closing in.

Arthur shoved that and the screaming, clawing pain in his lungs aside. He focused on his Throwing skill, his Makeshift Weaponry, and as hard as he could on his single temporary point of extra luck.

Then, he released the blade. It shot up so fast that it was a silver streak in the air, like a reverse lightning bolt from the ground to the sky.

The blue began to turn to the side, and the shield disappeared from in front of the Mind Singer to reappear right below the dragons. But it was a beat too late. The dagger had already passed and sunk, hard and true, into the blue's throat.

The blue let out a gurgled screech.

Arthur's ears popped as air returned around him. He and Cressida both half collapsed, wheezing in deep breaths.

Brixaby and Joy seemed to have handled the lack of air better. Brixaby surged forward with another Stunning Shout at the white dragon. But his breath was reedy, half choked, and it did nothing more than stagger the creature.

"We need . . . to take out the shimmers," Arthur gasped heavily, knowing there was no time for both.

"I got it," Joy said, scooping up her rider and helping her regain her seat.

"You will *not* face them alone!" Brixaby snarled at her. "One of those carries a Legendary card!"

Arthur glanced up, shocked. He hadn't felt that, but dragons were more sensitive to that kind of thing. To him, they felt like Rares, which meant one had likely poisoned itself with the higher card and was waiting for the right moment to spring it.

But Joy smiled. "Don't worry. I got a quest. We'll take care of the big meanies above. You get the Mind Singer."

Arthur was about to warn her again of the shield—it would stop anybody from attacking them from below. He was still gasping for air, and before he could find the words, Cressida and Joy disappeared into the shadows.

Of course. Their teleport power.

Perhaps it had something to do with his fire power needing air, but Laird had not gotten back to his feet yet. Joy and Cressida would be fighting the dragons above alone.

They'd be facing a *Legendary* alone . . .

But what choice did they have? Arthur's heart was heavy. They had to end the Mind Singer.

Arthur jumped up on Brixaby. For once, he was grateful that his dragon was so small.

He and Brixaby headed straight for the white dragon. Brixaby was half flying, using his wings to skim along the ground—a dark arrow headed straight for his enemy.

Finally, the Mind Singer defended herself directly.

Arthur felt her fear and rage slam into his mind and gouge in like claws. If it wasn't for the last vestiges of the mind-block card, and his own **Mental Shield**, he was certain his thoughts would've been turned to shreds.

But he wasn't completely unaffected. The world seemed to waver and shift and start spinning, even though he was certain his body stayed in place. The Mind Singer had reached in and twisted his perception around.

Brixaby fell hard, his wings thumping against the stone floor as if he were still trying to fly but was unsure of what direction to go.

Arthur reached into his Personal Space and grabbed his last resort: the purple apple.

Leaning forward, he shoved it into his dragon's mouth.

Brixaby bit down, chopping half of it off and swallowing.

Arthur took the other half, but before he could bite, the white dragon finally moved off of her nest. She snarled at them with a lower jaw that was already half rotted. Then she swiped at them with her claws.

The psychic-blocking apple must've had some effect because Brixaby was able to dodge to the side.

Arthur felt the world spin around him, even though his eyes insisted it wasn't happening. He slipped off Brixaby's side and managed to stay on his feet, but staggered straight into the side of the white dragon.

She began to turn, and Arthur desperately reached into his Personal Space for anything else from his bag of tricks.

His mind landed on a single chainmail rivet—one that he had kept back because he could feel it was badly forged, half rusted, and useless. But it was the only thing he had left.

In the timeless moment in his Personal Space, he crimped one end of the rivet to a point and ground it into his half apple. Sticky apple juice covered the rivet—he wished he'd had the common sense to save some of Joy's poison instead.

This would have to do.

Back in real time, with the rivet clutched between his pinched fingers, he dumped mana into it and aimed it straight for the Mind Singer. The world still twisted and spun around him—he had to focus entirely on his throwing accuracy and luck, and depend on the fact that he was only a couple feet away.

The white dragon flinched at the wrong second, and so did the Mind Singer. Her batlike wings half extended, as if she meant to fly off. The rivet missed her body and cut through the membrane wing. It was a tiny cut, but the rivet was coated in psychic-blocking apple juice. It struck her like poison.

The claws against his mind were blunted.

Which was good because at that moment, the last of his mind-block card anchor finally ran out. Only his **Mental Shield** was in effect, and it felt thin.

Her power hit him full on, and his mind was intimately close to hers. He felt her desperation, fear that he had gotten this close . . . but smug certainty, too. She had one last trick.

Arthur felt like he had just stepped into a trap.

His eyes flicked to the eggs that surrounded the white dragon. Why were these eggs here? Because she had already harvested mind-mage hatchlings?

He wasn't sure if this was his own inspiration or the fact that the scourgling's mind felt so close he could almost sense her thoughts. He *knew*, despite the fact that her powers were blunted, it didn't affect her cards. And she wanted Arthur to be here—would have rather had all his allies killed first, but this would have to do.

The Mind Singer activated a card. Due to his Counterfeit Siphon ability, he saw the spell.

New Counterfeit spell obtained: Mind Swap
Remaining Time: 59 Minutes 59 Seconds

Mind swap? She wants to be me? No, she wants my cards—

The card's power struck, and Arthur's mind felt . . . unmoored from his own body. For a moment, he was both himself and also sitting in an unfamiliar body, squatting on a white dragon he couldn't *stand*. The beast kept fighting him, whining over her eggs. Didn't she realize that she had been chosen out of the entire hive? Didn't she realize that she was blessed to be carrying him? To power him? When the feel of her scales burned against his feet?

His mind was mixed with the Singer's, unfamiliar notes dancing in his head. He felt his own hand reach to his chest, to his heart deck. Ready to draw out the cards.

No. The Mind Singer was in his body. A young, strong human body that no one would think twice at. Using his skin and the power of his cards, she would be able to travel the kingdom. All the kingdoms.

And that's when Brixaby's rage bit down on the Mind Singer with ghostly dragon teeth. Arthur's remaining link to his body was through his dragon's core. Their link had no boundaries, and Brixaby was not going to give up the cards. Or Arthur.

For a moment, Arthur felt like a chew toy tugged between two angry dogs. He was pulled into his body and out again.

Brixaby's nullification power began eating at the Mind Singer spell. It was a delicate working, and unraveled.

The Mind Singer's spell snapped, and Arthur was thrown back into his body.

But he was still close to the Mind Singer's thoughts and saw that a Rare-powered card, once activated, needed to spend its power.

The spell focused on the only other mind within range.

The white dragon howled in her own true voice. She rose up on her hind feet, shaking her head, fighting the swap with her own mind-mage powers. Her flailing forelimbs smacked Brixaby hard enough to send him skittering across the floor.

She nearly came down again on Arthur, but then her eyes went blank.

And a moment later, it was the Mind Singer who was screaming, flopping over and over. The former white dragon, now trapped in the body of her enemy.

The white dragon turned to Arthur. Her eyes blazed with the Mind Singer's hate. Through a ruined jaw, she half hissed, half sang, "This isn't over . . ."

Then she shrugged off the flailing scourgling and stepped on it.

It took one moment to harvest the cards, another to grab up a few eggs. Then she was flying away.

A white dragon with the scourgling's mind.

"No, stop her! Joy . . . Cressida . . ." Arthur scrambled to his feet, but he was completely out of tricks. She was a dragon, and by himself, he had nothing to stop her with.

Cressida and Joy were fighting a final battle with another pink dragon up above. As the white dragon flew past, remaining scourglings peeled off the ceiling and followed her. A terrible wave that escorted her up and up . . . and out a nearby tunnel.

She was gone.

Arthur staggered to Brixaby. His dragon had regained his feet, though he winced and held up one forelimb, not putting weight on it.

"What just happened?" Brixaby demanded.

"She tried to take over my mind—to take my cards. I'm not sure. She wants to be human. And now she's a dragon." It wasn't the most elegant way of putting it, but Arthur was still half stunned.

"A dragon? Impossible. Dragons are the antithesis of scourglings."

In that moment of connection, he'd caught how Mind Singer hated the way the white dragon's scales had burned when she sat on it. And now she lived in its mind? *That can't be comfortable.*

"She's a dragon now," Arthur repeated, still wrapping his head around the idea. The terrible implications. "I don't know if she will keep that body." He doubted it would be for long. The white dragon was quite damaged. "And she got away." The strength in his legs seemed to drain out of him all at once. He sank down next to Brixaby. "We lost."

"She is the one who just ran away," Brixaby said. "And we got the Legendary card she was holding in reserve. *We* won."

Arthur's head snapped around. "What?"

Brixaby nodded up above.

The pink dragon Joy had been fighting had tried to follow the Mind Singer. But black core poisoning had crawled up and down its limbs and made its way to its brain. It fell from the sky, helped along by a few necrotic slices from Joy. Falling from the sky like a broken thing, it hit the ground hard, just to the other side of the raised platform—luckily missing the remaining eggs.

"Told you I could handle it," Joy called from above.

Arthur stared. Even with the core poisoning . . . How? *How* had Joy and Cressida managed to defeat a Legendary? Why hadn't it used its power on them?

After a moment's thought, he had an answer. A Legendary seeking card would have even less combat capabilities than his Master of Skills.

Arthur stood and walked to the body. Sure enough, the dragon's chest began to glow with the strength of a Legendary card.

CHAPTER 58

The next few hours were a blur. Arthur did his best not to walk through them in an unthinking fog. Later, Brixaby insisted he had conducted himself as well as any Legendary rider should.

Arthur wasn't sure he agreed, but he appreciated the attempt to cheer him up.

Most of his attention was spent on rescue, organization of remaining resources, and the beginning of cleanup.

The scourglings had followed the Mind Singer like bees after their queen. Because she wore a dragon's body, no one still fighting outside the hive had stopped her. Most were already intimidated by the sight of a white dragon in principle.

Arthur questioned everyone he found who'd seen the white dragon leave, and received conflicting answers. There may have been illusions involved, so he couldn't be sure which direction she had gone.

If any of her scourglings or remaining thralls were portal users, it wouldn't matter. She could be anywhere in the world.

So, reluctantly, Arthur concentrated on the matters he could control: the rescue of the people and dragons who were left behind.

There was no denying the level of tragedy after all that had happened. The amount of dead hatchlings, piled up as if they were garbage, was a horror almost beyond telling. Their lives had been snuffed out before they'd had the chance to start.

And no one knew how many eggs had been lost.

One of the first tasks Arthur focused on once there was a vague semblance of order was to organize the earth-type dragons to search the tunnels for lost eggs. Many of the females, even the ones without helpful powers or were between current nest cycles, were eager to help. The instinct was strong.

Though not as demonstrative as the nesting mothers, the male dragons were more upset about the sight of dead hatchlings than the females. Laird had once mentioned that a male dragon's duty started when the eggs were hatched. Those instincts, too, were strong.

Brixaby refused to admit it, however.

It was agreed once the main cavern had been cleared out, the entrance tunnels were to be sealed. It was the best version of a burial they could give the lost hatchlings. The place had once been called the Amphitheater. It was now referred to as the Tomb.

However, there were glimmers of hope.

The Mind Singer had either managed to travel far enough away to lose a connection to her thralls, or, more likely, had cut her losses to consolidate what she had left.

Either way, the dragons who had not followed her had returned to their former selves. Without the Mind Singer's oppressive influence that had dampened their cards, the scourge-rot stopped advancing through their bodies. However, many would need healing.

Of this, the hive did have a few healers left. Some from their own number, and some who had come from Wolf Moon but hadn't managed to make it back through the portal.

Arthur and Brixaby bullied the few that were left to start tending to the worst of the scourge-affected.

Upon checking on them later, they learned that many of the people and dragons would still have scars, but the infection could be fully healed.

Then there was the problem of the cards.

Once it was learned there was a card harvest available, Brixaby had to use every bit of intimidation he could to keep people out of the Tomb until it was sealed.

Luckily, he excelled at intimidation.

Every scourgling that had fallen during that final battle had a full-fledged card. Some had two, and most had additional card shards in addition.

The Mind Singer's dragon-farming operation had been profitable. If word got out to the wrong people . . . Arthur didn't want to think of it.

However, not every card harvested from the hundreds of scourglings had come from a dragon hatchling.

Once the people and dragons were put under thrall, they were required to give up all cards except for their original in their heart or core. The extras were donated to the Mind Singer.

That helped explain why the scourge-sickness had taken root. Their bodies were in a mild state of shock from losing cards from their decks.

These cards, once located, were returned to their owners.

That still left a surplus of remaining cards.

Arthur did his best to try to portion them out as equitably as possible, though he was certain that some people likely got more than their fair share, and some ended with less.

He made a show of taking no cards for himself, mostly because he and Brixaby had taken pains to keep the Legendary card as secret as possible.

That left the matter of his retinue.

"So you're saying I should not be justly rewarded?" silver Tannai sniffed.

Arthur was getting a headache. "Of course you will be—"

"Did I not keep you topped up with mana? Follow you into the pits of the tomb, surrounded by scourglings?"

"Yes," Arthur said, annoyed.

"Did I not do all this without my own poor, hurt rider, who I left behind still injured from *your* attack—"

"Tannai." Arthur cut him off before he could get going. The longer he spent in the silver's company, the more he found he simply didn't like him. What a shame he had such a useful card. "I can't give you thirty cards. That's ridiculous. While you were a huge help—and we couldn't have done it without you—the entire retinue pulled together. Everyone was needed. Besides, you can't possibly fit thirty cards, even split between you and your rider."

Tannai pulled himself straight as if offended. "Of course not. It's only that both my females' nests survived. I would like to gift my hatchlings additional cards, when they're old enough."

That was . . . a little more noble than Arthur had feared. He eyed the silver. "How many eggs do you have?"

"Fifteen."

"Really," Arthur said flatly. "And if I send Brixaby to count them?"

"I have seven eggs in two nests," Tannai hastily amended. "But I mean to say the hatchlings will have seven, their mothers two, and me and my rider will be given six to split."

Arthur rubbed at his temple. Yes, he was definitely getting a headache. "You can pick out nine from the Common-Uncommon pile, and one Rare."

"I can't use a Rare. I'm an Uncommon."

"Sell it. That'll get you a handful of Uncommons if you're smart about it."

Tannai made a point of hemming and hawing but eventually agreed.

Arthur wondered if he really should have Brixaby check the number of eggs in those nests. His two mates might have laid seven eggs between them, but it didn't mean they'd end up with seven hatchlings, even in the best of times. And these weren't the best of times.

Arthur decided he didn't have the time.

He moved on to the next problem on his list: the human beings who'd been in the hive when it was taken over.

The ones whose heart cards had not been located were still suffering emotional and psychological shock.

However, they had been lucky in some ways. The Mind Singer had lesser plans for humans than for the dragons. They'd been kept as servants in the bowels of the hive, several levels below where Arthur had seen. This kept them away from the worst of the scourge-infected air, though some had come out with a touch of scourge-sickness.

Since many of them had been riders, they were able to reunite with their dragons. Seeing that had been touching.

The best of all had been Digger and his rider, Stefan.

Stefan was exactly as stereotypically big, burly, and barrel-chested as Arthur had imagined someone linked to Digger.

He closed giant bear-paw-sized hands around Arthur's own and shook his vigorously, thanking him over and over again.

Unfortunately, he and Digger declined to be part of Arthur's retinue. They were much more interested in helping the refugees settle into their sister hive, the Island Free Hive. That meant hollowing out new passageways and complexes in the sandy soil. Stefan and Digger were excited about the challenge.

Every resident of the Free Hive of the Waves was being relocated to Island Free Hive. It would not be safe to stay here long term with the scourge-rot taking a foothold. And no one wanted to live near the tomb of hatchlings.

So Island Free Hive had agreed to take them in, especially their newfound wealth in the form of cards. They needed it. From what Arthur heard, the Mind Singer had managed to sneak a hidden Legendary card out from under them.

Finally, after a full half day of work, Arthur was able to meet with the remains of the Free Hive of the Waves council.

They were not as effusive as Stefan had been, but he was thanked. Mostly, however, they were worried Wolf Moon Hive would expect a payment.

"No," Arthur said shortly. "All I want is for the people in this hive to recover." He sighed, his headache threatening again, even though he'd had the first one fixed by a healer. "I like the free hives, and I believe they have a place in the world. But . . . you need to learn how to defend yourselves. You need combat cards."

"What if this so-called Mind Singer comes back?" one of the councilmen asked with a chin thrust out aggressively. "Can we count on Wolf Moon Hive's assistance again?"

"I won't be in a position to help you," Arthur said.

They looked troubled. The man was about ready to protest but was shushed.

At least they hadn't treated him like a child. Maybe it was the lines of stress carved into his face.

Cressida made him rest after that. Arthur slept in somebody else's bed who hadn't been located yet.

When he woke, he found Brixaby by his side. The dragon had a smug expression on his face.

"I know where we're going next."

"Tell me," Arthur said, needing good news.

By the next day, Arthur had to admit to himself that he was procrastinating going back to Wolf Moon Hive.

First, though, he needed to return those who'd followed him from Mesa Free Hive.

The vast majority of the eggs stolen from Mesa had been located. Now almost every returning dragon wore slings made of linen to hold eggs for the journey. A couple of the smaller blues and purples just carried a precious egg within their claws.

Arthur convinced Tannai to top him up on mana again—mostly so he could copy his power for the last time, and had Brixaby locate the single remaining shimmer green who had portal powers.

First, however, he met up with Laird.

The red dragon had come out quite well in terms of cards. Most he'd harvested on the sly right after the battle with the Mind Singer.

Arthur would have been annoyed about that, but he knew Laird intended to rebuild his combat team. He needed cards.

"I also found an Uncommon card that filters minerals from soil," Laird told him. "That will help heal the damage left over from that saltwater dousing."

"Do you have someone in mind?" Arthur asked, thinking of Len and Tamya.

Laird shrugged a wing. "I'm sure the council will. They enjoy giving out plum gifts."

"If you still have any sway with them when you return," Arthur said. "Try to get them to come around on the combat cards."

"You know I will." Laird paused. "I once spoke to you about a card of prophecy that was rumored to be Legendary. Was that what you harvested down in the Mind Singer's chambers?"

"No," Arthur said.

The dragon looked at him for a moment, narrow-eyed, then seemed to like what he saw. "Good. That card belongs with the free hives."

He looked to the sky, where the green shimmer had just taken up position. It waited for Brixaby and Arthur to join up before the portal could be opened.

"I'm certain we will meet again," Laird said. "Do try to do some growing up before then. You're still nothing more than a tiny cub."

Horatio, of course, did have a thing or two to complain about.

"Everyone else has gathered a whole deck's worth of cards but me and Sams. Even your girlfriend."

"Cressida's not my girlfriend."

Horatio gave him a sly look. "Mind if I try my hand with her, then?"

"She is a noblewoman. You don't try your hand with her, you court her, and no, she wouldn't be interested in you," Arthur snapped. Though by the end, he knew he'd just fallen into Horatio's trap.

His friend grinned. "So you two are . . . courting?"

"No," Arthur grumbled. "I don't know what we're doing. Can we drop this?"

"She still has more cards than me and Sams," Horatio said. "Who is your best friend, exactly?"

"Don't act like I didn't offer you cards the other day. You were part of Joy's quest, just like everyone else."

"Sams won't take them. He calls them 'blood cards.' Can't say I blame him," Horatio said, "considering they came from the cores of dead baby dragons."

Technically, most intact cards came from dragon deaths, but Arthur didn't press it. "Cressida and Joy won't tell me what cards they harvested," he muttered. "I think Joy likes teasing Brixaby that she has something he doesn't know about. But Cressida just seems . . . embarrassed about her new card? I don't get it."

"You sure she's not trying to flirt with you, in a weird noblewoman way?" Horatio wagged his very dark, very bushy eyebrows at Arthur. "Maybe this is how she flirts."

Arthur gave him a flat look. Though inside, he wasn't sure.

"I have to ask . . . I'm still in your retinue, aren't I?" Horatio suddenly blurted. His amusement had dropped, and now he looked concerned.

"Of course," Arthur said, but then was forced to correct himself. "I mean, only if you want to be. But Horatio . . . I'm not going back to Wolf Moon Hive."

"I figured as much." Horatio smiled at Arthur's startled look. "You've been pulling long faces all day, and you're dragging your feet on opening that second portal to Wolf Moon. I know you're not afraid of getting in trouble. So what's the plan?"

For a moment, Arthur felt like he was twelve years old again, about ready to sneak out somewhere he shouldn't be going with his friend. "Plan?" he asked teasingly.

"You're not going to the hives. So where are we going?"

Arthur smiled at the sound of "we." Then he told him.

Arthur ended up delaying one more day under the guise of helping settle the people of Free Hive of the Waves in their new Island home.

At this point, he fully admitted he was procrastinating. He just didn't care. No one else could do what he and Brixaby could do with their powers. No one dared to countermand his orders unless they were outrageous.

It was good being a Legendary.

But finally, it was time.

The remaining Wolf Moon Hive dragons gathered in the sky. Arthur and Brixaby, alongside the green shimmer, opened a portal directly to Wolf Moon.

He let everyone go through first, then swung around and took one look at the island hive.

By now, everyone who could safely move had been evacuated to Island Free Hive. With the rest now returned to Mesa Free Hive and Wolf Moon, the sky was clear.

The only exceptions were a spot of yellow and a second spot of pink on the horizon.

Horatio and Cressida had quietly stayed back along with their dragons.

Joy roared out a goodbye that was echoed by Sams. Then the two turned. They had their own journey. It was a long one, and they needed to get started.

Besides, it was only goodbye for now.

Arthur directed Brixaby through the portal.

CHAPTER 59

Arthur was unsurprised to see a purple courier dragon with a golden sash waiting for him right on the other side.

Well, they hadn't come in quietly. Hive leadership would have been alerted by the portal and the missing dragons spilling out.

"What do you want?" Brixaby demanded of the purple.

The officious dragon puffed himself up. "Leader Whitaker demands to see you at once."

Brixaby snorted and shouldered past the purple, instead heading for Valentina's cave.

Elissa was drowsing on her ledge. In the full sunlight, she looked washed out. Her ribs were visible, and her joints looked a touch swollen. Arthur was certain she wasn't being neglected. She was just . . . old. Her body was failing her.

The dragon didn't crack an eyelid at them, and neither wanted to interrupt her rest. Brixaby landed as quietly as he could, Arthur dismounted, and they both walked by. Though she was asleep, Brixaby dipped his head to her in a brief nod.

Inside the cave, Arthur was unsurprised to see Valentina was bedridden.

Unlike her dragon, the old rider was awake. Propped up against pillows with her feet under blankets, her long white hair was out of its usual severe style and fell to her shoulders. She looked like she had just woken, though it was the middle of the day.

"So, you've returned. I was starting to doubt you would," she grumped.

"I have." Arthur stepped to her bedside and, glancing around, removed the Subtle Influence mind card from his card anchor. "I wanted to return this to you."

Valentina looked at it. Though Arthur knew her heart must be aching for the card to be replaced in her deck, she tore her gaze away and met his eyes directly.

"Whitaker has reported your conduct to the king. From the way he tells it, you single-handedly fed misinformation to leadership in order to lead our hive's dragons into a trap. Then, once there, you undermined his authority. He was forced to retreat." She flicked a hand. "Or that's how he tells it today. I'm afraid his grievances grow with every retelling."

Anger flashed through Arthur. Brixaby snarled at his side. But he had been expecting something like this. He forced himself to not snap something back at Valentina. This wasn't her fault.

His voice came out calmer than he expected. Almost amused.

"Has the king requested me, at my soonest convenience?"

"Not yet," Valentina said. "He does know what Whitaker is like, even if he does need to be reminded at times. But it's coming."

Arthur took a chance and told the truth. "He won't find me."

She snorted as if she was unsurprised by that. "You'd better hope not. Tell me, are you still loyal to the kingdom? Or have you joined those fluff-headed crafters in the free hives?"

"I'm loyal, and I haven't joined any free hive," Arthur said. "But my eyes have been opened. The world is bigger than I ever thought it could be. I want to see more of it."

He wasn't sure what her reaction would be. Mostly, he expected anger.

Instead, Valentina seemed to slump. She looked very fragile.

"Well, it will be interesting to see what Whitaker does—or doesn't do—when the fate of the entire hive is on his shoulders. I worry for the hive, Arthur. I truly do."

"Don't," Arthur said.

"My whole life has been dedicated to Wolf Moon Hive. I don't want it to fail."

"It won't," Arthur insisted. "At worst, another Legendary from one of the other hives will step in to help. Wolf Moon won't fail. And I will return. Valentina," he continued, hoping she would understand, "the scourge-eruptions are increasing, and no one knows why. It's more than just a cycle. All we have left in the world are safe patches, but even those are in danger. We have fewer Mythic-level dragons than ever before. If we're not careful, the balance will shift toward the scourglings."

"And you know how to fix it, do you? Oh, to be young and naive . . ."

"I don't, but I know how to start."

"How?"

Arthur nodded to Brixaby. The dragon projected his newest card for them to see.

Call of the Heart
Legendary
Seeker
This card seeks out the person or object who most closely can fulfill the
wielder's want or desire. There is no limit on distance. Once the target is
located, the wielder is shown the way through a map on the wielder's card
dashboard. This map is fully transferable from the wielder into another's
card dashboard but may not be transmitted further. This map does not
automatically update, and the card must be reused to update the target's
location. The same target may be refreshed once every twelve hours.
This card is part of the Call set. Search out other cards in this set to add to
your power.

"I asked Brixaby to search for something that will help our fight with the scourglings and help Wolf Moon directly," Arthur said.

"What is it?" Valentina asked. Her voice quivered.

"I don't know. It just shows a location."

Brixaby spoke up. "The map grows finer in detail the closer I become. We will find it, and we will return victorious."

"Also," Arthur added wryly, "I'm certain you're aware of my friend's pink meta-dragon powers? I have an outstanding quest to help an ally. It hasn't gone off through all the free hives I've visited. There's someone out there. Someone who can help."

Valentina leaned back against her pillows. She didn't look happy, exactly. But she was accepting. Reaching out, she patted Arthur's hand. "Go, before Whitaker finds you. He's an idiot, but he's a strong idiot, and he's been in a rage for three days."

Arthur had made another enemy. It seemed he collected more of those than cards. He didn't think he'd be welcomed back by the Mesa Free Hive Council, either.

"And Arthur," she added. "Take the damn mind card. I won't need it . . . whatever happens."

Reluctantly, Arthur slipped it back into his card anchor. "Thank you, Valentina."

"You can thank me by getting this whatever it is and coming back strong." Her eyes glittered. "You must be strong to face the king again."

He nodded and then exchanged a knowing glance with his dragon.

Arthur stuck the Subtle Influence mind card in his heart deck, at the same time deactivating the Nullify card that kept his Return to Start in check.

He and Brixaby spoke at the same time.

"Brix, you should give your cards to hive orphans."

"Arthur, go purchase a human-wing body-enhancement card."

Both sentences had weight to them, as they were both using the power of the Subtle Influence card.

It was only a Common, but as they were unwelcome suggestions, Return to Start counted them as an attack.

In a moment, Arthur and Brixaby were both transported away.

EPILOGUE

Arthur and Brixaby arrived a few moments later, well outside Mesa Free Hive. Right on top of the pebbles they had keyed to during the battle with the Mind Singer's dragons.

It was nighttime in this part of the world. Just after sunset.

Arthur turned to his dragon. "A human-wing body-enhancement card?"

"Even if we can now fly together, all proper beings should have wings of their own." Brixaby eyed him. "You wish me to give my cards to *orphans*?"

"I knew trying to influence you that way would be seen as hostile," Arthur said with a grin.

He knew his dragon, and Brixaby knew him well, too. Though Arthur wanted to grow stronger and truly master every secret of his cards, he was happy with who he was physically. He certainly didn't need wings.

Brixaby snorted at him, and then his eyes went briefly unfocused as he gazed inward.

"I updated my map. We are on the opposite side of the world from where we need to go."

"Doesn't matter," Arthur said. "We'll be there in a few minutes. Horatio and Cressida have a longer journey ahead of them."

"They have a copy of the map, and you were the one worried Crag's rider would capture them if they returned with us to Wolf Moon."

"I'm not taking any chances with hostages after what happened with the king," Arthur said, instead of admitting he might have over worried. "Let's get this portal open before we upset the Mesa Hive, too."

"Who cares about their feelings? We're a Legendary pair. What could they do to stop us?"

Arthur smiled and used the portal spell he'd copied using his Counterfeit Siphon card. There was plenty of time left.

He supposed he could have portaled back from Wolf Moon, but he wanted to make his escape as convoluted as possible in case they were somehow followed.

Arthur used his rapidly dwindling mana to rip a hole in the fabric of reality in front of him. Brixaby's new card supplied the destination.

It was bright daylight on the other side. The portal opened on top of a hill that looked down onto the sprawling city of a brand-new kingdom.

A place where neither he nor Brixaby would be known. An entirely fresh start, where a valuable, if unknown object waited for them.

And in a few weeks, Cressida and Horatio would join them. That would be enough time for Arthur to ensure he and Brixaby had truly gotten away clean, and Whitaker had no way to track them via portal.

Until their friends arrived, he and Brixaby planned to get started.

Still holding one edge of the fabric of reality like a heavy curtain, Arthur seated himself on his dragon. Together, they flew through and up into the air of a new kingdom.

ABOUT THE AUTHOR

Having selected banker as her profession and purchased sturdy oxen as well as all the ammunition she could afford, Honour Rae loaded her family into a wagon and set out to establish a homestead. Unfortunately, she could only keep two hundred pounds of the deer, elk, bears, bison, squirrels, and rabbits she massacred along the way. Soon, dysentery set in and attempting to ford the river proved to be a huge mistake. Somehow, Rae and her family pulled through—albeit with the loss of any extra wagon parts. The Oregon Trail conquered, and having made it to the Willamette Valley, she sat down to write this book.

THANK YOU

FOR SUPPORTING HONOUR RAE

CONNECT WITH THE AUTHOR
BY VISITING THE FOLLOWING:

 @HONOURRAE

 PATREON.COM/HONOUR_RAE

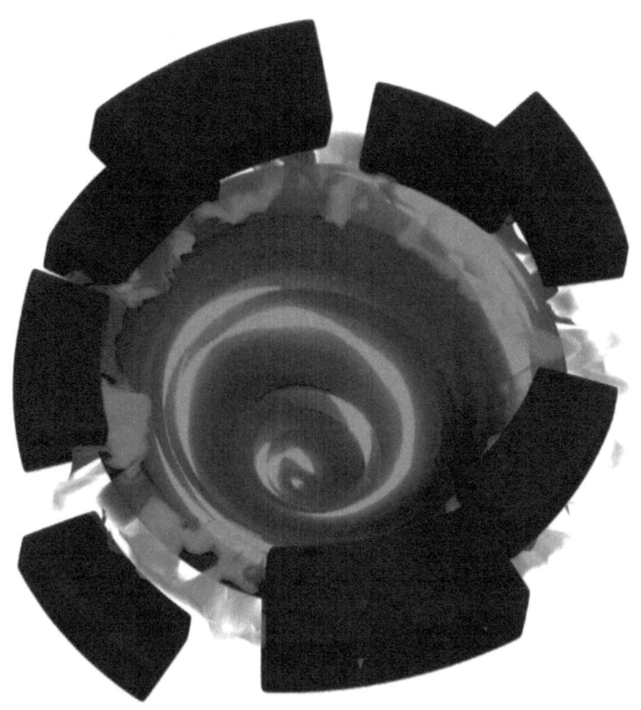

RESPAWN YOUR CURIOSITY

follow us on our socials

 podiumentertainment.com

 @podiumentertainment

 /podiumentertainment

 @podium_ent

 @podiumentertainment